THE KING OF DIAMONDS

Also by Simon Tolkien

Final Witness
The Inheritance

SIMON TOLKIEN

The King of Diamonds

HARPER

HARPER

An imprint of HarperCollins*Publishers*
77-85 Fulham Palace Road
Hammersmith, London W6 8JB
www.harpercollins.co.uk

This edition 2012
1

First published in the USA
by Minotaur Books 2011

ISBN 978-0-00-745418-1

Typeset in Sabon LT Std by Palimpsest Book Production Ltd,
Falkirk, Stirlingshire

Printed and bound in Great Britain by
Clays Ltd, St Ives plc

MIX
Paper from
responsible sources
FSC
www.fsc.org
FSC™ C007454

For Priscilla Tolkien
with love and gratitude

ACKNOWLEDGEMENTS

This novel was conceived in Tenerife, plotted in London, and written in Southern California. Anna Tolkien, Tracy Tolkien, Nicholas Tolkien, Marly Rusoff, Michael Radulescu, Thomas Dunne, Natasha Hughes, David Brawn, Lizzy Kremer, John Garth, Kevin Sweeney, Angela Gibson, and Anne Bensson have all helped in different ways with bringing it to fruition, and Peter Wolverton has, as always, been a quite wonderful editor. I am grateful to all of them.

PROLOGUE

THE OLD BAILEY

1958

'And so, Mr Swain, everybody might be guilty of this crime. Everybody except you? Is that right?'

The voice of Sir Laurence Arne, counsel for the prosecution, was laced with sarcasm as he uncoiled himself from his seat, slowly drawing himself up to his full height so that he was able to look down on the accused, to dominate him even before he had begun his cross-examination. He was a tall man, tall and thin, with a wide forehead set over small dark eyes. The boniness of his build and a long aquiline nose completed the birdlike effect that so many of Arne's fellow barristers had commented on over the years.

Like a bird of prey, thought the officer in the case, Detective Inspector Trave, sitting at a table at the side of the court behind the row of prosecution exhibits – the evidence that he'd carefully assembled during his investigation – handwritten note, knife, rent bloody clothing, each neatly tagged with its own case number. Yet again Trave was surprised to feel a stirring of sympathy for the defendant. David Swain looked like he hadn't slept in days. He shifted constantly from foot to foot in the witness box, running his hands through his unruly hair, unable to keep his focus on anyone or anything for very long. He was no match for Arne and Arne knew it. Now the prosecutor seemed to be almost playing with the defendant, like a spider before the kill.

'Because that's what you seem to have been saying in your interview with the police,' Arne persisted when the defendant didn't respond to his first question. 'Not me; not me; anyone but me.'

'Well, it's true. It wasn't me. And I was upset, disorientated. Anyone would have been in my situation,' said Swain. There was that same note of defiance in the young man's voice, of special pleading that Trave remembered from before. It wasn't going to win him any friends among the jury.

'But that's the point, isn't it?' Arne countered quickly, sensing the opening. 'Nobody else was in your situation. Nobody else had the motive you had; nobody else had the opportunity.'

'You don't know that. Ethan had found out something. That's why he wrote that letter to his brother before he came back – about needing to talk to him but it being too dangerous to put in a letter.'

'Someone wanted to shut Mr Mendel up before he could talk and so they framed you for the murder. Is that what you're saying?'

'Yes. A murder isn't enough; you need a murderer too.'

'I see. A nice turn of phrase,' said Arne, allowing himself a thin smile. 'Did you prepare that for our benefit, if you don't mind me asking?'

It was a cheap shot, thought Trave, but it had the desired effect. There was some nervous laughter in the courtroom, and Swain flushed deep red, his anger rising.

'All right, Mr Swain,' Arne went on after a moment. 'Let's look at your account of events and see whether what you say makes any sense, shall we? Let's see if we can find out who the real murderer was?'

Swain bit his lip, clenching and unclenching his hands on the top of the witness box. He clearly had no capacity whatsoever to conceal his emotions: anger and fear were written all over his pale face. And it didn't help that the hot-water pipes were doing such good work, overcompensating for the unseasonable temperatures in the world outside. Beads of sweat were forming in the defendant's hairline and over his forehead, and involuntarily he put up his hands and rubbed his knuckles in his eyes, trying to get some relief from the glare of the overhead lights illuminating the windowless courtroom.

'You admit to having been in a relationship with Katya Osman throughout most of last year, don't you?' asked Arne in a matter-of-fact tone of voice.

'Of course I do. She was my girlfriend,' said Swain, who was still trying to regain his composure.

'Until Mr Mendel came along.'

'Yes.'

'And then you lost control of yourself?'

Swain dropped his eyes, refusing to answer the prosecutor's question.

'Didn't you?'

Swain nodded. 'It hurt what happened. Anybody would have felt bad.'

'Ah, there you go again, Mr Swain: anybody and everybody. But we're not talking about anybody, are we? We're talking about you.'

'All right. Me. I felt bad – deep down bad. Is that what you want?'

Arne smiled, not answering the question. It was that same thin, humourless smile from before, and Trave noticed that Swain's hands had started to shake.

'And you felt so bad that you wrote letters to Miss Osman, threatening to kill her and Mr Mendel, didn't you, Mr Swain?' asked Arne after a moment. 'Not one letter, not two letters – lots of letters. And each one more violent than the last. You remember the letters, don't you? Miss Osman was kind enough to read some of them to us the day before yesterday.'

The defendant kept his eyes on the floor, refusing to meet the prosecutor's eye.

5

'No? You don't remember? Well, let me refresh your memory with some examples. March fourteenth – "I'll show you what pain is. You don't know the meaning of the word." April eighth – "If I can't have you, nobody can." And undated but received by Miss Osman on the twenty-ninth – "The last thing you'll see in this world will be that Belgian bastard's empty dead eyes." Not exactly ambiguous, these threats, are they, Mr Swain?' asked Arne, looking up at Swain from over the gold-rimmed, half-moon glasses that he had put on to read the letters.

It was a masterful performance. Arne had picked up one document after another from the pile on the desk in front of him, reading from them apparently at random, although Trave was quite sure that the prosecutor had in fact prepared each quotation carefully in advance. He was known for his thoroughness, his attention to detail.

'So would you have killed Miss Osman too if you'd had the chance?' he asked when Swain remained silent. 'That certainly seems to be what you are saying to her in these letters?'

'No, of course not,' said Swain, blurting out his answer.

'Well, that's certainly reassuring. You'd been to Mr Osman's boathouse before, yes?'

'Yes, I used to meet Katya there.'

'Because it was a private, out-of-the-way place where you knew you wouldn't be disturbed?'

'Yes, I suppose so.'

'Miss Osman's uncle didn't keep any of his belongings there?'

'No.'

'And you could get there without going through the main gate?'

'Yes, you go over a fence and then there's a footpath going round the lake. It wasn't locked.'

'In short, an ideal place for you to carry on your relationship with Miss Osman?'

'I suppose so.'

'And after she ended the relationship it would have been natural for you to assume that she would meet your replacement, Mr Mendel, there for the same purpose?'

'No, I don't know what you mean,' said Swain, stammering over his words.

'Oh, come on, Mr Swain, of course you do. You heard Miss Osman's evidence – she saw you in the trees. But that wasn't the only time, was it? You went right up to the window and watched them, didn't you? Watched them tangled up together in the same place where you had been with her only a few months before. Lying where you used to lie; doing what you used to do. How did it feel, Mr Swain? Tell us how it felt.'

'No, no, no!' shouted the defendant, finally losing control. 'No, I didn't. I swear I didn't.' He shouted – almost screamed – the words at Arne, but the prosecutor didn't respond. He didn't need to. He knew what the jury would believe.

It was a brilliant piece of cross-examination, thought Trave. Arne had no proof that Swain had watched Katya Osman and Ethan Mendel making the beast with two backs on the floor of the boathouse, but then again he didn't need any. The defendant's uncontrolled reaction to the accusation was enough. The picture was too powerful to be ignored. It was enough to drive a man to murder.

'You saw them and something broke inside you, didn't it? You decided to murder Mr Mendel. That was the only way to stop the pain, wasn't it?'

'No.'

'But then he went away. That must have been hard for you, Mr Swain – having to wait?'

The defendant didn't answer, and Arne went on

relentlessly: 'Except that suddenly, out of the blue, he came back and asked you to meet him at the very place where he'd hurt you so badly . . .'

'Yes. Why would he do that?' asked Swain loudly, interrupting.

'I don't know. I'm not Mr Mendel. But you obviously didn't give him a chance to explain, did you? Because he'd provided you with your opportunity. That's all you cared about. An opportunity to get even with him forever. In the very place where you had been betrayed. The place where your heaven had turned to hell. With a knife in the back. It must have felt like sweet revenge.'

'No, it didn't. I didn't kill him. I swear I didn't.'

'I can't hear you, Mr Swain. You'll have to speak louder.'

It was indeed hard to understand what Swain was saying. He was half-bent over in the witness box, and his words escaped from him in gasps. He was like a wild animal that had been wounded by a crack-shot hunter, thought Trave. He'd go on for a little while, but before long he'd be finished.

'I didn't murder Ethan,' he said, looking up at the prosecutor through reddened eyes. 'Someone else did.'

'At just about the same time that you were with him? That's the time-of-death evidence. You heard the doctor that came to court. You're not disagreeing with him, are you?'

'No, of course I'm not.'

'I'm glad to hear it. So let me get this right. You're beside the body of a man that's just been murdered, a man that you have repeatedly threatened to kill. And yet you're not the murderer. It's someone else. Is that your evidence?'

'Yes.'

'So why, if you're not the murderer, did you run away when Mr Claes told you to stop?'

'Because I knew how it would look. Because he had a gun.'

'No, Mr Claes shooting the gun is what made you stop. You ran because you were guilty, because you'd been caught red-handed. That's the truth, isn't it, Mr Swain? You're guilty as charged.'

Arne sat down without waiting for Swain to answer. He'd done all that he needed to. And the jury didn't take long to convict the following day. Trave remembered the end of the trial for a long time afterward. The way Swain collapsed in on himself; the way he had to be half-supported, half-carried out of the dock and down the stairs to the cells to begin his life sentence; the silence in the courtroom after he'd gone.

'Good work, Mr Trave,' the prosecutor told Trave afterward as he shook him by the hand on the courthouse steps. 'That boy's damn lucky not to swing. If he'd used a gun it would've been different.' Trave nodded glumly, wishing that he could share Arne's certainty that justice had been done. In spite of all the evidence, something still nagged at him about the case: a lingering doubt that no one else seemed to share. Policing was a lonely, miserable business at the best of times, he thought, as he headed across the road toward the car park and pulled his collar up against the biting wind.

PART ONE

1960

CHAPTER 1

Outside it was late summer. The red-brown leaves hung heavy on the trees in the woods beyond the house, and in the front courtyard silver water splashed down from the stone mermaids' open mouths into the blue-grey basin of the fountain to be reabsorbed, pumped back up and out again in an endless cycle. The courtyard was empty and it was the only sound. Above, the last golden light of the sinking evening sun glinted here and there in the polished glass of the three symmetrical rows of sash windows that ran along the façade of Blackwater Hall. All of them the same, except for one window high up on the left, a window with steel bars inside the reinforced glass. Behind it Katya Osman sat at her desk writing in her diary.

She wrote sideways with her body leaning over the book as if to conceal its contents, but this was clearly from force of habit, not necessity, since there was no one else in the room and the door was locked. Her long, unbrushed blonde hair fell down over the desk, and every so often she pulled it back behind her head with an irritated gesture. She was concentrating hard and she bit down on her lower lip as she wrote, occasionally looking up and out into the darkening sky beyond the bars of her window as if in search of inspiration. She had always been pretty but suffering had changed her. Her bright blue eyes, swollen from too much crying, had become larger and more luminous than ever before in her gaunt and ravaged face, and in the last few days she had almost stopped eating so that her clothes had now begun to hang off her body, as if they had grown out of her. She wore them carelessly – the buttons on her grey dress were unevenly fastened, and there were stains around the collar.

The room too was a mess. Clothes, dirty and clean, were everywhere, falling out of drawers, draped over the open doors of the wardrobe in the corner, and an overflowing ashtray competed for space with a framed photograph and a plate containing a half-eaten apple and an untouched sandwich on top of a crowded bookcase by the door.

'I cannot bear the pain any more,' she wrote. 'I feel like I'm going mad. I think it would be better to die than to carry on like this. But how? That's the question. Perhaps I can steal the matches from Jana when she comes in to feed me and then we'll die together, she and I. Burn until there's nothing left. There would be justice in that. But I know that at the last moment I won't be able to go through with it; I'll draw back – I know I will. Why? Why, in God's name, why? It's not fear of death that stops me. I know that. It's hope; hope for life. Hope is my curse. It always has been. I see that now. God, how much better I would be without it. How much . . .'

Katya stopped writing suddenly, her pen suspended in mid-air. Outside she could hear footsteps. She knew the sound of them – patent leather soles clicking on the wooden floor. They were coming down the corridor toward her door. Quickly she crossed to the bookcase and pulled out a thick book from the bottom shelf. Back in happier days Katya had hollowed out its interior to create a perfect hiding place for her secret diary. And then for years it had lain there forgotten until she'd begun to keep it again in recent weeks, adding almost daily entries in her tiny, spidery writing.

She'd just finished replacing the book and got back to her chair when she heard the key turn in the lock behind her and a tall thin woman dressed entirely in black came into the room.

Jana Claes had never been pretty, but then again she'd never claimed to be. Her nose was too big and her eyes too small for her pallid face, and her lack of any figure emphasized an enduring impression of semi-masculinity. She was almost fifty now, more than twice Katya's age, and, just as she had always done since she was a girl, she wore her hair, now greying, tied up in a severe bun at the back of her head. Katya had never seen her let it down; just as she had never seen her dressed in anything but black. Unmarried, Jana wore no jewellery except a small silver crucifix that hung on a thin chain around her neck. *Bloody hypocrite*, Katya always said to herself whenever she saw it.

The eldest of a family of five, Jana had had domestic responsibility for her siblings since the age of thirteen, when her mother was admitted to hospital one winter afternoon suffering from scarlet fever and had never come back home again. Life was a serious business. There was no room in it for frivolity or vanity. And in all the years that she had known the elder woman, Katya had never once heard her laugh.

Jana stood in the doorway surveying the room with her thin lips drawn back in an expression of unconcealed disgust.

'Why don't you clear this up?' she asked, speaking with the thick Flemish accent that Katya had come to dislike so much.

'Because I choose not to,' said Katya defiantly.

'It's horrible,' said Jana, advancing into the room and closing the door behind her. 'You have no self-respect.'

'Nor do you. You're nothing but a common gaoler. That's all you are.'

'It is for your own good.'

Katya snorted with contempt. 'Have you got a light?' she asked after a moment, taking a cigarette out of a battered packet lying on the desk. It humiliated her to have to ask, but she had no choice. Jana had taken her matches away after an accident with the bedclothes a week earlier, and she badly needed to smoke. Her hands were shaking as she held out the cigarette.

'No. Not now. I need to give you something to make you sleep,' said Jana, taking a syringe out of her pocket and removing the cover from the needle. 'Your uncle is worried about you. If you carry on having no sleep, you will be ill. It won't hurt, I promise. Just a little prick – that's all.'

Katya had gone white at the sight of the syringe. Her defiance disappeared like air from a burst balloon, and she backed away into the far corner of the room, terrified.

'No. Not that. Please not that,' she pleaded with her trembling hands held out in front of her in a gesture combining resistance and supplication in equal measure. 'It made me sick last time, don't you remember?'

'It was fine. You went to sleep and then you woke up and you felt a whole lot better,' said Jana, advancing slowly toward Katya with the syringe in her hand, the needle pointed at the ceiling. She tried to inject a soothing tone into her voice, but her words only seemed to make Katya more hysterical. She regretted coming alone now. There was a crazy look in the girl's eye like she was toppling over the edge into madness, and Jana wished that she'd brought her brother, Franz, with her, but she hadn't wanted to bother him. Like Titus, Katya's uncle, he had a lot of things on his mind. She'd wanted to show her brother that he could rely on her, and last time it had been easy with Katya. She'd been ill in bed and there'd been no trouble.

Reaching Katya, Jana took sudden hold of her arm and forced her down onto the bed. Katya felt the strength in Jana's hand. It was like a vice on her wrist, temporarily paralysing her. She felt the prick as the needle pierced her skin, and, as if in slow motion, she watched Jana's thumb move to press down on the stopper of the syringe. But then, at that precise moment, it was as if some outside force suddenly possessed her: a surge of adrenaline coursed through her body like a charge of electricity, filling her with an overpowering determination not to allow this withered old woman to treat her like she was nothing, a body to be drugged and starved and imprisoned in an attic room at someone else's whim. She pulled her arm away and pushed up suddenly with all her strength into Jana's chest, taking the older woman by surprise and sending her reeling back against the corner of the desk, where she sank down onto the floor. The syringe, half-full, fell out of Jana's hand and rolled away under the bed.

Getting to her feet, Katya looked down at her adversary. Jana wasn't moving. Perhaps she'd hit her head on the side of the desk. Quite deliberately Katya took aim and kicked Jana hard in the small of the back. Jana cried out and curled herself up into a ball on the floor.

'You deserved that,' said Katya with grim satisfaction. 'I'm not a fool: I know why you're trying to drug me. It's because someone's coming, isn't it? Just like before. And you don't want them to see me, don't want them to know what you're doing to me up here. Well, too bad. This time I'm going to talk. I'm going to tell them everything you've done. And when I've finished, I hope they lock you up and throw away the key. So you'll know what it feels like.'

Katya felt like kicking Jana some more but resisted the temptation. Glancing out the window, she saw that the courtyard was still empty, but nevertheless she felt sure that a car would soon be pulling up. And if she was to stand a chance of telling the visitor her story, she needed to find somewhere to hide until he or she arrived. For a moment Katya remained in the centre of the room, swaying backward and forward on the balls of her feet, her brow furrowed in

17

concentration, but then, drawing a deep breath, she seemed to make up her mind.

Crossing to the door, she smiled. The key was still in the lock. Jana hadn't taken it out when she came in, and so she wouldn't have to search the older woman's pockets and run the risk of another fight. It seemed like a good omen. With one backward glance, Katya closed the door, locked it, and then, with the key in her hand, ran away down the corridor. But before she'd reached the end she felt her legs buckle beneath her as the drug started to take effect, and she had to lean on the wall for support before she turned the corner and started down the stairs.

The first thing that Jana felt when she came to was the intensity of the pain in her head. Her right temple was throbbing so hard that she felt it would burst. It terrified her. Involuntarily she put her hand up to her hairline and felt blood seeping between her fingers. She opened her eyes and the room started to turn, spinning round and round, faster and faster. Quickly she closed them again tight shut, but it was too late. She was turning herself now, and, as she felt her stomach heaving upward, she leant over to the side and was violently sick onto Katya's ruby-red carpet. The movement and the retching made her suddenly conscious of a new hurt low in her back. For a while she lay motionless on the floor facing her own vomit while the two pains fought each other for supremacy until finally they fused together into one solid agony. And the pain was mixed up with shame and fear. She knew what she had done: she had messed everything up. She shuddered as she thought of what Franz would say when he found her. She had to get up, to warn them before this Vanessa woman arrived. Because she didn't know where Katya was. Not in the room certainly. The terrible, shameful retching had at least cleared her head

18

and she found she could open her eyes now without the furniture rising up to meet her. She took in the unmade bed, the syringe that had rolled away underneath it, a photograph of Katya's dead parents on top of the bookcase, and beyond it the door. It was closed. She felt in her pockets for the key, without success. Like a fool she must have left it in the door when she came in, and, if so, Katya would almost certainly have locked her in as she fled.

The pain came back in waves, and for a moment she thought she would pass out again, and perhaps she might have if she hadn't heard the sound of a car driving up and parking in the courtyard below. Now she knew she had almost no time left – a minute or two at most – before Titus opened the front door and brought his guest inside. And so, gritting her teeth, she dragged herself across the carpet to the door and then, putting her hand up to the handle, she found her worst suspicions confirmed. It was indeed locked. But she'd already thought of what to do. She reached down and took off her shoe and then, using all her strength, banged it on the door frame again and again, while she shouted out for help. After half a minute she came to the end of her strength and fell back in a swoon. But it was enough.

Two doors down and one floor below, Jana's brother, Franz, was sitting on his bed, polishing a pair of expensive black shoes. They were spotless, gleaming, and clearly didn't need polishing, but he still shined them every night, enjoying the ritual, the backward and forward strokes. He was in full evening dress, apart from his tie, and, just as he had been doing all day, he was thinking resentfully about Titus's ill-considered association with the policeman's wife, searching his brain for a way to get Titus to break off the relationship. Franz had his door shut, so he didn't hear Jana fall or Katya running in the corridor up above. He did, however, hear Vanessa Trave drive up into the courtyard and Titus come out to greet her. And it was probably the way he strained to hear their conversation down below that enabled him to catch the sound of his sister banging on Katya's door, crying out for help.

He ran upstairs, but he couldn't release her straightaway. He had spare keys to all the rooms in the house, even Titus's study, but they were back in his room, and so he had to return there to get the spare for Katya's bedroom. Once inside, he helped his sister onto the bed and listened patiently while she explained what had happened. He wasn't angry with Jana; instead he blamed himself. He ought to have gone with her to give Katya the injection. The fact that the girl hadn't resisted last time didn't mean she'd always be that way. And she'd obviously kicked Jana in the small of the back while Jana was down on the ground. He'd have a score to settle with little Katya when he found her, which had to be quickly. Vanessa Trave was downstairs, and she couldn't be allowed to know what was going on. Once again Franz clenched his fists in angry frustration. Why wouldn't Titus do what he asked? The woman was married to a police inspector for Christ's sake, the same police inspector who'd asked all those awkward questions after Ethan died, poking his nose into other people's business. So what if she and Trave were separated! They probably still talked to each other. Couldn't Titus at least have taken her somewhere else? No, no, always no. Titus was a law unto himself.

Franz looked down at his sister, trying to decide what to do. She was too badly hurt to help with the search. That much was obvious. And there was no time to lose.

'Stay here, Jani, I'll come back when I find her,' he said, speaking in Dutch. His voice was gruff but not unkind, and Jana picked up on her brother's use of his pet name for her.

'Yes, I'm sorry, Franz,' she said, sounding relieved. 'She went crazy. I didn't expect it.'

'I know. Rest now. I'll be back soon.' He picked up his sister's hand, held it lightly for a moment, and then let it go.

It was the nearest Franz Claes could get to tenderness or affection. Such emotions didn't come naturally to him. But he was fond of his elder sister. They went back a long way. And the idea of her being pushed around and kicked by bloody little Katya made him angry inside. He could feel the rage building like a knot in his stomach. But he had it under control. It was something he prided himself on – he was always in control of his emotions.

Franz went out into the corridor and stood there for a moment, listening intently. With his left forefinger he stroked a long white scar that ran down from the hairline above his left ear to a blotch of red puckered skin just below his jaw, but otherwise he was entirely still. Titus and the Trave woman were somewhere downstairs, too far away to be audible from where he was. It was Katya he was listening for. But he could hear nothing except the sound of his sister's painful breathing in the room behind him. He looked from one end of the corridor to the other, trying to decide which way to go. The house was old, full of unused cupboards and recesses where Katya could be hiding, and there were two staircases going down, one at each end of the corridor. After a moment he shrugged his shoulders and went to the right.

A few minutes later he began to be seriously concerned. He'd gone from room to room, systematically searching every crevice, every corner, but he could find no trace of Katya anywhere. What if he was wasting his time? What if she had got out of the house and was even now heading down towards the gate? The doors and windows were locked, but she could have slipped out the front door and past her uncle when he went out to greet Vanessa. He knew

21

Titus wouldn't welcome an interruption before dinner, but he felt he had no choice. There wasn't any time to spare, and he needed help if he was going to find the damned girl before she caused any more trouble.

As he'd anticipated, Titus and his guest were downstairs in the drawing room. It was the handsomest room in the house, with its views through high windows onto the rose garden and the valley beyond – a good place for a romantic encounter, Franz thought bitterly. As a rule of thumb, he didn't like women, but this one he disliked more than most. She was in the way, and she was a security risk. He wished that Titus had never clapped eyes on her.

He took a deep breath, knocked at the door, and went in. They were standing in front of the fireplace. Titus was holding Vanessa's hand but dropped it when Franz came in.

'What is it, Franz? It's surely not time for dinner yet,' he said, glancing over at the golden ormolu clock ticking sedately beneath the oval Venetian mirror on the mantelpiece. It was just after six o'clock.

'I know. I'm sorry, Titus, Mrs Trave. Something has come up. It won't take a moment.'

'Oh, very well. I won't be long, my dear.' Titus Osman made it a point never to raise his voice, never to depart from the elaborate rules of courtesy that he'd set for himself, but under an apparently unruffled exterior he was seriously annoyed by Franz's intrusion. For several weeks now he'd felt the right moment was approaching for a marriage proposal to Vanessa. The timing had to be right, and Titus was nothing if not patient, but she seemed particularly receptive this evening. The weather helped, of course. A warm late summer evening with the sun sinking gently into the pine woods beyond the lake. Perhaps he would take her out into the rose garden after dinner. Smoke a cigar; walk the carefully tended pathways hand in hand in the moonlight; tell her how he felt. But then again – perhaps not the cigar. The smoke might get in the way, particularly if they kissed. He liked the slow courtship that they had been engaged in, and he had enjoyed planning each move forward, continually adjusting his words and suggestions depending on her response, but now it was time to take their budding relationship to another level. He felt sure of it. Tonight was the night.

Of course, if Vanessa said yes, that still wouldn't be the end of the story. She'd need a divorce, and Titus knew how much Vanessa's husband hated him. But he had a strange feeling that that might make it more likely, not less, that Trave would cooperate if Vanessa asked him. The inspector had too much self-love not to want to take the moral high ground if it was offered to him. He was what the English liked to call 'an honourable man'.

However, Titus realized he was getting ahead of himself. First he had to deal with Franz, whose anxiety was obvious. Titus noticed how two bright red spots had appeared in the centre of Franz's pale cheeks, a sure sign of trouble. They talked in the hall. There was no chance Vanessa could hear. Titus had been careful to shut the door of the drawing room when they left.

'Katya locked Jana in her room,' said Franz. 'She attacked her when Jana tried to give her the injection. I don't know where she's gone. I can't find her. I've looked almost everywhere.'

'Christ, Franz. Can't I rely on anyone?' asked Titus angrily.

'We wouldn't have had the problem if you hadn't brought *her* here,' said Franz, gesturing with his thumb toward the drawing room door.

'It's my house. I'll do what I want in it.'

Franz met Titus's eye but otherwise didn't respond, and Titus paused, took a deep breath, and nodded.

'Is your sister hurt?' he asked.

'Yes, but she'll be all right. The point is she can't help us now. That's why I fetched you. It needs two of us to find the girl.'

'Yes, you were right. Could she have got outside?'

'Maybe, when you opened the door. But I think it's more likely she's hiding somewhere. If we don't find her, I'll go after her in the car. She can't get far; she's got no money.'

'All right. You carry on upstairs. I'll look down here after I've told Vanessa. I'm sorry, Franz. You were right to tell me.'

Katya stood at the back of a small closet under the stairs on the other side of the entrance hall from the drawing room. The coat rail running down the centre of the closet was only half-filled and she'd pushed the coats and mackintoshes to the front, creating a hiding place for herself at the back. One coat in particular reached down almost to the floor, and so she'd been all but invisible when Franz had peered inside a moment before. Now she stood holding on to the rail with both hands for support while she listened intently to Franz and her uncle through the half-open door. She felt terrible. Her right arm hurt constantly where Jana's needle had gone into her vein. The bitch – Jana deserved exactly what she'd got. Katya wished she'd kicked Jana a few more times when she'd had the chance. But some of the sedative must have got into her system. She had been fighting drowsiness ever since she got downstairs, and now she felt almost grateful for the pain throbbing in her arm since it was at least keeping her awake – but for how much longer she didn't know. Releasing her left hand from the rail, she squeezed her right wrist hard. Pain was good, and she wished that she had nails to dig into her skin, but she had bitten them all down to the quick long ago.

Damn them; damn them all! What right did they have to

24

treat her like this? She wished Ethan was here to help her. More than two years later and she still missed him as much as ever. So much for time as the great healer, she thought bitterly. She remembered how they had stood together in this same hall and how she had put her arms around his waist and buried her head in his chest and felt for a moment that her life was perfect – nothing needed to be added; nothing needed to be taken away. Everything was exactly right. But it had all been an illusion, a chimera made of delicate crystal glass that had shattered into a thousand tiny pieces a long time ago. Ethan had died with a knife in his back and she'd gone down to skid row and ended up a prisoner in her own bedroom, starved and terrified, without a friend in the world.

Except that now she had a chance, a small chance but a chance nonetheless. If she could just stay awake and escape detection long enough to tell this woman what had happened, then maybe someone would come and help her. So what if the woman had something going with her uncle. From what she'd overheard in the last few minutes, this Vanessa sounded normal, nice even. And Franz and her uncle didn't want Vanessa to know she was here. That much was obvious. Why else would they have got Jana to give her the injection?

Another wave of exhaustion swept over Katya. She hung desperately on to the coat rail, but there was no strength left in her arms and her legs were giving way beneath her. But then, just as she felt sure she was going to fall, she heard Franz above her head going up the stairs. She knew it was him because she could hear the unevenness of his steps; it was unmistakable the way he always dragged his left leg behind him as he walked. A war wound like the scar below his ear. Katya just wished that whoever had inflicted those injuries had had a truer aim and put an end to Franz Claes once and for all.

Franz was gone, but what about her uncle? Carefully she reached past the coats, pushed the closet door open a little further and peered out into the hall. Her uncle was standing with his back to her, stroking his beard as if lost in thought. It was unbearable. He'd told Franz he was going to search for her, so why didn't he? Instead, after a moment he turned and went back into the drawing room. Katya swayed from side to side. She needed air desperately. It was stuffy in the closet and the narrowness of the hiding place had started to make her claustrophobic. And she needed to know what her uncle was saying to this woman he'd invited over. Throwing caution to the winds, she went out into the hall and stood in a recess to the right of the drawing room door, listening. She was taking a terrible risk. She was in plain view from across the hall, and Franz or Jana would have seen her straightaway if they'd come down the stairs, but instinctively she knew that it was now or never if she was going to make her move. The sedative had taken hold, and she only had a little time left.

'I'm sorry, Vanessa. Something has come up and Franz needs my help for a few minutes. It can't be avoided, I'm afraid. Will you be all right?' It was her uncle's voice, and Vanessa answered.

'Of course I will,' she said. 'But would you prefer me to go? We can always rearrange.'

No, thought Katya desperately, clasping her hands together in silent prayer. *No, please don't go.* But she needn't have worried – her uncle came instantly to her rescue.

'Absolutely not, my dear,' he said. 'You would be breaking my heart if you were to go now. I've been looking forward to this evening all week.' Always the elaborate courtesy, Katya thought. He never changed.

'And so have I,' said Vanessa, sounding pleased. 'I'll be fine. How could I not be with this wonderful view to look at?'

'Thank you for being so understanding. I won't be long. Help yourself to another drink if you want one. Everything's over there on the sideboard.'

Katya couldn't believe how relaxed her uncle sounded. There was not a hint of panic in his voice. But he was a different person once he was outside in the hall. He glanced quickly from side to side, but not behind him, where Katya was standing, and then headed purposefully toward his study and the rooms at the back of the house. She had no time to lose. She went into the drawing room and closed the door softly behind her.

Vanessa had moved away from the mantelpiece and was now standing in front of the far window looking out into the twilight with a glass of wine in her hand. She turned around, putting her glass down when she heard the door open, and looked shocked when she saw Katya. The girl's haggard appearance was certainly alarming. White as a sheet, Katya stood swaying from side to side with a half-crazed, desperate look in her eye, and then suddenly leant forward, gripping the back of a sofa in order to stay upright.

Vanessa was frightened and her first instinct was to shout for help, but Katya saw this coming. Desperately she put her right forefinger up to her mouth, fastening onto Vanessa's eyes with her own, and the cry died in Vanessa's throat.

'Who are you?' Vanessa asked instead. And then, just as she'd finished the question, she realized she knew the answer. The girl was Titus's niece. She'd been at the dinner party here at Blackwater Hall that Bill had taken her to after David Swain's conviction – the first night she'd met Titus. She remembered being struck then by how pretty the girl was with her luminous blue eyes and her long blond hair arranged in an elaborate chignon. And her cheeks had been brightly flushed, perhaps from drinking too much champagne but also because she was excited at the outcome of the trial. There was nothing wrong with that. It was the reason for the gathering after all. But Vanessa remembered how it had seemed so personal for the girl. Swain, her previous lover, had killed Katya's new boyfriend in a fit of jealousy, and she clearly hated him for it. She'd almost been saying that life imprisonment wasn't enough, that the man deserved to hang. Perhaps she had actually said that. Vanessa couldn't remember. Well, the girl had certainly changed since then. Vanessa thought she would never have recognized this wraithlike apparition as Katya Osman if the girl's presence in Titus's house hadn't provided her with the connection.

Katya opened her mouth to speak but the words stuck in her throat. She felt sick and faint, and the room had started to revolve. Two great tears sliding slowly down her sunken cheeks bore silent witness to her inner distress.

Recovering from her initial shock, Vanessa crossed the room and put her arm around Katya, helping to hold her up.

'What's wrong?' she asked. 'What can I get you?'

'Water,' Katya whispered. 'Water.'

Vanessa couldn't hear her the first time and had to listen hard before she understood what Katya was saying.

'Yes, of course,' she said, getting up and going over to the drinks tray on the sideboard, but as soon as her back was turned Katya collapsed to the floor, taking a small ornamental table with her. Vanessa couldn't see any water and so she instinctively seized hold of a soda fountain, pulled down on the mother of pearl handle, and sprayed a jet of foaming water in the general direction of the girl's mouth. After a moment Katya coughed and opened her eyes, but she hardly seemed to know where she was. Vanessa knelt down beside Katya, supporting the girl's head in her hands. 'What's wrong?' she asked, repeating her earlier question.

Katya could hear Vanessa's voice, but it was very far away. She was sinking to the bottom of a deep, dark pool and

28

knew that talking would soon be beyond her, and so, with one last superhuman effort, she launched herself upward through the thick black darkness and into the light of her uncle's drawing room. She had come too far to stop now.

'They're . . .'

'Yes?' said Vanessa, putting her ear close to Katya's mouth so that her cheek brushed the wet soda water on the girl's upturned face.

'They're trying to kill me,' said Katya in a rush. But the struggle to get out the words was too much. The sedative that Jana Claes had half-injected into her vein upstairs finally did its work, and Katya collapsed back into Vanessa's arms, dead to the world.

CHAPTER 2

Vanessa reached up and took a cushion off the sofa and placed it under the girl's head, and then, letting go of Katya, she sat back on her haunches, wondering what the hell to do next. She'd come out for a pleasant romantic evening and had ended up within ten minutes of her arrival holding her lover's niece in her arms while the girl accused nameless assailants of trying to kill her. Vanessa closed her eyes, trying to think. It was all just so crazy. She knew Titus – he was a good man. She couldn't conceive of him as a murderer. And yet the girl had seemed so insistent, as if she would have done anything to tell Vanessa her message. 'They're trying to kill me,' she had said. But who was *they*? Perhaps it wasn't Titus at all, but his brother-in-law, Franz, whom the girl had been talking about. Franz and someone else. Certainly there was no blood relationship between Katya and Franz. Titus had told Vanessa very little of his family history, but she knew that Katya was the daughter of Titus's sister, whereas Franz was the brother of Titus's dead wife, about whom he never spoke.

Vanessa had met Franz Claes quite a few times during the last year and she had never warmed to the man. Titus didn't like to drive, and sometimes Franz would act as chauffeur, driving him and Vanessa to restaurants in the back of Titus's Bentley. She could make no criticism of his behaviour – Franz was always polite, and yet he never failed to make her feel uneasy when she was in his company. It wasn't his wounds, or at least she hoped it wasn't. Rather it was the way he avoided her eye and yet always seemed to be watching her. She'd noticed how he always kept

30

everything razor sharp: his too short slicked-down, jet-black hair; the crease in his trousers; the polish on his shoes. Everything was defiantly masculine, except that he felt feminine somehow underneath. He gave Vanessa the creeps when she thought about him. Not that she had very much. Franz Claes had been at the periphery of her life up until now.

She needed to talk to Titus. That was what she needed to do. He'd make sense of all this for her. She thought about going to look for him, but she didn't want to leave the girl on her own. Getting up, she went over to the door, opened it, and called out Titus's name several times. But there was no response. It felt awkward shouting in someone else's house, and she was just about to give up when she heard Titus's voice on the stairs, although she couldn't make out the words, and moments later he came into view. She went out into the hall to meet him.

As always, he looked entirely calm and self-possessed. There was not a wrinkle in his evening dress and he was coming down the stairs at his own pace, without rushing. The sight of her lover reassured Vanessa. Since the death of her teenage son, her only child, in a motorcycle accident three years earlier, Vanessa had convinced herself that the world was an entirely frightening, hostile place and that survival, not happiness, was the most that could be hoped for from life. Her husband hadn't supported her at all with her grief. Bill Trave might be good at his job, but he was hopeless at expressing his emotions or helping his wife to cope with hers. He'd locked himself away in a dark, inaccessible place after Joe died, taking refuge in his police work. Every day he'd acted like their son had never existed, turning in on himself to hide his grief, until she couldn't stand it any more. It was a crime – it was like killing their child all over again. Joe might only have been on the earth nineteen and a half years but they were the most important years of her life. He was her own personal miracle, wound about her heart forever, and she couldn't forgive her husband for denying him. She'd left her husband eighteen months earlier because she'd had to. She'd have died otherwise. And all she'd expected from life once she was on her own was some small easing of her sense of oppression. But instead Titus had come along and lifted her right up off her feet. The happiness was difficult, of course: it made her feel guilty because of Joe and because of her husband, and it didn't help that she'd met Titus because he'd been a witness in one of Bill's cases. But Bill was going to hate whomever she took up with, and she deserved the chance of a little joy before age caught up with her. Her new life might not be perfect, but it was certainly better than the death in life she'd been experiencing before. And recently she had begun to embrace it with both hands. Titus made her feel safe, and he made her feel desirable when she had never expected to feel that way again. He made her feel that she mattered.

'Are you all right, my dear?' asked Titus, seeing the anxious expression on Vanessa's face as she looked up at him from down below. 'I'm sorry to have kept you so long.'

'No, it's not that. It's your niece.'

'Katya?'

'Yes, she's in there,' said Vanessa, pointing toward the drawing room behind her. 'She was in a bad way. I gave her some soda water but she passed out.'

For the first time since she had known him, Titus went ahead of Vanessa through a door. Katya was where Vanessa had left her over by the sofa, and, as far as Vanessa could see, she was still unconscious. It was better that way, Vanessa thought instinctively. The expression of terror had left the girl's face and she looked quiet now, peaceful even.

Titus knelt beside his niece on the carpet and gently brushed her long, tousled fair hair back behind her head. Vanessa

32

noticed the tenderness of his touch; she saw the intense worry and concern plainly written all over his face. It was obvious Titus didn't mean his niece any harm. The idea was ludicrous, thought Vanessa, looking down at the two of them on the floor. Titus was Katya's protector, not her enemy.

In one fluid movement he picked Katya up in his arms and got to his feet. Vanessa noticed how little effort this seemed to require. Katya was a waif of a person, light as a feather. Titus laid her down softly on the sofa, keeping the cushion under her head to act as a pillow.

'Shouldn't we call a doctor?' asked Vanessa.

'No, it's not necessary. She has no fever. Come, you can see,' said Titus, beckoning Vanessa over and placing her hand on his niece's forehead. He was right. It felt cool, and she was breathing easily.

'This has happened before,' he went on after a moment. 'It is too little sleep that is the problem. You English have a word for it.'

'Insomnia?'

'Yes, insomnia. It is terrible for my Katya. She goes for many hours without sleeping and it makes her crazy. This evening my sister-in-law . . . no, is that right? The sister of my brother-in-law is my sister-in-law? Yes?'

'Yes, I suppose so,' said Vanessa, smiling in spite of herself. He often spoke to her like this, like a student of English asking questions of a teacher, and she sometimes felt that that he was half-teasing her, that he knew the answers to his questions before he asked them. Like now for instance. But she didn't mind. She knew that he was trying to calm her down, and she appreciated his thoughtfulness.

'Thank you,' he said with a small bow. 'So this evening my sister-in-law, Jana, tried to give Katya a sedative to help her sleep, but Katya struggled and became very angry. It is not fair because Jana was only trying to help.'

Vanessa had never met Franz's sister. Usually she and Titus met in town, and Jana had never come downstairs on the occasions when Vanessa had visited Blackwater Hall. In fact, looking back, Vanessa couldn't remember Titus ever referring to his sister-in-law before. It had been like she didn't exist. In other circumstances she would have liked to ask him more about Jana, but now wasn't the time.

'And yet it is not Katya's fault either,' said Titus, looking down sadly at his niece. 'She has never recovered from poor Ethan's death, you know.'

'Yes, I was remembering that that's when I last met her. It was here at the dinner party you gave after the trial.'

'The night when I first met you. A night I will never forget,' said Titus, bending over and kissing Vanessa's hand. She smiled again, but went on with her thought.

'She was so angry. That's what I remember. Furious with that man, Swain, for what he had done.'

'Yes, she wanted to kill him. Not that that would have brought Ethan back, of course. Having Swain convicted at the trial was the next best thing. But then, after it was over and Swain had got his sentence, she felt empty. There was nothing more to do and it was time for everyone to get on with their own lives again. But Katya couldn't. She had no sense of direction – she was like a ship without a rudder. And so she went into Oxford and lost control of herself. This is a beautiful city, but like all cities it has a bad side, an underbelly!'

Titus stopped for a moment, savouring the word, as if pleased that he knew such an obscure piece of English vocabulary.

'She went to places where a young girl should not go and she did things she should never have done,' he went on after a moment. 'She took drugs, Vanessa. Here, look.' Gently, Titus lifted the sleeve on Katya's left arm up to the shoulder

34

and pointed to the needle marks dotting the skin above her elbow. 'And that's not all. She sold herself.' Titus's voice broke, and he put his hand up to his eyes.

'I'm sorry, Titus. I had no idea. You don't have to tell me this,' said Vanessa. She felt appalled, horrified, by what Titus had had to bear.

'I'm telling you because I want to,' said Titus, reaching out and taking Vanessa's hand. 'Because I don't want there to be any secrets between us. Because you matter to me, Vanessa. You know that, don't you?'

Titus looked into Vanessa's eyes, sensing her response. But then suddenly the connection between them was broken as she looked away over his shoulder with a grimace, and, turning round, he came face-to-face with Franz, standing behind him in the doorway. *Like my damned shadow,* he thought angrily. Franz was in the way as usual, spoiling everything, just when he had had that instinctive sense that the moment had at last arrived to make a declaration to Vanessa. But then he remembered Katya lying unconscious on the sofa and he felt the injustice of his reaction. Franz was right to interrupt them. The girl couldn't stay here. She needed to be put to bed. There would be plenty of time for romance later.

'I'm sorry, Franz. I didn't see you,' he said in an even voice. 'I was just coming to find you to say that Katya was all right. Vanessa here has been kindly looking after her.'

Franz nodded toward Vanessa without saying anything. It was a formal gesture, like a military salute, empty of personal meaning.

'I'll take her up,' he said, crossing over to Katya, but Titus put up his hand in an authoritative gesture before Franz could take hold of her.

'No, Franz. This is a job for me, I think.'

Franz winced, stepping back as if he'd been struck. Vanessa

wondered at his sensitivity but then guessed intuitively that he didn't like being given orders in front of her.

Again Vanessa was struck by how light Katya seemed to be in Titus's arms. It wasn't just sleep the girl needed; it was food and drink. Vanessa knew it wasn't her place to interfere but she felt she'd have to say something to Titus later when they were alone.

'I'll be back in a moment, my dear. Just as soon as I've got my Katya tucked up in bed,' said Titus as he was going out of the door.

'No problem,' said Vanessa. 'I'm fine here.' But Titus was gone by the time she'd finished her sentence, and she found herself speaking instead to his brother-in-law, who stood facing her with his hand on the door handle.

He looked at her for a moment without speaking and then, bringing his feet together as if standing to attention, he bowed his head but not his back before turning around and leaving the room, pulling the door shut behind him. Vanessa half-expected to hear a key turning in the lock, but nothing happened, and she was left alone in a sudden strange silence.

A phrase she'd read years ago in some forgotten book floated unbidden into Vanessa's mind: 'Politeness is one of the most potent weapons in a civilized society.' Franz Claes didn't just make her feel uneasy, she realized. She actively disliked him as well.

Vanessa screwed up her eyes and shook her head, doing her best to clear all thoughts of Claes from her head. She preferred to think of Titus. She often found it difficult to summon an image, to accurately visualize a place or a person when they were not there in front of her, but with Titus it was different. He had impressed himself on her mind's eye from the first, long before they had started seeing each other. Nobody could say that he wasn't a fine figure of a man.

An inch more than six foot from the top of his thick wavy silver hair down to his Italian leather shoes. Generally she had never been attracted to men with beards, but with Titus it was different. The carefully groomed beard and moustache were an extension of his beautiful hair, and she liked the rough texture of it under her fingers.

She didn't know his exact age but she guessed him to be in his late fifties, and yet he was clearly physically very fit and never seemed tired or deflated. His bright blue eyes, perhaps his most attractive feature, were constantly alert, and sometimes it seemed as if they sparkled, lighting up his face.

He had beautiful taste. His clothes, his house, his possessions – everything was perfect. And yet worn and possessed with an effortlessness that Vanessa had never encountered before. He liked to show her things – between two high bookshelves in his study, for example, a tiny, terrifying painting of the Gorgon's head by Caravaggio that gazed at her malevolently out of its dark frame, or in the drawing room a silver box embossed with Cyrillic letters and a royal crest in which the last tsar had kept his cufflinks.

'You know the Bolsheviks told the imperial family to get ready to go out before they shot them. Perhaps this was the last of his possessions that the tsar touched at Ekaterinburg that morning.'

Vanessa remembered how Titus had held the box lightly between his two fingers, holding it up to the afternoon light, as he brought its significance to life with his words. It was the objects themselves, their beauty and their provenance, not his ownership of them, that he seemed to care about. He clearly knew an extraordinary amount about many different things and yet he always seemed interested in Vanessa's opinion; he was always trying to find out what she really thought. He would press her if he sensed she was just being polite until she had told him her true opinion, and then he would weigh her words, sometimes agreeing, sometimes disagreeing with her point of view.

On a visit to the house two weeks earlier he had elicited a lukewarm response from her to a standard-quality Italianate landscape hanging in the hall, and now on this visit she noticed it had been replaced with a wonderfully vivid, brightly coloured picture of one of the smaller canal bridges in Venice. She knew the place because she'd been there years before with her husband, and the memory had upset her for a moment before she rejected its poignancy with a surge of anger against the man she had left. She remembered the long silences at mealtimes, the empty space between them in their double bed; the way Bill had worked later and later hours down at the police station. He had had no interest in her opinion; he'd made her feel unwanted, useless, a dead weight. Not like Titus, who made her feel so vital – alive in every part of her mind and body.

And Titus was mysterious. She had to admit that was part of the attraction. She liked his foreignness, his elaborate courtesy and the slow deliberation with which he spoke, choosing his words carefully, as if weighing each one of them before use. She realized, of course, that she knew almost nothing more about Titus than what her husband had told her and what she had read about in the newspapers at the time of the Swain trial two years earlier. He was from Antwerp. He had made a fortune dealing in diamonds and had helped Jews escape from Belgium during the war, and then afterwards he had come to England, to Oxford, and become a philanthropist and an art collector, a man of influence and standing, well respected in the town, moving in its highest social circles. So why then would he want *her*? Vanessa had asked herself this question a thousand times since Titus first started showing interest in her eighteen months earlier, but she had never been able to come up with a satisfactory answer. Perhaps it was the thrill of the chase, the fact that she was so obviously unavailable; perhaps it was the challenge of bringing a smile to the face of someone who was so sad and lost; or perhaps it was just that Titus found her attractive. Perhaps she was beautiful and fascinating just like he said, lost to the world all those years, sitting at home in her North Oxford house, unhappily married to her misanthropic husband.

Vanessa got up from the sofa and went and stood in front of the fireplace, examining herself detachedly in the beautiful oval gold-leaf mirror that hung over the mantelpiece. Yes, she did look different. She could see that now. Better than she'd done in a long time. There was colour in her cheeks, a new lustre in her dark brown hair, and more flesh in her face and on her body, replacing that worn-down boniness that had made her avoid her reflection for so long. The truth was that she'd begun to look after herself since leaving her husband the previous year. She'd discovered she was a good cook. Bill had always seemed to want solid British fare, but now she was free to experiment. She enjoyed shopping in the Covered Market off the High Street, buying herbs and spices with exotic names and trying out recipes that she would never have dreamt of attempting back home in North Oxford. Sometimes her concoctions ended in disaster, but it didn't matter if there was no one there to criticize. It was all a learning experience, and by the time that Titus started coming to dinner, she found that she knew what she was doing, and it was obvious that the compliments he paid her on her cooking were genuine. Such a contrast to her husband, who had never said anything about the food she put in front of him; he was too self-absorbed to care about what he put in his mouth or what his surroundings looked like.

And she'd also begun to paint again for the first time in

as long as she could remember, taking advantage of the long summer evenings after work to ride her bicycle out onto Port Meadow with a folded-up easel across her back and her watercolours and paper in a canvas bag hanging from the handlebars. She'd been quite good once, or so her tutor at the art school that she'd attended for a year after college had told her, and she'd enjoyed the paintings and sketches she'd made on the sunlit holidays in France and Italy that she'd taken with Bill in the years after they were first married. In fact she didn't really know why she had stopped. Lack of encouragement perhaps. Whatever the explanation, it was certainly Titus's encouragement that had got her started again. She had hung one or two of her old pictures on the walls of the little flat that she'd rented behind Keble College, and he'd stood admiring them on his first visit, wanting to know the name of the artist. And then when he found out it was her, he'd insisted on taking her to an art supplies shop he knew down a tiny side street off George Street and buying her the materials to start again.

'It's a crime,' he'd told her in a voice that brooked no argument, 'to waste such God-given talent.'

And since then she hadn't looked back. The painting made her happy, and when she painted, she thought of Titus.

Vanessa's paintings now covered the walls of her flat, lighting it up with colour and life. It was a small place, just enough for her needs, but she'd grown to like it more and more as the months passed. She'd deliberately rented the flat unfurnished and then bought the furniture herself piece by piece. She didn't have much money. The temporary job that she'd taken on as a secretary and personal assistant to an overworked professor in the university's English faculty didn't pay well, but she had come to relish the challenge of shopping on a shoestring, finding treasures in secondhand stores that she'd never previously heard of, down narrow

40

side streets in parts of Oxford that she'd never visited before. She'd made her own home and she was proud of it. The flat, of course, was a million miles away from the grandeur of Blackwater Hall, but Titus genuinely seemed to like it there when he came to visit.

He had a way of making her seem special, and in his company she had begun to come alive again. It had been more than three years now since Joe died and she still felt the pain. It was there all the time but it was dulled. After it happened she'd spent more than a year feeling that the world was entirely without point, dragging herself through every day in a grey blur. She'd contemplated suicide more than once, even weighed up the pros and cons of the different possible methods of putting an end to her pain, but she saw now that she had never been truly serious. The will to live was too strong inside her. It had flickered for a while like a guttering candle, but it wasn't going to be extinguished. And her anger against her husband's silence, his refusal to try to move forward, was in a way the first sign of her recovery. Titus had arrived at just the moment when her desire for life had first begun to outweigh her guilt at living. And now she was halfway to falling in love.

CHAPTER 3

'You can't let them get to you, Davy. That's the point. Whether it's that bitch who put you in here, whether it's the screws, or whether it's the other cons, you've got to remember it's your life, not theirs. And you've got to keep it that way.'

Just as he had done every night for the previous two weeks, David Swain lay on his back in the dark listening to the voice of Eddie Earle coming down to him from the bunk above his head, and, as always, he felt that same odd mixture of irritation and gratitude. Irritation because Eddie kept calling him Davy – a nickname that nobody else had ever used and that David really didn't like – and because Eddie never seemed to stop telling him how to live his life. Gratitude because he gave David a sense of security that he'd been missing ever since he'd first arrived in prison following his arrest more than two years earlier.

It had got worse after his conviction – much worse. The judge had thrown away the key, had called him a coward, a knife-in-the-back murderer, and sent him down for life. And overnight David had become a number, an object to be moved around without explanation from cell to cell, from wing to wing, from gaol to gaol, until he'd ended up back where he'd started – in Oxford Prison. Days, months, years of terrible food and waiting in cold corridors, of boredom and claustrophobia banged up in tiny airless cells, had brought David full circle.

It didn't surprise him that he'd ended up back in Oxford. Nothing much surprised him any more. Prison was cruel, and here, locked away in the centre of his own hometown, it was just a bit more painful than anywhere else. That's all. A few hundred yards away on the other side of a thirty-foot brick wall surmounted with barbed wire, the world he'd left behind was going on without him, impervious to his absence. In the mornings he could hear the bells ringing in Magdalen Tower and in the afternoons he could see the tallest spires of the city's churches from the prison exercise yard. So near and yet so far; the proximity of the world outside was an exquisite torture.

And he was very different now from the man he'd been when he'd begun his sentence, less and less able to cope with the despair that was eating him up from the inside. Physically, he had survived. There had been pushes, punches, even a few kicks along the way, but he had got through them. And it could have been worse. David knew all about the mindless violence that was always waiting as a possibility around the next corner – God knows he'd seen it often enough, but so far he had avoided the worst by keeping his head down, not answering back, not getting involved.

Spiritually and emotionally, however, it was a very different story. Over time he had learnt to accept the arbitrariness of prison life: the endless petty rules that existed only to be broken, the lack of choice. And he had tried to get used to the strange combination of noise and isolation, his twin companions through the endless long days and sleep-interrupted nights. But underneath he had lost hope and purpose. His personality, already fragile and damaged at the time of his arrest, had disintegrated under the stress of prison life, and the anger and despair that raged inside him were now only kept in check by fear. He longed for someone to cling to as he sank, for someone to hold him up, and then, entirely unexpectedly one day, a friend appeared. He was called Eddie Earle.

With a smile David remembered the day that his new

cellmate had arrived. He'd been alone for over a week, ever since O'Brien, the previous occupant of the top bunk, had been transferred to the punishment block in D Wing for attacking another prisoner with a pool cue in the rec room. O'Brien had not been a bad cellmate. Tall, taciturn, and religious, with a permanent furrow etched across his massive brow, he'd actually gone so far as to give David a book called *JESUS FOR PRISONERS*. David hadn't yet read more than the first paragraph but he appreciated the thought. Gifts weren't a daily occurrence in HM Prison Oxford.

O'Brien's problem was his temper. It was what had got him put away in the first place. And he had an enemy on B Wing who'd been goading him for weeks. Something about taking too much food in the canteen, something stupid, but still O'Brien shouldn't have reacted. He only had himself to blame. And his departure had meant that David had had to start worrying again about who would be coming in next to share his ten-by-ten cell and stinking chamber pot. *Not some crazy*, he prayed after lights-out to a God he had no faith in whatsoever. *Not some fucking crazy psychopath*. But he needn't have worried. Eddie Earle, Easy Eddie as he liked to be known among his friends, was nothing like that at all.

Eddie had self-respect. If David had had to name one quality that singled out his new cellmate, that would've been the one he picked. He refused to be a number; he refused to give in to the system. David thought at first that this would lead to endless problems with the screws, problems that he could do without. But that wasn't how it worked out. Eddie had an easy way with him – it must have been how he'd got his nickname, and the screws laughed at his jokes and didn't seem to pick on him like they did with the other prisoners. Almost immediately this started to bring benefits for David because Eddie seemed to be able to get hold of anything he put his mind to. Soft toilet tissue, fresh fruit, magazines, and even on one memorable occasion two cans of beer appeared like magic in the cell. The screws turned a blind eye, and Eddie shared everything he got with David. 'Because that's what cellmates do,' he said.

'You've got to take care of yourself. That's the secret,' Eddie announced on that memorable afternoon when they'd sat on David's bunk and raised their cans of Special Brew in a toast to the poster of Elizabeth Taylor in a sultry, low-cut dress that Eddie had put up on the opposite wall.

'Liz has to, you know,' he went on musingly. 'Imagine the time she spends every evening with her paint bottles and stuff getting ready to go out to one of them Hollywood parties. Monty Clift's outside, walking up and down getting all sweaty and impatient, but, oh no, she's got to get it right. Eyebrows, makeup, lipstick. Not a fucking hair out of place. And you know why, Davy? You know why?'

It was a rhetorical question and David sat sipping his beer, halfway to heaven with the taste of it, waiting for the answer.

'Because she cares about herself. That's why.'

'Not that easy in here though, is it?' said David, sounding a note of realism. It was a long way from HM Prison Oxford to Beverly Hills, California.

'No, it ain't,' said Eddie, agreeing. 'But I'll tell you this much – looking after yourself when you're inside is where it's most important. Because in here is where they're trying to take your pride away every minute of the day. I should know – I've been in prison enough times. The point is, Davy, it doesn't matter where you are – Hollywood or Her Majesty's pleasure. You've got to keep your head up. That's what I do. And it's what you'll do if you've got any sense. Why do you think I'm working out down in the gym during association? Why do I try and eat proper food?' said Eddie, jabbing his finger over at the two rows of apples and pears carefully arranged on the rickety shelves under Elizabeth Taylor's poster.

'I've noticed you spending a lot of time looking in the mirror, Eddie. I suppose that's the same thing,' said David, trying to inject a lighter note into the conversation. He didn't really disagree with Eddie's take on how to survive prison life but it was instinctive for him to rebel a little whenever he found himself being lectured about anything. And Eddie was indeed almost obsessive about his personal appearance. He spent ages every morning stooped in front of the broken piece of glass screwed to the wall at the back of the cell, combing his jet-black hair until the parting was razor straight, and he insisted on the barber who came round to shave the prisoners every morning taking extra care with the long sideburns that he'd grown in the style of Elvis Presley. David had learnt very early in their relationship that the two great loves of Eddie's life were America and show business.

David regretted his words as soon as they were out of his mouth. Sipping his beer, he felt more warmly disposed to Eddie than ever before at that moment and he had no wish to rock the boat or give him offence. But he needn't have worried. Eddie had a very thick skin.

'Yes, taking care of what you look like's important too. Of course it is, like I said before,' said Eddie, refusing to be put out of his stride. 'It's like my old auntie used to say when I was a kid – take care of your skin if you want to feel comfortable in it.'

David had begun to notice in recent days how Eddie's aunt, like Elizabeth Taylor, was becoming an increasingly frequent visitor to their conversations.

But it wasn't all Eddie. He knew how to listen too, and perhaps it was this quality more than any other that drew

David to his new cellmate. David had two years of anger and frustration built up inside him, and it helped to let some of it out. Or rather he thought it helped. Talking about Katya and Ethan had seemed like a relief to begin with. He'd not been able to talk to anyone about how he felt until now. People didn't discuss personal stuff in prison. It was one of the unwritten rules. But Eddie was different. He wanted to know about what had happened, every last detail of it.

Lying on their bunks after lights-out, they had long, whispered conversation into the small hours. Their positions, one on top of each other, so close and yet invisible to each other, disembodied voices in the semi-darkness, made it easier to talk somehow. And so David had told Eddie his story, or his version of it at least – about how Katya had thrown him over and how that made him feel, about Ethan, and about Katya's coming to court and reading out his letters one after the other, looking over at him in the dock with such hatred in her eyes.

And Eddie was sympathetic, so sympathetic in fact that his words of comfort made the pain worse, not better, turning David's slow-burning anger into rage so that he couldn't sleep at night for the thought of Katya and what she had done to him.

Sometimes, waking up in the pale light of day, David did draw breath and wonder why Eddie seemed to care so much, but then Eddie himself provided the explanation. David's experience with Katya fitted in with Eddie's whole view of the opposite sex. It was another proof for his well-developed theory that women were the root of all evil. He made an exception for his dead aunt and a screen goddess or two, but the rest of them were all the same. They teased men with their tight skirts and their painted faces, promising paradise with a look of the eye or a turn of the hip, and then, once they had their victims hooked, they turned them loose just to watch their pain.

'For the fun of it, just for the fucking fun of it,' said Eddie, whose first experience of evil women had been his tart of a mother who had abandoned him at his grandmother's so she could carry on with the life of debauchery that her pregnancy had briefly interrupted. And then the grandmother had not been much better, beating Eddie with her stick whenever he came home late from school and dosing him with horrible homemade medications to keep his insides clean. Only his great aunt, his grandmother's younger sister, had shown him a little kindness, but that was only when the old woman's back was turned, and it hadn't been enough to stop him running away at the first opportunity. He'd gone to his mother but she wouldn't have him. And from there he'd begun a series of relationships that all ended in disaster, culminating in marriage to a cook in one of the colleges, who'd turned him in to the police when she found out he was using the basement of the matrimonial home as a warehouse for fencing stolen goods.

'Fucking bitch. The only thing I miss about her is her apple pie,' said Eddie, who then promptly turned and spat out the unwanted memory into a corner of the exercise yard. The night was over, giving way to a cold, miserable morning with the sun lost behind a thick blanket of grey clouds, and the prisoners of A Wing had been turfed out into the open after an unappetizing breakfast of overcooked porridge and dried toast. David shivered, wishing he'd brought his coat from the cell.

'Visit; visit for Earle!'

One of the screws was shouting down at them from the top of the staircase leading up to the new building over beyond B Wing, the one housing the rec room and the gym.

'Aren't you the lucky one? That's your second in a week,'

said David, unable to keep the envy out of his voice. He couldn't remember when he'd last had a visit. His mother was too ashamed to come and his friends all seemed to have forgotten him. Out of sight; out of mind.

'It's business, Davy. I told you that before,' said Eddie, clapping David on the shoulder as he turned to go. 'Just because I'm banged up in here doesn't mean I ain't got things going on on the outside; things I need to hear about from time to time.'

Left on his own to make a final circuit of the yard, David lit his last cigarette and inhaled the smoke deep into his lungs in an effort to blot out his frustration. Eddie had business on the outside because he was going to be getting out in a year or two. He had something to look forward to, unlike David, who had a lifetime of barbed wire and prison walls in front of him. *Like being buried alive*, he thought bitterly.

On the way back to A Wing he felt a tap on his shoulder and turned round to find his ex-cellmate, O'Brien, towering above his head. He looked thinner than before and his eyes were sunk deep in their sockets. D Block had clearly not agreed with him.

'You got a new cellmate, I hear,' said O'Brien as they approached the white wrought-iron stairs leading up to the landings above.

'Yeah, Earle; Eddie Earle. He's all right,' said David defensively. It wasn't his fault O'Brien had had to move out.

'No, he's not all right. I know him. He'd sell your bloody grandmother if he had the chance,' said O'Brien. There was an urgency in his voice and a wild look in his eye that David found alarming.

O'Brien moved away as they reached his landing, but, turning round, had time for one last warning before he went into his cell: 'You watch your back, Swain, you hear me. Or he'll have you.'

Back in his own cell, David felt unnerved by his encounter. O'Brien did seem a little crazy, but then again why should he be so worried about Eddie? The question gnawed at David for the rest of the afternoon, partly because he too had his doubts about his new cellmate. Why was he so friendly? Why was he so interested in David's life story? Why did he seem to care so much? David needed answers. And the only way of getting them was to ask Eddie himself.

'Good visit?' asked David, looking up from *Jesus for Prisoners* as Eddie was let back into the cell an hour later.

'Yeah, all right. What you been doing?'

'Nothing much. Talking to O'Brien.'

'Who?'

'Irish guy who was in here before you. Big guy, into Jesus, got a temper. He doesn't like you.' 'Oh?'

'Yeah, says I ought to watch my back.'

'And so you should, Davy. So you should. Anyone who doesn't do that in here's a fucking idiot.'

David couldn't see Eddie's expression. He had his back to the bunks, doing something over by the shelves.

'Do you know him?' David asked

'Yeah, I think I know who you mean, if it's the same guy. Jesus Joe he was called when I last saw him. Down in Winchester nick a couple of years back. We've crossed paths once or twice. He doesn't like me and I don't like him. That's all. Nothing to write home about.'

There was a casual note in Eddie's voice that sounded forced somehow. It was like he knew more than he was saying.

'Why doesn't he like you?' asked David, persisting with his questions.

'I don't know. He's stupid and I'm not. I nick stuff and he listens to the Ten Commandments. Thou shalt not steal; thou shalt not take the Lord's name in vain,' said Eddie, imitating O'Brien's deep Irish voice surprisingly well. 'You know what I mean.'

Turning round, Eddie stood looking down at his cellmate for a moment and then came and sat down beside him on the bottom bunk.

'Got you worried, has he, this Irish bloke?' he asked, looking David in the eye.

'No, not really. It's not that. It's just, well, it's just I don't get why you're so interested in me, why you keep asking me all these questions, why you're nice to me. I mean other cons aren't like that. Some of them are all right, but . . .'

'They're not like me?' said Eddie, finishing David's question for him.

'Yes.'

David felt good and bad all at the same time. Good because he'd got out the question that he needed to ask. Bad because he didn't want to give Eddie offence, and he hoped he hadn't. Eddie was the only friend he'd got in this God-forsaken place and he didn't want to lose him.

'So, if I say I'm nice out of the goodness of my heart, it won't do for you?' asked Eddie with a smile.

David shook his head, feeling relieved. At least Eddie didn't seem to be taking it the wrong way.

Eddie eyed David meditatively for a moment. He looked like a bookmaker weighing up the odds. And then, as if making a decision, he leaned over and clapped David on the shoulder.

'All right, Davy, I'll tell you why I'm nice. But don't you go blabbing if you don't like what I say.'

He put his forefinger up to his lips, and David nodded.

'Okay. I'm nice to you because I like you, but it's also because I need you.'

'Need me!' David sounded shocked. It was the last thing he'd expected to hear. Eddie was the resourceful one, able

51

to get almost anything he wanted from God knows where. What could he possibly need David Swain for?

'To escape,' said Eddie, answering the question.

Escape. It was the thought that was always at the outer edge of David's consciousness, that he wouldn't let in because he knew there was no way out of this hell and thinking about it would send him crazy. And yet here it was, spoken aloud as if it was something possible, something that could actually happen. David felt his heart beating like a hammer inside his chest; he put out his hand and held on hard to the metal ladder leading up to the top bunk as if to prevent himself falling, even though he was sitting with his feet on the ground.

'I need you because it'll take two of us to get out of here, and I think you want it as much as I do. If there's one thing I've learnt it's that you've got to want to escape more than anything else in the whole world if you're going to have any chance of success. Do you want it that much, Davy? Do you?'

David didn't answer and so Eddie went back on the attack.

'Don't you want to see that Katya woman one more time and tell her what you think, tell her how you feel? Or maybe you're happy to let her sit there in that great fine house of hers laughing at you while you rot away in here?'

Eddie looked at his cellmate expectantly. David swallowed hard but he still didn't respond. And yet Eddie knew he'd found his mark. There was a fire in David's eyes. They were wider open than they'd been since his arrest. He'd been thinking of the world outside – of air and water and trees and grass, but now he thought of Katya and his mouth twisted in a grimace. Eddie was right. She had these things every minute of the day. *Fuck her*, he thought savagely. *Fuck her*.

'Yes, I want out of here,' he said. 'I want it so much it hurts.'

52

'All right,' said Eddie, looking pleased. 'That's what I thought. But you'll have to do as I say. It won't be easy. Escaping's no piece of cake.'

David nodded and then looked up instinctively at the tiny window set high in the back wall of the cell. It was tiny, far too small for a man to fit through, even if he could find a way of sawing through the three thick metal bars cemented inside the frame. There was a ventilation shaft in the ceiling above the window, but that too was a hopeless cause. The aperture was a third the size of the window. And the cell door was three inches of solid steel that couldn't be unlocked from the inside. The only opening in it was a spy hole near the top, the so-called Judas hole, through which the screws could watch their charges without being seen themselves.

Not easy! Getting out of here was downright impossible. It was stupid to even think about it.

Eddie smiled. He knew what David was thinking. He'd watched his cellmate's expression change from hope to despair as his eyes travelled around the cell.

'Don't worry, Davy,' he said. 'It's not this cell we're getting out of. It'd take more than a year to dig your way out of here. Even if we had the tools, which we don't.'

'How then?'

'You know they're going to be painting the gym and the rec room over in the new block next week?'

'No.'

'Well, they are. They're putting up scaffolding tomorrow on the top floor. They need it because the ceilings are so high.'

'How do you know?'

'A little bird told me. It doesn't matter how I know. What matters is they're doing it,' said Eddie impatiently.

'Sorry.'

'The point is, Davy, the scaffolding's an opportunity for

us. And opportunities are your best chance. Not tunnelling away for a year and a half just to find yourself moved to another wing when you're still chiselling away in the small hours.'

'How's it an opportunity?'

'Because we can use it to get at the rec room ceiling, punch a hole in that, and climb out onto the roof. And then down into the rear yard.'

'But that's thirty feet. More maybe.'

'Twenty-eight I reckon. We'll use dust sheets. They put down plenty of them when they painted the canteen last month, and they're bigger than the sheets we have in the cells.'

'How do we get out of the rear yard?' asked David, growing more sceptical by the minute. 'There are two bloody great walls to go over once you're out there. If you get out there. And the perimeter one's more than thirty feet. I know it is. I've seen the top of it over the roof of the new block from the back of the exercise yard, so it's got to be higher than the rec room. How do we go thirty feet up in the air, Eddie? I doubt the builders left too many footholds.'

'We don't need any footholds. There'll be a rope ladder and a car on the other side. I've got connections, or have you forgotten that?'

'So why do you need me if you've got connections?'

'Because they're on the outside, not in here,' said Eddie, sounding as if he was running out of patience. 'Until we get to the perimeter wall we're on our own. And so I'll need you to keep a lookout and help me over the first wall. I'm a lot more worried about that one than the other one, to be honest.'

'Why?'

'Because we've got to find a way to get up it without a ladder. Down's easy, it's up that's the problem. But don't worry. I'm working on it,' said Eddie, tapping the top of his head with his forefinger.

David sat back heavily, resting his head on the wall behind him, trying to digest the information he'd been given. He felt like he'd been put through a wringer, catapulted from one conflicting emotion to another with no time to catch his breath and think. He'd felt excitement at first as he dared to think about escape for the first time as a real possibility, then doubt and anger too that he had let down his defences and allowed himself to be suckered into believing in miracles, and then the beginning of a new thought – that maybe Eddie did know what he was talking about, that maybe he could get them out of here.

'How do you know about all this escaping stuff?' he asked.

'Because I've done it before.'

'What? Got out?'

'Once yes, twice no. You need some luck too, you know. And I don't use violence. Not like your religious friend,' said Eddie, pointing over at David's discarded copy of *Jesus for Prisoners*.

'Does violence help?'

'Sometimes, but it's hard to get weapons in from the outside. You can fake them, of course. Dillinger got the better of fifteen Indiana state troopers back in the Thirties. Used a dummy gun he'd made in the carpentry shop; whittled it out of wood and blackened it with shoe polish. But I prefer not to be seen on the way out if I can help it.'

'Why do you do it?'

'Escape, you mean? Because it gives you hope, keeps you alive. It's easy to lose yourself in here. Why do you think they have those suicide nets hanging under the landings out there? And this time it's also because I need to. I've got debts I couldn't collect before I got sentenced and now I'm running out of time.'

Eddie got up and went and stood under the window,

looking down at his cellmate. He took a shilling coin from his pocket and passed it up and down between the fingers of his hand several times before he broke the silence.

'So, are you in?' he asked. 'I need to know, Davy, because that scaffolding's not going to be there forever and I need to make my plans. And if it's not you I'm going with, I'll need to find someone else.'

David didn't answer at first. Part of him still didn't believe escape was possible. This prison was like a bloody fortress even if it was in the middle of the town. But then again, what did he have to lose? So what if he got a few more years added on to his life sentence. He'd be an old man anyway if he ever got out, way past his sell-by date.

'All right, I'll do it,' he said. 'But once we're out, I want money and a gun. Not a fake one like that American bloke's. A real one with bullets inside. Can you get that for me?'

Eddie looked hard at his cellmate, pursing his lips. Once again David was reminded of a bookmaker weighing up the odds. And then all at once Eddie seemed to make up his mind. He nodded, walked over to David, and held out his hand to seal their agreement.

CHAPTER 4

Vanessa smiled at her reflection in the mirror above the drawing room fireplace and then closed her eyes, willing Titus to return. And, as if in answer to her prayer, the door behind her opened and she turned around to find him crossing the room toward her.

'I'm sorry, my dear. This wasn't what I had in mind for our evening,' he said, taking Vanessa's hand and leading her over to the sofa where Katya had been lying prostrate a few minutes before.

'Is she all right? She seemed ill, Titus, really ill. Shouldn't she go to hospital?' Vanessa spoke in a rush. It was as if she hadn't realized until now how much Katya's sudden appearance and collapse had upset her.

'No, she's fine now. She'll sleep through until morning. She's had a sedative. Katya's her own worst enemy, you know. She won't eat; she won't sleep. She could be back to her old self if she just tried a little, but she won't. As I said before, it's like something snapped inside her after Ethan died and now she's determined to go the same way. Except that I won't let her,' Titus added defiantly.

Vanessa squeezed Titus's hand, unsure of what to say. She wasn't used to him opening up to her like this. She felt the pain in his voice, his vulnerability, and her heart ached in sympathy. The last thing she wanted to do was to upset him further, but she felt she had no choice. Certainly it seemed far-fetched that Franz or anyone else was plotting to murder the girl behind Titus's back, but Titus deserved to be told what his niece had said. But then, just as she was about to speak, Titus forestalled her.

'When Katya was down here did she say anything, Vanessa, you know, before she passed out?'

Vanessa didn't answer immediately, taken aback by the apparent telepathy between them. It was uncanny the way their minds seemed to be moving in tandem.

'I only ask because I have to know what she's planning to do. I'm the only one stopping her from going back on the streets. And I don't think she'd survive another relapse.'

'She said: "They're trying to kill me." She didn't say who. But she really meant it. I could see that. It cost her a lot to get the words out.'

'Did she say anything else?'

'No, just that. But who did she mean, Titus?' Vanessa asked, suddenly urgent. 'Could it be your brother-in-law's doing something to her without you knowing? I don't like the way he looks at me sometimes. It's like he hates me for some reason.'

Vanessa gripped Titus's hand as she spoke. She'd kept a lid on her aversion to Franz Claes for too long and now it suddenly erupted into the open. She felt Titus stiffen beside her, taken aback by the intensity of her emotion. He didn't reply at first but instead released her hand gently, picked up her glass and his own, and went over to the sideboard, where he methodically mixed them two more drinks, standing with his back to her. Then, picking up one of her hands, he wrapped it around her glass.

'Drink,' he said. 'You need it. We both do.'

Vanessa did as he asked. The alcohol did make her feel better, but she continued to look up at Titus expectantly.

'Two questions, Vanessa, which both need answers,' said Titus. He spoke slowly, choosing his words with care. 'As to the first one, no, no one in this house is trying to kill my niece, least of all Franz. And yet it doesn't surprise me to hear that this is what she believes. She is being kept in this house against her will, and without the drugs that she craves, she has to use her mind and think, which is terrible for her.'

'Why?'

'Because she is what you English call highly strung and her thoughts are full of pain – the death of her parents in the war, the loss of her home, the murder of Ethan, her guilt over his death.'

'Why should she feel guilty? It wasn't her fault that that man Swain went crazy.'

'No, but she thinks it is. And I can understand why she feels responsible. If she'd not started a relationship with Ethan, then Ethan would still be alive today.'

'But that makes no sense. We're not Hindus. People have to be allowed to decide who they want to be with.'

'Like you and me,' said Titus with a half smile. 'I wonder what your husband would have to say about that.'

'He doesn't like it – of course he doesn't – but that doesn't mean he thinks people shouldn't be free to choose.'

'Even when they're married?'

'Yes, even when they're married. And your niece wasn't,' Vanessa added pointedly.

'Yes, you're right,' said Titus with a sigh. 'Katya shouldn't feel guilty, but that doesn't change the fact that she does. I just wish I could get her to see things differently. As I said, she's her own worst enemy.'

'Well, what about getting someone else to talk to her? Maybe a psychiatrist could help?'

'Don't you think I've tried?' said Titus bitterly. 'She won't speak to anyone.'

'There must be something you can do.'

'Only what we are doing. Giving her our love and keeping

her out of harm's way. And hoping that time will heal her wounds, of course. I'm a great believer in that.'

Titus was silent, lost in his troubles, but Vanessa stayed quiet, certain that he had more to say. It was unusual for him to talk about himself and she didn't want to interrupt his train of thought. And yet when he spoke again it was to change the subject.

'You asked me about Franz,' he said. 'I am sorry you don't like him. He's not an easy person, I know. And he's not at his best with women. But it's not because he doesn't like them or doesn't like you. I assure you of that. It's rather that he feels uncomfortable because he doesn't know what to say. You see, his mother died when he was very young and his father was away, and it was really left to his older sister, Jana, to bring him up. She did her best, but she couldn't be his mother – if nothing else she was too young. And then afterward he was in the army . . .'

'The Belgian army?'

'Yes. For ten years before the war. He did well, but it left its mark. I suppose you could say he has all the virtues and the vices of the well-trained military man. He can be awkward in company, especially with the opposite sex, and he tends to see everything in – how do you say? – in black and white. But he is loyal and true; a man of honour. And there is nothing he would not do for me, Vanessa.'

'Why?'

'Because years ago I was able to help him when he needed help, because once upon a time I was married to his sister, because . . .'

Titus broke off in midsentence as if turning away from an unwanted memory. Vanessa couldn't remember how she had first heard that Titus was a widower, but she'd known it for as long as she'd known him. And yet his dead wife had always been an invisible presence. There were no family photographs in the house that she'd ever seen and he'd never mentioned her until now.

'What was her name?' Vanessa asked. Her voice was quiet, almost a whisper, and she felt for a moment like a child pushing open a forbidden door.

'Amélie.'

'Was she beautiful?'

'Yes.'

'Do you miss her?'

'Sometimes. My child too. But it is painful and so I try not to think about them.'

'Your child! I never knew you had a child.' Vanessa was rigid with astonishment.

'Yes, a son like you, but younger. It is part of what draws me to you, I think, Vanessa. That we have both suffered, both lost what was dear to us. Life is never the same after that.'

'But why didn't you tell me before? When I told you about Joe?'

'Because that conversation was about you, not me. I wanted to know how you felt, not to tell you about me.'

Vanessa sat back in the sofa, trying to cope with the confusion of her emotions. It made no sense that Titus should not have told her about his loss when she told him about hers, and yet it also made perfect sense because of the person he was. She vividly remembered the evening sitting up late in front of the fire in her flat when she'd described the terrible night of the motorcycle accident to Titus and told him in broken words about the shroud of meaninglessness that had hung over her ever since. She remembered the way he'd listened to her so quietly, so intently, so that she felt able to talk about what had happened, about what it meant, for really the first time since the accident. And she realized now that she couldn't have talked like that, couldn't have

61

unburdened her soul, if the conversation had been about him as well as her. She felt a sudden wave of emotion, of gratitude toward this man about whom she still knew so little.

'What happened to them? Your wife and child?' she asked, leaning toward Titus with sympathy and concern written all over her face.

'They died in the war. Back at the beginning when the Germans came in. Nothing special about it. There was a lot of bombing and many people lost their families back then. You go out, you go to work, you come back, and what do you find? Rubble. Yes, you English have the right word for it. *Le mot juste.* In the morning a house, a home; in the evening rubble.'

Titus had closed his fist while he was speaking, and now he suddenly opened it empty, like a circus conjuror. And with a bitter, twisted smile he got up and went over and stood by the window, looking out. It was almost dusk and hard to see past the lawn and the rose beds to the lake and the line of trees beyond.

'*Tramonte* the Italians call it,' he said musingly.

'What?'

'The twilight, the in-between time. It means "across the mountains" in English. And I suppose you could say that that's where I've come from, Vanessa. Across the mountains. Bringing what I could out of the flames. Katya, my niece, more damaged than I am, whom I must try to protect however much she hates me for it, and Franz and Jana. Yes, Franz, Vanessa,' said Titus, looking at her apologetically. 'He is my family too, and I cannot turn my back on him even if I wanted to.'

'But I wasn't asking you to do anything like that,' said Vanessa, raising her hands in protest. 'Your life is your own; it's not for me to interfere.'

'But that's where you're wrong, my dear,' said Titus,

coming back over to the sofa and raising her right hand to his lips. 'I want you to interfere; I want you to be a part of my life. Not just now but for always.'

Vanessa looked into Titus's bright blue eyes and knew exactly what he was saying. She felt like a swimmer being borne out to sea on a riptide. She was falling in love with a man whom she hardly knew. *Whom she hardly knew* – an inner voice repeated the words inside her head, holding her back almost against her will.

'I'm married, Titus,' she said in a soft voice.

'Yes, and your husband hates me,' said Titus with a sigh.

'No, he doesn't. He just hates what you represent. Bill's always been a fair man. It's one of the things he prides himself on.'

'Well, then maybe he'll be fair to us and give you a divorce. Won't you ask him, Vanessa?'

'I don't know,' said Vanessa, sounding upset. It distressed her to hear Titus talking about Bill. Because she'd spoken no less than the truth. She did believe her husband was a fair man. He might be unable to express his emotions or to cope with his son's death; he was certainly unbearable to live with; and yet he was fundamentally decent – good even. It wasn't that she wanted to go back to him. She was sure of that, but she and Bill had been through a lot together; they'd been happy once, and something inside Vanessa rebelled at the thought of the divorce court, of a legal end to everything that had gone before.

And yet here was Titus offering her a new life, entirely unlike the one she'd left behind. He would take care of her; love her; encourage her to express herself in a way in which her husband had never been able to do. He was wealthy, influential, a man of the world. There would be no more scrimping and saving at the supermarket, no more worrying about the next bank statement. Surely her marriage was over? It was eighteen months since she'd left her husband. Did her independence, her tiny little flat, mean so much to her that she'd turn down the chance of becoming Mrs Osman? Or was it simply that she no longer believed in happiness, didn't want to put the possibility of it to the test?

'I don't know,' she said softly. 'I don't know, Titus. You must give me more time.'

'Of course,' he said. 'All the time that you need, dearest Vanessa. It's enough for me that you will think about it. Love will take care of the rest.'

Titus got to his feet with a smile. He was not discouraged. He'd watched the storm of conflicting emotions pass across Vanessa's face, and he sensed how close he was to obtaining his heart's desire.

CHAPTER 5

'Why do you want a gun?' asked Eddie as they completed another circuit of the exercise yard. Several hours had gone by since they had reached their agreement to escape, but they were both still in a state of unnatural excitement.

'Because that bastard Claes had one,' said David. 'On the night I didn't kill Ethan Mendel. You remember.'

'So you're going back there?'

'Yeah, but not for long. You don't have to take me if you don't want to.'

'No, I'll take you. It's on the way out of Oxford. But what you do in there's your business.'

'Fine.'

Here, in the exercise yard, they were in the very centre of the prison and the high walls of the wing buildings surrounding them formed a barrier against the wind that was blowing hard across the city outside, but they still wore the collars of their jackets turned up high against the unseasonable cold, leaning their heads close together when they spoke to hear what the other was saying. Halfway round each circuit, David glanced up at the top of the rec room block on the other side of the yard. It seemed impossibly high to come down from, but at least the roof was reasonably flat so there was less risk of slipping down the tiles on the other side and breaking one's neck on the ground below.

And Eddie had been right about the scaffolding. A gang of workmen had just been finishing carrying the poles in through the door to the gymnasium on the ground floor when they'd come out for afternoon exercise, and now David could see their heads moving across the barred rec room windows up at the top of the building as they assembled the scaffold.

'How are we going to get in there? The rec room's going to be out of bounds while they're painting it,' he asked, leaning toward Eddie again and pointing across the yard.

'Yeah, but not the gym,' said Eddie. 'They're painting the rec room first and then the gym. That's what I heard and it makes sense if you think about it. One's on top of the other, and they don't want both out of use at the same time; otherwise, what are they going to do with us? So all we've got to do is slip up the stairs from the gym during evening association and then wait until everyone's back in their cells.'

'Except us! How the hell are we going to get past the head count?' asked David, suddenly raising his voice so that several prisoners nearby turned and looked over at them with curiosity. He couldn't believe that he hadn't thought of this before. The screws went round the cells, landing by landing, every evening before lights-out counting the prisoners, making sure they were all there. Except that he and Eddie wouldn't be; they'd be hiding under a dust sheet over in the rec room, waiting to be caught. Like sitting ducks.

'Keep your fucking voice down, can't you?' said Eddie angrily, pulling David over toward a set of steps leading up to B Wing, where they sat down. 'People have ears, you know. Of course I've thought about the count. Do you think I'm an idiot? We'll make dummies and put them in our beds, and then we'll go at the weekend when they're under-staffed. Association's later on Fridays and Saturdays and they do a lot less checking.'

'Yeah, but what happens if they talk to us, ask us something?' asked David, refusing to be reassured.

'Well, we'll be asleep with the lights out and we'll just

have to hope they don't. Like I told you before, you need some luck to succeed with something like this.'

David sighed, thinking about the succession of events that had brought him to where he was now. If there was one thing he wasn't, it was lucky.

Uncharacteristically, Eddie went to sleep early that night, but David tossed and turned in his bunk, thinking of Katya. Now that he had allowed himself to start thinking of escaping his prison walls, David's obsession with the girl who had betrayed him had returned in full force. Once again the vision of her locked in naked embrace with that Belgian bastard returned to haunt him. The thin, hawkeyed prosecutor at his trial hadn't known that he'd looked in at them through the grimy boathouse window; he'd only guessed. But it had been a bull's-eye guess. David had lied at his trial – said he'd never seen them together. How could he have done otherwise? But he couldn't hide behind the lie now. The memory of that spring afternoon returned in Technicolor to haunt him, and he saw them again, coupling like a pair of beasts on the ground. Two or three seconds he'd looked. No more than that, but it was enough for the memory to last a lifetime.

David remembered how he'd fallen back from the windowsill and run blindly down to the lakeside, fallen on his knees, and vomited his lunch down into the grey water. There they were behind him in the boathouse intertwined, interlocked. In the same place where Katya had met with him the year before. But they hadn't writhed on the floor like animals. Kissing, holding hands, but nothing like that. It wasn't an act of love; it was an act of hate. That's what it was. A way of saying he didn't exist. And it was the same hate she'd shown him in the courtroom when she'd read out his letters with such contempt, when she smiled at him after he got his sentence and was led off to the cells like a dog. He hated her himself now; with every fibre of his being he hated her, just as much as he'd loved her before. She'd trampled on him, robbed him of everything he had, and now she was going to have to look him in the face and tell him why. Suddenly still, David closed his eyes tight shut, clenching his body in anticipation of that moment.

Two nights later, working by torchlight in the darkness, they started work on the dummy heads. Eddie had been busy in the interim purloining what he needed, and, not for the first time, David was impressed by his cellmate's resourcefulness. He had got carrots and flour from the kitchens and a spare prison-issue blue-and-white shirt from the laundry, which he had torn into small pieces.

'That's for the inside of the heads when I've got the outsides ready,' said Eddie, who was standing over the sink in the corner mixing his ingredients. Page by page, he was tearing up O'Brien's *Jesus for Prisoners* and adding it with practised hands to the flour and water mush to make papier-mâché.

'What are the carrots for then?' asked David curiously.

'To give the heads some flesh colour.'

'What about hair?'

'Paintbrushes! I got two out of the rec room last night. The workmen leave them behind when they go home,' said Eddie, looking even more pleased with himself than usual as he pulled back his mattress to reveal his ill-gotten gains. 'You can start pulling the bristles out while I'm doing this.'

'How was it over there?' David asked. They'd been working steadily for a little while and David had now finished with the first paintbrush and started work on the second.

'Great,' said Eddie, breaking off from humming a discordant version of Elvis Presley's 'Love Me Tender' as he looked up from the sink. 'They've got all the dust sheets we need in there, which helps because we can't use the sheets in here – we'll need them for covering the dummies. The scaffolding's up near the ceiling, just where we want it, and there's an old half-broken tubular chair in a corner that'll work perfectly for a grapple. You know, to get over that first wall. It's looking good, Davy, really good.'

An hour later Eddie was ready with the first head. He'd sculpted out a crude nose and ears and now he used a tube of glue that he'd stolen from God knows where to add bristles from David's pile to make hair and eyebrows.

'It'll do,' he said, turning the head from side to side. 'We can use a pen to touch them up at the end after they've dried.'

'How long'll that take?'

'Twenty-four, thirty-six hours maybe. Don't worry. We've got time. It's the screws finding them that bothers me. We'll have to keep them under the bunks and hope there isn't a cell search. That's all.'

'Hope we're lucky, you mean?'

'Yeah, and stop sounding like a doubting Thomas all the time, okay? It's getting on my nerves.'

It was unlike Eddie to sound so irritated for no reason. The tension must be getting to him too, David realized.

They went as planned on the Saturday night. When the cell doors were opened for evening association, Eddie had the dummies ready in the bunks. They'd broken up their two wooden chairs and covered them with their jackets and bunched up bedclothes to simulate their bodies, and then they'd laid the papier-mâché heads in profile on the pillows. The effect was better than David had anticipated, but Eddie, eyeing his handiwork with a professional detachment, was less confident.

'They'll work okay if the screws are just doing a quick

check through the Judas hole, but if they come in here, we've had it,' he said, giving the dummies a final dissatisfied look before they left the cell for what they hoped would be the last time. David's heart was beating so fast he felt it would burst.

Eddie had been right: There were less screws on duty than usual – just one out in the yard and another at a desk in the corner reading a newspaper, nowhere near the doorway at the other end of the gym that opened onto the darkened stairs leading up to the rec room above. And there'd been no head count going in, which made it a lot less likely there'd be one going out. But these positive developments didn't help David calm down, and he soon began to find the waiting almost unbearable. Eddie had been adamant that they should stay downstairs until almost the last minute since there would be far less chance of their being missed that way, and he seemed to have no problem passing the time chatting to the other prisoners and joining in a game of basketball down the other end of the gym, but David couldn't take his eyes off the clock on the wall. Time seemed to have stopped; the minute hand didn't move at all, and he kept looking toward the stairs and then over at Eddie, waiting for him to give the signal for them to go.

At quarter past seven, fifteen minutes before the end of association, Eddie came over. He looked furious.

'What the hell are you doing, Davy?' he asked in an angry whisper. 'Hopping from one leg to the other gazing up at the bloody clock – you might as well go and tell that screw over there exactly what we're planning. Do something for Christ's sake. Anything. Just stop looking shifty.'

Eddie moved away before David could answer, and for the next ten minutes David walked the perimeter of the gym, keeping his head down, only glancing up occasionally at Eddie, never at the stairs. Until, at twenty-five past seven, he felt a tap on his shoulder and, seconds later, saw Eddie slip through the doorway and up the stairs. No one seemed to have noticed, and a minute or two later, he followed.

Eddie was at the top of the stairs holding a small half-sized gym mat folded up in his hand.

'What do you want that for?' David asked.

'You'll see.'

The door to the rec room was locked, but Eddie seemed to have expected that. He took a thin piece of wire from out of his pocket, fiddled inside the keyhole for a moment, and then opened the door with a gentle push.

'Piece of cake,' he whispered before beckoning David to follow him inside. The rec room looked very different from when David had last seen it. Dust sheets covered the furniture, the pool and the ping-pong tables, and a scaffold on wheels stood in the corner, leaning up against the far wall. There were no ladders. The workmen must have taken them with them when they left for the day. Outside the windows the sun had almost set over the exercise yard, leaving the big room in an eerie twilight.

Through the open door they heard the guard's whistle down below, signalling the end of association, and then came the sound of the prisoners spilling out into the exercise yard and crossing over to A Wing, until finally the door of the gym shut with a bang, a guard's voice shouted 'good-night', and they were left alone in sudden silence.

'All right. Let's get to work,' said Eddie, crossing over to the scaffold with a determined look on his face. 'Come on; give us a hand, Davy. We need to move this. We don't want to be visible through the windows, do we?'

Gently, they trundled the scaffold over to the centre of the wall and then, once Eddie was satisfied with its position, he started clambering up its side toward the top. Halfway up he stopped, bent down, picked something up from one of the planks, and then let out a suppressed whoop of delight. He had something metal in his hand, but in the half-light David couldn't make out what it was.

'We're in luck,' said Eddie, waving the thing in the air like it was some kind of trophy, his face creased with a wide smile.

'What is it?' asked David from below, irritated by his own incomprehension.

'A scaffolding clip, you idiot. They must have had one over that they didn't use.'

'How does it help us?'

'For making a hole so we can get up through there,' said Eddie, pointing at the ceiling. 'It's going to have a bit more weight behind it than our paint brush handles, isn't it?'

David nodded. He resented being spoken to like he was some bottom-of-the-class schoolboy, but he could see the point. The clip would help; it was a good omen.

Once he was up on the top of the scaffold, Eddie beckoned down to David to follow. It was a high room and the ceiling suddenly seemed impossibly far away, and David cursed the workmen under his breath for taking away their ladders. It didn't take him long to realize that he was a far less skilful climber than his cellmate. He lacked the strength in his upper arms to haul himself up between the bars and he found it hard to balance on the narrow footholds. Two-thirds of the way up, he got stranded, unable to go up or down, and Eddie had to come down and help him the rest of the way.

'Now maybe you can see the point of why I work out in the gym every day,' said Eddie with a self-satisfied smile as he pulled and lifted David up onto the top level. He seemed to have forgotten his earlier ill humour now that he'd found the clip and they were under way with the escape.

'What about keeping a lookout?' asked David.

'No point. If anyone comes up here, we've had it anyway. Unless you can think of an explanation of why we're making a bloody great hole in the rec room ceiling after lights-out, of course,' Eddie added with a grin.

Now, lifting the clip above his head, Eddie punched it up into the ceiling, and David joined in beside him using the wooden paint brush handle that he'd brought from the cell. Almost immediately a great cloud of white plaster mixed up with horsehair fell on their heads, half-blinding them. Wiping the dust from their eyes, they looked at each other and burst out laughing.

A pair of snowmen up to no good, that's what we are, thought David. The adrenaline coursed through his veins and he suddenly felt absurdly happy.

Bit by bit the plaster came away, and soon the hole above their heads was large enough for them to see through to the roof space above.

'I'm going up to take a look,' said Eddie. 'I won't be long.'

Standing on David's hands, he hauled himself up through the opening onto the rafters above, and for a moment all David could see from below was the beam of Eddie's pocket torch travelling across the timber underside of the roof. It seemed a long way away.

But Eddie had lost none of his confidence when he came back down.

'It'll work,' he said. 'There are a couple of planks across the beams where we can stand. We're lucky it's a flat roof. It's going to make it a lot easier. You finish off the hole. I'm going down to get the dust sheets and the chair.'

'What chair?'

'The one over there in the corner. The one for the grapple, remember?' said Eddie, pointing down to a cheap swivel chair behind the door. It was missing one of its wheels, and David was surprised it hadn't been thrown away.

Clambering up and down the scaffold like a human monkey, Eddie brought the gym mat and four of the dust sheets up from below, and then tied a last one around the base of the chair and pulled it up to the top, where he positioned it under the hole in the ceiling that David had just finished widening.

'Right, you first. I'll hand you the stuff once you're up there,' said Eddie, holding the chair steady as David got on it and put his head up into the dark roof space above, feeling with his hands for the rafters on either side so he could lever himself up. But then he froze. Down below, someone, it had to be a screw, was rattling the handle of the gymnasium door.

For what seemed an eternity but was in fact less than a minute, David stood motionless on the swivel chair, his feet and legs in the rec room, his head and upper body in the roof space above.

What an idiot, he thought to himself. *What an idiot I was to think we could get away with something as harebrained as this.* He'd not yet done any time in the punishment block, but he'd heard enough about it to feel sick to his stomach at the prospect.

But then Eddie's voice came from below his feet.

'It's all right, he's gone. Just some screw doing his rounds, checking the doors are locked. That's all.'

Relief flooded through David, leaving him weak at the knees, and he had to use all his strength to haul himself up through the hole. But there was no time to relax as Eddie started handing him up the mat and the dust sheets straightaway before following himself, pulling the swivel chair up after him by the dust-sheet rope to which it remained attached.

'I thought we'd had it,' said David, wiping the sweat from his brow. His hands were shaking uncontrollably.

'Yeah, well, you were wrong. You need to calm down, keep your nerve. That's what you need to do. Because up there we're going to have to be even more careful,' said Eddie, shining his torch over the underside of the roof above their heads. 'We can't risk even one of those slates falling off. You hear me?'

'Yeah, I hear you,' said David, breathing deeply in a vain attempt to slow his racing heartbeat.

What helped was work, and soon they set to again, punching up through the timber frame of the roof and prising away the tiles one by one. It was harder work than it had been with the ceiling down below, and David felt mentally and physically exhausted when they finally got up onto the roof an hour later. But the evening air revived him. He inhaled it deep into his lungs and felt the excitement rekindling in his chest as he looked out over the lights of the city. Nearby, the thick stone walls of St George's Tower, the ancient keep of Oxford Castle, loomed out of the shadows, and above them the moon hung high in the eastern sky, shedding a pale light on the prison buildings down below. On one side was the exercise yard from which they'd come, on the other an open courtyard with buildings on three sides, and beyond that the two high walls that stood between them and freedom.

'Okay, we need to get back down out of sight,' said Eddie after a moment, looking at his watch. 'We've got two hours to wait before they're here. And I hope to God there's some cloud cover when we go. We'll be sitting ducks if we have to cross that yard in this light,' he added with an angry backward glance at the moon.

The waiting was awful, worse than anything that had gone before. Sitting, perched precariously on a crossbeam in the semi-darkness, David watched as Eddie worked and reworked the knots in the two dust-sheet ropes.

'There must be easier ways of doing this,' he said, adjusting his position for the hundredth time. He'd never felt more uncomfortable.

'There are,' said Eddie, nodding. 'Impersonation's the best if you can get away with it, but you need a lot of luck. Johnny Allen, the mad parson, was the best. You must've heard of him. He was in all the papers a few years back.'

David shook his head.

'It was brilliant. He was a strangler, one of those ones that can't help themselves, and so they put him in Broadmoor, you know the loony bin for the criminally insane. High security though – guards round the clock and all that. Well, he was a bit of a song-and-dance man Johnny was, and he used to entertain the crazies on Saturday evenings with a vicar routine, dressed up in an old black suit and a stock and dog collar. And this went on for nine or ten years until one Sunday morning he got out of bed, got into his outfit, and just walked out. Simple as that. Screws didn't recognize him and thought he'd been holding a service or something. Bye-bye maximum security, hello London,' Eddie added with a grin.

Above their heads the church bells out in the city tolled three times, and Eddie glanced at his watch, looking suddenly serious.

'Quarter to twelve,' he said in a low voice. 'Time to go.'

Moving carefully, they climbed back up onto the roof, hauling their equipment after them. The moon was just as bright as before and Eddie shook his fist at it half-heartedly.

'Well, I suppose at least we'll be able to see what we're doing. Even if half the prison can too,' he said, sounding resigned.

Slowly, laboriously, Eddie paid out the first of his

dust-sheet ropes until the bottom hung three or four feet above the ground.

'Are you sure it'll hold?' asked David, looking over doubtfully at the nearby drainpipe to which Eddie had tied the top end.

'Yeah, and I'll be holding on to it too. I'm the one who should be worried. It'll just be me and that drainpipe when I go down. Now get on with it. We haven't got all day.'

Halfway down the wall, David stopped, hanging on to the rope for dear life. He remembered his first swimming lesson and his father telling him how nothing was as bad as it looked. Well, he was wrong, he thought. Halfway down the rope it looked a lot worse than it had done from on top. He had too much imagination. That was the problem. He could feel his bones shatter on the concrete down below even while he was still hanging here in mid-air. Eddie's voice, hissing down at him from above, broke through his panic.

'Listen, Davy, keep going or I'm letting go. You hear me, you fucking idiot?'

David heard. Half-grabbing, half-falling down the dust sheet, he hit the ground a second later, shaken, bruised, but with nothing broken as far as he could tell.

There was no time to recover. Eddie was already lowering the swivel chair on the end of the second dust sheet. It turned quicker and quicker as it made its descent, knocking several times against the windowless wall of the gymnasium, but eventually David had it in his hands, and Eddie let go of the rope, letting it fall to the ground. Quickly he followed, coming hand over hand down the dust sheet on which David had hung suspended a minute earlier, waiting to die. He had the small gym mat folded up inside his shirt.

'What the fuck happened back there?' he asked in an angry whisper as soon as he reached the ground. 'Are you trying to get us caught?'

'No, of course not. I panicked. That's all. I'm not a climber like you.' David sounded as if he was about to cry.

'All right, all right. I'm sorry,' said Eddie, swallowing his annoyance as he realized that it wasn't helping anyone. 'Look, the wall over there's a lot lower than this one. It's only the wire we've got to worry about and that just hurts, it's not scary.'

'And then?' asked David, looking over at the wall beyond, the perimeter wall of the prison. It was way higher than the first; higher than the wall he'd just come down.

'There'll be ladders. I already told you that. But we've got to get there at twelve,' said Eddie, glancing anxiously at his watch. 'That's the time they said they'd put them over, and they can't leave them hanging there for long or someone'll see them. So come on, let's go. Follow me and keep your head down, for Christ's sake.'

'What about this?' asked David, tapping the end of the rope they'd just come down.

'It'll just have to stay there. I know. I don't like it any more than you do, but we've got no choice. With any luck, we'll be out of here before anyone sees it.'

And so, leaving the dust-sheet rope hanging down from the roof behind them, a hostage to fortune, they took off round the edges of the courtyard, staying in the shadow of the buildings and doubling down almost to their hands and knees as they passed underneath lighted windows. One was open and they could hear voices inside laughing, but somehow they got past it without incident until finally they crossed open ground to the wall they had to climb. Eddie ran along the side of it a little way, looking for the place they'd be least exposed. Then, once he'd made his decision, he got up on David's shoulders, raised the swivel chair above his head while David held the dust-sheet rope to which it was attached, took several practice swings, and then threw

78

the chair up and over the wire on the top of the wall. The noise of its impact on the other side was louder than they'd expected and they froze for a moment in a strange eight-foot tableau of man on man, but nothing happened, and Eddie dropped back down to the ground.

'Okay, start praying,' said Eddie in a whisper as he took the rope from David and started gently pulling the invisible chair back toward him. At the top of the wall it wobbled and then caught in the wire. Eddie pulled it harder but it didn't move; it was secure. Silently he pumped his fist, and drew a deep sigh of relief. Still no one seemed to have heard them.

'All right, I'm going up first, and I'm going to put this down on the wire. It'll make it easier to get over,' he whispered, pointing to the folded-up gym mat inside his shirt. 'Don't worry, okay. Just do what I say, and you'll be fine.'

Whatever the reason, whether it was Eddie's words of encouragement for which he felt absurdly grateful, or whether it was that he found going up easier than going down, David got up to the top of the wall without a problem. And then the moonlight helped with finding a place to stand on the mat while Eddie switched the dust-sheet rope to the other side of the wall. The barbs tore into David's shirt and trousers, digging into his skin as he began his descent, but he hardly noticed the pain as he concentrated on lowering himself down to the ground.

And then, standing under the wall at the bottom, he suddenly felt hope surge again inside his chest. The prison was out of sight behind his back and they were so close to freedom now that he felt he could almost touch it with his hand. Never in all his life had David been through so many mood swings in such a short space of time.

But Eddie seemed more worried, not less. He kept walking up and down, looking up at the wall above them and then glancing at his watch.

'Five past bloody midnight,' he burst out. 'Where the hell is he? That's why we waited, so as not to have to sit here in the fucking sterile area waiting to be caught.'

'Sterile area?'

'Yeah, sterile. No prisoners allowed. Just screws, walking up and down with fucking guard dogs. God, I hate dogs. Come on, come on,' he said, hopping from one leg to the other, gazing up at the wall.

And suddenly, as if in direct answer to Eddie's call, a man appeared in the moonlight above them and threw down two rope ladders toward them.

'Okay, go, go!' shouted Eddie.

David didn't know why he suddenly shouted when he'd been always whispering up to now. Perhaps he'd already seen the guard and the dog coming round the corner, but David was only a little way up when he heard the mad barking just beneath his feet. There was the sound of a whistle and people were calling, screaming, crying out, but he couldn't make out the words. All he knew was that he had to climb. Near the top he felt someone, it had to be the screw, pulling at the rope from down below and he was half-blinded as a searchlight beam swung round and picked him out. He looked up and there was Eddie taking aim with his pocket torch in his hand. It came down past his head and it must have hit its mark because David heard a cry and suddenly felt the tugging stop. He climbed two rungs, three rungs, forcing his feet forward up the ladder and then suddenly Eddie's hands were around his wrists pulling him up on to the top of the wall where the man had put down a piece of old carpet to cover the wire.

'Stop! Come back now!' someone was shouting at them from down below, but his voice was drowned out by the noise of dogs barking and running feet. David didn't wait. He was already halfway down the ladder on the other side when the prison alarm bells started to go off. He'd never heard anything like it. It was a noise like the end of the world, and the bells were still ringing in his ears when he got to the ground and jumped in through the open back door of the waiting car.

CHAPTER 6

Immediately the car screamed into motion, throwing David back in his seat as it hurtled down the street and around the corner.

'We did it; we did it!' shouted Eddie, punching his hand up into the roof of the car in celebration. It must have hurt but Eddie didn't seem to notice. He was wild with delight. But the driver, the man who'd saved them, showed no emotion. He sat hunched over the wheel, his eyes fixed on the road ahead.

David felt numb, but looking down, he saw that his hands were trembling uncontrollably. He couldn't believe they'd actually escaped – it had been such a close-run thing. He could still hear the shouting and the barking and the alarm bells reverberating in his ears, and he kept looking back over his shoulder expecting to see police cars in pursuit.

'Don't worry about it,' said Eddie, catching his eye. 'They won't have seen our number plates. The wall was in the way. And thank God for my torch, eh? I thought you'd had it there for a moment when that screw was pulling on the end of your ladder. But then Corporal Crackshot here takes aim and hits the bastard right on the nose.'

David smiled weakly. As always, Eddie was at his happiest when he was singing his own praises, but David didn't begrudge his friend his moment of triumph. He knew that without Eddie he'd be rotting back in gaol, one more day into his life sentence, whereas now he was free, free to go where he chose, and he knew where he was going. The outside air rushed against his face through the open window as they sped down New Inn Hall Street, and he clenched his fists, breathing in deeply as he thought of Katya and what lay ahead.

They parked in the station car park. The driver of their car had still said nothing and Eddie had made no effort at introductions. Sitting behind him in the back seat, David had not even seen the man's face. Now, without turning around, he reached in the pocket of his coat and took out a set of keys, which he handed to Eddie.

'Which one?' Eddie asked. It was curious the way Eddie and the driver seemed to have so little to say to each other, thought David.

'The red Triumph. The one over there,' said the man, pointing to his right. 'It's got a full tank.'

'Thanks. Come on, Davy,' said Eddie, opening his door and beckoning David to follow. 'We need to get a move on.'

Shutting the door, David looked back through the car window, anxious to get at least one look at this stranger who had done so much to help him escape, but it was as if the man had read his mind. In the minute since he'd parked, he'd turned the collar of his coat up around his ears and pulled his hat down over his forehead so that all David got to see was a flash of the man's black beard before he was gone, driving back down to the road and picking up speed as he went around the corner and disappeared from sight. But the man's voice stayed in David's head. It had been high-pitched, effeminate sounding, not at all what he would have expected from one of Eddie's friends.

'Who was that?' asked David, getting into the Triumph beside Eddie, who already had the engine on.

'You don't need to know,' said Eddie in a voice that brooked no argument. 'Do you still want to go to this Blackwater Hall place?'

'Yes. That was the deal, remember. You promised me,

Eddie,' said David. There was an edge of panic to his voice, as if he was about to lose his self-control.

'All right, all right, I remember. There's no need to get all crazy about it. Just try and relax, okay?'

Eddie drove out of the city over Magdalen Bridge and headed out on the Cowley Road at a precise thirty miles per hour. David still kept looking over his shoulder, scanning the night for police cars.

'Can't you go any faster?' he asked impatiently.

'And get caught for speeding after all we've been through? No way. That's a sucker's game.'

David leaned forward, drumming his fingers on the dashboard.

'Where's the gun?' he asked feverishly. 'You promised me a gun.'

'In there under your fucking fingers. And can't you stop doing that? It's driving me crazy.'

'Sorry,' said David, opening the glove compartment and taking out the nickel-plated revolver that was lying inside.

'Christ, there's a whole lot of money in here too,' he said, holding up a see-through bag containing a large bundle of banknotes.

'What the hell?' said Eddie, sounding angry suddenly. 'That's not supposed to be in there.'

'Where's it supposed to be then?'

'With our clothes in the back, away from the gun,' said Eddie, keeping his eyes on the road as he jerked his thumb behind his head toward a small suitcase lying on the back seat. 'The gun's loaded, so be careful, okay?'

David nodded, barely listening. A strange calm had settled down on him since he'd taken hold of the small snub-nosed revolver that he now held cradled in the palm of his hand. Having it made him feel different inside. It meant the end of being told what to do; he could give the orders now. He thought of Claes's scarred, waxy face, and his hand clenched involuntarily around the handle of the gun. The polished wood felt smooth and hard. It would be different this time.

They passed the Morris car factory on the left, its blue towers illuminated by the moonlight, and David remembered how the bottom of the Cowley Road used to be full of bicycles at five o'clock as the workers swarmed out of the factory on their way home. Like India, or how he imagined India anyway. But now the road was deserted and they were all alone in the night. Under a bridge and past a few straggling houses and they were out in the open countryside. David felt his heart hammering inside his chest: Katya was out there in the darkness only a mile or two away with no idea of what was coming her way.

'Left, left,' he shouted at the last moment as the turn to Blackwater came into view, but Eddie seemed to know already, and soon they were climbing the hill that David remembered so well. Past the church and out of the village until they came to the bend in the road and the fence beside the path that led up to Osman's boathouse; the last place that he'd been as a free man.

'All right, turn off here,' said David. 'You can park under the trees. If you keep your lights off no one'll see you from the road.'

'Unless they're looking,' said Eddie. 'I'm waiting here half an hour, okay, like we agreed. Until five past one. Provided no one comes. If you're longer than that, it's your lookout because I'm out of here.'

'Fair enough,' said David. 'But then I'll need this too.'

Reaching into the glove compartment, he opened the bag with the money and helped himself to a wad of notes. Looking at Eddie defiantly, he stuffed them in his pocket.

'Just in case,' he said. 'I won't be long.'

But he never saw Eddie again as a free man.

David was grateful for the moonlight, but still there was little risk of his getting lost. He'd been down the path to the boathouse many times. Always the boathouse, never the house, he reflected bitterly, except on that one occasion when Katya had had the place to herself and even then she was as nervous as a cat. Because her uncle didn't think he was good enough, didn't like the fact that he didn't go to the university and had a common name like Swain. Not like that bastard, Ethan. To the manor born he was, until he got that knife in his back. Just there. Standing outside the boat-house, David looked down to the water's edge, to where Ethan's body had lain, and then beyond to where the moon was shining silver ripples down onto the black surface of the lake. Everything was quiet. There was no wind in the trees, just the sound of the dark water gently lapping against the dock. It was an evil place, David thought. Beautiful but evil. Like Katya.

Gripping the gun in his hand, David turned away from the lake, heading into the woods. He picked his way carefully, but it wasn't long before he came out into the open and paused, looking across the lawn toward the side of the house. There were no lights on in the windows that he could see, and there was no sound either. The mermaid fountain in the front courtyard must have been switched off for the night. This was the best place to cross the lawn, but still David hesitated, hating to risk himself out in the open, imagining unseen eyes watching from the shadows. But he had no choice. He knew that. He'd come too far to stop now. And so, steeling himself, he burst from the trees, running with his head down across the moonlit grass. He made it to the other side, but in his haste he'd forgotten about the rosebushes growing under the windows. They tore into his prison shirt and trousers and he had to bite his lip hard to stop crying out as he disentangled himself from the thorns.

He was outside the window of Osman's study. He tried opening the sash without success – he could see it was fastened by a catch in the centre. But if he could just reach his hand through the pane above, he could open it. One blow would surely break the glass, and if everyone was asleep upstairs, and the door was shut, then maybe no one would hear. He had to take the chance. The first time he hit the pane with the butt end of the gun it only cracked, but the next time the glass shattered. David stood motionless in the darkness, waiting for lights, waiting for shouts, but nothing happened. Somewhere out in the trees an owl hooted, but otherwise the silence was as complete as before. Nothing stirred. Quickly he knocked the rest of the broken glass out of the pane and then, wrapping his hand in the sleeve of his torn shirt, he reached through the opening and turned the clasp, pulling the bottom half of the window gently up toward him.

Carefully, he climbed inside and then extended his arms in front of him, moving gingerly forward like a blind man. Katya had shown him the room when she gave him a tour of the house on that day when her uncle was away, and he thought he remembered a reading lamp on the corner of the desk. Seconds later he felt its shade and pressed down, searching for the switch. It clicked and suddenly the study was bathed in a pale green light. David blinked, getting his bearings. There was a big painting over the mantelpiece above the fireplace, some biblical scene it looked like. Probably valuable like everything else Osman owned, David thought bitterly, taking in the rich luxury all around him – the thick Axminster carpet, the rows of leather-bound books with golden titles on their spines, the silk curtains.

David remembered his damp, dark, evil-smelling cell back in Oxford Prison and the contrast between the two rooms made him angry, made him want to smash something. But that wasn't why he was here. He needed a torch, some light to guide him through the house. But there was nothing on the desk apart from the lamp and a telephone, and the drawers were just full of useless papers except for the top one in the centre that was locked. Stealthily, David ventured out into the corridor, leaving the door open behind him to give a little light, enough to see the shape of the long oval table in the room opposite. And on the table were candles, a whole line of them: tall white candles in high silver candlesticks. More suited to an altar than Osman's dining table, David thought inconsequentially as he felt in his pocket for his matches.

Now, with the light, everything was easier. With a candle held aloft in one hand and the gun gripped in the other, he walked slowly down the corridor to the front hall, and stopped suddenly stock still at the foot of the wide ornamental staircase, gazing up into the luminous green eyes of a black cat sitting in the middle of the fourth stair up, barring his way. The animal seemed disembodied, indivisible from the surrounding darkness. For a moment they stared at each other without moving, but then David sensed the cat's back beginning to arch as if it was about to spring, and instinctively raised the gun and candlestick in front of his face to ward off its attack, but instead it ran past him down the stairs. He felt its fur against his leg before it disappeared behind him into the shadows on the other side of the hall.

David felt his legs trembling underneath him and breathed deeply several times, exhaling his fear into the darkness before he steeled himself to the task ahead and began slowly to climb the stairs. Pictures and portraits lined the walls, but David looked neither to his right nor his left, concentrating all his attention instead on the ground beneath his feet, taking each step as if it might be his last. He knew where he was going. Katya had taken him to her room on that day when she had shown him the house. It was halfway down the top-floor corridor on the left. You had to lean down when you went inside because there was a slope in the ceiling. He remembered lying on her narrow bed; he remembered the taste of her kisses on his mouth. Her nervousness about him being there, about her uncle coming home and finding them, had made the afternoon more exciting than any of their previous encounters. His heart had pounded inside his chest like it was going to burst. Just like now.

Walking down the corridor almost on tiptoe, he thought he heard something – a rustling or a movement behind him. He turned, hesitating whether to go forward or back. Perhaps it was someone sleeping behind one of the closed and half-closed doors that he had passed. He had no idea who else slept up here. But now all was quiet again. Softly, he moved forward, coming to a halt outside Katya's door.

Here comes a candle to light you to bed,
Here comes a chopper to chop off your head.

The words of the old nursery rhyme came unbidden into his head, and he smiled as he placed the candlestick carefully on the floor, put out his hand, and opened the door.

CHAPTER 7

Detective Inspector Trave woke with a start. He'd been deeply asleep, fighting the noise of the telephone ringing insistently beside his bed.

'What is it?' he asked blearily, still half-inhabiting the dream he'd been having: a bad dream that had been recurring lately in which shapeless shadows were coming toward him on a cliff's edge and there was nowhere left to hide. His Dunkirk dream he called it, remembering 1940, when the world had gone up in flames. Who was to know if it wouldn't happen again?

'Sorry to wake you, sir,' said a young, brisk voice on the other end of the line. 'It's a murder: young female shot in the head. At a place called Blackwater Hall. It's outside Blackwater village on the London Road.'

'Blackwater Hall,' Trave repeated, coming fully awake.

'Yes, that's right. Do you want directions? I've got them here.'

'No, I know Blackwater Hall. Get hold of Adam Clayton for me, will you? Tell him to meet me there.'

'He's already on his way, sir. He was on night duty when we got the call.'

'Good. Thanks,' said Trave, replacing the receiver.

Homicide at Blackwater Hall. It wasn't the first time he'd heard those words. *And people aren't murdered in the same place twice for no reason*, he thought as he got dressed, made himself a triple-strength cup of coffee, drank it in three gulps, and went out into the night.

Trave drove quickly through the empty streets and out

into the dark countryside while his mind raced, remembering people and events that he'd been trying for a long time to forget. It was like the door of a lumber room had finally given way under the weight of what was stacked up behind it. Images from the past passed quickly in front of his mind's eye like a succession of ghosts – Ethan Mendel lying dead, with the lake water lapping around his dark hair and his outstretched arms; David Swain's hollow face collapsing in on itself as the jury foreman announced the guilty verdict; Titus Osman's smug eyes twinkling behind his manicured beard as he entertained his guests at that dinner party after the trial, with Vanessa sitting on his left, listening to the bastard's tall tales with such rapt attention.

Why had he taken Vanessa that night? Trave asked himself the same useless question for the thousandth time. Useless because he knew the answer. He hadn't wanted to go. The Mendel case had left him feeling obscurely dissatisfied, a viewpoint evidently not shared by the jurors, who had taken less than two hours to convict. But Creswell, his boss, had insisted, and Trave had taken Vanessa with him to Blackwater Hall because he didn't want to go on his own and because he felt guilty that she never went out; that he'd not been able to help her at all through those long, hard months and years after their son, Joe, died. Trave had had his job to fall back on, but she'd had nothing. Just him, and he'd been no support, worse than no support in fact. They'd grieved soundlessly and separately, trying to avoid each other in the passages and corridors of their empty house until their marriage withered away and died. Not with a shout; not even with a whimper. In a cold and weary silence.

He and Vanessa were finished long before the night that he took her to Osman's to celebrate the end of another successful case. He realized that now. And yet she had looked so delicate, so fragile, that evening in a white dress that she hadn't worn in years. He remembered her laughing in the bedroom before they left, saying that perhaps losing weight wasn't such a bad thing after all, and he remembered how she'd bent her head to allow him to fasten the faux pearl necklace that he'd bought her as a present twenty years earlier, after Joe was born. His hands on her neck replaced by Osman's hands – Osman, who could afford to pay more for a necklace than Trave earned in a year. Trave shuddered, braking hard to avoid the line of police cars with flashing lights parked in a line on the road up ahead. They must be searching the woods, he thought, as he turned through the open gate and drove up between the tall, moonlit trees to Osman's house.

Clayton was waiting for him in the entrance hall. The whole place was ablaze with lights, and there was the sound of people running up above, although the hall itself was temporarily empty except for a uniformed policeman standing guard outside the closed door of the drawing room. It was a room that Trave vividly remembered from his previous visits to Blackwater Hall, when he was investigating Ethan Mendel's murder. The views across the gardens and the woods to Blackwater Lake were among the most beautiful he'd seen from any house in the county. But for now the drawing room could wait; he had other business to attend to.

'Where is she?' he asked, dispensing with any greeting. He was a man in a hurry tonight.

'Who?' asked Clayton, thrown off balance for a moment by the suddenness of the question.

'Katya Osman. I assume she's the young female shot in the head who's brought us all out here tonight.'

'Yes, that's right. She's in her bedroom up on the top floor. It looks like she was shot while she was asleep. The owner's in there,' said Clayton, pointing to the door of the drawing room on the other side of the hall. 'With the other two residents: Mr Claes and his sister.'

'They can wait,' said Trave curtly, making for the stairs.

'They say it's a David Swain who broke in here and killed her,' said Clayton, running to catch up with his boss.

'He can't have done. He's in gaol serving a life sentence. I'm the one who put him there.'

'I know. They're saying he's escaped.'

'How?'

'I don't know. I've got Samuels making enquiries. Mr Osman thinks he was transferred back to Oxford Prison earlier this year.'

'Oh, he does, does he? How do you know about Swain?'

'Well, everyone was talking about his trial at the station a couple of years back when I first got posted down here. About him and this girl and the Belgian bloke he knifed – a sort of love triangle gone wrong is what I heard.'

'You could call it that, I suppose,' said Trave with a grimace, thinking of his own situation.

'So when they mentioned Swain down there, I remembered that this was the place. Where it happened, I mean.'

'Well, good for you,' said Trave. He could feel the anger growing inside his chest as they got closer to the top floor, but lashing out at his subordinate didn't make him feel any better. It was a useless anger born out of years of frustration. In his experience most murders could have been prevented before they happened, but by the time he arrived on the scene it was always by definition too late. He could find the killers and get them locked up in a cell somewhere, but he couldn't bring the dead back to life.

And it was worse when he knew the victim and she was young like Katya Osman, he thought, as he stood beside her bed, looking down at her pale, ravaged, pretty face, at the neat little hole in the centre of her forehead rimmed crimson with her dried-up blood.

Bedrooms were private places; in bed you were supposed

to be safe, inviolate, free from the attentions of the bogeyman. 'Matthew, Mark, Luke, and John guard the bed that I lie on.' He remembered the prayer from his childhood: his mother's voice intoning the words in the semi-darkness; his voice following hers. But no one had guarded Katya's bed when it mattered. No one had been there to protect her.

It was unbearable. Trave swallowed and closed his eyes hard, feeling for a moment like one of those parents that he had to take down to the hospital morgue from time to time to identify the remains of their dead child. And yet his days as a parent were over. He was a policeman now. That was what was left to him. He looked down again at the dead girl on the bed, past her sunken cheeks and into her unseeing blue eyes. He remembered Katya's eyes. They had been her best feature. Large and luminous, eyes a young man could fall into. But now the light had gone out of them and they stared sightless up at the ceiling.

'You were wrong about her being asleep, Adam,' he said without turning around. 'She saw whoever it was before she died. She saw the gun. She wasn't spared a thing. She knew.

'If the eye was like a camera and we could just unroll the film,' he went on musingly, talking to himself as he leant over and closed Katya Osman's eyes forever.

He was about to turn away, but something made him linger, picking up the girl's hand from where it lay, lifeless, on the coverlet.

'Look at that,' he said, beckoning Clayton over to join him at the bedside.

'What, sir?'

'Her nails. They're bitten down to the quick. And she must weigh half of what she did when I last saw her,' he added, pulling back the quilt to expose Katya's upper body.

'Close to malnutrition I'd say,' said a voice behind him.

It was Davis, the police doctor, standing behind them in the doorway, dressed in his own personal uniform of brown corduroy jacket and silk bow tie. The outfit never changed – in all the years he'd known him, Trave couldn't recall ever seeing Horace Davis wear anything else.

'Not the first time we've run across each other here after hours, Bill,' said the doctor drily, taking Trave's place beside the dead girl.

'No,' said Trave. They were alone now. Clayton had left the room to talk to a uniformed policeman who'd been waiting outside in the corridor for some time, trying to attract his attention.

'Who is she?' asked the doctor.

'Katya Osman. She is or was the girlfriend of the corpse you were here for last time.'

'And them?' asked Davis, nodding toward the photograph that Trave had idly picked up from the top of the bookcase: a laughing woman with a scarf around her head holding on to the arm of a bald-headed man wearing an old suit and round-rimmed glasses; behind them the sea and a sense that the wind was blowing them off balance.

'Her parents.'

'How do you know?'

'I asked her about them before. She showed me the photograph.'

'And where are they now?' asked the doctor, continuing his examination of the dead girl as he carried on the conversation.

'Dead. In the war. I don't know how.'

Davis looked up, picking up on the bitterness in Trave's voice.

'Different, this one, is it?' he asked.

Trave put back the photograph, saying nothing, but Davis nodded as if he understood.

'She was beautiful,' he said, looking down at Katya. 'It's a waste. That's what it is. A bloody awful waste.'

He turned away from the bed, resuming his professional air as he snapped his battered old medical bag shut.

'She's been dead just over an hour, so I'd put the time of death at about half past twelve, give or take a few minutes. And whoever did it knew what they were doing, although I suppose that's obvious,' he added, pointing to the wound in the centre of Katya's forehead.

'Oh, and you should also take a look at this,' he said, beckoning Trave back over and pulling up Katya's left sleeve to expose the puncture marks above the elbow. 'She's been injecting or someone else has been doing it for her.'

'Are any of those from tonight?' asked Trave.

'I don't know. But the autopsy'll tell us. I'll let you know. I hope you catch the bastard, Bill,' Davis added, looking back for a moment as he went out of the door. 'Whoever did this isn't one of our usual punters.'

'No,' said Trave to himself. 'No, that he's not.'

Clayton waited patiently while Trave stood over by the window, looking out into the night. There were other things he needed to explain, including the news he'd just heard outside, but he knew better than to interrupt his boss while he was lost in a train of thought.

'Something's been happening in here,' said Trave without turning round.

'Happening, sir?' Clayton repeated, sounding mystified. Of course something had happened. A young woman had been shot in the head.

'It's too damned tidy. I remember when I went round the house after the Mendel murder, this room didn't look anything like it does now. Everything was strewn about everywhere: clothes, makeup, magazines, books – you name it. A typical girl's bedroom. This is like a room in a hospital. Or a gaol,' he added, taking hold of the steel bars over the windows with his hand. 'What the hell are these for, I wonder?'

Clayton had no idea.

'All right, so tell me about Swain. Anything new?' asked Trave, turning back from the window with a sigh.

'Yes, he's definitely escaped. And it was from Oxford Prison. Samuels got through to them a few minutes ago. Swain's with a man called Earle, apparently. They got over the wall.'

'Earle. Eddie Earle?'

'Yes, that's right. Edward James Earle. Doing five years for deception,' said Clayton, glancing down at the piece of paper in his hand. 'Do you know him?'

'Yes, I know him. He's a confidence trickster, quite a good one, specializes in conning old ladies out of their life savings. Easy Eddie he likes to be called – easy with other people's money.'

'They had help,' said Clayton. 'Apparently someone threw rope ladders over the perimeter wall, and they think there was a getaway car.'

'How long ago? Have you got a time?'

'Just after midnight. They'd have had time to get here, sir.'

'I know,' said Trave. It made no sense but Clayton thought he sounded disappointed.

'All right,' Trave went on after a moment. 'So where are they now?'

'Earle, I don't know. No one's seen him as far as I know. And I'm pretty sure Swain's not in the house. I've had the place searched from top to bottom. But he could be some-where out in the grounds. I've got people looking, but it's difficult in the dark. To be sure, I mean. And he may be wounded. We don't know.'

'Wounded?'

'Yes. The owner's brother-in-law, Franz Claes, says he fired two shots at him in the corridor out there. The first one hit the door and the second one hit the wall at the far end, just by the turning to the stairs, but it may have touched Swain on the way. It was too dark for Mr Claes to see, apparently. But the bullet holes match his story.'

'We'll need to get ballistics to compare the bullets with the one over there,' said Trave, pointing at Katya. 'Not that I'm holding my breath.'

'Sir?'

'Nothing. Don't worry about it. How did Swain get in?'

'He broke the window in the study downstairs, and I reckon that's how he got out too. All the other doors and windows seem to have been locked when we got here. Oh, and he tore his clothes on the rosebushes outside. There's a bit of shirt we've recovered. Blue-and-white stripe, like prison uniform. I'll have it checked out.'

'Anything missing?'

'Can't be sure yet, but the owner hasn't noticed anything, except a silver candlestick that the intruder took upstairs from the dining room, to light his way. He left it outside the door before he came in here. I've got it being dusted for fingerprints. And the study too, sir. Photographs as well.'

'Good. You've been very professional, Adam. Just what I would have hoped. Well, I suppose we'd better go and talk to our friends downstairs. See what their story is,' said Trave, making for the door.

Clayton felt pleased. He didn't often get praise from his boss, so when it came, it was worth savouring. But he also felt uneasy. There was something Trave wasn't telling him, he thought, as they went downstairs. In normal circumstances he'd have expected the inspector to have a modicum of sympathy for the owner and his family after what they'd just been through, but instead, Trave's attitude seemed to be bordering on hostile before he'd even clapped eyes on them.

'Who do you want to see first?' asked Clayton once they were back in the hall. 'There are just three of them – the owner and his brother-in-law and sister-in-law. No servants – none of them live in apparently.'

'Claes – the one with the gun,' said Trave immediately. 'Doesn't he say he was the first one on the scene?'

Clayton nodded and was halfway to the drawing room door when Trave's voice stopped him in his tracks.

'Wait. We haven't decided *where* to interview them yet. Where's more important than the order they go in right now.'

'You don't want to interview them where they are?' asked Clayton, looking puzzled.

'Osman? No, anywhere but in there. That's his lord-of-the-manor room.'

'His what?'

'The place where he struts about entertaining high society, feeling like a million dollars. No, we need to put him on edge, put him at a disadvantage when we talk to him.'

Trave stroked his chin musingly, and Clayton kept quiet. None of this made much sense as far as he was concerned. The training book said you should put witnesses at ease in order to get as much out of them as possible, not put them through the third degree. Unless they were suspects, of course, but Titus Osman wasn't that. If anything, he was a victim. His niece had just been murdered, for God's sake. However, Clayton knew better than to question his boss's methods. Trave was the best detective on the Oxford force when it came to getting results.

'What about Osman's study?' Trave asked, looking up. 'Are forensics still working in there?'

'Yes. I told them to start downstairs so you and the doctor could see the deceased first. I hope that was right?'

'Yes, no problem,' said Trave distractedly. 'But tell them to finish in the study before they go anywhere else. We'll interview Claes and his sister in the drawing room, and then see Osman in the study when forensics are done in there. We may have to wait a bit but that doesn't matter.'

Franz Claes sat bolt upright on the edge of the sofa, facing Trave and Clayton, who sat side by side on the matching sofa opposite. The empty fireplace was between them. Claes was short, no higher than five foot two or three, and his forward position meant that he could at least keep his feet on the floor, although Clayton felt that Claes would have preferred a straight-backed wooden chair to the comfort of the sofa in any event. He was that type of man.

'When did you get dressed, Mr Claes?' asked Trave.

'After calling the police and making sure Swain was no longer in the house.'

It was a strange first question to ask, thought Clayton, but Claes didn't appear surprised by it. He seemed alert, ready for anything that might be thrown at him. And to be fair, Clayton had been surprised too when Claes had answered the door dressed semi-formally as he was now, in blazer, starched white shirt, and trousers, with not a hair out of place. He even looked as if he had shaved. His cheeks were entirely smooth and hairless even though it was the middle of the night.

'And so you were the first to see Mr Swain?' Trave continued.

'Yes, I heard him as he went past my bedroom door. It was slightly open.'

'It's on the first floor as I recall,' said Trave.

'Yes, at the opposite end of the corridor to Mr Osman.'

'Why do you call him Mr Osman? He's your brother-in-law, isn't he?'

'Titus then,' said Claes, nodding as if he had lost an insignificant point in a game that had barely begun. 'As I say, I heard a noise. My light was off but I had not yet fallen asleep, and so I got up and went outside.'

'Wearing?'

'Pyjamas. I took my gun with me.'

'And where was that? Do you sleep with it under your pillow, Mr Claes?'

'It was in the top drawer of my desk,' said Claes, apparently unruffled by the close questioning. His English was surprisingly good, thought Clayton. He spoke slowly and with an accent, but he was clearly fluent.

'Is this the gun?' asked Trave, holding up a Smith and Wesson revolver now neatly packaged in a see-through plastic bag.

'Yes.'

'And you've got a licence for it, have you?'

'You know I have, Inspector. It's the same gun I had two years ago. It's not the first time we've discussed it, you know,' said Claes with a half-smile. It was not an attractive smile, thought Clayton. It was partly the way in which the tightening of Claes's facial muscles threw into sharper relief the ugly scar that ran down the left side of his face, but it was also because there was no warmth in the man. His eyes were cold too, grey and watchful and somehow disconnected.

Trave had been quiet for a moment, but now he pursed his lips as if coming to a decision.

'All right, Mr Claes. You tell us what happened in your own words. I'll try not to interrupt you.'

'Thank you,' said Claes with a nod. 'Once outside my room I heard someone walking on the floor above, and so

I climbed the stairs and looked around the corner. There was a candle burning on the floor outside Katya's room. It's about halfway down the corridor on the left-hand side. Her door was half-open and the light was on inside. It was then that I heard the shot. Almost immediately a man came out. I could see it was Swain. I recognized him from when I stopped him before down by the lake, and from his trial. He was standing still for a moment, and I shot at him, but he saw me and ducked back behind the door. And immediately he ran away down to the end of the corridor, toward the other set of stairs, and I fired again, but I don't know whether I hit him or not. And then he disappeared.'

'What was he wearing?' asked Clayton, speaking for the first time.

'A blue-and-white shirt, some jeans maybe. I'm not sure about the trousers.'

'Were the clothes torn?'

'I don't know. There was no time to see things like that.'

Trave looked at Clayton impatiently, drumming his fingers on his knee as Clayton made a note in his report book.

'So Mr Swain disappeared,' Trave said, leaning forward. 'Did you follow him?'

'Yes, but not to catch him up. It would have been impossible: he was running and I have a problem with my leg' – Claes tapped his left knee – 'so I shouted down to Titus to warn him, and then I went downstairs myself. Titus was in the corridor outside his bedroom. We looked down here and it seemed like Swain was gone, so we went back up to Katya's room.'

'Together?'

'No, Titus went first. I looked in all the rooms first because I wanted to make sure Swain wasn't hiding somewhere.'

'What would you have done if you'd found him?'

'Whatever was necessary, of course,' said Claes. There

was a cold, clipped tone to his voice that Clayton found oddly disconcerting, chilling even.

'And so when you didn't find him, you went back upstairs and found Miss Osman shot in the head. How did that make you feel, Mr Claes?' asked Trave.

Claes didn't answer for a moment. It was as if he was nonplussed by the question, as if he'd prepared himself to say what had happened but not how he felt about it. Clayton didn't think that Claes was the type of man who spent much of his life discussing his feelings.

'I was sorry. Of course I was sorry,' he said slowly. 'But there was nothing I could do.'

'No, there wasn't, was there?' said Trave, sounding unconvinced. 'Miss Osman hasn't exactly been a high priority in this house recently, has she?'

'I don't understand.'

'The doctor says she's badly undernourished; she's got puncture marks all the way up one arm; and there are steel bars on her windows. What have you got to say about that, Mr Claes?'

'She had got herself into trouble in the town,' said Claes, choosing his words carefully. 'My brother-in-law was looking after her, but she was unwilling.'

'Unwilling?'

'Yes, often she would not eat. She was not grateful.'

'Grateful! For being kept a prisoner in her own home?'

Claes shrugged his shoulders.

'Why did you try to shoot Mr Swain?' asked Trave, changing the subject.

'Because I was frightened of what he was going to do next. Titus was downstairs and he had already shot Katya.'

'You didn't know that.'

'He was coming out of her room. I'd heard the shot. Anyone would have assumed it.'

Clayton silently agreed, thinking that he'd have definitely taken a shot or two if some armed man was running around his house shooting people. But then again he didn't keep a gun in his bedroom. Not like Franz Claes.

'It's not the first time you've tried to put a bullet in Mr Swain, is it?' Trave observed.

But Claes was ready for this.

'No, Inspector, it is the first time. After Mr Mendel was murdered, I fired my gun to stop Mr Swain running away, not to hit him. This time it was different.'

Trave didn't argue. He was stroking his chin again, thinking, and Clayton was just wondering whether this might be the signal for him to take over, when Trave asked his next question. It was not one that Clayton had expected.

'Where does your sister sleep, Mr Claes?'

'On the top floor, further along the corridor from Katya's room.'

'I see. Further down the corridor. Well, then let me ask you this: Why did you fire twice down that corridor when you must have known that there was a serious risk that she would come outside and be hit?'

Claes didn't answer. There was a flush in his cheeks: it was the first time during the interview that he'd looked really discomforted.

'You could have killed her, couldn't you?' said Trave, pressing the point.

'It was a moment of stress,' said Claes, finally answering. 'I didn't have time to think,' he finished lamely.

'You didn't think,' repeated Trave with a withering smile. 'Well, thank you, Mr Claes, for your assistance. That'll be all for now. But please don't leave the house without telling us. We may be needing you again.'

Claes stood, bringing his polished shoes together with an audible click; nodded his head once to the two policemen; and limped to the door. He went out without looking back.

'Slippery bastard,' said Trave. 'He's play-acting with that limp. He walked a lot quicker last time I saw him.'

'Why do you dislike him so much, sir?' Clayton felt compelled to ask the question. He hadn't warmed to Franz Claes during the interview, but most of what the man said made sense, even though it was strange he hadn't thought of his sister when he fired those shots. It was Trave's hostility that was more puzzling.

'It's not that I like or dislike him; it's that I don't trust him. He's got secrets – that much I can tell you.'

'Secrets?' repeated Clayton, surprised.

'All right, *a* secret,' said Trave. 'He was picked up in a vice raid a few years back – before the Mendel murder. A man called Bircher was running a whole lot of underage boys out of an old tenement house in Cowley. The detective I talked to said they were going to charge Claes, but then orders came down to let him off with a talking to, because it was a first offence or something like that. I don't know the ins and outs of it, but Osman obviously got involved – spun some sob story or other, made a donation to the police benevolent fund. I don't know. It's ancient history now. Let's see what the sister's got to say.'

CHAPTER 8

Out in the hall Jana Claes sat on a high-backed wooden chair awaiting her turn in the drawing room. She had had time to get dressed and was now wearing her usual coal-black outfit with her greying hair tied up in a bun at the back of her head. Her pale face was even more wan than usual, but otherwise there was little to indicate that it was the middle of the night and that she had been woken by a murder committed only a few yards away from where she slept, except perhaps that the stillness of her hands seemed forced, as if inside she was rigid rather than relaxed, trying hard to hold herself in check.

She kept her eyes on the ground, only looking up when her brother came out of the drawing room and stopped for a brief moment beside her chair.

'Be careful of the old one. He'll try to trap you,' he said, speaking in an undertone in rapid Dutch. 'Remember what I said.'

She nodded: a small but clear inclination of her head, and Claes turned away toward the stairs, apparently satisfied, just as Clayton came out into the hall.

'Miss Claes,' said the policeman, holding the door of the drawing room open. 'We're ready for you now.'

Reaching behind her shoulder, Jana unhooked the handle of a walking stick from the back of her chair and got slowly to her feet.

'Do you need a hand?' asked Clayton, reaching forward instinctively to help Jana up.

'No!' Jana almost shouted the word, recoiling from the

policeman's touch, and Clayton gave her a wide berth as she went past him into the drawing room.

Trave was standing in front of the fireplace with his back to the door. He'd been thinking about his wife and Osman; imagining them standing in this room where he was now; picturing Osman's long, tapering fingers on Vanessa's arm as he showed her his possessions. Trave shuddered. He knew the man. Osman was a collector, and now Vanessa was being added to the collection. Involuntarily Trave picked up a pretty Dresden china ornament from the mantelpiece, a milkmid with a jug, and held it in his fist, thinking about how satisfying it would be to throw it down, smash it in the fireplace at his feet, but at that moment Jana, entering the room, caught sight of Trave's reflection in the mirror above the fireplace, and, perhaps sensing what was going through his mind, she shouted at him from the doorway: 'Put it down.'

Trave was surprised at himself afterwards that he so meekly obeyed the woman's command. Perhaps it was an association with his childhood – his mother had hated him touching her ornaments, her 'precious things' as she called them.

He didn't turn round immediately but instead took a moment to pull himself together, watching Claes's sister in the mirror as she came slowly into the room, leaning heavily on her stick. She hesitated after a few steps, perhaps embarrassed at her outburst, before going on to the sofa, where she sat awkwardly, keeping firm hold of the stick as if ready to get up and leave at a moment's notice. She looked out of place in the room, and Trave thought he knew why. This was Osman's territory, and Jana would only come in here to clean and dust, not to sit on the sofa and make conversation.

'I am sorry,' she said, speaking slowly and with a heavy foreign accent. 'The china, it is expensive and I look after it.' The apology was reluctant, Trave thought. She would have remained silent if she'd felt she had a choice.

'I quite understand,' said Trave, resuming his seat beside Clayton on the sofa opposite. 'All this must be very distressing for you.'

'Yes.'

Trave looked at Jana Claes with interest. He'd interviewed her two years before when he took her statement after the Mendel murder, but she'd had little to say then. Her evidence had been straightforward: she'd gone out shopping with Katya in the afternoon and so neither of them had been present when Mendel met his death down by the boathouse. She knew very little of the murdered man and had never met his assassin, David Swain. And yet now it was different. Jana Claes had been living with Katya Osman for years. She knew things: how the house worked, what Katya's life had been like in her last months, and it was Trave's job to get the information out of her if he could. But it wouldn't be easy. That much was obvious. With her eyes fixed on the carpet, she looked the very image of an unwilling witness.

'Okay,' he said, beginning his questions in a far more friendly tone than he'd adopted with Jana's brother. 'Detective Clayton and I are trying to put together a picture of what happened here tonight, and so we'd like you to tell us everything you remember.'

'I went to bed. I woke up because there was a shot. Then there were more, two more. And people running. And then it was quiet again. Titus, Mr Osman, came into my room and took me to Katya. Then my brother, Franz, was there too. I did not touch her. They said to wait. After, I got dressed and you came.'

Trave watched Jana carefully. There was a rehearsed feel to her words, and he was struck by her failure to articulate any emotional response to the murder. Was it shock or her difficulties with the language or something else?

'You sleep only two rooms away from Miss Osman. Isn't that right?'

'Yes.'

'So the gunshots must have been very loud?'

'Yes.'

'How long would you say there was between the first shot, the one that woke you up, and the others?'

'I don't know. I was sleeping.'

'Enough time to get out of bed?'

'Yes.'

'But you didn't go outside?'

'No, I was frightened.'

'Yes, I can understand that.' Trave nodded and then stayed silent for a moment, with his forehead creased as he debated where to go next with his questions.

'Tell us what you do here, Miss Claes. Other than look after the china,' he said with a smile.

'I take care of the house. I tell the servants what to do. My brother-in-law, Mr Osman, he likes things done . . .' Jana stopped, searching for the right word, and Trave came to her assistance.

'Properly?'

'Yes.'

'And does Mr Osman pay you for your help?'

'No, of course not.' Jana looked insulted.

'He gives you nothing?'

'I have an allowance, but that is because I am family; it is not pay. And I do not need money,' she added.

'Oh, and why is that?'

'I stay here. I do not go out.'

'Then who does the shopping?'

'The servants. That is their job. Like I told you.'

'But you went shopping with Miss Osman on the day Mr Mendel was killed, didn't you? I remember you telling me that last time we met.'

Jana looked disconcerted. Two small red circles appeared in her pale cheeks, and she swallowed before answering Trave's question. She was clearly nervous underneath her cold exterior.

'That was different,' she said. 'Katya needed something in the town, and my brother asked me to go with her, to keep her company.'

'But generally speaking you never go out? Is that right?'

'Yes.'

'Never, Miss Claes?'

'I go to church. On Sundays,' Jana said reluctantly, as if she had been forced into an admission she didn't want to make.

'Ah, yes, I thought you might,' said Trave. He'd noticed the crucifix that Jana wore around her neck and he remembered her bedroom from when he'd gone round the house two years before, after Ethan Mendel's murder. He remembered the room better than its owner in fact: the heavy oak furniture; the absence of ornamentation and personal possessions; the plainness of the walls, except above the bed, where a tortured Christ hung in bloody agony on a thick wooden cross. A nun's room, he'd thought at the time. Or the room of someone who wanted to be a nun but had been thwarted in her ambition.

'And who takes you to church? Do you drive yourself?' Trave asked, keeping his tone casual and ignoring Clayton's restless stirring by his side. There'd be time to get back to tonight's events later on.

'No. My brother takes me.'

'And does he accompany you inside?'

'No, he waits.'

'I see. And at the end of the Mass, you take communion, yes?'

Jana didn't answer but instead put her hand up to the silver cross on her chest. Trave could have sworn that it was an unconscious gesture, and he felt almost sorry for her for a moment.

'Do you?' he asked insistently.

For a moment Jana didn't answer, but then reluctantly she raised her eyes to meet Trave's and shook her head.

'And do you go to confession; do you tell the priest your sins, ask for God's forgiveness?' Trave went on remorselessly.

Again Jana shook her head. 'No,' she said softly, her voice almost inaudible.

'Well, Miss Claes, do you want to tell me why?' asked Trave in a soft voice as he leaned forwards towards her.

But this time Jana didn't answer, keeping her eyes fixed on the floor, and Clayton felt compelled to intervene. Trave was sounding like a member of the Spanish Inquisition, not a policeman investigating a crime. This was England – Miss Claes's religious beliefs were her own affair.

'How well did you know Miss Osman?' he asked.

'I know her a lot. I look after her,' said Jana, switching her attention to the younger policeman with obvious relief.

'How do you mean? Look after her?' asked Clayton, surprised by Jana's choice of words.

'I give her meals. I clean her room. I wash her clothes. I look after her.'

'Why?'

'Why? Because Titus asks me to. It is for a woman, not a man to do this.'

'But why did Miss Claes need looking after? That's what I'm asking you.'

'She was not well. She had done bad things.'

111

'And so you kept her a prisoner in her room to stop her doing them again. Is that right?' asked Trave, returning to the attack. 'With bars on the windows and a key in the door?'

'No. No key.'

'And fed her bread and water. That was for her own good too, was it?' went on Trave remorselessly. There was a tough edge to his voice now, as if he'd decided to blast the truth about Katya out of Jana Claes with a full frontal assault.

But Jana was unyielding. 'I give her good meals. On a tray,' she said, sounding genuinely annoyed. She'd let go of her walking stick now and was clasping and unclasping her hands in her lap. 'It is not my fault she does not eat what I give her.'

'And what else did you do?' asked Trave. 'Did you inject her with drugs? In her left arm, above her elbow?'

'I gave her a sedative to help her sleep. Before; not tonight.'

'How many times?'

'Twice. That's all.'

'Think carefully about what you're telling me, Miss Claes,' said Trave slowly, fixing Jana with a hard stare. 'I'll ask you one more time. Is there something you want to tell me about Katya Osman, about what happened here tonight?'

'No!' Jana Claes almost spat out the word. She looked angrily from one policeman to the other and then took hold of her walking stick and got up.

'I am tired,' she said. 'I need to rest.' Clayton went over to the door and held it open for her, and as she went slowly by, he could have sworn that she was biting her lip and that there was a tear in the corner of her eye.

David Swain sat at the top of a small hill with his back to a big horse-chestnut tree, looking down on the road below, which was illuminated by the lights of a myriad of police cars and vans parked in a long line running almost the whole length of Osman's property. The house behind was also lit up, like a beacon in the night, and to the left the moon was palely reflected in the dark waters of Blackwater Lake.

The police were searching the grounds. David could hear them, their voices calling to one another in the woods. They had to know about his wound, or at least suspect, or they wouldn't be hunting him like this, like some wounded fox gone to ground with a telltale blood trail left behind. Soon they would cross to his side of the road and start climbing up the hill, and by then he would have to be gone. But where? Yet again David searched his mind for a plan, but he could think of nothing beyond the here and now. The pain in his left shoulder was too great. He had no idea whether Claes's bullet had hit him or merely grazed him as he turned the corner at the top the stairs. All he knew was that it hurt and that his arm felt soft: it made him sick to his stomach to even touch it. When he'd got to the top of the hill he'd ripped away the left arm of his already-torn shirt to make a tourniquet, but it didn't seem to have stopped the blood. He could feel it seeping down the side of his body, and, reaching across, he took the wad of money out of the left pocket of his trousers and transferred it to the right. It was all he had: the money and the gun and a head start.

David shivered: in the last few minutes he had started to feel icy cold despite the fact that it was a reasonably warm night for the time of year, and he wished now that he'd been able to bring his jacket from the prison, but Eddie had insisted on using them for the dummies in the beds. Stupid bastard! Yet again David cursed his erstwhile friend through his chattering teeth. Why hadn't Eddie waited like he said he would? David knew from his watch that he'd only been gone twenty-five minutes – less than the half hour they'd agreed, but there'd been no sign of the car when he'd got back to the road. Nothing at all: just the empty woods and an owl hooting overhead. Easy Eddie! – easy with his word, easy with his friends. David clenched his fists in anger and felt the pain in his shoulder shoot down his arm. He knew he had to stop thinking about Eddie. It was only sapping his strength, and, God knows, he had little of that left.

He lay back against the tree and closed his eyes. Unconsciously he ran his fingers over the smooth red-brown surface of one of the chestnuts that were lying strewn on the ground at his side. It felt reassuring somehow, perhaps because it reminded him of his childhood. At school he and his friends had threaded thin pieces of string through the soft centres of the conkers, as they called them, and then fought with them in the playground, taking it in turns to smite the other's chestnut until one of them burst and the other survived to fight another day. *Conkers.* David remembered an especially hard nut that had once been his most treasured possession, the veteran of countless fights, a legend in its own time but now long forgotten – in a drawer somewhere perhaps, mouldering. In that house on the other side of Oxford, where his mother, old before her time, lived with Ben Bishop, who drove a bus and treated him like he didn't exist. It wasn't David's home any more, hadn't been for a long time, but for now he couldn't think of anywhere else to go. Ben worked on Sundays, and he needed someone to clean his wound, to let him rest for a few hours and get back his strength while he decided what to do, and surely to God his mother couldn't deny him that. The police would come looking of course, but maybe not tonight, not while they were busy searching for him in the undergrowth. It was a bad plan. He knew that. But it was better than no plan at all.

Using the trunk of the chestnut tree for support, David hauled himself to his feet and took a last look at the road below and the lights from the house hidden in the trees: Osman's house and inside it Katya, dead with a bullet in her head. Then, with a heavy sigh, David tucked the gun in the waistband of his jeans, pushed the wad of banknotes deep into his pocket, and set off down the other side of the hill towards Blackwater village.

It was difficult to see his way even in the moonlight, and once or twice he stumbled, almost losing his footing on the uneven ground. With each step he felt more light-headed, weaker at the knees, and, when he looked up, the stars seemed to be rushing through the sky as if he was looking at them through a black-and-white kaleidoscope. Reaching the empty road, he staggered a few hundred yards to a crossroads at the beginning of the village and then sank to the ground, exhausted, in the shadow of a garden hedge.

He was awoken in the first grey light of dawn by the noise of a lorry's engine only a few feet away from where he was. The driver waited a moment or two, no doubt for the cross-traffic to pass, and then drove away into the night. Across the road in the light from a street-lamp David could see the Blackwater village store. There was food in the window – biscuits and loaves and even a birthday cake, and David suddenly felt ravenously hungry. He hadn't eaten since six o'clock the night before, and not much then. Saturday-night dinner in Oxford Prison was always the worst of the week: the cooks went home for the weekend, and the cons got food reheated from the night before.

David remembered the shop now: he'd passed it on the bus ten times or more on his way to meet Katya at the boathouse in happier times. Katya and he had even been in there once, on a hot summer's day more than three years ago now, standing in line behind a gaggle of children from the village as they queued to buy peppermints and ice creams from Mrs Parsler, who had to climb up on a tiny stepladder to reach down dusty jars of sweets from a shelf high above her head. Her husband's name was on the sign above the door, and no doubt the two of them were now fast asleep behind the drawn curtains in their flat overhead. David was so hungry that he thought for a moment of smashing the shop window and taking the food from inside, but he resisted the temptation: if he was going to be caught, it wouldn't be for something as stupid as that. Sleep had at least temporarily cleared his head, and he realized that he hadn't any more time to waste. He needed help with his shoulder and he was too weak to go on much longer; certainly he was too weak to walk into Oxford. And there was no point trying to steal a car since he had no idea how to hot-wire the ignition. No, he'd have to get someone to drive him, and there was only one way of doing that.

He stood waiting in the shadows, holding the gun inside his pocket. Nothing moved. The village was entirely quiet, its inhabitants blissfully unaware that they would be on the front page of the national news by the end of the day. And then, just as the church bell had finished tolling the hour of five, David saw lights coming up the road toward him. It was now or never. As the car slowed to a stop at the junction, he walked out into the headlights and waved his uninjured arm above his head.

He was in luck. The driver wound down his window and leaned his head out.

'What's wrong, mate?' The man sounded nervous, frightened even. David wasn't surprised. He had to look like something out of a horror film, dressed in his blood-soaked, ripped-up prison clothes.

'I've been in an accident,' said David, improvising. 'A car hit me when I was crossing the road. I need to get to a hospital. Can you take me?'

'I don't know about that. Why don't you knock on one

of these doors, ask someone to call you an ambulance? I'm sure they will.'

It was the answer David had anticipated. He hadn't seriously expected that a passing motorist would give him a lift at five in the morning looking like he did, but the conversation had given him time to edge round toward the driver's door of the car, and now he rushed forward and pulled it open, pointing the gun at the side of the man's head.

'Give me the keys,' he said through gritted teeth. 'I'll shoot you if you don't.'

The man didn't obey at first. He sat with his hands rigid on the steering wheel, obviously in shock, and it was only when David thrust the barrel of the gun against his right temple that he leant forward, turned off the engine, and handed David the keys with a shaking hand. On the man's other side a young woman in a party dress sat frozen in fear, her eyes fixed on the gun.

With the keys in his pocket, David pulled the handle of the door to the back seat, but nothing happened. It was obviously locked.

'Open it,' he shouted. 'Open the fucking door.' But the man did nothing. Perhaps shock had immobilized him again, or maybe he couldn't face the thought of having the gun pointing at the back of his head. David didn't care. His frustration boiled over, and he wanted to hit the man, to pistol-whip him until he did what he was told. And maybe he would have done if the woman hadn't intervened. Leaning across the back seat, she lifted the lock and David got in.

'All right,' he said, tossing the keys over the man's shoulder into his lap. 'Now drive. We're going to Oxford.'

'We! Why we? Why can't you leave us here and take the car? Please, please do that.' The man had got his voice back, but he was quite clearly terrified out of his wits. He stumbled over his words, and the woman didn't look any better: David

117

could see her hands shaking in her lap. But David felt no sympathy or guilt. Instead he felt a curious sense of disconnection from himself. The panic and desperation that he'd experienced earlier up on the hill had disappeared, and now it was as if he was watching himself, as if he wasn't really here at all. And besides, there was no time to argue. That much was obvious. There would be more police cars coming this way soon, joining the manhunt down the road.

'Do as I say,' said David, louder this time. 'Shut your fucking door and drive. I'll use this thing if you don't. I promise you I will.'

'Do what he says, Barry. Please!' The woman's voice rose almost to a scream on the last word. David could clearly see that she was about to have hysterics. But the man made no move to start the car.

'All right,' said David, taking a deep breath and making a conscious effort to speak in a calm and measured voice. 'I can't take the car and leave you here because you'll go straight into that shop over there, wake up Mr and Mrs Parsler if they're not awake already with the noise we're making, and get them to call the police. I need a head start, and that's why I need you to drive. Okay? Twenty minutes: that's all I need, and then you'll never see me again. I promise.'

David didn't know whether it was his words or the way he said them that had the desired effect, but the man seemed to relax. He sighed audibly and his shoulders slumped.

'Put that thing down then,' he said, turning his head to look at David over his shoulder. 'I can't drive with that pointing at me.'

Carefully, David put the gun down on the seat beside him and covered it with his hand. The man nodded, pulled his door shut, and put the keys in the ignition, and, as they pulled away, David saw that the lights had come on in several of the neighbouring houses, including above the window of the general store opposite, and inconsequentially he thought how the night's events might at least be good for the Parslers' business.

They drove in silence. The woman kept looking back at David and the gun on the seat beside him, but he didn't pay her any attention. He was lost in thought, working out what to do, racing over the possibilities, calculating his chances, and all the time his shoulder hurt him more and more as he felt waves of hot and cold rush through his body. He wondered how much time he had left before he passed out.

Halfway down the Cowley Road, he told them where they were going. 'The railway station,' he said. 'Take me to Oxford Station.'

It felt strange to be back in the station car park again, parked only a few yards away from where Eddie and he had arrived from the prison so elated five hours earlier. It seemed impossible that it was such a short time ago. Where was Eddie now? David wondered angrily, thinking of his cellmate driving away through the night to a new life in his red Triumph, but then he dismissed the thought from his mind. He had more important things to think about now, like laying a false trail. He needed to concentrate. Everything depended on him getting it right in the next few minutes.

'Well, aren't you going to go then?' asked the man, looking back at David in the driving mirror. 'Twenty minutes: that's what you said. We've done what you asked.'

'I need to know when the first train leaves for London. That's when I'm going. Go and look on that board over there. It'll say.'

'I don't need to look,' said the man. 'The first one on a Sunday's at twenty to six.'

'How do you know?'

'I've been on it before.'

'Well, twenty to six it is then,' said David, settling back

119

in his seat. And they relapsed into silence. The man, Barry, sat rigid, staring straight ahead at the big Victorian clock over the station entrance, but his companion kept looking back at David. She seemed less frightened now, as if realizing that if he was going to do anything to them he'd have done it already. She was pretty in an odd sort of way, David realized. All dressed up in her party frock with a ribbon in her hair at the end of an evening that he'd turned into a nightmare.

'What's your name?' he asked.

'Lucille,' she said. 'What's yours?'

'David.' He liked the way she said her name. Not Lucy – Lucille. A bit of class. 'Pleased to meet you,' he added, making the words sound like a joke. And she smiled, as if appreciating his effort to lighten the tension. But Barry didn't see it that way.

'Shut up,' he said, turning toward her. 'Don't talk to him, Luce, all right?'

But she was having none of it. 'Shut up yourself,' she said. 'You don't own me.'

David smiled. 'So you're not married?' he asked.

'No way,' she said. David could sense Barry bristling with irritation in the seat in front, but she hadn't finished. 'What did you do?' she asked. 'We saw all those police cars back there before you . . .' Her voice tailed off, but David had picked up on her greedy curiosity and felt suddenly disgusted.

'It doesn't matter,' he said. 'It doesn't matter what I did.'

He looked up at the station clock. It was time.

'Give me your jacket,' he said, tapping Barry on the shoulder.

'No.' Barry sounded defiant, angry even.

'Give me your fucking jacket,' David shouted, losing his temper. And his anger had the desired effect. The man took off his jacket and passed it back to David, while the woman cowered in her seat, her fear returning as she saw the gun in his hand.

'Right,' said David. 'I'm going. Don't follow me and don't call the police. Okay?'

He didn't wait for an answer, just got out of the car and walked quickly into the station without a backward glance. He was sure they would call the police, but maybe not straight away. And probably not from the station either. He should have time.

He asked the clerk at the ticket office a whole lot of questions about train times, about the cost of first- and second-class tickets, and even about whether there was a dining car, hoping that the man would remember him when the police came asking questions later, and then, with a single ticket in his pocket, he crossed the bridge to the London platform. And when the train arrived several minutes later, blocking the view across the tracks from the ticket office and the car park, he slipped away unnoticed through a side exit, climbed over the barrier, and walked away towards the canal with the collar of Barry's jacket pulled up around his ears.

CHAPTER 9

Trave sat behind the big mahogany desk, across from its owner, Titus Osman, who was dressed in an expensive coal-black suit and tie. The desk's surface was covered with a light film of white fingerprint powder but was otherwise bare except for a telephone, a green-shaded reading lamp, and a photograph of Katya in a silver frame. It had been taken several years previously, and she looked nothing like the emaciated waif she had since become. Clayton sat to one side of the desk with notebook and pen at the ready; opposite him, on the other side of the room, the glass from the shattered window pane lay in pieces on the pale blue Axminster carpet. Outside, Osman's red and white roses were just beginning to be visible in the first grey light of dawn, and beyond the dew-covered lawn the sound of the police search teams shouting to each other in the woods was distantly audible.

'I'm sorry for the wait, Mr Osman,' said Trave. 'This room is where the intruder broke into your house and probably got out too, and so I wanted to bring you in here so that you could see if anything is missing or has been moved about. And I'm afraid that meant waiting until forensics had finished.'

'No problem, Inspector. It gave me time to get dressed and compose myself a little,' said Osman evenly.

'And yet you look surprised,' said Trave, noticing Osman's raised eyebrows and the quizzical look on his face. 'May I ask why?'

'I suppose I am unaccustomed to being interviewed on

the wrong side of my own desk,' said Osman with a thin smile. 'But it doesn't matter; it is Katya, my niece, who matters. It is horrible, quite horrible, what has happened. I cannot believe it, cannot credit it.' Osman shuddered and put his hand up to his face, running his fingers across his eyes.

Trave couldn't tell whether Osman had been crying. There was certainly redness around his pupils, but whether from tears or rubbing was anyone's guess.

'I'm sorry, Inspector,' said Osman, taking a deep breath and shaking his head as if trying to pull himself together. He glanced around the room. 'Nothing appears to have been taken as far as I am aware. I have not had time to check the drawers in my desk.'

'Why do you keep the top one locked?' asked Trave. He kept his eyes fixed on Osman as he asked the question.

'Because its contents are private.'

'Private to me?'

'Yes, Inspector: private even to you. And frankly I can't see their relevance to what has happened here tonight.'

Clayton, shifting in his seat, silently agreed.

'Look, my brother-in-law has told me that he saw David Swain outside my niece's room tonight – the same man who murdered my guest, Ethan Mendel, two years ago,' Osman went on, leaning across the desk. 'I thought that Mr Swain was safely locked away in prison, but perhaps he has escaped. Has he, Inspector?'

'Yes, he's escaped,' said Trave in a flat, expressionless voice.

'I see,' said Osman, sounding unsurprised. 'Well, then, perhaps it is Mr Swain that we should be talking about. Not my private correspondence.'

'I'll decide which questions to ask, if you don't mind, Mr Osman,' said Trave coolly. 'Perhaps you wouldn't mind explaining why you felt the need to keep your niece imprisoned in her room?'

'The bars on her window were for her safety,' said Osman patiently. 'And her door wasn't locked, Inspector. If it had been, Mr Swain wouldn't have been able to get into her room tonight, would he?'

'Perhaps not. But then can you explain why she seems to have been suffering from malnutrition and has needle marks all up one arm?' Trave spoke harshly, not bothering to keep the anger out of his voice.

'The marks are from the drugs she took when she was in Oxford before I got her back here last month, and she is thin because she refused to eat. It wasn't for want of trying. It broke my heart to see her like that, but she was stubborn like her mother, my sister.'

'So I assume you got professional help?'

'Yes, of course. My doctor has been here regularly to see her.'

'Is he a psychiatrist?'

'He's a doctor, a good doctor.'

There was an uneasy silence. Once again Clayton found himself puzzled by the way that Trave was pursuing the investigation. Certainly there were questions that needed to be asked about the deceased's physical state, but there was no real evidence that she'd been imprisoned in her room, and there was nothing to justify Trave's ill-concealed hostility to Osman and his family.

'Can you tell us what you know about what happened here tonight?' Clayton asked, speaking for the first time.

'Certainly,' said Osman, transferring his attention from Trave to the younger policeman with a smile. 'I went to bed at about eleven. I heard gunshots . . .'

'How many?'

'Several. I can't be sure. I was asleep. I got out of bed

124

and opened the door of my bedroom. I heard Franz shouting my name, and then at the same time someone was rushing past me in the corridor. He was running very fast, and instinctively I backed away into my bedroom or he would have knocked me over.'

'Did you see who it was?'

'No, he was too quick.'

'He?'

'I had the impression it was a man. As I say, he was very quick.'

'Were the lights on?'

'Yes. It was dark outside when I opened the door, and so I turned on the light in the corridor. I wish I hadn't now as it must have helped Swain find his way downstairs.'

'And where is your bedroom, sir?' asked Clayton.

'Just above where we are now, off the first-floor corridor. It's on the far left side of the house as you face it from the front.'

'Thank you,' said Clayton, making a note.

Osman looked benevolently at Trave's assistant, and Trave looked even more irritated than before. 'So what happened next?' he asked, taking over the questioning.

'There was quite a lot of noise coming from downstairs, but then it stopped; and, at about the same time, Franz came down the flight of stairs nearest my bedroom. As you probably know, there is a staircase at each end of the house leading from the first to the second floors, but only one central staircase coming up from the ground floor, and I'd heard the intruder running down that one,' said Osman, glancing over at Clayton, who was busy writing in his book. 'Franz had his gun with him, and so we came down here and found the window broken over there. It seemed like Swain had gone, and so I left Franz to look through the other rooms while I went back upstairs and found Katya.

125

She was . . .' Osman's voice broke, and he covered his face with his hand for a moment, mastering his emotion.

'How do you think Swain knew where he was going?' asked Trave, once Osman had had a chance to compose himself. 'Has he been here before tonight?'

'Never with my permission. Once without, but that's all as far as I know. Katya had him in the house when I was away on business, and she even took him in her bedroom. I was very angry when I found out about it afterwards.'

'Why?'

'Because it is my house. I make the rules,' said Osman, as if he was stating the obvious.

'But why wouldn't you let him in the house in the first place?' asked Trave. 'What didn't you like about Mr Swain?'

Osman paused, thinking about his answer before he gave it.

'My niece has always had a tendency to mix with the wrong kind of people,' he said slowly, choosing his words with care. 'It became a great deal worse after Ethan's death, when she got into quite a lot of trouble in Oxford, but the problem was there before. Ethan's death hit me particularly hard because I had thought that Katya had at last found someone suitable.'

'But in what way was Mr Swain unsuitable?' asked Trave, persisting with his question.

'He was without roots, without academic background; he was living hand-to-mouth.'

'And Ethan?'

'He had been to university in Antwerp and done well. He'd lost his parents, but I knew why, and his grandmother, who brought him up, is a solid, respectable person. Ethan had a future – a bright one, until Swain took it away from him. I was right about Swain, you see. He turned out to be worse, much worse, than I thought he was: nothing more or less than a cold-blooded murderer. But being right doesn't help in the end. Katya is dead, and all I ever wanted to do was protect her. You see, she was my last blood relative. Everyone else died in the war. Franz was my wife's brother, and so he and Jana are family too, but it is not the same.'

'And yet you were able to save other people you knew from the Nazis, were you not, Mr Osman?' asked Trave, leaning forward. 'People like Ethan Mendel and his brother.'

'Yes, I was lucky: I had the money and the contacts, and so when the deportations began in Belgium I was able to help some of my Jewish friends to escape.'

'But you couldn't save everyone; you had to choose, didn't you? Who to help, who to leave behind,' Trave went on insistently. 'Like in that picture you've got up there over the mantelpiece. It's from Exodus, isn't it? The Angel of Death going through the streets, passing over the doors of those who were to be saved, exercising the power of life and death. Is that why you bought that picture, Mr Osman? So that it would make you think of having that power again?'

Osman looked furious for a moment, fighting to retain his self-possession. But then he smiled crookedly, as if he'd thought of the perfect riposte.

'I have the picture in here because it reminds me every day of what happened in my country,' he said slowly. 'And because it is beautiful, a true work of art. I wouldn't expect you to understand that, Inspector, but Vanessa certainly thinks it has quality. She was admiring it just the other day, and I have great faith in her judgement.'

Trave seemed to flinch as if he'd just been hit. His cheeks flushed, and Clayton saw how his boss's fists clenched hard on the surface of the desk. He remembered the rumours, the station gossip from the year before about Trave's wife walking out on him. Vanessa was her name. Clayton was sure of it. Was that the same Vanessa whom Osman was talking about now? It certainly seemed like it.

The door opened, but not to a human visitor. It was a cat, long and sleek and black with two distinctive white markings on either side of its green eyes. It was a most beautiful creature, thought Clayton, who had never been an animal lover. Coming to a halt beside Osman's chair, the cat arched its back, as if delighting in its own suppleness, and then jumped into Osman's lap with an easy, precise leap and sat facing Trave across the desk.

'Hullo, Cara,' said Osman, scratching the cat delicately behind its ears. 'I was wondering where you'd got to.' The cat purred, blinking its eyes at the two policemen, and Clayton had a sudden sense that Trave was now the one on the wrong side of the desk, that it was the inspector who was being interviewed, not the owner of the house.

'Cara spends much of her time outside, hunting in the woods. And I like that, that she's independent. But today it's no fun for her out there with the grounds full of strangers,' said Osman, looking out through the broken window toward the sunrise. 'Better for her to stay inside, I think. Do you need me for anything else, Inspector? If not, I'll go and give Cara her breakfast.'

Trave shook his head, and Osman got up to leave, but at the door Trave called him back.

'There is just one last thing, Mr Osman. Do you have a burglar alarm?'

'Yes, but I only use it when I'm away.'

'And why is that? You have many valuable items in this house, don't you?'

'Yes. Perhaps I am too trusting. But – how is it you English say? – hindsight is a wonderful thing. I'm here if you need me, Inspector.' Osman smiled and went through the door, preceded by his cat.

'How bloody convenient,' Trave burst out once the door was closed. 'The bastard might just as well have left the window open.'

'I don't know about that. Aren't you exaggerating a bit, sir? A lot of people don't use their alarms when they're at home, you know,' said Clayton mildly.

Trave grunted, continuing to look thunderous, and once again Clayton felt disturbed by his boss's obvious animosity toward the occupants of the house. Questions had to be asked, but the interviews with Titus Osman and his family had seemed at times more like interrogations. Just now, for instance, Trave's questioning of Osman's motives for helping Jews in the war seemed like a gratuitous personal attack for which Clayton could see no justification. Trave's approach to the case made no sense, particularly when there was an obvious suspect with motive aplenty who was now on the run from the police. There had to be an explanation. Did it have something to do with Vanessa, Trave's wife, who'd left him for another man? Clayton remembered how Trave had seemed to get so angry when Osman mentioned her name. What was Osman's connection to Vanessa? Clayton wondered. He knew that sooner or later he was going to have to ask his boss what it was all about. He couldn't do his job properly if he didn't have the full picture. But at the same time Clayton shied away from the prospect. Trave was a private man, one of the most private men Clayton had ever met, and the thought of invading his boss's privacy on a subject as sensitive as his failed marriage made Clayton feel distinctly uneasy. He'd have to find the right opportunity, but it certainly wasn't now, not with Trave sitting behind Osman's desk, looking like thunder.

Later that morning Trave and Clayton went for a walk down to Osman's boathouse, where Ethan Mendel had met his end two years before. Trave's mood seemed to improve as soon as he was outside the front door of the house. He rubbed his hands together, took a deep draught of the fresh morning air into his lungs, and set off across the lawn at a cracking pace, with Clayton following in his wake.

Soon they entered the woods. Above their heads squirrels were running in the tall trees through which the sun shone down, dappling the ground below with a play of shadows and light. Trave and Clayton were walking on a thick carpet of pine needles that deadened their footsteps, and their voices seemed unnaturally loud in the surrounding silence. The search team had obviously moved on to the other side of the road.

Trave seemed to know where he was going. At a fork in the path he took a left turn without hesitation and then stopped dead in his tracks so that Clayton had to suddenly brace himself to avoid falling over his superior officer. Osman's cat was sitting on a low, leafless branch of a pine tree that jutted out from its fellows, half-blocking their way. Clayton laughed uneasily. It was a ridiculous idea, but the creature really seemed like it was guarding the path. It sat entirely motionless, staring at them out of its unblinking eyes until Trave picked up a handful of pine needles and threw them at the cat's head. With an enraged squawk, Cara leapt from her perch and disappeared into the trees.

'Gone to report me to her boss I expect,' said Trave morosely as they carried on down toward the lake.

'Why do you dislike him so much?' asked Clayton, remembering how he'd asked exactly the same question at the end of their interview with Claes earlier that morning.

'Because he's so smooth and insincere, because he's a snob, because he's so bloody pleased with himself, because he's got that iceman, Claes, in tow. What do you want me to say?' asked Trave angrily. His irritation seemed to have returned in spades following their encounter with the cat.

'I don't think he was insincere,' said Clayton, taken aback by his boss's venom. 'He seemed genuinely upset about his niece. That's what I thought anyway.'

'He's a better actor than the other two. That's all,' said Trave shortly. 'Didn't you notice how Claes and his sister seemed so unsurprised at the way I went after them? It was almost as if they expected it. And what about all their monosyllabic answers when you'd expect them to want to help? Jana's more worried about the bloody ornaments than a girl with a bullet in her head at the top of the house.'

'She's shocked.'

'Maybe. But I'd say they all sounded rehearsed, like they were reading from a script. And don't tell me they're foreign, that English isn't their first language, because I know that.'

'Well, it isn't,' said Clayton stubbornly. 'And if it's all so rehearsed, then why didn't Osman say he saw Swain in the corridor? Isn't that what you'd have expected?'

'Because that would be over-egging the pudding, wouldn't it?' said Trave impatiently.

They took a turn in the path and came out beside the lake, leaving the woods behind. At once Clayton was struck by the utter stillness of the dark blue water. Its glassy surface stretched perhaps half a mile across to a line of weeping willow trees on the far shore, and beyond that a meadow, where a herd of black-and-white cows stood in a group, dully eating the grass in the shadow of a grove of conifers growing further up the bank.

'Does all that belong to Osman too?' asked Clayton, pointing at the lake.

'No. The boundary of his property is this path as it runs along the side of the lake and then through the trees over there to a fence by the road. But the boathouse is his, even though he never seems to use it,' said Trave, pointing to a single-storey black wooden building with a tarred convex roof that they were now approaching. Clayton had not noticed it at first since it was set well back from the water and was thus heavily camouflaged by the surrounding trees.

The boathouse was set on wooden struts, and an old rowing boat, pushed into the crawl space underneath, was partially visible. Above, the door was unlocked, and they went inside. There was a deal table and two chairs in the centre of the room but no other furniture apart from a bookshelf in the corner, its shelves empty except for a few well-worn Agatha Christie paperbacks. The air smelt musty as if from long disuse, but the electric lightbulb overhead worked and there was a sink and a small refrigerator behind a partition at the back.

'It's even got a phone line,' said Trave, picking up the receiver mounted on the wall by the door. 'Line's dead now,' he added. 'But it wasn't when Ethan died. Claes called the police and the house from here while he was holding Swain at gunpoint – very convenient.'

'Where was the body?' asked Clayton.

'Out there,' said Trave, pointing through the open door toward the lake. 'Face down, half in the water, half out. He'd been stabbed in the back, but the killer took the knife out and threw it in the lake, so there were no prints.'

'Tell me about him, about Ethan,' said Clayton, sitting down on one of the chairs at the table and looking up at Trave expectantly. It had to be why his boss had brought him here, after all – to tell him about what had happened here before, to fill him in on the background. He couldn't say he wasn't interested.

'He was twenty-four years old when he died,' said Trave. He remained standing by the door, looking out at the morning sunlight glittering on the surface of the lake, and he spoke in a slow, flat voice, as if he was describing distant events. 'He was a Jewish boy from Antwerp, which is, as you probably know, the world centre for diamonds – for cutting them, polishing them, selling them, you name it. And before the war it was the town's heyday. Everyone wanted Antwerp diamonds. Osman made his fortune trading in them, and from what I can gather, Ethan's father did well too. The two of them were friends. But then the Nazis came, looking for Jews, and Osman started helping them escape. Across the border into Switzerland; and then, when that became too difficult, down through Vichy France and into Spain; and, from there, by boat to Cuba, places like that. I've no doubt he was well rewarded for his pains.'

'How do you know that?' asked Clayton suspiciously.

'I don't. It's an assumption. Call it my natural cynicism if you like. Anyway, sometime in 1942 Ethan and his younger brother, Jacob, and their grandmother got away, but the parents waited. I don't know why. And when they went the next year they got caught crossing the border with false papers and were sent to Auschwitz. By the end of the war they were dead. I don't know the circumstances, but one can assume the worst.'

Trave paused, noticing how Clayton had turned away, biting his lip. Trave wondered whether Clayton had seen any of those films that they'd all watched at the end of the war, films about Auschwitz and Treblinka, Majdanek and Sobibor, those terrible places in the east where the world had changed forever. Clayton was young – he couldn't be more than twenty-seven or twenty-eight, Trave thought, but that didn't mean he hadn't seen the pictures. It was only a few months ago that the Israelis had captured that bastard, Eichmann, living it up in Argentina.

'And so the war ended and the two brothers came back

to Antwerp with their grandmother,' Trave went on in the same flat monotone. 'Ethan went to university and got a very respectable degree, just like Osman told us this morning, and then sometime towards the end of 1957 he took his savings out of the bank, crossed the Channel, and came to stay here with his family's benefactor, Titus Osman. His fairy godfather,' Trave added with a dry laugh.

'Why?'

'Good question. According to Osman, Ethan was here because he wanted to thank Osman personally for saving his life, but that wouldn't have required more than a short visit. He stayed on because almost immediately after his arrival he began a passionate relationship with Osman's niece.'

'Who had been seeing David Swain . . .'

'Exactly: meeting Swain here in this pretty little boathouse for romantic trysts whenever her uncle was looking the other way,' said Trave musingly, looking around the spartan room. 'Anyway, to cut a long story short, Swain got crazy about being thrown over and wrote Katya a lot of very unpleasant letters, which she later produced at his trial.'

'Were they threatening?' asked Clayton.

'Oh yes, very. Bursting with motive, if that's what you mean,' said Trave with a smile. 'David Swain was the living definition of an angry young man.'

'So what happened next?'

'Ethan left. I don't know why, and I don't know where he went exactly, although the stamps in his passport show that he spent three days in France and then just over a week in West Germany before he came back on an early morning flight from Munich to London. He arrived here at Blackwater at about twelve o'clock according to Osman. And five hours later he was dead.'

'Did Osman know he was coming?'

'Yes, apparently Ethan called ahead from Heathrow – the

telephone records confirmed that afterward. Katya wasn't home when he got here – she was out all day shopping with Jana, but Osman told me when I took his statement that Ethan seemed happy and excited to be back. They ate lunch together, and then Ethan drove into Oxford in the afternoon – and that was the last Osman saw of him. He didn't see Ethan come back – he said that that must have been because he was working in his study at the back of the house – and he could shed no light whatsoever on the note that Swain received later that afternoon.'

'The note? What note?' asked Clayton, not following.

'The note Ethan supposedly left stuck in the doorbell outside Swain's lodgings in Oxford asking Swain to meet him at the boathouse at five o'clock. It was found on Swain after his arrest, and he gave it as his reason for being where he was.'

'Standing over the body,' said Clayton.

'Yes.'

'And then running away until Claes fired his gun in the air to stop him,' added Clayton, remembering what Claes had told them up at the house.

'Yes. And Swain didn't argue with that at his trial – he said he panicked. I know it looks bad,' said Trave reluctantly. 'Everything pointed to David Swain as the murderer – motive, presence, even the knife we got out of the water was similar to other kitchen knives in his flat. It was one of the easiest cases I've ever had to put together, and maybe it was that that bothered me. It was as if everything fitted together too well. The people here, Claes and Osman, had an answer for everything just like they do now, and I couldn't shake them on the facts, however hard I tried. And then Swain didn't help himself of course. He sacked his barrister a month before the trial, which didn't give the new one much time to get up to scratch, but not even the best counsel could have done much with a case like that. The jurors came back unanimous after less than two hours. Not a reasonable doubt among them. The verdict didn't surprise me; it just left me feeling uneasy – like an itch that wouldn't go away. Afterwards I tried to put the case behind me. You have to do that in this job or you lose focus and nothing gets done. But I couldn't for some reason . . .'

'Why?' asked Clayton.

'A few things: the way Claes just happened to come round the corner of this boathouse with a gun in his pocket at exactly the time specified in the note; the fact that Katya was sent out shopping for the day; but most of all, I think, it was the note itself that worried me,' said Trave reflectively. 'Whichever way I looked at it, it made no sense that the first thing Ethan did after he got back from his European trip was to go and see a person who hated him, a person whom he didn't even know, and that then, instead of suggesting a meeting in Oxford where he already was, he left a note asking Swain to come out here at five o'clock the same day.'

'Maybe he was going to propose to Katya and wanted to straighten things out with Swain before he did,' suggested Clayton.

'But he didn't need to,' said Trave, warming to his theme. 'Ethan had no responsibility to Swain. Katya had finished with Swain long before. The note nagged at me. I couldn't make any sense of it, and Swain couldn't shed any light on the bloody thing either when I went to see him . . .'

'You went to see him!' repeated Clayton, sounding surprised. 'When?'

'A couple of times last year. He was still up in London then, in Brixton Prison pending transfer. But he wasn't any help – just went endlessly on about the injustice of it all and how much he hated Katya Osman. And so I came back out here a couple of times, even though I knew I was wasting my time – I got nowhere with Osman and Claes, and there was no evidence to justify a search warrant, although I doubt I'd have found anything worthwhile even if I'd got one. The diamond business is a secret world at the best of times, and Osman's got a castle wall built around his share in it. I thought I was on to something at one point when I found a neighbour of Swain's who said she'd seen a man with a beard hanging around near Swain's flat on the day of the murder, but then she didn't recognize Osman when I showed her his photograph, and so that was that.'

'Where did you get the picture?' asked Clayton.

'Out of a magazine. Our friend up at the house is quite a celebrity in these parts, you know – always willing to reach into his pocket for a good cause, always available to cut a ribbon, say a few words. You know what I mean,' said Trave with a twisted smile.

There it was again – the unexplained animosity toward the owner of Blackwater Hall. It alarmed Clayton more each time he saw it. What Trave had told him about the case was interesting, and there was certainly something strange about the note the dead man had left for Swain, but Clayton had seen enough police work to know there were always a few loose threads left hanging at the end of every investigation. The note didn't make Swain's conviction unsafe. In fact, the more Clayton heard about it, the more the Mendel murder sounded like an open-and-shut case. And yet Trave hadn't been prepared to let it drop. Why? Had the answer got something to do with Trave's wife and this man, Osman? Once again Clayton remembered how Trave had looked in the study when Osman had said the name Vanessa. Clayton vividly recalled the way his boss's fists had involuntarily clenched on the desk, the scarlet flush that had spread across his face, and Osman's look of smug self-satisfaction as if he'd just downed an opponent with a knockout blow.

Clayton didn't much like the man either, but that wasn't the point. This was a murder inquiry he and Trave were conducting, and personal feelings couldn't come into it. It had to be without prejudice.

Trave could be a hard taskmaster, and the last thing that Clayton wanted was to get on the wrong side of his boss, but he felt he had no choice in the matter. He had to ask Trave about his wife's connection to Osman if only to get some reassurance before they went any further with the investigation.

'Mr Osman mentioned something earlier that I wanted to ask you about,' Clayton began nervously.

'Yes, what?' asked Trave, sounding distracted. He was obviously still thinking about Ethan's murder.

'Well, he said something about someone called Vanessa, and I wondered . . .'

Clayton broke off, alarmed by the change in his boss's demeanour: the name had registered on Trave's face like an electric shock.

'You wondered what?' asked Trave, staring angrily at his subordinate.

'I wondered if . . . well, if it was Mrs Trave he was talking about,' Clayton finished lamely.

Trave was silent for a moment, breathing heavily, and then, when he spoke again, his voice was hard and cold.

'Yes, Constable, Titus Osman *was* referring to my wife, the same lady who has left me and taken up with him, as you must know full well given that you choose to spend your time listening to station gossip instead of doing your job.'

'I'm sorry, sir. I asked you because I didn't know – about her and Osman, I mean. I knew she'd left, that she was no longer with you, but I didn't know the other. I promise you, I didn't,' said Clayton, stumbling over his words.

'Well, now you do. What of it?' asked Trave brutally.

'Well, it's just, it worried me, sir, that it might affect things, the inquiry . . .'

'Cloud my judgement, you mean?'

'Yes, sir.'

'Well, it won't. Are you satisfied now?'

Clayton nodded, and he would have said more, but for the fact that they were at that moment interrupted by someone tapping on the half-open door. It was Watts, one of the detectives who'd been helping organize the search.

'What do you want?' asked Trave furiously, rounding on the newcomer in the doorway.

'I'm sorry, sir,' said Watts nervously. 'It's just I thought you ought to know. The switchboard called. A man that matches Mr Swain's description hijacked a car in Blackwater village a few hours ago and made the people in it take him to the railway station.'

'The station – which station?' asked Trave.

'Oxford. They think he took the first train to London apparently. Oh, and he's got a gun. He threatened them with it.'

'A gun. Anything else?'

'Yes, they say he was wounded – there was blood around his left shoulder and he was holding his arm like it was hurting him, apparently.'

Behind Trave, Clayton got to his feet. It was the news they'd been waiting for – independent evidence that Swain had been here during the night – and armed too. Now surely there could be no doubt about the identity of their main suspect.

'Put out an alert,' said Trave. 'Nationwide. You know the drill. And Adam, you come with me,' he said, turning to Clayton. 'We've got work to do.'

* * *

Titus waited until the police had cleared out of his study before he telephoned Vanessa and told her what had happened.

Vanessa was aghast, remembering Katya's desperate face in the drawing room ten days before, the way she'd struggled so hard to convey her message. 'They're trying to kill me,' the girl had said. And now she was dead, murdered in her bed.

'I need to see you,' said Titus urgently. 'Can I come over?'

Twenty-five minutes later he was sitting beside her on the sofa in her living room. The weather had turned cold, and she'd lit a fire before Titus called so the room was warm. But he still shivered, as if the shock of what had happened was only now beginning to penetrate his skin. He was different to how she'd ever seen him before – like something inside him had broken, and his voice had a faraway feel, even though he was sitting beside her.

'It's such a waste,' he said with a sigh. 'Such a terrible waste. She'd have got better if she'd just had a little bit more time. I know she would. She had so much to live for, and now it's as if she never was. You should have seen her, Vanessa. Like a rag doll in her bed, with all the life blown out of her by that swine. And her beautiful face such a mess too, such a damned, God-awful mess.'

Titus shuddered, and Vanessa reached over and took his shaking hand, wishing she could find some way to comfort her lover, but she could think of nothing to say to mitigate his pain. Death of the young was unbearable. Because it was avoidable, because of what might have been and now would never be. She knew these things from bitter personal experience.

'It's how we parted that I cannot bear,' said Titus. It was obviously hard for him to speak, and the words caught in his throat. 'If she'd had a bit more time to recover, then we

140

could have been friends again like we were when Ethan was alive. She'd have got her hope back. But instead she saw me as her enemy; she wouldn't understand why I was keeping her at home. And your husband doesn't understand either, or rather he doesn't want to understand.'

'My husband. What's my husband got to do with it?' asked Vanessa, not understanding the connection for a moment.

'He's the man in charge, what you English call the officer in the case,' said Titus bitterly. 'I know – it's crazy,' he added, seeing the look of surprise on Vanessa's face. 'Anyone else would have handed the investigation over to another detective given his personal interest. But oh no, Bill Trave knows best.'

'What's he done?' asked Vanessa, feeling alarmed.

'Interrogated me and my family like we were the criminals. That's what. He accused us of deliberately starving Katya, of hurting her. And he even asked Jana, my sister-in-law, why she didn't take communion or go to confession when she went to church. Can you imagine? The other policeman stopped him, or I don't know what else he'd have said.'

'That's not like Bill,' said Vanessa, shaking her head. 'He always took pride in his work. That's the one thing that kept him going, I think.'

'Well, maybe his jealousy of us has changed all that. I am sorry for what has happened to him. Truly I am. I bear him no ill will, but I need him to be a policeman now, to catch this maniac who has done this terrible thing, not use my niece's death as an opportunity to . . .'

'Settle the score,' Vanessa said, finishing Osman's sentence for him when he couldn't seem to find the right word. 'I have to say I find all this hard to believe, Titus. That Bill should be so unfair. He was on the radio while I was waiting for you to come over, appealing for help finding Swain. It's

141

a pity you didn't hear him. It might have made you feel better.'

'It does make me feel better,' said Titus, sounding just as upset as before. 'Once Swain is under lock and key then maybe everything will settle down. But, in the meantime, Vanessa, I need to ask you something. A favour. You have to help me.'

'Help you how?' asked Vanessa, looking puzzled.

'Help me by not telling your husband about what Katya said to you. She was out of her mind with misdirected anger and grief that night like I told you before, and she didn't know what she was saying. The evidence against Swain is overwhelming. He was in Katya's room with a gun – Franz and Jana heard him fire it. But your husband refuses to see it that way. I know it's wrong, but I didn't feel able to tell him that I was keeping Katya at home against her will. It was for her own good, but I know he'd just have used it against me. I know what he's trying to do – he's looking for any excuse to build a case against me because he hates me, Vanessa. You know he does.'

Titus looked hard at Vanessa, willing her to look him in the eye and give him what he asked, but she looked away into the fire, knitting her brow. She didn't like it. She'd been brought up to tell the truth and this felt all wrong. But then again Titus wasn't asking her to tell a lie, only to keep information to herself, and maybe the thought of it made her feel bad just because anything less than one hundred per cent truthfulness always made her uncomfortable. And Titus was right – the case against this Swain man did seem overwhelming. Why did she need to make Titus's life hell for no reason just when he needed time and space to recover from the terrible wound that Swain had inflicted upon him? What would it do to their relationship if she got Titus into trouble just when he needed her the most, if she denied him the first major sacrifice he'd ever asked of her? Vanessa still hadn't made up her mind whether she wanted to marry Titus, but she had no doubt in her mind that she didn't want to lose him.

And yet it was unlike Bill to be unprofessional. And it certainly was a strange coincidence that Katya should have been so convinced that nameless people were trying to kill her less than two weeks before she met a violent death. Vanessa thought of Franz Claes's cold smile and shivered, wondering not for the first time if Titus knew his brother-in-law as well as he claimed.

'Let me think about it,' she said, looking up. 'I know this has been a terrible shock for you, Titus. But it's a shock for me too.'

'I understand,' said Titus, drawing a deep breath as he tried to hide his disappointment. 'Will you talk to me before you do anything, though, Vanessa? Can I ask you that much?'

'Yes, of course,' she said. 'If you only knew how much I want to help you, Titus, if you only knew . . .'

She stopped, struggling with her emotions.

'I know,' he said. 'You don't need to tell me. I already know.'

And as they sat hand in hand on the sofa watching the fire burn down to glowing broken embers, Vanessa felt she'd never loved anyone as much as she loved Titus Osman at that moment.

CHAPTER 10

David Swain hurried through the deserted streets in the early light. He felt cold and hungry, but none of the shops or cafés that he passed were open yet, and most of them would stay closed all day. Sunday was not a good day to be on the run, he thought, with sour humour. And his shoulder was hurting worse than ever, with pains that shot down his arm and left him weak at the knees so that all he could think about was his mother's house and the distance that still separated him from his destination. It wasn't a solution – he knew that. His trick at the train station might buy him a little time, but the police weren't going to assume he'd gone to London forever. Sooner rather than later they'd come knocking at his mother's door, and his stepfather would hand him over without a second's thought. Because Ben Bishop hated him and his mother did what her husband told her to do, which had to be why she'd never visited him in gaol even after he'd been moved back to Oxford Prison at the beginning of the year. She wrote to him, she'd even sent him a couple of bars of chocolate, but she never came to see him. And what use were letters? No use, except that in her last one she'd told him about Ben getting a bit more money from working on weekends, driving his Number 19 bus round the Oxfordshire countryside, 'providing a service to rural areas' as David remembered his stepfather pompously describing his work when he'd first appeared on the scene seven or eight years ago in his ill-fitting suit and tie, trying to worm his way into David's mother's affections. And it hadn't taken him long, thought David bitterly; less than a year to move in and take over, to wipe the past from David's childhood home like it had never existed. But on Sundays he worked, and David's mother couldn't refuse to help her son for a few hours. That's all he needed: enough time to clean up the wound, eat, and grab a little sleep, and then he'd be on his way like he'd never been in the house at all. Ben would never need to know.

David was utterly exhausted by the time he got to the turning to his mother's street. He felt himself tottering from side to side, hanging on to street lamps and garden walls for support like he was a drunk on his last legs returning from an unusually excessive night out on the town. He looked down at his watch – half past six. He'd have to wait and keep watch – his stepfather couldn't have left for work yet. Crossing the road, he retrieved yesterday's *Daily Express* from a litter bin and sat down on a bench with the newspaper held up over his face to hide his features. He was too tired to read more than the headlines: *US presses ahead with Polaris submarine program: More nuclear missiles fired from underwater.* The bomb, always the bomb – the shadow over all their lives. There were times when he was younger when David had thought about nothing else. He'd seen the pictures of Hiroshima and Nagasaki and read the reports of what had happened after the atomic bombs were dropped on the unsuspecting Japanese down below, and fear of the Russians had kept him up through countless sleepless nights, thinking about the Politburo leaders in their brown fur caps standing on top of the Kremlin wall, watching the tanks roll by on May Day with unreadable expressions on their Slavic faces. But now for a moment he almost welcomed the thought of a war that would wipe everything out, leaving nothing behind.

He woke up with the sun in his eyes. More than an hour had gone by, and now he had no way of knowing whether his stepfather was still in the house. Cursing his stupidity, David threw the newspaper off his chest, turned the collar of the stolen jacket up around his neck, and started to walk slowly down the street toward his mother's house. Stopping just before the low box hedge in front of the next-door neighbour's garden, he knelt down as if to tie his shoelaces and peered round the corner. He took in the front garden – a postage stamp patch of carefully mown grass bordered by two rows of red chrysanthemums growing at precisely equal distances from each other, and beside it, parked on the tiny drive, his stepfather's brand new lilac-green Ford Anglia motor car, its owner's proudest possession, gleaming in the early morning sunshine. And then, edging forward, the front bay window of the nondescript little house that had once been David's home came into view. Framed in the centre, David's stepfather was at that moment finishing his breakfast. As David watched, Ben Bishop removed his napkin from where he'd had it tucked into the front of his shirt and dabbed it around the corners of his heavy-lipped mouth. Then, getting up from the table, he pulled his braces up over his big shoulders and put on his bus driver's jacket that had been hanging over the back of the chair before he disappeared from view as he walked away from the window into the interior of the house. *The bastard must be just about to go to work*, thought David as he retreated back down the street and, sure enough, five minutes later, David caught sight of Ben with both hands on the wheel of his car as he turned carefully onto the main road, headed for the bus depot.

Back at the house, David suddenly felt an attack of nerves, and his hand shook as he pressed the bell and heard it chime behind the frosted glass of the front door. And all at once, before he'd had any time to compose himself, there was his mother standing two feet away from him, wearing the same pale blue housecoat that she always wore, with a pack of John Player Navy Cut cigarettes in the breast pocket, and a lit one in her hand that she dropped in shock on the doormat when she saw who it was who'd come to call. David reached down to pick it up, and, as he straightened up, he saw how the expression on her face had changed from surprise to fear, almost panic.

'Don't worry,' he said, trying to keep the irritation out of his voice. 'I know you're not pleased to see me, but I only need a few hours. I'll be gone long before he gets back.' He held the cigarette out to her like it was a peace offering, but she shook her head and so he threw it back behind him onto the path where it burnt uselessly, the blue-grey smoke curling up into the cold morning air. And still she said nothing, just stood staring at her son like he was some kind of horrible apparition.

'Well, aren't you going to invite me in?' he asked, injecting a false cheeriness into his voice. 'I used to live here, you know – once upon a time.'

'You've escaped,' she said in a dull, flat voice. It was a statement, not a question.

'Yes,' he said. 'I've escaped, and I've hurt myself too. Here, in my shoulder. And I need your help, Mother. Please.'

Suddenly he swayed in the doorway, stumbling over his words as his legs began to buckle beneath him, and instinctively she put her hand under his arm and supported him over the threshold, before he fell to the floor in a dead faint.

He came to on the hallway carpet. There was a cushion under his head, and a boy whom he didn't at first recognize was squatting down beside him holding a glass of water. The boy was wearing the most enormous pair of glasses that David had ever seen – he thought they were an illusion at first as his surroundings swam in and out of focus – but behind the glasses were eyes exactly the same colour as his own. David knew who the boy was now: it was his half brother, Max, Ben Bishop's son. He'd doubled in size since David had last seen him nearly three years before and grown a thick mop of curly black hair on top of his head, and his skin was oddly pale, as if he spent all his time inside.

'You fell over,' said the boy. He spoke slowly and with an extraordinary seriousness, as if he was disclosing a vital piece of information.

'Yes, I fainted.'

'Fainted? I don't know *fainted*.'

'It means "pass out". Like when you crack your head,' David added lamely. But Max seemed to understand, and it was almost as if David could see the boy's mind working as Max carefully added another important word to his store of vocabulary.

'Do you want some water?' asked Max, holding out the glass, and David took it gratefully in both hands, swallowing the water down in great gulps.

'Where's . . .' David hesitated, unsure of what name to call his mother, but Max came to his rescue.

'Mum?' he said. 'She's in the kitchen. She's getting you something. I've already had my breakfast: toast and jam and cornflakes.' Max counted off the items like he was making a list.

'Sounds good,' said David, smiling.

'Mum': the way Max said the silly one-syllable word touched David suddenly. He and this strange boy had something in common, something vital, and for a moment David felt a deep sense of kinship with this half-brother of his that he hardly knew; for a moment he didn't feel quite so all alone in the world as he always did.

His mother's stern-sounding voice brought him back to reality. 'Can you walk?' she asked.

'I think so,' he said, getting gingerly to his feet.

'Well, you'd better come in the living room if you want me to look at this wound of yours. The light's better in there.'

He lay down on the sofa, the same sofa where he used to sit listening to the radio after school what seemed like a lifetime ago, and his mother knelt down next to him, placing the tin box in which she kept her medicines beside her on the floor. He remembered it from his childhood – the bright red cross emblazoned on top of the white tin and, inside, the bandages and elastoplasts and little bottles with strange-sounding names on their labels. He remembered how the box had frightened him and made him feel safe all at the same time.

Clearly it was an object of fascination to Max as well. The boy's eyes seemed to get even bigger when his mother opened the box, but that was all he got to see.

'Go and do your homework, Max,' she said. 'You know what your father said.' Reluctantly the boy obeyed. He looked back for a moment at the door. David weakly raised his hand in a farewell gesture, and the boy responded word-lessly in kind.

'Making friends I see,' said David's mother. There was no pleasure in her voice, and David sensed her hostility.

'Is that a crime?' he asked, rising to the challenge.

'No, but escaping from prison is.'

You don't know the half of it, thought David. He had his eyes tight shut, determined not to complain about the pain as she helped him out of the stolen jacket and the ripped-up prison shirt underneath and washed the dried blood away from his shoulder with a wet sponge.

'What happened?' she asked.

'Someone took a shot at me.'

'Why?'

'Because I was escaping,' he lied. 'I could feel the blood

afterwards, but I don't know if the bullet's in there. Can you see?' he asked, clenching his teeth and his fists, setting himself against the agony as she probed the wound with her fingers.

'It's superficial,' she said eventually. 'It'll heal if you give it a chance.'

He let out his breath in small gasps, physically experiencing his relief as his mother began to dress and bandage the wound. If Claes had really got him with that second shot, then he'd have needed a doctor, and David knew he hadn't a hope of finding that kind of help without getting caught, however much money he had in his pocket. Now he still had a chance.

He closed his eyes, daydreaming of freedom, of foreign cities – places he'd never been, where nobody would know him or ask questions – and then suddenly came to when his mother shouted out his name. He looked up: her face was contorted with rage, but there was fear there too, and the beginnings of despair. She was holding the gun in her hand, dangling it between her fingers and thumb like it was something diseased, and he realized what a fool he'd been to forget his mother's mania for order, for hanging things up. He should never have let her anywhere near the jacket.

'Give me the gun,' he said. 'I need it.'

'Not in my house you don't. Do they know you've got this?'

'Yes.'

'Have you used it?'

'No. I tell you I haven't,' he added, half-shouting when he saw the look of disbelief written all over his mother's face, but the repeated denial did nothing to soften the severity of her expression.

'Well, it doesn't matter what you did with it. They'll shoot you when they come if they know you've got it. And me too. And Max. He's only six years old. Doesn't that mean anything to you? Why did you have to come here, David? Why?' Her voice was rising all the time. Soon she would start to scream.

'Because there was nowhere else. I told you I wouldn't stay. Just something to eat and a few hours sleep and I'll be gone, I promise. And they won't come here today. They think I've gone to London. I made it look like that at the station. For Christ's sake I'm your son. Doesn't that mean anything?'

She looked at him long and hard and then over at the brass clock ticking above the fireplace.

'Ben works half days at the weekends, so you can stay until one o'clock,' she said. 'But not a minute later. And this stays in here until you go,' she added, putting the gun in the top drawer of the old bureau in the corner where she kept her papers. 'I'll get you some clothes and make you something to eat.'

He sat at the table in the same place where he had watched his stepfather finishing his breakfast half an hour earlier. Ben Bishop's oversized shirt and cardigan hung off him like a scarecrow, but at least they were an improvement on the torn, bloody shirt he'd had on up to now. And the breakfast was wonderful. It was hard not to eat too fast. David hadn't realized just how hungry he was until he started putting the food in his mouth.

His mother stood in the doorway of the kitchen silently watching him as she smoked yet another cigarette. He remembered how she never seemed to sit down: it was as if she couldn't allow herself to relax for one moment from the endless round of cooking and cleaning and washing that she'd devised for herself because otherwise . . . Otherwise what? The world would end? Well, that was probably going to happen anyway, David thought grimly, remembering the newspaper headlines he'd read earlier.

'Thank you,' he said when he was done. 'That was the best meal I've ever had.' He wasn't exaggerating.

She ignored the compliment. He couldn't read her expression. She didn't seem frightened or angry any more, but there was a distance between them that he couldn't seem to bridge.

He looked over at the mantelpiece, from which the photographs of his mother and father on their wedding day and of him as a boy of Max's age had long since disappeared. Consigned to the bureau, he supposed, gathering dust.

'Do you miss him?' he asked.

'Who?'

'Dad. It's like he was never here.'

'No,' she said, responding to the question but not the comment.

'Why?'

'Because he was like you: always full of ideas, never settling to anything. Ideas don't pay the bills,' she said with finality.

'Not like Ben, though. I doubt he's had an idea in his life.'

'He's solid,' she said, not taking offence.

David nodded. He understood what his mother meant. It couldn't have been easy for her all those years, worrying about debts and eviction notices, although it had to be said that the old man had done better toward the end, with his own one-man business and a second-hand white van with SPARKS ELECTRICS painted on the side to prove it. Much good it did him: the van was where he'd died – a heart attack on his way to a job in Abingdon. 'Painless,' the doctor had told them at the hospital, 'but lucky he was stopped in traffic at the time, now wasn't it?'

'Have you got a cigarette?' David asked. His mother handed him her packet and lit one herself too. The acrid smoke felt good in his lungs, and the shared cigarettes broke down the barrier between them for a moment so that they seemed almost like old comrades, free of the bonds of their failed mother-son relationship.

'The old man's ideas didn't do me much good either, you know,' said David reflectively. 'All those crazy plans for my future like I was going to be a university professor or something. This is the last town he should have been living in. Those bloody dreaming spires went to his head.'

'He wanted the best for you.'

'No, he didn't,' said David bitterly. 'He wanted to live his life again through me. That's what he wanted. It's why he spent his last penny and yours too sending me to that posh school – so I could learn to speak like the upper classes, be one of them. And you know what they called me there, Mum? Sparky! Maybe he should have thought twice about sending me to the same place where he changed the light-bulbs, but I expect they gave him a special rate – cut price fees for Sparky Swain's son. I never stood a bloody chance in that place – that's the truth.'

'You did all right in your first lot of exams.'

'Yes, to keep him happy. But what was the point in that if he was going to die? What was the point in any of it?'

'I don't know, David. I'm not God. Like I said, he wanted the best for you. You're the one who chose to throw it all away. You could have made something of yourself if you'd wanted to.'

'So it's all my fault, is it?' David asked angrily.

'You make your bed, and you lie on it,' said his mother. The finality of the platitude infuriated him, even more so because he couldn't think of a cutting response.

'Why didn't you visit me in prison?' he asked. It was the unspoken question that had been hanging in the air between them ever since he'd arrived.

'Because I couldn't,' she said simply. 'I wanted to, but Ben wouldn't have it, and I didn't want to go behind his back.'

And David knew she was telling no more or less than the truth. Honesty was his mother's great redeeming quality, and, as had happened so often in the past, his anger bounced off it and evaporated.

'You can sleep in your old room,' she said. 'I'll wake you when it's time to go.'

'Thanks,' he said, getting up. And on impulse he bent over and kissed her on the cheek on his way to the door, and then left without waiting to see her reaction.

Upstairs, David washed in the tiny bathroom. Just like in the rest of the house there was not a speck of dirt anywhere – even the taps gleamed in sterile glory. David opened the medicine cabinet over the sink, looking for aspirin, and found some behind a bottle of men's hair dye. He smiled, amused for a moment by the thought of his stepfather trying to keep his non-existent looks, and then caught sight of his own reflection in the mirror. He looked awful – haggard, with great dark circles under his staring eyes, the living image of a man on the run, a convict on his last legs. He needed to sleep.

His old bedroom had become Max's room, distinctively Max's room. The bed and most of the furniture were still the same, but every surface was covered with careful arrangements of toy soldiers and Dinky cars and different species of furry animals. There was something oddly touching about this great assembly of disparate objects and creatures, and yet the room was still disturbing to David's peace of mind. Here he'd played and read and slept, done his homework with his father, and been tended to by his mother when he had the measles. He'd had a family and a purpose and a life, and now he'd come back here a fugitive from justice, an outlaw like in those John Wayne movies he used to watch at the cinema when he was a kid. David closed his eyes, but sleep wouldn't come. Outside a cacophony of Sunday-morning church bells pealed out, calling the faithful to worship, and he tossed and turned on the bed, tormented by the memory of Katya lying on her bed with a bloody hole in the middle of her pretty forehead and the gun shaking in his hand like it had a life of its own.

David opened his eyes and saw Max in the doorway. The boy looked worried, and his eyes behind his oversized spectacles seemed even larger than before.

'You cried,' he said, 'like you were having a nightmare or something.'

'I was,' said David apologetically. 'But it's all right now. I like your room, Max.'

'Do you?' The boy seemed immoderately pleased, as if nobody had noticed the place before.

'Yes, I do. All your things – it's quite an arrangement you've got going. Which is your favourite?'

'Toy or animal?' asked Max seriously. He'd come into the room now and was standing beside the bed.

'Both.'

'Well, that's easy. I like Fluff the most of the animals,' he said, picking up a worse-for-wear black-and-white teddy bear from the top of the bookcase. 'I like to sleep with him, but Dad says I need to stop because I'm growing up. And my best toy . . .' – Max looked around the room, carefully weighing his decision – 'is . . . my robot,' he finished with a flourish, holding up a silver flat-faced, cone-headed android with an elaborate control panel in what would otherwise have been its stomach. Robbie the Robot was engraved on the back over the compartment for the batteries.

'Yes, good choice. I think that's the best one too,' said David admiringly. 'Is Robbie your favourite character?'

'Yes, one of them.' Max seemed distracted, like he wanted to say something but couldn't find the right words.

'What is it?' asked David.

'This was your room too, wasn't it, when you were a kid?'

'Yes, it was once, a long time ago. But it's yours now. And you've got it looking a lot better than I ever did.'

'Have I? Thanks,' said Max. Once again David had that same sense that the boy was filing away what he'd just heard for later inspection. It was a funny trait, but it appealed to David for some reason.

'I've got to go to sleep now,' he said. 'But our talk's made me feel better, so I promise you – no more nightmares.'

Max nodded and left the room still carrying the robot and the teddy bear, and downstairs David could hear the muffled sound of the television being turned on – a new addition since he'd last been here. It was true – the conversation with his half-brother had helped – he felt calmer, easier in his mind, and, turning over, he fell into a deep dreamless sleep.

He woke with a start. His mother was shaking him. 'You've got to go. Ben's back.'

'But I thought you said one o'clock,' he said, looking blearily at his watch. It was only five to twelve.

'I know I did. He's back early. That's all. I've made you some sandwiches,' she said, holding out a plastic bag. 'You can go out of the back door. He won't hear you if you're quiet.'

'What about my gun?' he said, pulling on his clothes.

'Leave it. I'll get rid of it. And I'll tell them you haven't got one when they come. They won't shoot you if you haven't got a gun.'

There was an urgent, pleading note in his mother's voice, and it gave him some comfort in the days and weeks afterwards to know that she'd cared, but now it didn't make any difference: he had to have the gun.

Downstairs he heard his stepfather's barking voice mixed up with the sound of the television.

'I'll keep him in the living room. You go through the kitchen and out the back. The door's open,' she said from the doorway.

'I need the gun,' he told her again, but she'd already left.

Dressed in his prison jeans and shoes and his stepfather's oversized shirt and cardigan, topped with the jacket he'd stolen the night before, David tiptoed down the stairs, holding the bag of sandwiches in his hand. Stopping halfway down, he listened to the voices in the living room across the hall and felt for a moment like he was a child again, eavesdropping on his parents in the half-light after he was supposed to have gone to bed, except that he was fifteen years older now and he needed the gun in his mother's bureau. It was just behind the living room door.

Ben had been holding forth about a road closure some-where, something to do with a change in his bus route and coming home early, but now he wasn't talking any more, and David could hear the news summary being read on the television – more about missile tests and the elec-tion coming up in the United States – *Kennedy or Nixon; Nixon or Kennedy – who the hell cares*? thought David. But maybe Ben did; maybe he was watching up at the other end of the room; maybe there'd be time to sneak in and take the gun out of the bureau without Ben's seeing him at all.

The door was already open, and Ben *was* watching the television, sitting in the big armchair, dressed in his bus driver's uniform with his back to David and the window. Max was on the sofa looking at a book, and David's mother was nowhere in sight. Slowly, stealthily, David opened the bureau drawer inch by inch, but it made no noise, and there was the gun inside, just where his mother had left it, lying on top of a bundle of old letters. It felt good to have it in his hand again; holding it made him feel empowered, safe. He straightened up, ready to go, and looked at his face staring back at him from the television.

'. . . escaped from Oxford Prison late last night and is now wanted for a murder committed in an isolated country house outside the village of Blackwater shortly afterwards,' intoned the impassive voice of the newsreader, talking over the blown-up photograph they'd taken of David at the police station after his arrest two years earlier.

David gasped involuntarily, and Ben turned round, getting to his feet and letting out a bellow of rage as he caught sight of his stepson standing in the corner of the room behind him, but the gun in David's hand, pointed at his midriff, brought him to an abrupt halt.

'What do you want?' he asked through a deep exhalation of breath. He was obviously terrified.

'Shut up and sit down,' said David, ignoring the question. 'I need to see this.'

The picture on the television had changed. Now there was some kind of press conference going on with lights flashing and a whole bunch of microphones held up toward a thin, tired-looking man with a receding hairline. He was wearing a creased, crumpled-up suit, and his tie was on crooked. David remembered him: it was the policeman who'd been in charge of his case before, the one who'd come to talk to him in Brixton Prison last year before his transfer down here. He had an unusual name – Trave, Inspector Trave. That was it. David remembered the way the man's eyes had been sad and focused all at the same time, like he was trying to see past David, through a glass darkly, and failing in the attempt.

'He's armed and dangerous,' Trave was saying. 'Members of the public should call the police immediately if they

158

see him, and he should not be approached under any circumstances.'

'Where is he? Any ideas?' asked a reporter, pushing his microphone up toward the inspector.

'He went to Oxford Railway Station this morning and bought a ticket to London. We don't know for certain if he was on the train, but he may well have been.'

'What about the murder?' asked another invisible journalist. 'Can you give us any more detail?'

'She's a young woman in her early twenties who's been shot in the head. She was killed with a single bullet,' said Trave. He seemed uncomfortable or impatient maybe, like he wished he was somewhere else.

'Was the victim known to the suspect?'

'Yes, known.'

And the television cut away from the press conference to a photograph of Ethan Mendel, but now David couldn't hear what the newsreader was saying. His mother was shouting, telling him to get out, telling Max to get behind her into the kitchen. But David stood his ground. He felt sorry, wished it hadn't come to this with his pig of a stepfather involved, but he'd had no choice. She shouldn't have taken away his gun.

'Give me the keys,' he told his stepfather.

At first Ben didn't understand, or perhaps he didn't want to.

'Give me the keys to your fucking car,' David shouted, brandishing the gun. All his anger at this interloper, this man who'd taken over his home and treated him like dirt, came rushing to the surface. He felt like shooting Ben Bishop, putting an end to him once and for all.

Ben looked at the gun and saw the rage in David's eyes. It hurt him harder than anything he'd ever had to do to hand over the keys to his most prized possession, but in the end his fear won out. He took the keys out of his pocket and tossed them at his stepson's feet with a look of hatred in his eye.

David picked them up off the floor and then went over to the telephone on top of his mother's bureau and yanked its cord out of the wall. He hadn't got anything with which to cut the wire, and so he put the phone in the bag with the sandwiches that his mother had made for him.

'Have you got an extension?' he asked. His stepfather shook his head. Maybe he was telling the truth; maybe he wasn't. David didn't have the time to check. He needed to go. He looked over at his mother, took a step toward her, and then stopped, sensing her fury.

'I'm sorry,' he said, 'I didn't do this thing. I promise you I didn't. Katya was dead when I got there. I took the gun to protect myself. The man there shot at me last time, and I needed to defend myself. I needed . . .'

'You're lying,' she said, interrupting him in a harsh, unforgiving voice. 'Lying like you always do, but it won't help you this time, David. This time you've gone too far, and you'll have to pay the penalty. Now get out of my house and don't come back. You've done enough to me and mine for one lifetime.'

There was nothing he could say. It was like his mother was a stranger suddenly, like she had no relation to him any more as she stood across from him in the kitchen doorway, protecting her son from the man with the gun, white-faced, willing him to be gone.

He looked around the room one last time, as if committing it to memory, and then turned on his heel and walked out, leaving the front door open behind him. He unlocked the car and got in, turned the key in the ignition, and waited a moment. It gave him a sudden savage pleasure to sit there in his stepfather's seat feeling the engine purring underneath him. And then, just as he'd put the car in gear and was about to drive away, Max came running out of the front door with Robbie the Robot clutched in his hand.

David wound down the window.

'I want you to have this,' said Max. 'Because . . .'

'We're brothers?'

Max nodded. David had never seen anyone looking so upset and so determined all at the same time.

'Thank you, Max,' he said, placing the robot carefully on the passenger seat beside the gun and the bag containing the sandwiches and the telephone. 'I'll take good care of him. And . . .' He paused, searching for the right words, but they wouldn't come. 'I'm sorry,' he said. 'Tell your mother I'm sorry. This isn't how I wanted it to be.'

Turning away and looking over his shoulder, he reversed out of the drive, and then, pausing for a moment, he stared over at the door where his mother was standing with her arm around her younger son. And she remained there, tight-lipped, immobile, as he stepped on the gas and drove away.

CHAPTER 11

Adam Clayton pulled down on the lever and watched the low-quality black coffee slowly filling the Styrofoam cup that he was holding under the nozzle of the hot-drinks machine. It was his third visit to the coffee machine that morning, and each cup had tasted worse than the one before, but he needed the caffeine to stay alert as he combed through the reports from the Katya Osman case that now covered every inch of his desk in the room he shared with Trave across the corridor. It was hard work, and he wasn't sleeping well. Partly it was the pressure that always comes with a new inquiry, particularly one as high-profile as this; partly it was the continuing unease he'd felt with Trave ever since he'd voiced his anxieties in Osman's boathouse two days earlier about Trave's reaction to his wife's ongoing relationship with the owner of Blackwater Hall. Clayton wished now that he'd kept quiet. Trave had not referred to the subject again, and so there was no opportunity to apologize or make amends, but he'd clearly not forgotten his junior's implied doubts about his professionalism. Ever since their conversation, he'd treated Clayton with a new businesslike reserve, and the frostiness of the atmosphere had started to undermine the younger man's confidence, making him realize how much he'd depended up to now on his boss's goodwill and support.

And yet Clayton also felt a growing sense of injustice. He'd never have brought up the issue of a conflict of interest if Trave hadn't treated everyone at Blackwater Hall like they were murder suspects, not witnesses. No wonder Claes and his sister had been less than forthcoming when Trave had started in on them straight away, giving them the third degree. And Osman had seemed genuinely distraught when they'd talked to him in his study across from the broken window through which this Swain character had come bursting in with his gun a few hours earlier. Swain was there in the house at the right time and with the right motive. Everything pointed to him, and yet Trave remained obviously dissatisfied, distrusting the accumulating evidence. Why? There was no reason for it. Unless . . .

'You look like shit, lad. Something wrong with your love life?'

Clayton turned to his left and saw Inspector Macrae looking up at him from a chair in the corner. He'd obviously been too preoccupied with his troubles to notice that he wasn't the only one in the break room when he'd come in earlier. But Macrae was like that – always there when you were least expecting it, popping up with some unnerving comment that you couldn't think of an answer to. He was new at the station, transferred down from up north when old Inspector Finney retired. And Clayton and the other junior detectives were wary of him – he came with a reputation for getting results and not caring too much about how he got them. He seemed to have a way of always looking for the bad in people. It was more than cynicism, more like a perpetual sneer. It set Clayton on edge, and he tried to give Macrae as wide a berth as possible. Today he was the last person that Clayton wanted to talk to, but he could hardly turn his back on the man. Macrae was an inspector and Clayton was a junior detective, right down at the bottom of the station totem pole.

'No, sir, I'm all right,' Clayton said, forcing himself to sound friendly, like he was feeling on top of the world. 'Just a lot of work suddenly. That's all.'

'Well, sit down and tell me about it, lad,' said Macrae, patting the empty chair beside him. 'Perhaps I can help.'

'No, the work's not a problem. It's just I've got to give Inspector Trave a progress report when he comes in,' said Clayton nervously. He stayed fixed to the spot by the coffee machine but looked longingly toward the door.

'Ah yes. Bill Trave can be quite demanding when he wants to be. I've seen that for myself. Giving you a hard time of it, is he?' asked Macrae with a smile, clearly enjoying Clayton's discomfiture.

'No, sir. Not at all.'

Macrae nodded knowingly as if he understood that Clayton wasn't telling him the truth because he couldn't, and then pointed again to the empty chair. Clayton sat down. He had no choice.

He'd never been so close to Macrae before, and Clayton felt an instinctive repulsion that he couldn't quite explain to himself. It wasn't that the man was ugly or smelt bad. Quite the opposite in fact: Inspector Macrae was a good-looking man in the prime of life, dressed in a far more expensive suit than Trave had ever worn. He wore his hair carefully combed back *en brosse* from his high, unwrinkled forehead and, to the extent that he smelt of anything, it was expensive Italian aftershave. But there was something weird about the way his waxy skin was pulled so tightly across the bones of his face like it was a mask with only his small, watchful grey eyes seeming to hint at the true personality underneath; and his hands were strange too – long, scrupulously clean nails on the end of tapering fingers and thumbs that Macrae kept perpetually in motion, moulding, stroking, kneading invisible shapes. An artist's hands or a strangler's, Clayton thought. Not a policeman's.

'An interesting case, this Blackwater murder, from what I've been hearing,' said Macrae, looking not at Clayton but beyond him into the middle distance.

'Yes,' said Clayton non-commitally. He was not deceived

164

by Macrae's languid manner – the inspector clearly had an agenda of some kind.

'Two press conferences already I see, so it's quite high-profile.'

'Yes, I suppose so.'

'Well, it's got all the ingredients, hasn't it? A beautiful girl gunned down in a country house owned by a rich foreigner, a dangerous armed suspect on the run who's killed before and may well do so again. What more could you ask for? A bit more exciting than your average, run-of-the-mill hit-and-run, eh, Constable?'

Clayton nodded, waiting to see where Macrae was going.

'And I suppose Trave's the natural choice given that he was in charge last time there was trouble over there.' Macrae paused and then went on musingly: 'But there's talk, you know, that he's got something of a personal interest in the case – something about his wife and Mr Osman. Have you heard about any of this? Rumours, station gossip – I don't pay much attention, of course, but I wonder if it's something that might affect his approach.'

Clayton shook his head, keeping his eyes resolutely on the floor. He knew what Macrae was after now. A case like this with a lot of news interest followed by a quick, dramatic arrest could do wonders for an ambitious inspector's career.

'*Adversely* affect his approach,' Macrae said softly, leaning closer and forcing Clayton to look him in the eye. 'What do you think, Constable?'

'I don't know, sir. We're doing the best we can,' said Clayton stolidly. He might have some private concerns about his boss's having a conflict of interest, but that sure as hell didn't mean he was going to share his anxieties with a snake like Macrae.

'We certainly are doing our best,' said Trave brightly

from the doorway, appearing as if from nowhere. 'And while we really appreciate your interest, Hugh, we can't stay to chat. We've got work to do, haven't we, Adam? Come on.'

Clayton hadn't obeyed an order with such alacrity in a long time. He practically ran out of the break room, leaving Macrae with an angry look on his face and a scarlet flush that was beginning to suffuse his pale cheeks. Clayton had no idea how much his boss had heard of what Macrae was saying, but Trave's timing had been perfect, and he certainly seemed to be in a far better mood than he'd been since the case broke. The frostiness of the previous two days seemed to have been consigned to the past.

'So what's new?' asked Trave once he'd hung up his jacket and sat down, adjusting himself to his favourite position, with his chair teetering on its back legs and his feet lightly resting on the edge of his desk. Clayton had never once seen him lose his balance.

'Ballistics report is as you expected,' said Clayton, picking up the top file from his desk. 'The bullets in the door and the wall at the end of the corridor match Claes's gun; the one that killed Miss Osman doesn't. It's a standard bullet apparently – could be fired from most types of handgun.' Trave nodded, looking unsurprised. 'And the rest of the fingerprint evidence has come back,' Clayton went on. 'There are matches to Swain's prints on the desk in the study and on the reading lamp . . .'

'What about on the photograph?' asked Trave.

'The one beside the reading lamp?'

'Yes, the one of Katya.'

Clayton turned a page, running his finger down the list of items. 'No, nothing. Just Osman's prints – they took them for elimination.'

'Interesting. Carry on.'

'Well, upstairs you already know about. Swain's prints are on the candlestick and the door of Katya's room.'

'On the handle?'

'Yes. And the door itself.'

'So he was there. Well, that's not exactly a surprise, is it? We knew that already, but it's curious he didn't wear gloves, wouldn't you say?'

'Perhaps he couldn't get hold of them in the prison.'

'Maybe. But he got himself a gun, didn't he? A little bit more difficult to lay your hands on inside than a pair of gloves I'd say.'

Clayton nodded, picking up another pile of reports. 'Clothes,' he said, looking at the top one. 'They've matched the torn piece of clothing that we found in the rose bushes outside the study window to a standard-issue prison shirt.'

'So what?' said Trave dismissively. 'It doesn't add anything, does it? Like I said, we already know Swain was there. Have you seen the autopsy report?'

'No.'

'Not as bad as the autopsy itself,' said Trave with a grimace. 'I thought I'd spare you that.'

'Thank you,' said Clayton, and he meant it. He'd always had a queasy stomach, and he still hadn't got used to attending post-mortems. He still remembered with shame the first one he'd been to with Trave when he'd had to run out of the room to stop himself being sick.

'Anyway,' said Trave. 'It didn't help us. She ate a small amount of supper – chicken and peas – about four hours before she died, and then got killed with a single shot to the head at about twelve thirty, give or take fifteen minutes either way. There's no evidence she took drugs in the forty-eight hours before her death or that she was sedated.'

'What about the needle marks on her arm?' asked Clayton. 'Did you find out anything about them?'

'Yes, sources say she was a drug addict for most of last year and the first half of this, although I doubt she was injecting all that time. Anyway that means there's no way of knowing whether Jana Claes is telling the truth about only sedating the girl on two occasions,' said Trave, sounding disappointed.

'But Osman was telling us the truth then, wasn't he? About why he brought her home for her own good?' asked Clayton. It hadn't escaped his attention how Trave appeared to be downplaying Katya's drug use as if it was an inconsequential detail rather than important corroboration of the history of events that Osman had given them when they'd questioned him after the murder.

'Yes, I suppose he was,' said Trave, looking irritated. It was clearly a reluctant concession.

'The crime-scene guys found nothing of significance in Katya's room,' Clayton went on after a moment, glancing down at the last report he had in his hand.

'Yes, someone had been doing some spring cleaning out of season in there, I'd say,' said Trave with a hollow laugh. 'Well, none of that seems to have taken us much further,' he added with a sigh. 'I better tell you what I've dug up. The woman at the telephone exchange says there were two calls to Blackwater Hall that evening, both from the same public call box in the centre of town. Came through at 12.20 and 12.21. Both times the phone rang six times; both times nobody answered. Interesting, eh? I went out to Blackwater and asked Osman about the calls, and he says he doesn't know anything about them – says he must've been asleep, and there are no phone extensions upstairs. He's right about that – I checked.'

'What about Claes and his sister?'

'Jana says she was asleep too, but Franz is a different story. You remember he said he was still awake when he first heard Swain in the corridor outside his room and that his door was slightly open, so he could hardly say he didn't hear the phone. But he told me each time he went to go downstairs the phone stopped ringing and so he went back to bed. And then when I asked him why he hadn't told us about the calls the bastard said it was because I didn't ask him. Can you believe it? Anyway that's not all. It turns out there's been trouble out at the Hall already this summer – an attempted burglary back in July. Yes, exactly,' said Trave, responding to Clayton's look of surprise. 'Another piece of information our friends out there decided to keep to themselves. Harrison, one of the uniforms, came and told me about it yesterday. There was an emergency call in the afternoon from a woman with a thick foreign accent – obviously Jana, so Harrison went out there and the burglar was gone. Claes said he'd caught him in Osman's study and punched him a couple of times before the bloke hit him back and got away through the window. The burglar was wearing gloves, unlike our friend, Swain, and so it went down as an unsolved.'

'Did he take anything?'

'Osman says not.'

'What's the description?'

'Well built, six foot, Caucasian male in his early twenties, clean-shaven with short dark hair, wearing jeans and a dark blue jersey – could be anyone, could be you apart from the clothing. Oh, and the glasses: he left them behind apparently. They fell off when Claes punched him. Harrison checked them out – they're a German make, but the burglar didn't say anything, so there's no way of knowing where he's from.'

'He got in the same way as Swain?'

'Yes, through the study window, although it was open at the time – the burglar probably thought no one was home because Osman's Bentley was out being serviced and the gates had been left open for some reason. I agree – the house is isolated and it's an obvious target, and this burglary's probably got nothing to do with the murder. But still, it's interesting – something else that doesn't add up, like that note I told you about – the one Swain got before the first murder. Here, I made a copy,' said Trave, opening the top drawer of his desk and handing Clayton a piece of paper. 'The original's in London locked up with the other trial exhibits, but this is on the same kind of writing paper. And it's definitely Ethan Mendel who wrote it. We did a comparison.'

The sheet of thin, light-blue paper was about five inches by four and looked like it had come from a standard-size, unlined letter-writing pad, but almost all of the top third had been torn off in a strip running diagonally from high on the right side of the sheet to lower on the left. The paper was wrinkled as if from frequent handling, and the ink had begun to fade a little, but Clayton clearly recognized the handwriting as Trave's, even though Trave had sloped his letters to imitate the original.

I need to see you.
Meet me at the boathouse at five.
Ethan.

Clayton read the note twice, turned it over, and saw that there was nothing written on the other side. He handed it back to Trave with a puzzled look on his face.

'What do you make of it?' asked Trave.

'Written in a hurry . . .'

'Why do you say that?'

'The handwriting's rushed. The paper's torn . . .'

'Yes, but look carefully: the sheet of paper's taken from the top edge of the writing pad; it's not torn across the middle like you'd do if you just needed a scrap. It's from a

Basildon Bond writing pad – like this one,' said Trave, taking an unused pad out of his drawer. 'And look – each sheet comes off really easily from the top as you get to it in the pad. It's more difficult to tear it than it is to pull it off whole. You try.'

Clayton had to agree. The perforation made it hard to tear a sheet – any pressure and the whole sheet came away in his hand. You could only get a torn sheet like the one the note was written on by covering the top of the sheet with one hand and then tearing with the other, and even then it was awkward.

'What about if you tear out one of the sheets from the middle of the pad?' Clayton asked, experimenting with one.

'I've tried that – you can't keep any of the very top of the page because of the sheets on top. It tears lower down. Look.'

Trave was right. The whole top edge of the sheet had stayed inside the pad.

'All right, so either Ethan tore it from the top deliberately, which I agree is unlikely, or he used a piece of paper that had already been taken out of the pad. In fact, he must have done it that way,' said Clayton, warming to his theme. 'He wouldn't have taken the note with him since he was hoping to find Swain at home, but then, when Swain didn't answer, Ethan took this piece of paper that he already had out of his pocket and used it to write the note. That's what happened,' said Clayton, looking entirely satisfied with his explanation.

'But why would he then tear a strip of paper off the top?' asked Trave, unconvinced.

'I don't know. Maybe he started the note one way and then changed his mind.'

'Or maybe someone else changed his mind for him,' said Trave.

Clayton knitted his brows, thinking. He had to agree – the note was certainly odd. Like Trave had said before: Why would Ethan leave an urgent note for a person he didn't know, a person who hated him, immediately after he'd just got back from a trip to Europe? But then again that was life: not everything was always going to make perfect sense, and the note didn't change the fact that Swain had been caught almost red-handed standing over the body of the man whom, by his own admission, he hated above all others in the world. Just like he'd been in Katya's bedroom with a gun two nights ago and she'd ended up with a bullet in her head. Clayton knew it was Swain they should be concentrating on, and yet they hadn't talked about the hunt for him once since Trave had come in. Perhaps Trave was coming to that or perhaps he wasn't. Perhaps Macrae was right – maybe Trave wasn't the right person to be running this particular murder enquiry.

Clayton shuddered involuntarily, thinking of Macrae, and suddenly there Macrae was again, framed in the doorway with a smug smile drawn across his pale face.

'Sorry to interrupt your little tête-à-tête, Bill,' he said, not looking as if he was sorry at all. 'But Creswell wants to see you in his office – now.'

'Thanks, Hugh. Be right along,' said Trave, raising his hand in friendly acknowledgement. 'Toad,' he added under his breath once Macrae had gone, as he put on his jacket and straightened his tie.

'Did you know Inspector Macrae before he came here?' asked Clayton curiously. Macrae's earlier reference to Trave's work methods had not escaped his attention.

'In a manner of speaking,' said Trave ambiguously. And he left the room before Clayton could ask him any more about the station's new inspector.

*   *   *

172

Looking up for a moment, Detective Superintendent Creswell waved Trave to the seat opposite his desk and then went back to the letter he was writing. Trave wasn't offended: he knew Creswell wasn't intending to be rude; it was simply that the superintendent was a methodical, orderly man who liked to finish one task before he started another. As Creswell's pen moved steadily across the page, Trave glanced around the room, taking in the hat and coat hanging on a stand behind the door; the framed certificates and awards charting Creswell's steady rise up the ladder of promotion; a photograph of the superintendent in dress uniform standing next to the Queen Mother when she'd visited the station five years before; and, on the desk, a studio portrait of Mrs Creswell, a statuesque, philanthropic lady popularly known as 'the dragon', who insisted on having her husband home by six o'clock every night and 5.30 on Fridays. Creswell had been a thorough but unimaginative detective for most of his life, and now he was an excellent administrator who trusted his officers to get on with their work and didn't interfere unless he had to. And when he thought about it, which wasn't very often, Trave was sorry that Creswell would soon be retiring since it seemed highly unlikely that he would get a more decent, supportive boss than the one he had at present.

'I'm sorry, Bill,' said Creswell, looking up. 'Endless paperwork – that's all my life seems to be these days. Makes me nostalgic for my detective days – out on the job, asking awkward questions, making breakthroughs.'

Trave smiled. He thought it improbable that the superintendent had any wish to go back in time and start getting his hands dirty with criminals and lowlifes again, but he appreciated the friendly intent behind his boss's words.

'You wanted to see me about something?' he asked.

'Yes, this Osman case. You'd better fill me in on what's been happening.'

'No breakthroughs yet, I'm afraid. But we're working hard. We're following up every lead, and we've got Swain's photograph out everywhere – it shouldn't be too long before we pick him up.'

'Where do you think he's hiding?'

'Well, he's not with Earle because he was alone when he went to his mother's. My guess is he's not too far. We found his stepfather's car at the railway station, but he already tried to trick us that he took the train to London on the morning after the murder, and I don't see him running the risk of public transport now after all the press coverage. He's not stupid.'

'Maybe not, but he's certainly dangerous, waving this gun of his around, threatening to shoot people. The switchboard's jammed with terrified old ladies convinced he's hiding in their garden sheds. It's unbelievable that two of them could escape like that. I don't know what kind of outfit the governor thinks he's running over there – Oxford's supposed to be a high-security prison.'

'They had help, sir. How much I don't know yet, but someone definitely threw rope ladders over the outside wall, and there was a getaway car. There are no descriptions because it was dark and they were too quick, but Earle had quite a few visits in the last month and there might be a connection. The prison says that Earle's visitor was the same man each time. You have to show ID at the gate, and he gave them his driver's licence. Had the name Macmillan on it apparently.'

'What? Like the Prime Minister?' asked Creswell, laughing.

'Yes,' said Trave with a smile, 'although this was Robert Macmillan, not Harold. And there was an address in Headington. But surprise, surprise, it turns out that there's no Robert Macmillan who's ever lived there, let alone applied for a driving licence.'

'What about what he looked like? Can't they give you any help on that?'

'Not much. They get a lot of people through there for visits. Best they can come up with is average height, average build, in his thirties or forties, with a black beard. They're positive about the beard, but it may well be false, of course.'

'Like the driver's licence.' Creswell paused, tapping his pen on his desk. He looked uncomfortable, as if he had something to say but was having difficulty finding the right words to say it. Trave was surprised. Creswell was usually direct, even outspoken – it was something Trave had always liked about his boss.

'I wonder if it might be better if you had some help with this, Bill,' he began eventually in a tentative voice, keeping his eyes on his pen. 'Inspector Macrae . . .'

'Hugh Macrae and I wouldn't work well together, sir,' said Trave, interrupting. 'I don't like his methods and he doesn't like mine.' Trave wasn't surprised that Macrae was trying to interfere – he was ambitious, desperate to get his name linked with any big case that came along, and the best way to stop him was to head him off at the pass by taking a firm line with Creswell.

'He came well recommended on his transfer,' said the superintendent defensively. 'The problem you had with him is a long time ago now. There's been a lot of water under the bridge since then.'

'People don't change,' said Trave stolidly.

'Well, they've got to be given the chance,' said Creswell. 'Hugh Macrae gets results. You can't deny him that.'

'That doesn't mean they're the right ones,' said Trave. 'Remember what happened before.'

'Yes, well, like I just said, that was a long time ago. Now please, Bill, let's not get sidetracked. It's this case, not

Inspector Macrae, I want to talk to you about,' said Creswell testily. 'I've got no problem at all with you tracking down Swain and this Earle character – you seem to have all that well under control. It's the . . .' Creswell hesitated. '. . . the Blackwater side of things that concerns me.'

'I don't understand,' said Trave, who had begun to have an inkling that he did.

'Well, it's delicate and I'm sure you don't want me to have to spell it out.'

'No, please do. I'd like to hear it.'

'Oh, very well,' said Creswell, putting down his pen with a look of irritation. 'I'm sure it's not news to you that your wife . . . that Vanessa's seeing Titus Osman, and that obviously puts you in an awkward position out at Blackwater Hall or whatever the bloody place is called.'

'Only if I let it, sir,' said Trave doggedly. 'With respect, I've been doing this job a long time, and I know how to be professional about it.'

'I'm sure you do,' said Creswell impatiently. 'But you're also clever enough to see that it's not just what you do but what you're seen to do that matters.'

'Has somebody been saying something, sir?'

'Yes, since you ask. I've had the chief constable on the phone this morning. Apparently he knows Osman socially, and Osman let it slip at some university gathering last night that you'd put him and his family through the third degree. Asked his sister-in-law whether she went to confession, suggested to Osman that he'd been starving his niece.'

'She was suffering from malnutrition,' said Trave. 'It's in the autopsy report.'

'Fine, so you needed to ask the question. But no more, okay?'

Trave stayed silent, but his dissent was obvious. Creswell sighed, running his hands through his thinning hair, and

176

eyed his subordinate with a look that seemed to mingle exasperation and sympathy in equal measure.

'Look, Bill, I'm going to talk to you frankly,' he said, taking off his glasses and leaning back in his chair. 'We've known each other a long time you and I, and you're a good detective, probably the best one I've got, but you've got faults too, just like everyone else. You're stubborn and sometimes you over-complicate. You poke around in the shadows because you don't like what's going on right in front of your face. And I don't want to see you doing that with this case. It's plain as a pikestaff that this Swain character murdered the Osman girl, just like he killed that Belgian bloke two years ago. He's got the motive, he's got the gun, and his prints are all over the shop from what I hear. So get out there and find him and leave Osman and his family alone – okay?'

Creswell gave Trave a long, searching look, but Trave dropped his eyes.

'Well?' asked the superintendent.

'They're part of the investigation,' said Trave. 'I can't just ignore them.'

'All right, don't ignore them. But treat them like witnesses, not suspects. Buy a pair of kid gloves if you have to.'

Trave nodded and got up to go, but at the door Creswell called him back.

'How's Clayton getting on?' he asked.

'Good,' said Trave. 'He's enthusiastic, works hard.'

'Glad to hear it,' said Creswell. 'One for the future, I'd say.' He gave a small grunt of satisfaction and pulled another file towards him across the desk.

'Everything all right?' asked Clayton as Trave came back in the room.

'Yes, no problem,' said Trave. 'But more work for you,

Adam, I'm afraid. I've been talking to Creswell about the escape, and we both think we ought to find out a bit more about the mystery man who helped them over the wall, the one with the getaway car. Might help with finding Swain and Earle too.'

Clayton nodded, looking enthused. Swain was who they should be focusing on. He had no doubt about that.

'What I want you to do is take Earle's rap sheet over to archives and get a list of all his co-defendants and then pull up their mug shots if they're known,' Trave went on. 'And then try and find out about any other associates he's had and do the same with them. Once you've got some pictures, you can take them down to the prison and see if they can match any of them to the man who's been so busy visiting Earle this last month. I'll be here if you need me. I'm going to see how we're getting on with this manhunt of ours.'

Clayton left with a smile on his face and a renewed sense of purpose. As soon as the door was closed, Trave reached for the telephone and put a call through to the stenographers' department at the Old Bailey. He wanted to know if they could hurry up his request for a copy of the trial transcript in the case of *Regina versus Swain 1958*. He needed it top priority, he told the woman on the other end of the line – for the purpose of an ongoing murder inquiry.

CHAPTER 12

It was in a basement down an alley off Wardour Street and called itself the Monte Carlo Casino – even had a cracked neon sign outside and a big burly doorman with tattoos on his meaty fingers, but that's where its pretensions stopped. Down the steep narrow stairs, under the low ceilings, it was dark and cavernous and smoky and nobody asked any questions as long as you had the money to play. And Eddie had the money: a roll of blue and red bank notes bulging in the pocket of his trousers and three tall piles of yellow and blue chips stacked beside his right hand. Without even hesitating, he nodded for another card, and the dealer turned it over – the king of diamonds, the king of jewels, symbol of wealth and power – Eddie's lucky card. He won again and leaned back in his chair, smiling, stretching his arm around the waist of the girl who was half-standing beside him, half-sitting on his knee, watching him play, drawn like a magnet to his luck.

She felt warm and soft, even more so when he let his hand stray up to where her breast began, pronounced under the low-cut red dress she was wearing. And she didn't protest, even seemed to like it, folding herself more into his side. He had no curiosity about her as a person at all – he didn't even know her name, but he liked her animal proximity and the intent way she was watching him – watching him win. Because tonight he was on a roll – he could feel the luck flowing through his veins, empowering him, transforming him from a nobody, a number on a prison governor's list, into a force to be reckoned with – Easy Eddie, who'd gone through the roof and over the wall of Oxford Prison and ended up here in Soho on a Friday night holding the world in the palm of his hand.

Almost a week had gone by since his escape and Eddie was feeling more secure with every passing day. He'd bought himself a hat and a pair of thick glasses to go with his new suit of clothes, and without shaving he was now halfway to having a full beard. He looked a different person from the man in the police mug shot that had been in the papers a couple of times immediately after the escape, and, anyway, since then David Swain had been getting all the publicity, which was hardly surprising given what he'd got up to within an hour of getting out, whereas Eddie had kept his head down and his hands clean since he'd got to London. It wasn't his fault that Davy was an idiot, Eddie thought contentedly as he ordered another drink and one for the girl too.

'I don't mind if I do,' she said in a put-on classy voice that didn't fool Eddie for a minute. He'd been in enough basement gambling dens in his day to know where the hookers and good-time girls came from, but it didn't put him off. It was where he'd come from too: raised by his crazy grandmother in an evil-smelling flat above a grocery shop on the wrong side of Oxford. And he liked the way this girl looked – blond hair and blue eyes with big lashes and pouting red lips and her dress clinging to her skin like a sheath.

'How old are you?' he asked as he watched her sipping from her glass – she'd ordered Babycham, a little girl's drink.

'None of your business,' she said in a 'don't ask no questions and I won't tell you no lies' kind of voice that made Eddie tighten his hand on her thigh.

'Go on,' he said. 'Tell me.'

'Twenty-one – like the game,' she said in a way that made

it sound like she was ready for anything. 'Aren't you going to ask me my name?'

'All right. What's your name?'

'Audrey,' she said with a simper. 'Like the actress.'

'Like the actress,' Eddie agreed. It made him want to laugh: this two-bit girl imagining herself like Audrey Hepburn. Eddie knew all her movies, had seen some of them twice or even three times; he even knew some of her lines by heart. Audrey Hepburn was a goddess of the silver screen – up there on Mount Olympus with Elizabeth Taylor and Marilyn Monroe, available for admiration, for staring at, loving even from afar, but never to be seen in the flesh or touched. But this girl, this Audrey, she *could* be touched, and Eddie suddenly wanted her with a hard need that came on him unawares.

'I'm hot,' he said. 'Let's get some air.' And standing up, he felt her eyes watching his hands as he filled the pockets of his jacket with the Monte Carlo chips and then exchanged them for bright new banknotes at the caged window by the door.

She held his arm up the steps, uncertain of her footing in her high heels, and then reached down for his hand as they came out into the night. He still hadn't told her his name.

They walked up Wardour Street past a line of people queueing outside a dimly lit cinema to see a late-night screening of Alfred Hitchcock's *Psycho* – 'the most frightening film ever' screamed a poster by the door – and on past shops with blacked-out windows, crowded Chinese restaurants, and girls in doorways calling out to passers-by. The cold air made Eddie's head swirl after the heat of the casino, and he stopped at an off-licence and bought a bottle of Bell's whisky.

'Where are we going?' asked the girl.

181

'Home,' said Eddie, and he squeezed her hand as he guided her across the road and down a side street to the dark, nondescript tenement house where he'd been staying for the last week.

But she stopped outside on the pavement, refusing to go any further.

'I need the money first,' she said, looking him in the eye for the first time. And he saw how she looked different now out under the streetlights – not flirtatious, fluttering her eyelashes, hoping to pass for Audrey Hepburn, but shrewd and calculating – a lot older than twenty-one.

'What money?' he said. 'I thought we were friends.'

'Yeah, we're friends,' she said quietly, not bothering to conceal her East End accent any more. 'But I need the money first. That's all.'

'How much?' he asked, feeling flat all of a sudden, like all the air had gone out of him. He wasn't an idiot – he'd known who she was and what they were doing, but he'd wanted the illusion too, at least until it was over. Was that so much to ask?

'Twenty pounds,' she said. And he reached into his pocket and counted off the money, not caring that it was more than she was worth, and then turned round, preceding her through the door and up the dimly lit stairs. And the girl followed in her high-heeled shoes, holding on to the bannister for support.

He couldn't. However hard he tried, he couldn't. Maybe the trying was why he couldn't or maybe it was the alcohol or the way she'd turned the whole thing into a sordid business transaction, lying on the bed and staring out the window while he tried and tried. He remembered how he'd felt in the casino – like he had the world in the palm of his hand, like he was the fucking king of diamonds. And now here he was – failing at what every other man could do, in a seedy lodging house with a girl who didn't care whether he lived or died. She was just like all the others. Except worse maybe – she hadn't even asked him his name: he could read the indifference in her stupid, over-made-up eyes.

Eventually he gave up, pulled back, and poured himself another glass of whisky from the half-empty bottle on the bedside table. He drank it with his back to her, sitting on the side of the bed, listening to the sound of her washing in the sink, putting on her clothes, getting ready to go. And leave him. Just like they always did. Every last one of them. Always the same.

'Fuck you,' he said, turning round to look at her standing by the bed, balancing on one foot as she bent down to put on her shoes. 'Fuck you, Audrey.'

'Not much chance of that, pal,' she shot back. And he could hear the contempt in her voice, see the derision in her eyes. And suddenly something inside of him broke. He'd fucking well show her he was a man. If he couldn't show her one way, he'd show her another, and picking up the whisky bottle in a tight grip, he smashed it down on the side of her head.

She saw the blow coming at the last moment. Not in time to get out of the way, but in time to put her arm up to protect her eyes. And she didn't fall but ran out of the door screaming, while he sat back heavily on the bed with the remains of the broken bottle in his hand and one of her high-heeled shoes lying on the floor at his feet.

They kept him in West End Central overnight, charged him with the assault, and then sent him back to Oxford in a police car, wedged between two huge uniformed officers in the back seat who said nothing all journey, just gazed straight ahead like they were a couple of stood-down robots. But Eddie enjoyed the ride, notwithstanding his cramped conditions. There was an escort car up in front with its sirens blaring and its lights flashing, clearing them a way through the traffic, and he felt important again, like he'd felt in the Monte Carlo Casino the previous evening when he'd been winning all those blackjack hands, before he got railroaded by that stupid girl. A spasm of hatred contorted Eddie's face for a moment as he remembered the look on her face before he smashed her with the bottle. The fucking bitch had got exactly what she deserved, even if it had meant getting nabbed.

But Eddie's anger was passing. He had a talent for living in the present and he hadn't really expected to stay on the run forever. He hadn't told David, but he knew that almost all escapers got caught again within a few days. He'd done well to last a week, and he looked forward to the new respect he'd have back at the gaol for his daring escape – it was almost worth the extra time they'd tack on to his sentence, if they did add any on, that is. Maybe he could make a deal – he was pretty sure the police would be interested in what he had to tell them about Davy Swain and their late-night chats about that Katya girl, even if it was that self-righteous copper, Trave, who was in charge of the investigation – he was the one who'd busted Eddie the last time, put him away for fencing stolen goods. Self-righteous or not, coppers were like everyone else – they knew which side their bread was buttered on.

And it was Trave who met them at the back door of the police station dressed in a suit that was even more creased and crumpled than the one Eddie was wearing. He looked like he hadn't had any sleep, and he looked angry. Not self-righteous but angry. Like a man on a mission. It worried Eddie, but he wasn't going to let it show. 'I want my hat,' he said, hanging back, insisting on his rights. 'It's mine. They took it off me in the car.'

At a nod from Trave one of the burly policemen retrieved the hat from the front seat, and Trave shoved it down hard on Eddie's head so that it covered his eyes.

'Welcome back, Eddie,' he said, leading the way inside. 'We've got some talking to do, you and I.'

But Trave waited to start the interview until Adam Clayton had got back from the prison. It was Clayton's second visit there in three days, but this time he was no more successful than the first. He'd drawn a blank with all the mug shots.

'The prison officer who checked in Earle's friend's no fool. I think he'd recognize him if he had the chance – I just haven't been able to show him the right photograph. That's all,' said Clayton ruefully. 'Maybe Earle'll help us.'

'I wouldn't hold your breath,' said Trave. 'Easy Eddie's got a big mouth when it comes to talking about himself, but I don't see him selling his friends down the river just because we ask him to and say please.'

And so it proved, although it wasn't for want of trying. Trave controlled his irritation and instead plied Eddie with cigarettes and coffee in the station's only unchipped mug, and soon Eddie was singing about his daring escape – in fact once he got started they couldn't shut him up, and Clayton's hand started to ache as he wrote down how Eddie worked out how to use the scaffolding in the rec room and made papier-mâché for the dummies in their beds, how he measured the sheets and used the broken chair as a grappling hook to get over the inner wall. But then, just when he'd got to the vital point in his story, Eddie shut up tight as a clamshell. However hard Trave pressed him, he wouldn't say who'd helped him and David Swain over the outer wall, wouldn't say if it was the same man who visited him at the prison, wouldn't say who that was either, until in the end Trave lost patience.

'Do you know how much trouble you're in?' asked Trave, leaning across the table into Eddie's cigarette smoke. 'You took Swain out to Blackwater Hall, you and your bearded friend, didn't you?'

'No, I told you. We split up.'

'There wasn't time for you to split up. You drove him out there in the getaway car, and you gave him that gun. That's what happened, isn't it?'

'No.'

'And you know what that makes you, Eddie, don't you? An accomplice to murder.'

'I didn't know nothing . . .' Eddie stopped in mid-sentence and swallowed hard. He took another cigarette from the packet on the table and lit it from the one he already had. Clayton noticed how his hands were shaking.

'You knew,' said Trave. 'You've already told us how Swain kept you up at night going on and on about Katya Osman and how much he hated her . . .'

'That don't make me no accomplice,' said Eddie, interrupting.

'It does if you helped him. And if you want to help yourself now, you'll tell me who put you up to this.'

'Nobody did. I got out because I wanted to get out. I've done it before, you know.'

'Not when you're coming to the end of your sentence you haven't, and not with help from outside. What made this time different, Eddie?'

'Nothing made it different. I don't like prisons. That's all.'

'All right, I'll tell you what made it different. David Swain – that's who. You didn't need to take him along – in fact it doubled your chances of getting caught.'

'I needed someone to be a lookout; to hold on to the ropes . . .'

'No, you didn't. You've already told us all about your heroics, remember – the planning, the split-second timing. And you know what – Swain didn't get a mention. He was the invisible man. Except he was the reason you got the outside help – the rope ladders and the car and the money. Where did you get all this money, Eddie?' asked Trave, producing a large see-through plastic evidence bag stuffed full of banknotes. 'There's over a thousand pounds here.'

'Gambling. You can ask that girl. That's why she went home with me. Because she could see how much I'd won.'

'Home. Yes, I wondered about that. What were you doing in someone's house, I wonder? A friend of a friend, was it?'

'It was a bedsit. They're safer than a hotel. People don't ask questions.'

'I'm sure they don't, but whose bedsit? That's what I'm asking.'

'And I'm not saying. I'm not ratting on my friends. I told you that already,' said Eddie defiantly.

'He doesn't need to,' said Clayton, speaking for the first time. 'It's in the report from the London police. The whole house is divided up into bedsits, and they talked to a couple of the tenants. Landlord's a John Birch. Usually collects the rent in person on the first day of the month. Doesn't have a forwarding address . . .'

'Birch or Bircher?' asked Trave, interrupting. Clayton picked up on the sudden expectancy in his boss's voice – he'd seen how Trave had gripped the edge of the table with his hand when he heard the name.

'I don't know. It could be either. Here, you can look yourself,' said Clayton, handing Trave the document that he'd been reading from. 'The report's obviously been written up in a hurry.'

Trave glanced down at the page and then fixed Eddie with a hard stare. Clayton noticed how the cigarette had started to shake again in Eddie's hand and how the colour had gone out of his cheeks.

'Who's Bircher?' asked Trave.

'I don't know. Never heard of him.'

'How did you find that house?'

'A friend told me about it.'

'A friend. What friend?'

'I'm not saying. Like I told you: I'm no rat.'

'Tell that to the old ladies you've conned out of their life savings,' said Trave angrily. 'Tell that to the poor girl you hit with that bottle last night.'

'She had it coming,' said Eddie with a sneer.

'What? Because she has to earn her living going home with people like you? You didn't think she'd go to the police because of who she was. That was your big mistake, wasn't it?'

'I don't have to listen to this,' said Eddie. 'I've changed my mind. I want a lawyer, and until I get one I'm saying nothing.'

'Interview suspended at twelve thirty-one,' said Trave smoothly, looking at his watch. 'You can have your solic-itor, Eddie, but we're not finished. I can tell you that much.'

'Come on,' said Trave, looking back at Clayton over his shoulder as he picked up his coat and went out the door of their office. 'We've got work to do.'

'Where are we going?' asked Clayton, half-running down the corridor to keep up with Trave.

'Where do you think? Archives first – to get Bircher's picture – and then down to see your friend at the prison. I hope he's not gone off duty by the time we get there.'

They were in luck. Bircher was on parole and so his file was live. He'd been released on licence the previous year after doing three years of a five-year stretch for running the rent-boy ring that Claes had got caught up with. He'd kept girls in another house too apparently – quite an operation. He'd stayed out of trouble since getting out, which seemed to be something of an achievement, given that he had a string of previous convictions going back to when he was eighteen a quarter of a century earlier – most for pimping, a few for low-level fraud. He was living at an address in Oxford according to the parole record – there was no mention of the tenement house in London. And pinned to the front of the file were his arrest photographs – front on and in profile. Average height, average build, average-looking except for a thick black beard.

'Gotcha,' said Trave under his breath as he signed for the file.

It didn't take long for the visits officer to identify Bircher as the man who'd visited Eddie Earle on four different occasions in the month before Earle escaped, but Trave wasn't satisfied. He insisted on seeing the prison governor and wouldn't take no for an answer, until, half an hour later, the two policemen found themselves seated on uncomfortable hard-backed chairs in the governor's second-floor office. Opposite them the governor, an unfriendly, balding little man, sat bolt upright with his hands palm down and immobile on the desk in front of him, looking like he was about to have his photograph taken. Behind his head, a picture of the young Queen in a pearl-white dress adorned with a blue regal sash gazed down at them, while to her right a large laminated sign ordered inmates not to smoke and to stand in the presence of the governor. Above the door a wall clock ticked loudly, measuring out the time with thick black hands.

The one window in the office looked directly down onto the concrete exercise yard in the centre of the prison, bleak and deserted in the gathering gloom of the autumn afternoon, and beyond that, above a long brick building lined with tiny barred windows, Clayton glimpsed the top of the high perimeter wall. He wondered if that was the way Earle and Swain had gone when they escaped, and was struck with admiration for a moment at their audacity in finding a way out of this hellish place.

'What is it you want to ask me about, Inspector?' asked the governor, looking up at the clock behind his visitors' heads. 'I do my rounds at two o'clock and I'm a punctual man, so please be brief.'

There was a nasal, clipped quality to the governor's voice that stopped just short of outright rudeness. Clayton put it down to the governor's wanting to avoid having to answer any more questions about the escape – it wasn't hard to imagine that he'd already taken a lot of flak over what had happened, and he didn't look like someone who'd welcome being in the line of fire. But Trave wasn't in the least deterred – Clayton couldn't remember ever seeing his boss this fired up before.

'I want to ask you about David Swain and Edward Earle, the two prisoners who escaped last weekend,' said Trave. 'I want to know who put them in a cell together. Whose decision was it?'

'It was nobody's decision,' the governor shot back without hesitating. 'It was standard administration. Swain's cellmate was sent to the punishment block because he was caught fighting, and so Earle replaced him. It's not our practice to keep cells in single occupation, Inspector. Space is at a premium here.'

'But why Earle? Why put a known escaper in with a maximum-security prisoner?'

'There are a lot of high-security prisoners here. Earle had to go somewhere.'

'Why? Why couldn't he stay where he was? Why not put a new arrival with Swain?'

'Because we didn't. That's why. We move prisoners around. It's our policy. I don't know what you're implying, Inspector, but . . .'

'I'm not implying anything,' said Trave interrupting. 'Two men have escaped from your prison. One of them is a convicted murderer who's still on the run, and I need to know how they came to be put together. That's all.'

'And I've told you how,' said the governor, rising from his chair. 'Now, if you'll excuse me . . .'

But Trave stayed anchored to his seat, ignoring the governor's attempt to terminate the interview.

'How many visits are convicted prisoners allowed each month?' he asked.

'Two,' said the governor, reluctantly resuming his seat. 'Two every four weeks.'

'So why did Earle receive four last month?'

'I don't know,' said the governor, sounding genuinely surprised. 'It's the first I've heard of it. If it's true, there must have been some kind of mix-up.' Clayton noticed how the governor's cheeks had become suffused with a deep red flush and wondered whether this arose from embarrassment or anger or a combination of the two.

'It is true,' said Trave, pushing his advantage. 'Your visits officer just confirmed it to us. He showed us the book.'

'Well it won't happen again. I can assure you of that.'

'I'm sure it won't, except that it sounds a bit like locking the stable door after the horse has bolted. Have you any idea what harm these mix-ups of yours have caused?' asked Trave, leaning forward suddenly across the desk and giving his anger free rein. 'If they are mix-ups . . . I haven't even started looking into how Swain and Earle got out of your so-called maximum-security prison . . .'

'What do you mean by that?' asked the governor, whose plump hands had now curled into tight fists as he retreated back into his chair in the face of Trave's attack.

'What do you think I mean?' Trave shot back, returning the governor's hostile stare.

The governor opened his mouth to respond but then thought better of it, breathing deeply in an effort to regain his self-control.

'I don't know why you have chosen to be so offensive, Inspector,' he said at last in a self-consciously dignified voice as he got up from his chair and went over to the door. 'But it is not conduct that I will tolerate in my office. Please make an appointment if you have any further questions. Or even better, put them in writing.' He now had the door open and stood waiting for them to leave.

Outside Trave wrinkled his nose in disgust. 'Prig,' he said, spitting out the word like it was a bad taste. 'Another one who knows more than he's saying.'

Clayton followed his boss to the car, wondering where they were going next. He soon found out: instead of returning to the police station, Trave drove out of town on the Cowley Road, pressing his foot down on the gas as they weaved in and out of the busy afternoon traffic.

'Shouldn't we have another go at Eddie first, now we've got the ID on Bircher?' Clayton suggested, holding on to the dashboard to prevent himself flying forwards as Trave came to a sudden halt at a red light, narrowly missing a car coming from the right.

'No, let him stew for a bit,' said Trave in a tone that brooked no opposition. 'Claes is the connection – it's him we need to talk to now.'

'Connection? So you really think Claes used Bircher to

spring Swain out of gaol just so as to set him up for Katya's murder?' asked Clayton doubtfully.

'Maybe,' said Trave, sounding the opposite of doubtful. 'And maybe Claes wasn't acting on his own either.'

'You mean Osman was in on it too?'

Trave nodded.

'But why would they go to all this trouble to frame Swain?' asked Clayton. 'Katya was sick, mentally unbalanced. They could easily have faked a suicide.'

'Sure, but that would've given me the opportunity to go straight for Osman's jugular, wouldn't it? He's got too much to hide to risk that, whereas this way Swain's the focus of the investigation. And if I start asking any awkward questions out at Blackwater, all Osman's got to do is have a chat with the chief constable and I'm off the case.'

Trave glanced over at his companion, catching the look of disbelief on his face. 'Osman did it to prove he could do it. That's what I think,' he said quietly. 'It's the same reason he does everything. To show he can.'

Clayton bit his lip and said nothing. He didn't agree at all with his boss's handle on the case, and he didn't like the hard set of Trave's jaw, the white-knuckled grip with which he held the steering wheel, the angry edge to his voice. As far as Clayton could see, there was precious little evidence against Claes and none whatsoever against Osman. Trave wanting him to be a murderer didn't make him one. All the evidence pointed toward David Swain, and this surprise visit to Blackwater Hall felt like at best a wild-goose chase, at worst a serious mistake. But Trave was the man in charge – it was his call where they went next and when. Clayton had infuriated his boss once already by questioning his methods, and he wasn't going to do it a second time unless he had to. Clayton was independent-minded, which was why Trave liked him as an assistant, but he was no mutineer.

And so he kept his peace and hoped for the best as Trave made a sharp left turn and headed up the road toward Blackwater Church, where it stood silver-stoned and serene at the top of the hill, looking down on the lush green landscape all around.

CHAPTER 13

Franz Claes opened the front door before Vanessa had even got out of her car and came down to meet her on the steps. He took her coat in the hall and showed her into the drawing room, explaining that Titus was tied up with something in his study. He offered her a drink, which she refused, but then, just when she'd expected him to leave, he closed the door and came and sat down opposite her on the sofa. It made her feel nervous. Up until now he had always seemed keen to shun her company, treating her with an icy polite-ness that barely concealed an obvious antipathy, and she wondered what it was that had changed his attitude today.

'Perhaps I'll change my mind about that drink,' she said. 'A glass of wine would be nice.'

'Certainly,' said Franz, crossing to the sideboard and opening a bottle with quick, practised movements, and then, as he held the glass out towards her, he caught her eye and held it.

'It's obvious you've got something to say to me, Franz,' she said. 'Why don't you tell me what it is and put me out of my suspense.'

He nodded, smiling thinly as he resumed his seat. 'It's about Titus,' he said. 'I am worried about him.'

'Because of what's happened?'

'Yes. He is under very great strain, and the police inspector, your husband, he is making it worse.'

'What? More since last Sunday?' asked Vanessa, trying not to show how perturbed she felt. She'd only seen Titus once since the previous weekend for a hurried lunch in

Oxford, and he hadn't referred to her husband then or when they'd spoken each evening on the telephone. He'd obviously not wanted to worry her.

'Yes, he comes here almost every day, insulting Titus, treating us like we are the criminals when he should be trying to catch the real murderer,' said Franz, allowing his anger to show through. 'Swain killed Katya just like he killed Ethan Mendel. I caught him doing it.'

'I'm sure Bill's doing his best to find him,' said Vanessa, trying to inject her voice with a sense of conviction that she did not entirely feel. 'The manhunt story's on the radio every day.'

'I am afraid that I do not share your confidence, Mrs Trave,' said Claes coldly. 'It has been a week and they have found nothing. And yet your husband won't leave us alone . . .'

'Well, what do you want me to do about it?' Vanessa burst out, unable to contain her exasperation. 'I'm sure it hasn't escaped your notice that I've been separated from my husband for eighteen months. I can't tell him what to do, and he wouldn't listen to me even if I tried.'

'I know. I understand this,' said Claes, bowing his head. 'Inspector Trave is a law to himself. It is not your fault that you are his wife.'

'No, it isn't,' said Vanessa, bridling. It was one thing for her to leave her husband, quite another to stand by while Franz Claes insulted him. 'He's a good policeman. I know that much,' she added angrily.

'Maybe once upon a time he was good, but not now. He is treating us like this because of you and Titus, and that is not being a good policeman. I know this.'

'All right,' said Vanessa, controlling her temper. 'If what you say is true then maybe Bill is in the wrong, but I still don't see why you're telling me about it. You just told me there was nothing I could do.'

'Yes, but there is something you can *not* do,' said Claes quietly.

'What do you mean – *not* do?'

'Titus told me about what Katya said to you in here. She lied of course, but it doesn't matter – if your husband hears about it, he will never leave Titus alone. He will arrest him. It is just the excuse he is looking for. And Titus will be disgraced even though he is innocent. I ask you – is that justice?' asked Franz, leaning forward and looking Vanessa in the eye. He hadn't raised his voice, but she noticed how his bony hands were clenched together in his lap. She felt like he was looking inside her, and it made her heart beat fast. A cold sweat broke out on her forehead.

'Titus has told me that he asked you to say nothing,' Franz went on after a moment. 'And he says that you are thinking about his request, but it is not enough to think, Mrs Trave. You must decide to do what is right; you must protect Titus from your husband.'

Vanessa drew a deep breath, trying to keep a lid on her inner turmoil. All week long she had been agonizing over what to do. She believed in Titus and wanted to help him, but then each time she resolved to do as he asked and stay silent, Katya's desperate face appeared in her mind's eye, and she remembered the terrible struggle that the girl had gone through to convey her message. 'They're trying to kill me' – what if it was Claes and his invisible sister that Katya had been talking about? Was that why Claes was appealing to her now – not for Titus's sake, but to protect himself?

'Does Titus know about you talking to me about this?' she asked.

Claes shook his head, and she was inclined to believe him. Titus was too considerate of her feelings to allow Claes to pester her – he knew how much she disliked his brother-in-law.

'Well?' Claes asked, looking at her expectantly. 'Can we count on you?'

'I'll talk to Titus about it,' she said. Claes flushed, but bit back the angry response he'd been about to make when the door opened and Titus came in.

'I'm sorry,' he said, looking surprised. 'I only just now saw your car outside, my dear. I had no idea you were already here. Has Franz been looking after you?'

'Oh, yes,' said Vanessa holding up her glass. 'He has been most attentive.'

After lunch, Titus lent Vanessa a pair of Wellington boots and they walked out across the lawn to where the path opened up in the pine trees leading down to the lake. Titus's cat, Cara, followed them a little way but then turned aside, entering the woods at a different point, engaged on a hunting expedition in the undergrowth. Vanessa was not sorry to see the animal go. She found it unnerving the way the cat stared at her out of its unblinking green eyes whenever she visited the Hall. Once or twice she had tried to stroke the creature, but it had got up each time and stalked away, impervious to her well-intentioned advances.

It had been raining earlier and the ground was still wet underfoot. There were patches of thin mist floating in the damp air and the autumn cold tingled on Vanessa's skin, making her feel irrationally nervous and uneasy. And yet Titus seemed in better spirits than she'd seen him since the murder. She'd been distressed by the change in him when she'd seen him the previous Sunday and then again in the middle of the week. Then there'd been thick dark circles under his eyes and he'd spoken in disjointed sentences as if his mind was constantly wandering away into desolate places where she could not follow. And afterwards, on her own, she'd thought of him as an old tree bent over to the ground in a winter storm. The image frightened her, making her worry whether he would recover from the blow of his niece's violent death, as she selfishly realized how much she'd come to depend on her lover's strength and self-assurance. But then today, as if in answer to her prayers, there was a spring in his step again and a glow in his eye. He seemed almost like his old self again.

'Having you here makes such a difference,' he told her, squeezing her hand as they passed under the trees and left the gardens behind.

'I'm glad,' she said. And she would have liked to have said more except that she felt self-conscious suddenly. It was as if another separate Vanessa was standing off to one side under the trees watching Titus and her pass by along the path. She hoped that he wouldn't ask her about his marriage proposal or what she intended to do about what Katya had said. She felt upset by the pressure Claes had put on her back at the house – being in the drawing room had reminded her of Katya and how she'd suddenly appeared in the doorway ten days earlier swaying from side to side. It haunted Vanessa that Katya had known what was coming and yet nobody had been able to protect her from her fate.

'I keep wishing I could have done something,' said Osman, as if reading his companion's mind. 'I wish I'd known . . .'

'About Swain? How could you have known he'd escape? Prisons are supposed to keep people in, not let them out,' said Vanessa, quick with words of reassurance. 'You can't blame yourself.'

'I know, but it's hard sometimes,' he said and then stopped, suddenly silent as the trees opened out in front of them and they found themselves standing on the edge of the lake. Here the mist was thicker, shrouding the far bank and absorbing a flock of geese into a grey-white invisibility almost as soon as the birds had passed overhead, leaving only their raucous calls borne back to Titus and Vanessa on the breeze. Vanessa shivered, and Titus put his arm around her.

'Blackwater Lake can seem like an evil place on days like this,' he said, 'but then within an hour or two the wind will chase the clouds away, and it knocks me back with its beauty. Its changeability reminds me of home, I think. That's why I like it so much.'

'Home? Belgium, you mean?'

'Yes. Antwerp and the River Scheldt and Flanders – where I came from, where I made my fortune.'

'Selling diamonds?' asked Vanessa, genuinely curious. Titus had never told her about how he had made his money before. The subject had not come up for some reason.

'Yes, diamonds, always diamonds. I fell in love with them before I dealt in them and perhaps that was why they have been so good to me. They are in my blood, Vanessa. I can close my eyes here now and I'm back there, back in the attic workshops before the war with the rows of men on stools in their white shirts and black waistcoats cleaving the stones, sawing them, cutting them with a precision that you cannot imagine – each one of them an artist – or sitting among the dealers in the bourse or at the Diamond Club on the Pelikaanstraat, bent down over the jewels so all you could see were their wide-brimmed hats.' Osman laughed, as if shaking off the intensity of his recollection.

'Why don't you go back there if you miss it so much?'

'I don't know. Because I have made a new life here; because I have enough money now to last me a lifetime; because there are too many bad memories over there, too many people that died when they shouldn't have done. Except that now they are dying here too,' added Titus with a bitter smile.

'Come on, let's go back,' he went on after a moment. 'You're cold and this isn't one of the lake's better days.'

200

They walked slowly back through the woods without speaking, the sound of their footsteps muffled by the pine needles that carpeted the ground, each lost in their own thoughts, until, coming out on the other side, Titus shivered as he looked up toward his house and reached for Vanessa's hand.

'Thank God we're together,' he said. 'I don't know where I would be without you.'

Vanessa felt a sudden wave of protective love for Titus. She raised her head, waiting for his kiss, but the kiss never came. From across the lawn there was the sound of a car coming fast, much too fast, up the drive and then the screech of its brakes as it emerged into the front courtyard and screamed to a halt. Titus set off across the lawn at a run with Vanessa following in his wake, and she turned the corner of the house just in time to see her husband beginning a shouting match with Franz Claes at the foot of the front steps. Further back, a young man whom Vanessa recognized as her husband's assistant, Adam Clayton, was standing beside the open door of Trave's old Ford car, looking as if he knew that something bad was about to happen but was powerless to prevent it.

'Where's Bircher? Tell me where he is right now,' shouted Trave. He was no more than a foot from Claes, who was standing ramrod straight, refusing to give ground.

'I don't know who you're talking about,' said Claes evenly. He seemed strangely calm, and there was even a faint smile playing around his thin lips: Vanessa sensed to her surprise that he was actually enjoying the situation.

'You're lying,' yelled Trave. 'Bircher was the one who set you up with those boys and he's the one who you used to spring Swain out of gaol.'

'Spring – what's spring?' asked Claes with a sneer. He spoke the word with derision. It was obvious that he was trying to provoke Trave, whose hands had bunched into fists, whereas Claes kept his hands firmly in the pockets of his trousers. Osman clearly sensed what was coming and chose this moment to intervene.

'Inspector, please calm down. I'm sure we can sort this out,' he said.

Trave wheeled round to his left, aware of Osman for the first time. He opened his mouth to speak and then closed it, seeing his wife behind Osman's shoulder. It was one thing to imagine Titus Osman with his hands on Vanessa; it was quite another to see them together in the flesh. A current of rage surged through Trave, momentarily blacking out his reason, and, taking two steps forward, he punched out at Osman with all the force he could muster. But instead of connecting with cheek and eye and bone as he had hoped, Trave's hand flailed through thin air. Osman had seen the blow coming and had had time to duck out of the way, and then, just as Trave was readying his arm for another punch, Clayton came from behind and pulled Trave backwards towards the car. Taken by surprise, Trave lost his balance and fell over onto the ground with a thud.

Sprawled on his back, Trave looked up into the grey indifferent sky and felt a terrible humiliation. He'd broken every rule in the book; he'd made a fool of himself in front of Vanessa; he'd played into the hands of his enemies. He sensed them all looking down at him and closed his eyes tight shut. He could imagine the different expressions on their faces: contempt and, even worse, pity, and triumph too. He knew he was finished unless he could prove a connection between Blackwater Hall and the prison escape, if there was one . . . But Trave refused to acknowledge the possibility that he might be mistaken. He felt sure that the vital piece of evidence was there, just out of reach. He'd come to the wrong place – that was all; he'd allowed his anger to swamp his reason. Clayton had been right – it was the police station that he should've gone to from the prison, not here. Eddie was the key. Trave saw that now as clear as day. He could offer Eddie a deal, lean on the cocky bastard until he coughed up the truth. Except that Trave would never get the chance once Creswell got to hear about what he'd done in the last two minutes. And that was only a matter of time. Osman would complain, and Clayton would have to make a report to Creswell once he got back to the station. He'd have no option. Trave would do the same if he was in Clayton's shoes.

Trave knew what he had to do. He had to get out of here now and leave Clayton behind, and then trust to luck that no one could get hold of Creswell on the phone before he'd had a chance to talk to Eddie. Picking himself up from the ground, he looked over at Vanessa, trying to make her understand that he was sorry, that he hadn't meant it to turn out this way, but she refused to meet his eye, and instead reached out and took hold of Osman's hand.

All right, to hell with you too, he thought as he turned away, running toward the car. He got in and reached over to lock the passenger door just as Clayton took hold of the handle, and then, throwing the car into gear, he drove in a fast arc round the mermaid fountain in the centre of the courtyard and away down the drive. Overhead there was a clap of rolling thunder, and rain started to fall in heavy drops down from the leaden sky.

Trave had Eddie back in the interview room within five minutes of his return to the police station. He took a young uniformed constable in there too so that there'd be a witness and a written record if he managed to get Eddie to talk.

'I told you I wanted a solicitor,' said Eddie defiantly.

'And you can have one once you've heard what I've got

to say,' said Trave. 'You don't have to say anything if you don't want to. I've just read you your rights.'

Eddie lit a cigarette from the open packet that Trave had left lying on the table and breathed the smoke in deep. He glanced over at Trave and then looked away. He seemed even more nervous than he'd been earlier, Trave noted with satisfaction.

'All right, so what is it?' Eddie asked.

'The visits officer at the gaol picked out Bircher as the man who came to see you four times in the last month, the same John Bircher who's a friend of Franz Claes, who lives at Blackwater Hall. Does that name mean anything to you, Eddie? Franz Claes?'

'Maybe.'

'What do you mean maybe?'

'Swain mentioned him a couple of times.'

'And what about Bircher? Did he mention Claes?'

Eddie looked at Trave and said nothing.

'Bircher, Eddie. The man with the beard. Here, let me refresh your memory.'

Trave already had Bircher's photograph face-down on the table. Now he turned it over and slid it across to Eddie, who flicked his eyes down to it for a moment before looking away.

'He's the one who helped you over the wall, isn't he, Eddie? Got you a car, got you money? Gave you a place to stay in London? Why, Eddie? Why would he do all that?'

Eddie ground out his cigarette in the ashtray and began chewing his thumb nail. 'You've got nothing,' he said, spitting out the words. 'Nothing.'

'Not yet maybe. But I'm only just beginning. I've been in this game long enough to know there's always evidence if you know where to look. And I know where to look now. I'll find Bircher, and if he talks, I won't need you. You'll be hung out to dry, Eddie. Conspiracy to murder: you'll be an old man when you get out.'

He was getting to Eddie. Trave could feel it. He was an expert at this: playing his man like a fish, reeling him slowly in. He saw the telltale signs: the beads of nervous sweat forming under the hairline on Eddie's forehead, the way Eddie chewed his nails and smoked hungrily on yet another cigarette. Not much longer now, provided Eddie knew something, of course. But he had to. Trave had no room left for doubt.

'You talk, Eddie; you testify against Claes and Bircher, and I'll protect you,' said Trave, leaning across the table. 'Immunity from prosecution, early release, a new start, you name it.'

Trave knew he was going out on a limb. He needed authority to make these kinds of offers, but there was no time for that now. Time was the one thing he didn't have. And he was close if he could just catch Eddie's eye. But Eddie had withdrawn into himself – he was bent over, chewing his nails, eyes on the floor. Trave longed to take hold of Eddie and shake the truth out of him, push him up against the wall, make him confess, but he knew he couldn't. He'd been an honest copper too long to change his ways now.

'What do you owe them?' asked Trave insistently. 'Nothing,' he said, answering his own question. 'Think of yourself, Eddie. Don't be the fall guy.'

Eddie looked up, and Trave tried to read the conflicting emotions written across his face. Fear was there, but what else? Indecision? Hope? Eddie opened his mouth, about to speak, and closed it again. He was no longer looking at Trave but over Trave's shoulder toward the door that had just opened. Turning round, Trave saw Creswell in the doorway and behind him, waiting like a vulture, Macrae.

'I need to see you, Inspector. In my office,' said the superintendent. It was an order, not a request.

'I'm coming,' said Trave, hoping Creswell would give him a minute or two more with Earle. That was all he needed. But it was a vain hope.

'Now, Bill,' said Creswell in a voice that brooked no opposition.

Trave looked across the table at Eddie Earle one last time and knew he was beaten. He got up to go and then, just as he was turning away, Eddie shot him a look of hatred. 'I'm no rat,' he said, spitting out the words. 'I told you I'm no rat.'

Trave sat in Creswell's office, looking utterly deflated. Macrae had tried to come into the room too, but Creswell had at least put a stop to that. The superintendent seemed sad more than angry.

'Mr Osman called, told me what happened out at Blackwater,' said Creswell. 'You're off this case, Bill. And there may be more trouble. I don't know. I'll do my best for you. You can count on me for that. You're a damned good policeman, and you've been put under more strain than anyone should have to cope with. I feel responsible: I should have replaced you on day one.'

'I insisted.'

'Yes, you did. But that doesn't mean I had to listen to you.' Creswell paused, shaking his head. 'What a mess! What a bloody awful mess!'

'Who's getting the case?' asked Trave, although he already knew the answer.

'Hugh Macrae . . .'

'Christ!'

'I don't want to hear it, Bill,' said Creswell – there was a warning note in his voice. 'He'll find Swain . . .'

'Yeah, and that's not all he'll do . . .'

'Enough!' said Creswell, banging his desk. 'I'm in charge of this police station, not you, and I'm not interested in your opinion of Inspector Macrae. You've caused enough trouble round here for one day. You should be bloody grateful I'm standing by you. Stay away from this case, you hear me?'

'I hear you,' said Trave, bowing his head. 'And I am sorry, sir, for what it's worth. I don't need you to tell me what an idiot I've been.'

'No, you don't,' said Creswell, sounding appeased. 'Go home, Bill. Have a drink; have two drinks. Do whatever it is a workaholic like you does to relax. And then forget this case – like it never happened, all right?'

'Yes, sir,' said Trave, getting up.

But Creswell called him back just as he'd reached the door. 'Clayton'll work with Macrae,' he said. 'For continuity. Once it's over you can have him back.'

'Good,' said Trave, nodding.

'Good?'

'Yes, good. Thank you, sir. I'll go and have that drink now,' said Trave, closing the door.

He passed Macrae in the corridor on his way out of the station, walking by him like he didn't exist. Macrae paused for a moment and then went over to the window, and his mouth twisted into a smile as he watched Trave get into his car down below. And then, as Trave drove away, he began softly singing to himself an old Great War soldiers' song, one of his favourites: 'Oh, we don't want to lose you but we think you ought to go . . .'

CHAPTER 14

Adam Clayton was still half in shock about all that had happened when he was called into Inspector Macrae's office early on Monday morning.

He'd hardly slept for two nights. His exhausted brain was like a broken film projector that he couldn't switch off, endlessly rerunning the scene of his boss's self-destruction in the courtyard outside Blackwater Hall. Each scene was worse than the next: Trave shouting at Claes; Osman intervening; Trave punching, missing, falling on his backside like a schoolboy when Clayton pulled him back; the look of scorn and disgust on the face of Trave's wife; and the mad rush to the car before Trave drove away, leaving Clayton standing there in the rain looking like an idiot.

To give Osman credit, he'd made it a lot less awkward afterwards than it might have been. He'd calmed everyone down; thanked Clayton profusely for his intervention; and even shown some sympathy for Trave, calling him 'the poor inspector' or something like that; and then finally insisted that Claes drive Clayton back into Oxford. Osman had opened the back door of the Bentley for him, and so he'd ended up sitting behind Claes in the back seat, looking like he was some millionaire magnate being chauffeured around town until they arrived at the police station and he returned to being a humble detective constable again.

Trave had been in Creswell's office when Clayton had got back; and then, unlike Macrae, he'd missed Trave's sudden rushed departure after his interview with the superintendent was over. However, it didn't take long for the station's gossip mill to start to grind, and by the time the day was over, everyone seemed to know that Trave had been taken off the Blackwater case and been replaced by Inspector Macrae. And, whether he liked it or not, Clayton had a new boss.

'Good morning, lad,' said Macrae, waving him to a seat behind an empty desk opposite his own. 'That'll be your place. Used to be Jonah's, but he's kindly agreed to let you have it, haven't you, Jonah?'

Police Constable Joseph Wale, sitting silently on a chair in the corner, nodded curtly. He was a big man and the chair seemed too small for him, making Clayton wonder if it might break under Wale's weight if he stayed sitting on it too long. Wale was a recent addition to the Oxford force. Rumour had it that he'd been a not-very-successful professional boxer in London who'd joined the police after he'd been knocked out one too many times and found that he couldn't get any more fights. It had soon become apparent that Wale was a loner. As far as Clayton knew, he hadn't made any friends since his arrival – except Macrae, who had taken an immediate and unexplained shine to the new recruit, given him the nickname Jonah (which Wale surprisingly didn't seem to resent), and adopted him as his unofficial assistant.

'Jonah would be the first to admit that paperwork's not his strongest suit, wouldn't you, Jonah?' asked Macrae, glancing cheerfully over at Wale, who gave another brief nod. Clayton thought he had never seen Macrae looking happier: he was wearing a garish white flower in the buttonhole of his jet-black suit jacket – Clayton wondered what it was; it looked like a weird hybrid of a rose and a snowdrop.

'So record-keeping'll be your department, Constable,' Macrae continued, turning back to Clayton. 'But don't

209

worry – Jonah has a lot of other talents, some of them quite unexpected. I think you'll find he turns out to be a very valuable member of our team.'

'I'm sure I shall,' said Clayton, who had no idea what Macrae was talking about.

'Good. Now, before we begin, Constable, a word of caution. If it was up to me, Bill Trave would have been suspended for what he did the day before yesterday. He's brought the whole of the Oxford police force into disrepute.' Macrae paused, looking Clayton in the eye. Clayton flushed and was about to rise to the challenge, feeling a sudden instinctive rush of loyalty to his old boss, but then thought better of the idea and bit back his response. Macrae was watching Clayton carefully and now smiled icily, leaving Clayton with the uncomfortable impression that the inspector had read his mind.

'But it's not up to me,' Macrae went on in the same steely voice. 'And Inspector Trave lives to fight another day. But he has been taken off this case, removed from it once and for all. And what that means is that you're not to talk to him about it. Your loyalty's to me now, Constable. Do we understand one another?'

Clayton felt the eyes of not just Macrae but also the silent Wale on him. He resented the aspersions on his professionalism implied in Macrae's words, and it angered him that Macrae should have raised his concerns in front of a junior officer like Wale, but at the same time it was true that Trave had made an unholy mess of the Osman case. The investigation needed to follow the evidence, not spurious coincidences, and that meant focusing on David Swain. Trave hadn't been prepared to do that, and it was right that he had been replaced. Clayton knew that his personal antipathy toward Macrae shouldn't get in the way of doing his job. Catching Swain was the priority. Macrae had a reputation for getting results, and he was entitled to rely on Clayton's support for achieving them.

'You can count on me, sir,' said Clayton.

'Thank you, Constable,' said Macrae, looking pleased. 'Now fill me and Jonah in on what's been happening. You'll find we're good listeners.'

Macrae wasn't exaggerating. Wale remained characteristically silent throughout Clayton's briefing, and Macrae only asked one or two questions. Curiously, he seemed most interested in the fact that Trave had visited Swain twice in Brixton Prison the previous year.

'So Trave doesn't just think Swain is innocent of the Mendel murder, he's also gone and told him so?'

'I don't know if he actually said that,' said Clayton. 'He told me he wanted to see if Swain could shed any light on the note or the other aspects of the case that he was worried about, but Swain couldn't.'

'And he went twice. You're sure of that?'

'Yes.'

'Interesting.' Macrae stroked his chin with his long, thin forefinger for a moment, thinking, and then nodded as if he'd come to a decision. 'Thank you, Constable,' he said. 'You've been most helpful. And now . . .'

'Now, sir?' asked Clayton when Macrae didn't finish his sentence.

'Now, let's have a press conference,' Macrae said, snapping his fingers with sudden energy. 'Two o'clock this afternoon sounds good. And get as much media as you can over here. Jonah'll help you with the phoning. He's good at that.'

David lay on his bed listening to the radio. It was his ninth straight day inside the shabby hotel at Number 10 Parnell Avenue, and he didn't know how much longer he could stand it. The physical pain in his shoulder had largely

211

disappeared now that the wound caused by Claes's bullet had almost entirely healed, but the mental anguish that he was suffering now was fast becoming unbearable. Every minute of every hour he sat waiting for a knock on the door or the sudden shout from a police megaphone. His body was rigid and his mind was exhausted with the waiting. It was worse, far worse, than the prison. O'Brien might have been a religious maniac, and Eddie was a treacherous, lying bastard, but at least they were human beings he could talk to, and there was a life of sorts outside the cell – in the canteen or the exercise yard or the rec room. Here the fear intensified when he went outside. Hunger and claustrophobia had driven him out to the convenience store at the end of the road three times since he'd moved in. He'd worn his jacket collar turned up around his face, and he hadn't shaved since his escape, but still the last time he'd been in there he could have sworn that the little Indian man behind the counter had been about to recognize him. David's hand had been shaking as he took his change, and it had been all he could do to stop himself from running away down the street.

Now he was trying to make his meagre supplies last, but it was hard without a fridge or a cooker. A diet of stale sandwiches and cold sausage rolls was beginning to take its toll: every day he thought with greater longing of the breakfast that his mother had cooked for him on the morning after his escape, and he was even becoming nostalgic for the stodgy food they served in the prison canteen, but for the present his fear remained stronger than his hunger, and he wasn't prepared to risk a café or a restaurant.

He'd been lucky up to now. He knew that. He'd driven away from his mother's house in a panic, without any kind of plan, knowing he couldn't stay in the car too long: every policeman in Oxford would be looking for it once Ben had phoned the police with the registration number. And so he'd driven frantically through the Oxford suburbs looking for a place where he could lay low for a while, but he'd seen nothing suitable until he made a random turning off Botley Road onto an entirely unmemorable street called Parnell Avenue and came to an abrupt halt outside the Bella Vista Hotel. The house was not 'bella' and it certainly had no 'vista'. It was run-down and in bad need of a coat of paint, and the view across the road was of a builder's yard bordered by a piece of waste ground. But it was perfect for what he needed, and inside, the half-asleep man behind the reception desk didn't even ask him for ID once David had taken out his roll of banknotes and volunteered to pay two weeks in advance.

Upstairs he'd sat in his room and waited for nightfall, and then, under cover of darkness, he'd driven the Ford Anglia over to the railway station and abandoned it in the car park yards from where Eddie and he had got into the red Triumph the night before, overdosing on adrenaline. And then he'd walked back to the hotel through the deserted side streets. And he'd been there ever since, lying on his bed looking at the wall, eating stale sandwiches, listening to the radio that came with the room.

Two days ago he'd heard on the news about Eddie's arrest in London. That had shaken him. He'd be next. He knew that, unless he could come up with a plan. But he couldn't, however hard he tried. He still had the gun. His mother had told him to get rid of it, but he'd hung on to it. He couldn't face them taking him alive because he knew what they would do to him in the end. David was under no illusions: he knew what would happen. He'd be charged, he'd be tried, and he'd be convicted just like before, but this time they wouldn't send him to prison for the rest of his days. No, they'd truss him up like a turkey and hang him from a gallows, break his neck with the snap of a noose. It was the punishment prescribed by law for killing with a gun, and David knew he'd get no mercy because this was his second time around. For a second murder he'd definitely swing.

The rope: David had nightmares about it every night, waking up in the small hours, screaming for air with his hands outstretched, pushing away invisible black-masked strangers; and then, turning on the light, clutching his racing heart, he'd catch sight of Robbie the Robot on the night table gazing back at him out of his protuberant android eyes and remember where he was.

David thought about his half-brother often. It gave him a strange but intense comfort to know that the little boy with the oversized glasses and the utterly serious view of the world was out there only a few miles away, arranging his toys and creatures in the room that had once been David's own. David thought that the moment at the end when Max had come out of the house holding Robbie the Robot in his outstretched hands was one of the best in his whole sorry life. But then he also wondered whether he would have any more moments like that. He wondered when his luck was going to finally run out.

The quiz programme that he'd been half-listening to came to an end, and now Frank Sinatra was singing: 'New York, New York . . .' David changed stations, irrationally irritated. He'd always wanted to go to New York and climb the skyscrapers, and now he was about as likely to go there as the moon. But Radio Luxembourg was no better – more stupid music. David twisted the tuning knob again and went rigid. A man with a cold, Scottish-sounding voice had just spoken his name.

'David Swain . . . a change in direction . . . taken over the investigation from Inspector Trave, who had for personal reasons formed the mistaken impression that Mr Swain was innocent . . . we will redouble our efforts to find Swain . . . appeal to the public for their help . . .'

David only caught the words in snatches. His head was suddenly full of a great rushing wind and he swallowed hard, thinking he was going to be sick.

The noose was tightening. He could feel it. It wouldn't be long now unless . . . unless maybe this policeman, Trave, the one with the sad eyes who thought he might be innocent, could help him . . .

Trave had taken Creswell's advice the previous evening: he'd gone home and had a couple of drinks; and then, when that didn't help, he'd had several more, sitting morosely in his living room armchair in front of an unlit fire, feeling sorry for himself as he mechanically turned the pages of dusty photograph albums, looking at old pictures of Vanessa and his dead son. Eventually, soon after he'd reached the halfway point in the whisky bottle, he'd fallen asleep in his clothes and had then woken up in the first light of dawn, feeling like death. But it wasn't in his character to give in to adverse circumstances for very long. He'd always been one of those who carry on struggling until they reach the finish line even though the race is already over. He remembered at school how he'd had so much trouble learning to swim that his parents had despaired of him, but he'd carried on flailing and failing on his own until the day finally came when he'd been able to stay afloat.

And so he fortified himself with two cups of strong black coffee and took a brisk walk around the deserted golf course at the end of the road, filling his lungs with the cold sharp air of the early morning before returning home to work for hours in the garden in the autumn sunshine – weeding the flower beds, mulching the roses, raking the leaves from off the lawn – until he felt almost human again. He slept well on Sunday night and took the day off on Monday to complete his recovery. And he'd just come in from the garden and was sitting down to a late lunch in his shirt sleeves when the telephone rang.

'Turn on your radio. Two o'clock news,' said an oddly familiar voice.

'What? Who's this?' said Trave, but the line had gone dead, and he couldn't put his finger on where he'd heard the voice before. It was frustrating, but he stopped thinking about the mystery caller once the voice of Hugh Macrae came on the air.

Trave couldn't believe what he was hearing. For reasons best known to himself, Macrae had taken it upon himself to tell the entire country that Trave hadn't done his job properly for personal reasons. Trave felt the same boiling anger that he'd felt outside Osman's house two days earlier. He ran upstairs and pulled on his suit and tie and then drove at breakneck speed across town to the police station, running two red lights on the way.

The car park was full of reporters and media men leaving the press conference. Several of them recognized Trave and called out to him, asking for a comment, but he pushed past them up the steps without replying and found himself face-to-face with Clayton in the foyer.

'Did you hear that? Did you hear what he said?' asked Trave. He was red in the face, breathless with indignation.

'Yes, I'm sorry,' said Clayton. He seemed embarrassed by the situation, almost tongue-tied.

'What the hell's Macrae playing at?' asked Trave. 'Do you know?'

'I can't talk about the case,' said Clayton, looking stricken. 'I said I wouldn't.'

'But I've got a right to know . . .'

'No, you haven't. You've got no right at all,' said Macrae,

coming up behind Clayton's shoulder and planting himself squarely in front of Trave. 'You've been taken off this case once and for all. I'm sure you can find something else useful to be getting on with . . .'

'You bastard,' shouted Trave, clenching his fists, his reason overwhelmed by another surge of fury.

'What? You're going to hit me as well now, are you?' asked Macrae with a sneer. 'First the star witness and then one of your fellow officers – where's it going to end, Bill? That's what I'd like to know.'

Trave couldn't contain his rage. He hated Macrae just as much as he hated Osman. He wanted to smash them both, pummel them into oblivion. *But not this way*, protested a small, half-smothered voice somewhere inside his brain, and Trave realized suddenly where he was going: he was destroying himself, not his enemies, with his mad anger, and so with a supreme effort he fought to regain his self-control, willing his fists and his teeth to unclench. Breathing deeply, he looked Macrae in the eye. 'This isn't over,' he said quietly. 'It's only just begun.' And then he turned his back on his adversary and walked away toward his office without waiting for a response.

He passed Jonah Wale in the corridor. Noticing the smirk on Wale's face, Trave realized who his mystery caller had been. He thought of turning back to have it out with the man but then decided against the idea, realizing that he'd only demean himself by such a confrontation. Ten minutes later the switchboard put through a call from a public call box. It was David Swain.

'Can I trust you? How do I know I can trust you?' The voice on the other end of the line was rushed, breathless, choked up with fear.

'Because I don't think you committed these crimes. There

217

are too many coincidences that just don't add up,' said Trave urgently. 'Listen – I want to help you. That's why they've taken me off the case. But I can't unless you tell me what happened out at Blackwater. I need to know what happened, David.'

'I can't tell you. Not here. It's a phone box, for Christ's sake. I'm in the middle of the bloody street. Someone'll see me, someone'll . . .' Swain's voice rose and broke off, and Trave could sense the young man's growing panic.

'All right, all right,' said Trave soothingly. 'We can meet. That'll be better anyway. Anywhere you like. Anywhere . . .'

There was silence on the other end of the line. It sounded like someone was breathing, but Trave couldn't be sure it wasn't his own breath: he could feel it coming out of his lungs in gasps. And then, just as Trave was about to give up, Swain spoke again: 'St Luke's School, down by the river. Do you know it?'

'Yes.'

'There's a cricket pavilion. I'll meet you there.'

'When?' asked Trave.

'Tonight, at ten o'clock – no – half past ten. If you're not alone, you won't find me, so don't bother looking . . .'

'Don't worry. It'll just be me . . .' Trave began but then broke off. The line had gone dead, and he knew he was talking to thin air.

Trave's hand was shaking as he replaced the receiver. Unanswered questions cascaded through his mind. Why had Swain called him? What did he want? And why now? It had to be because of the press conference, because of what Macrae had said. Trave smiled suddenly, struck by a wonderful thought: What if it was Macrae's big mouth that was going to give Trave the break he'd been waiting for for so long? Swain might know something that would blow the case apart, and, if so, Trave would have Macrae to thank for giving him the opportunity to hear it.

218

There were hours yet before he was due to meet Swain, and Trave tried to distract himself by tackling the mound of paperwork that had grown rapidly all over his desk during the previous week, but his heart wasn't in the task, and he gave up after half an hour and picked up his coat to go home. He drove out of the car park almost on automatic pilot and so didn't notice the nondescript Mini that slipped out after him and followed him home.

St Luke's was an old private secondary school founded in the second half of the nineteenth century by an evangelical philanthropist who had made an enormous fortune manufacturing steel couplings for steam locomotives. Trave passed a statue of the man dressed incongruously in a Roman toga standing in the centre of the entrance courtyard with the legend FUNDATOR carved in capital letters on the plinth underneath, and then turned right through an archway that took him out onto the playing fields that ran in a swathe of green down to the river. He'd been to the school twice several years earlier, both times to interview a teacher who'd been a witness to a hit-and-run on the Banbury Road, but the place had been very different then, full of the shouts of schoolboys running to and fro in their black-and-grey uniforms. Now it was half-term and the school was deserted, with no lights visible in any of the windows.

Guided by the moonlight, Trave picked a path past the wooden goalposts and nets that rose up like ghostly shapes in the semi-darkness, dividing one football pitch from the next. In the distance he could make out the weathercock on the top of the school cricket pavilion. Trave remembered the weathercock from his previous visit: it was a representation of Old Father Time, a miniature Grim Reaper complete with sickle. To Trave's left a tall yew hedge divided the playing fields from a small side road, and he grimaced in

219

momentary irritation when he noticed a gate halfway along, realizing that he could have saved himself a lot of trouble by parking his car on the other side and accessing the playing fields that way.

A hundred yards further on Trave stopped in front of the pavilion. The cricket season was now over, but the scores of the last match of the summer were still displayed on the façade – Batsman 1, Batsman 2 – meaningless white numbers on a black background, which Trave could barely make out in the moonlight. Beyond, the grass sloped down gently to a row of poplar trees lining the riverbank.

The door of the pavilion was open, but Trave didn't go in. He'd been too revved up all day since Swain's phone call to properly think through the implications of this clandestine meeting. He'd rushed headlong towards it, and now, standing on the brink, he suddenly hesitated, realizing the extent of the risk he was taking. Creswell wouldn't be able to save him this time if it came out that he'd arranged a meeting with an escaped prisoner, the main suspect in a murder inquiry. And he wondered too what he stood to gain by taking the risk. What could Swain tell him that he didn't already guess? But he'd never know if he didn't ask. It was too late now to turn back, and, throwing caution to the winds, Trave walked up to the door and went inside.

Immediately he found himself in almost pitch darkness, and instinctively he put out his hand, feeling for an invisible light switch.

'Don't,' said a disembodied voice somewhere to Trave's right. 'Keep your hands by your side. I've got a gun, remember.'

'What, are you going to shoot me?' asked Trave, suddenly angry. 'I'm the only friend you've got, you idiot.'

'All right, all right, I'm sorry,' said David. 'I'm scared. That's all.' A match flared, illuminating the young man's face for a moment as he lit a cigarette. He looked terrible – haggard, worn out, a shadow of the person that Trave had visited in Brixton Prison the previous year.

He was sitting in the corner on a bench consisting of the top of a set of two-tiered footlockers that ran the length of the room. Trave felt his way along the wall and sat down beside him.

'I used to go to school here, you know,' said David, now invisible again apart from the red glow of his cigarette.

'No, I didn't,' said Trave. St Luke's wasn't the kind of place that he would have pictured as Swain's alma mater.

'Too upmarket for a kid like me, eh?' said David, catching the note of surprise in Trave's response. 'Well, you're right. I never fitted in here. They could tell I wasn't one of them from the day I arrived. I used to hide out in here when it got really bad, unless they were playing cricket, of course. Then there was nowhere to go. Cricket's such a stupid game . . .' David broke off, his bitterness filling the room.

'David,' said Trave, reaching out and touching the young man's arm in an effort to connect. 'You've got to tell me what happened. Like I told you, I can't help you unless you tell me everything.'

'If you can help me! I'm an innocent man – white as the bloody Christmas snow, and that hasn't helped me any these last two years.'

This was going to be more difficult than he'd thought, Trave realized. Swain was clearly at the end of his tether.

'Here, have a drink of this,' said Trave, taking a small hip flask out of his pocket and holding it out toward David. 'It's brandy. It'll help.'

Trave felt David's trembling hand on his for a moment as the young man reached for the flask, and then he heard David cough violently as he swallowed the alcohol.

'Thanks,' said David, keeping hold of the flask.

'No problem. Right, let's start at the beginning – tell me what happened from when you and Earle got out of the prison. There was a man with a beard, right?'

'How do you know that?'

'It doesn't matter. Where did he take you?'

But David didn't get to say where Bircher had driven them. There was the sound of a car approaching at speed across the grass outside – it had to have come in through the gate in the hedge that Trave had noticed earlier. It screeched to a halt, and then suddenly the pavilion was full of white light from the car's headlights, and David had dropped the hip flask and the cigarette and was reaching in his pocket for the gun. Trave saw the silver barrel at the last moment and lunged forward to grab hold of it, but David sensed him coming and got to his feet, pulling away. He took a step toward the door, raising the gun in readiness to shoot, and then fell suddenly forward, tripping on Trave's hip flask where it lay on the floor. As if in slow motion, Trave watched the gun fly out of David's hand and hit a footlocker on the right. He saw Swain recover his footing and bend down, reaching for the gun, and at that moment, knowing he had no time, Trave threw himself onto the ground like he was bellyflopping into water, covering the gun with his body. Surprised, David lost his balance and fell over Trave's prone body, ending up sprawled out at right angles to Trave on the floor.

Trave was the first to recover. Everything hurt, but at least he could move his limbs. He pulled the gun out from under his chest and got slowly to his feet.

'We know you're in there. Come out with your hands up. You too, Trave.' It was Macrae outside, shouting at them through a megaphone. Trave could hear the conceited triumph in the Scotsman's voice despite the amplified distortion of his mouthpiece. Trave felt like he was going to be sick.

'Bastard,' said David, looking up at Trave from the floor. 'I should never have trusted you.'

'And I should never have come,' said Trave bitterly. 'This was just as much a trap for me as for you. God, what a fool I've been.'

'One minute,' shouted Macrae. 'And then we're coming in.'

'They'll shoot us,' said David. 'Maybe it's better that way.'

'For you maybe,' said Trave brutally. But Swain was right: Macrae might try to murder them if he could find an excuse. It was unlikely, but it was still possible.

'Adam Clayton, are you there?' shouted Trave, keeping out of sight behind the door. 'Are you there, Adam?'

There was silence and then the noise of people talking outside. Trave couldn't make out the words. And then a nervous, familiar voice came over the megaphone: 'This is Clayton. What do you want?'

'I've got Swain's gun,' shouted Trave. 'I'm going to throw it out. Once you've got it, we're coming out too.'

Trave lobbed the revolver underhand out into the light and waited until he heard the sound of someone picking it up. And then he went over to Swain and took him by the arm. 'Come on,' he said. 'It's better this way.'

Surprisingly Swain didn't resist. 'What does it matter? I'm dead meat anyway,' he said, and Trave thought he'd never heard such resignation in a man's voice.

And then, blinking, they walked out into the light.

PART TWO

1961

CHAPTER 15

New Year's Day dawned fresh and cold and was soon suffused in bright hard winter sunlight. A light coating of seasonal snow still covered the grass and flower beds in Trave's garden, and two robins sitting on a black branch of the leafless apple tree over by the far wall made the view from Trave's bedroom window look almost like a Christmas card. But Trave was unmoved. He felt neither festive nor ready for turning over new leaves or making New Year's resolutions. There was no Christmas tree and there were no cards or decorations in the old North Oxford house that once used to be a family home.

He hadn't seen or heard from Vanessa since the day he'd disgraced himself out at Blackwater Hall three months earlier. What a fool he'd been! First with Osman and then with Macrae, who'd baited his hook with a few well-chosen words to the press and then reeled him and Swain in like a pair of floundering fish. And now Swain was awaiting trial in London – a trial he couldn't win, and Trave was suspended on half pay, pending the outcome of a disciplinary hearing that he couldn't win either, while Macrae swanned around Oxford Police Station like he owned the place and Osman ran his manicured hands over Vanessa's body . . . Trave closed his eyes tight, using all his mental strength to shut out the obscene images that had once again floated unbidden into his mind. The telephone ringing in the front room was a welcome distraction.

It was Clayton. 'Bircher's dead,' he said, sounding excited. 'Fell from the top of a multi-storey car park in the centre of town last night. Or was pushed . . .'

'Welcome to 1961,' said Trave.

'Can I come over?'

'For some free advice from an ex-copper with time on his hands? Why not?'

'Thanks.'

Trave got dressed and took a cup of coffee into the garden, where he felt the sharp winter air prickle against his unshaven cheeks. He looked back toward the house and felt reassured by the line of his footprints in the snow. They were a proof of his existence, like the bite of the cold snow on his hand as he moulded it into a ball and threw it at the shed in the corner. The snowball exploded into a mass of white flakes and a couple of birds flew, cawing wildly, up into the cloudless blue sky. And Trave felt suddenly ashamed – that Bircher's death should make him suddenly feel alive or even perhaps that he should be alive at all when others lay dead and unavenged. He thought of Katya Osman lying stretched out on her bed with her eyes open, seeing nothing at all. He remembered the scene with a terrible, crystal clarity, and he shuddered at the recollection as he went back inside and closed the door.

It wasn't the first time that Clayton had seen his old boss since Trave's suspension from duty on the morning following Swain's arrest, and the events of that night had in fact played a big part in ending their brief estrangement. Three months later Clayton still remained disturbed by what had happened.

Macrae had been ecstatic on the way back to the police station. 'Two birds with one stone,' he'd kept repeating in a sing-song voice as if Trave were a criminal too like Swain, instead of what he actually was: a good, honest policeman sent off the rails by an emotional strain that even the most balanced person would have found almost impossible to cope with. Clayton had felt desperately sorry for Trave as he'd come stumbling out of the cricket pavilion with Swain and stood there in the glare of the car headlights, shamed in front of the junior officers from the station that Macrae had brought along for support. Clayton remembered how they'd all turned away from Trave, shunning him like he'd got some infectious disease. All of them except Wale and Macrae, whom Clayton had heard afterward over by the cars hissing in Trave's ear: 'It's over *now*, you moron. Over and out.' But Trave hadn't responded, just stood slumped over like a beaten man while Jonah Wale laughed out loud. It was the first time Clayton had ever heard the man's laugh – an animal laugh, full of a vicious, unreasoning cruelty, devoid of all human compassion.

Clayton had anticipated that they would interview Swain when they got back to the police station, but Macrae was having none of it. 'Let's not be hasty, Constable. He needs his dinner and his eight hours' sleep first. Just like you. Go home and get some rest. We'll talk to him in the morning.' Clayton had hung around for a while, writing up his report, but Macrae and Wale had outwaited him and eventually Clayton had gone home.

And the next day Swain admitted everything, or rather agreed with every suggestion that Macrae put to him in the interview room. He'd insisted on Eddie driving him out to Blackwater Hall; he'd taken the gun from the car and broken in through the study window, and then he'd gone upstairs and shot Katya in the head because she'd betrayed him with Ethan Mendel and it was her evidence that had put him away before. And then when he'd got out to the road, Eddie was gone, so he'd flagged down a car in Blackwater village and forced the driver to take him back to Oxford, where he'd holed up in a cheap hotel until he was caught.

And that was that. As full and frank a confession as any investigating policeman could wish for. Except that Clayton was left obscurely dissatisfied. He felt that Swain had confessed too easily. He'd sung like a canary but without any variation in the notes. There'd been no intonation, no emotion in Swain's voice when he answered Macrae's questions except that his eyes seemed to keep flickering over to Wale, who sat motionless in the corner, saying nothing, looking off into space.

Clayton had been sufficiently concerned to wait until Macrae had left the station for the day and had then gone to see Swain in his cell. But Swain had refused to talk to him, lying on his bunk in a foetal position with his face to the wall, shivering, even though the radiator was on and it wasn't cold. And the sergeant who'd been on desk duty the night before just shook his head and suggested he take his questions to Inspector Macrae when Clayton asked him if he'd heard anything untoward.

'There wasn't a mark on him that I could see,' Clayton told Trave a week later when his doubts and anxiety had driven him over to his ex-boss's house for the first time since Swain's arrest.

'But you don't need to leave a mark if you know what you're doing,' Trave said, laughing at Clayton's naïveté. 'There's other ways of breaking a man . . .'

'Like what?'

'Squeezing his genitals, half-drowning him in a bucket of water, threatening his family. It wouldn't have taken much to break Swain. I saw him, remember, and he was already on his last legs in that cricket pavilion. And Macrae's not averse to a bit of coercion where it suits his purpose.'

'How do you know?'

'Because a few years back he put an innocent man in gaol for a murder he didn't commit. The man did three years before the conviction was overturned and he got a Queen's pardon.'

'Did you have something to do with that?' asked Clayton, remembering the oblique references that Trave and Macrae had both made earlier in the investigation to some kind of shared past.

'Yes, by accident at first,' said Trave. 'I had a murder down here in which the killer left the same calling card as in Macrae's case.'

'What was it?' asked Clayton, curious.

'A shilling coin on the victim's tongue. You know, like they used to do in Roman times to pay the ferryman to take the dead across the River Styx. Don't you kids learn anything in school any more?' asked Trave, shaking his head in response to Clayton's look of bemusement. 'Anyway, I remembered about the other murder up north, and I went and looked up the evidence. It was really weak apart from a confession extracted by guess who?'

'Macrae?'

'Exactly. And once I was able to tie my man to the first murder, then that was it for Macrae's conviction.'

'What happened to him?'

'Macrae? Nothing as far as I know. The man who got the pardon said that Macrae had tortured him into confessing, but there was no physical evidence of that and the fact that his confession was false didn't prove that Macrae had forced it out of him.'

'It just made it very likely,' said Clayton.

'Yes. And that obviously didn't help Macrae's climb up the greasy ladder, for which he's blamed me ever since. This Osman case was his chance for payback, and you can't take it away from him – he grabbed the opportunity with both hands,' said Trave with a rueful smile.

'Why didn't you tell me this before?' asked Clayton.

'Because Creswell asked me not to, and I agreed with him. I didn't want Macrac transferred down here, but once it happened I wasn't going to make things worse by a lot of backstabbing. It had been a long time since I'd crossed swords with him and I didn't realize that he's a Scotsman with a long memory.'

The conversation with Trave increased Clayton's sense of unease about the case, and his anxieties intensified soon after when the ballistics report came back from the lab with the news that Swain's gun could have fired the bullet that killed Katya Osman but was now entirely loaded with blank ammunition. Clayton had expected Macrae to be concerned at this development, but he dismissed it with a shrug of his shoulders.

'It's an old trick, lad,' he said. 'Kill your man with a gun, load it with blanks like it never happened, and then play the innocent.'

'But where would he get the blanks?'

'Anywhere. It's not difficult. The evidence is self-serving. It won't make any difference.'

And then, just as he was turning away, Macrae noticed the look of disappointment on Clayton's face.

'Don't go lily-livered on me, Constable,' he said with a sneer. 'You don't want to end up like old Trave, do you? Flushed down the toilet at fifty?'

There seemed to be nothing Clayton could do to change the direction of events. Swain was charged with murder, and Eddie got an even better deal than Trave had dangled before him. The charges for the assault on the girl in London were dropped and leniency was promised for the escape, in return for Eddie's testifying at trial about the threats he'd heard Swain make against Katya and about how he'd seen Swain enter the grounds of Blackwater Hall at around half past midnight on the morning of Sunday, 25 September, armed with a handgun.

Swain had pleaded not guilty, but everyone at the station

agreed that the trial would be a formality and that it was only a matter of time before Swain went to meet his maker.

'It's not like the old days with all that dangling and strangling,' said Macrae, sounding disappointed. 'They've got it scientific now so it snaps their necks in a second.'

They were in Macrae's office on the morning after the arraignment. Suddenly Clayton jumped, hearing a loud snap. And then he looked back over his shoulder to where Jonah was sitting in the corner. Wale met Clayton's stare and then leaned forward and snapped his fingers again hard. And Macrae laughed like it was the funniest thing he'd ever seen.

After this episode Clayton started going over to Trave's house a lot more in the evenings after work. But it didn't help. Trave was depressed and felt as impotent as Clayton. And then Christmas came and the new year, and John Bircher fell off the top of a multi-storey car park and broke his head into three different pieces on the concrete down below.

'Perhaps he jumped,' said Clayton without conviction. 'That's what Macrae says.'

'What? Felt sorry for his sins, couldn't stand to live with himself any more?' asked Trave with a hollow laugh. 'I don't think so. Bircher was as black-hearted as they come: look at his rap sheet. No, someone got worried because he knew too much – arranged to meet him and then gave him the heave-ho.'

'It wouldn't be that easy. Bircher was a big man, you know.'

'Maybe whoever did it had a gun.'

'Like Claes, you mean?'

'Maybe. But you'll never prove it.'

They were sitting on either side of the old dining table in Trave's living room, each nursing a glass of neat whisky. Trave sighed and relapsed back into his own thoughts; and then, as if coming to a decision, he got up and went over to an open-top bureau in the corner of the room and brought back a thick file crammed with well-thumbed, typed papers. There was a label on the front: REGINA VERSUS DAVID JOHN SWAIN, CENTRAL CRIMINAL COURT, 1958.

Trave dropped the file on the table in front of Clayton and leant down over him, rapidly turning the pages until he got to one towards the end headed EVIDENCE OF JACOB MENDEL.

'Here, read this,' said Trave. 'And then we'll talk.' And Clayton began to read:

DEFENCE COUNSEL, MR RELTON: *You are the younger brother of the victim in this case, Ethan Mendel?*
WITNESS: *Yes.*
COUNSEL: *When did you last see your brother?*
WITNESS: *November last year. He left our home in Antwerp to go to England.*
COUNSEL: *Why?*
WITNESS: *He was going to see Titus Osman.*
COUNSEL: *Why?*
WITNESS: *Osman knew my father before the war. They both dealt in diamonds. My family – we are Jews, and after the German invasion it became unsafe. More and more unsafe. Osman – he was called Usman then – helped my brother and me escape with our grandmother to Switzerland in 1942, but my parents waited. I don't really know why. And then the next year, when Osman tried to help them, they were caught crossing the border into France and the Germans sent them to the deportation camp at Malines. And from there they went on a train to Auschwitz. And they died. Ethan wanted to know more about what happened to them and so he went to see Osman in England.*

COUNSEL: *Did you hear from Ethan after he left?*

WITNESS: *Yes, he telephoned my grandmother and me at Christmas, and he wrote us postcards. He said that he was staying longer than he'd expected and that he had met a girl, Katya, who was Osman's niece. He said he was happy. And then at the start of May I got a letter from Ethan which was different. He said that he had found out something important, too important to tell me about except face-to-face. He said that I should come to England and talk to him. But I did not go to England because Katya telephoned to say that Ethan was dead – murdered. His body came back to us on an aeroplane.*

COUNSEL: *Did Ethan say anything else in his letter about what he had found out?*

WITNESS: *He said it was dangerous. That's all.*

COUNSEL: *You have the letter with you, Mr Mendel?*

WITNESS: *Yes.*

Witness produces handwritten letter in postmarked envelope.

COUNSEL: *This will be exhibit 33, my lord. It's dated May 4 of this year and postmarked Munich, West Germany – the day before Ethan Mendel's death.*

JUDGE: *Yes, very well – exhibit 33. Is that all, Mr Relton?*

COUNSEL: *Yes, my lord.*

JUDGE: *Very well. Do you wish to cross-examine the witness, Mr Arne?*

PROSECUTION COUNSEL, MR ARNE: *Yes, my lord, just a few questions. You have no idea what it is that your brother wished to talk to you about, do you?*

WITNESS: *No, but I'm pretty sure it was . . .*

COUNSEL: *Please don't speculate, Mr Mendel. We are*

solely concerned with facts here, not guesses. Do you know David Swain?

WITNESS: No.

COUNSEL: Do you know anything about letters written by Mr Swain to Katya Osman?

WITNESS: No.

COUNSEL: Do you know anything about David Swain's movements on the day of your brother's murder?

WITNESS: No.

COUNSEL: Do you know anything about your brother's movements that day?

WITNESS: No, of course I don't. I was in Belgium when my brother was murdered. I already said that.

COUNSEL: Yes, you did. And the point I'm making to you now is that you don't know anything about what happened to your brother because he never told you anything, and you weren't even in this country when he was killed . . .

WITNESS: I know he'd found out something . . .

COUNSEL: But you don't know what it was. Your letter leads us precisely nowhere. It's not evidence.

WITNESS: But . . .

COUNSEL: Thank you, Mr Mendel, I've no more questions. I'm sorry that you've had such a wasted journey.

WITNESS: I don't care what's evidence or not evidence; I care about who killed my brother. Ethan died because he'd found out something, and I'm going to find out what it was.

JUDGE: Please just answer the questions, Mr Mendel. Do you have any re-examination, Mr Relton?

DEFENCE COUNSEL, MR RELTON: No, my lord.

JUDGE: Thank you, Mr Mendel. You may step down.

'Pretty effective piece of cross-examination I'd say,' said Trave, catching Clayton's eye as he looked up at the end of the page. 'Jacob Mendel had no real probative evidence to give, and the defence looked stupid for calling him. That's what I thought at the time anyway, but since then Jacob and his mysterious letter have gnawed at the back of my mind. It's like Ethan's note – an itch that won't go away.'

'Why?'

'Because the letter and the note don't make any sense. Think about it: Ethan goes to West Germany and finds out something dangerous and important – so important that he can't put it in a letter but instead asks his brother to cross the Channel so that they can discuss it face-to-face. Then he rushes back to England and immediately goes off to Oxford to see a man he's never met. And when he doesn't find Swain at home, he doesn't wait; instead he leaves an urgent note setting up a meeting at Osman's boathouse for five o'clock the same day.'

'You mean – how would Ethan have known Swain would get the message?' said Clayton thoughtfully.

'Yes. Unless whoever left the note knew Swain was at home and that's why he left it – because he didn't want to be seen.'

'Because whoever it was wasn't Ethan at all, but someone pretending to be him.'

'Someone setting a trap,' said Trave, nodding.

'Why didn't you tell me about the brother before?' asked Clayton.

'Because, like the prosecutor said, Jacob's evidence didn't go anywhere, and then you made it pretty obvious that you thought I was chasing my tail when I told you my concerns about Ethan's murder after Katya was killed,' said Trave with a dry smile. 'I'm telling you now because it seems like you've got more of an open mind, and also – well, also because I've decided to do something about Jacob.'

'Do something?' repeated Clayton, sitting up, suddenly alert.

'Yes, I'm going to go to Antwerp and try and find him.'

'Why, if he doesn't know anything?' asked Clayton, surprised.

'Because he might know something now. Look what he said at the end of his evidence,' said Trave, tapping the page with his finger. '"Ethan died because he'd found out something, and I'm going to find out what it was." Perhaps he's done just that. I remember him at the trial. He was angry and upset, but determined too. He didn't need to come all the way to London to give evidence, but he did. I don't think he's someone who'd give up easily once he'd set his mind to something.'

'Like you,' said Clayton wryly, raising his eyebrows.

'Like me,' agreed Trave. 'The point is, Adam, I know in my bones that Swain's not guilty. He's a hot-headed fool, but he's no murderer, and I'm not going to rest until I've proved it.'

'And I suppose that's also your only way to get your job back,' said Clayton, looking quizzically at his ex-boss.

'Yes, there's that too,' said Trave, agreeing with a wry smile of his own. 'Creswell's agreed to postpone my disciplinary hearing for a month, but I can't see the Chief Constable showing me much mercy once he's finally got me in his sights.'

On the other side of town, Macrae was working late in his office, reading through the documents in the John Bircher file. After a few minutes he gathered together the incident reports, the attending doctor's statement, and the three hideous photographs of Bircher's smashed-up body lying on the concrete outside the entrance to the car park, fastened them together with a paper clip, and replaced them in the cardboard file. Then, picking up a red pen, he wrote SUICIDE in thick capital letters across the front, added his initials, and pushed the file to the other side of his desk.

The door opened and Detective Constable Wale came in.

'Well?' asked Macrae, looking up.

'Clayton's been to Trave's house again. I followed him there this evening. He stayed inside more than an hour. You want me to talk to him?'

Macrae looked across the desk at his assistant and ran his eyes over Wale's thick arms and heavy, oversized hands. The sight of them always gave him pleasure, and he hesitated for a moment, stroking his chin. He liked the thought of Jonah trying out a few of his techniques on that self-righteous little sneak, Clayton, but he knew that it wasn't worth the risk of the runt going squealing to Creswell.

'No, Jonah. It's a tempting suggestion, I must admit, but I think we'd better leave Constable Clayton alone for now. Keep watching him though. He'll hang himself if we give him enough rope – save us the trouble.'

Macrae knew that it wouldn't be long now before Creswell retired, and who better to take over as superintendent than the up-and-coming Inspector Macrae? And then, once he had the power, he wouldn't waste any time: he'd shake up this sleepy police station and teach Clayton and his like a lesson that they'd never forget.

CHAPTER 16

Trave crossed the Channel on the early morning ferry to Calais and then took the train to Antwerp. He had never been to the city before and was unprepared for the baroque grandeur of the central railway station, with its gilt and marble interior and huge metal and glass dome. It was like a cathedral – there was even a rose window above the entrance, surmounted, however, not by Christ in glory but by a golden clock. In Antwerp the trains ran on time.

Trave had obtained an address but no telephone number for Jacob Mendel from the lawyers who had acted for David Swain at his first trial two years earlier. The house was in the Jewish Quarter, which ran in a tangle of crooked streets south from the station. It didn't seem too far on the street map that Trave had brought with him from England, and so he decided to walk. Almost immediately he found himself in a strange, utterly foreign world. It was the lunch hour, and crowds of Hasidic Jews thronged the pavements in their dark suits and white shirts, with curled sidelocks emerging from under their black felt hats. Everywhere was a hubbub of activity: cafés and synagogues and kosher delicatessens, and on Pelikaanstraat Trave passed by endless diamond shops with narrow storefronts and glittering wares watched over by morose merchants sitting perched on stools behind thick reinforced-glass windows.

Trave soon felt hopelessly lost amid a sea of trams and bicycles. The roads with their long Flemish names all seemed to twist and turn into one another, and he had just made up his mind to stop and ask directions when he looked up and saw that he was standing opposite the side street that he was looking for. Jacob's house was halfway down – a nineteenth-century apartment building constructed around a small cobbled courtyard. There were names on the letter-boxes, but Mendel was not one of them, and Trave was about to start knocking on the apartment doors when a voice called to him from behind in a language he didn't understand.

He turned around and found himself looking down at a small elderly woman with a bent back and a black scarf covering her hair. She was standing a few feet away in a low doorway under the entrance arch that Trave hadn't noticed when he came in. She had a walking stick in her hand.

'I'm English,' he said hopefully. 'I am looking for Jacob Mendel.'

Surprisingly the old woman seemed to understand.

'No Mendel here. Why you want him?' she asked suspiciously.

'To talk to him about his brother. I'm a friend.'

'Friend! Everyone says that,' she said with a sneer.

'Well, I am one,' said Trave. 'Jacob wants to find out who killed his brother, and I want to find out too. I want to help him.'

The old woman looked at him blankly and Trave realized with a sinking heart that she hadn't understood a word he'd said. Her English was obviously very limited, and Trave didn't know a word of Dutch.

'Parlez-vous français?' he asked, switching to French, but the old woman ignored him. Instead she looked him up and down, staring intently, and then waved her walking stick toward his feet. For a moment he thought she was going to attack him with it, but then realized that she was giving him an instruction: 'You wait,' she said, and then turned around and went back through the doorway behind her.

She emerged again a minute later, holding out a big book, a piece of paper, and a pencil. Trave opened the book and found that it was written in incomprehensible lettering, which he assumed to be Hebrew.

'I can't read this,' he said, pointing to the text and tapping the side of his head to try to make her understand his ignorance.

Impatiently she pulled the book back, closed it, and pushed the blank piece of paper down on top of the cover and made as if to write.

'You write,' she said. 'Then you come back.'

'When?'

'Four,' she said, holding up four fingers. 'Maybe.'

Trave nodded and began to write:

> *Jacob – I am the police inspector who was in charge of David Swain's case. Like you I do not believe Swain killed your brother. Perhaps we can help each other to find out who did?*
> *William Trave*

When he was finished, Trave caught the old woman's eye as he handed the note back to her.

'Please,' he said, pointing to his chest. 'I mean good.'

'Yes, yes. Friend,' she said, and Trave took comfort from the fact that at least she didn't pronounce the word with the same derision with which she'd spoken it earlier. 'Now you go,' she ordered. And Trave went.

With more than two hours to kill, he wandered the streets in a state of distraction. Would Jacob come? Would he know anything? Trave had no answers to his questions. He began to feel hemmed in by the rows of tall medieval guild houses in the old town with their myriad of leaded windows, and so he headed west toward the river. Leaning on the parapet,

Trave gazed out over the wide expanse of the Scheldt and watched as the afternoon turned from blue to grey in a moment as a bank of low clouds came funnelling up the river from the North Sea. He shivered suddenly, feeling the January cold in his bones, and turned to go back.

The old concierge was waiting for him under the entrance arch. 'Badge,' she said. 'Show me badge.'

Trave complied, and she examined his credentials for a moment before beckoning him inside her doorway. Trave took off his hat and followed her into a surprisingly spacious room with two windows overlooking the main street through which the last of the winter sunshine was picking a golden, glowing path across the spotless wooden floor. There was no sign of Jacob Mendel, but on the other side of the room an old lady with bright blue eyes was sitting in a rocking chair beside a brightly burning fire. Trave could see that she must once have been very beautiful, but now her skin was wrinkled and pulled tight over the bones of her face so that it seemed as if she was made of antique porcelain, like the teacup she was holding in her hand. She was dressed entirely in black with her silver-grey hair tied up into a bun at the nape of her neck, and an enormous white cat lay stretched across her lap, apparently fast asleep.

'Excuse me for not getting up, Mr Trave,' she said in accented but otherwise perfect English, gesturing to an armchair facing her on the other side of the fire. 'Mrs Morgenstein's cat does not like to be disturbed. Would you like tea?'

Trave shook his head as he sat down, but the concierge handed him a cup regardless, before vanishing behind a curtain into the interior of the apartment.

'It seems I have no choice in the matter,' he said wryly. 'Mrs Morgenstein was a lot more formidable earlier.'

'Yes, she can be quite frightening when she chooses,' said

the old lady, smiling. 'But it's because she's protective – she's the kindest person when you get to know her. I miss her since we moved. And her cat.'

'We?' repeated Trave, looking perplexed.

'I'm sorry, Inspector. I don't mean to talk in riddles. I'm Aliza Mendel, Jacob's grandmother. I expect you're wondering where Jacob is?'

'Yes.'

'He's gone, I'm afraid. Where I don't know. It's nine months now since he left, and he is my last living relative, so you can understand why I am worried.' Aliza screwed up her eyes, resisting a spasm of pain that momentarily contorted her features. 'It is why I am here, Inspector: to ask you if you find Jacob to give him a message from me.'

'What message?' asked Trave. He wanted to help the old lady if he could. He remembered what had happened to Jacob's parents, her son and daughter-in-law, in the war.

'Tell him to come back to Antwerp and stop digging into the past. No good will come of it. I know that.'

'I'll give him the message if I find him, but I doubt he'll listen to me. He's a determined young man. I remember that from watching him at the trial when he gave his evidence.'

'Yes – determined, headstrong, foolhardy. And obsessed too – obsessed with the letter Ethan wrote to him before he died. Jacob can't stand it. That's the problem. He can't bear it that his brother wanted to tell him something but died before he had the chance. I suppose he thinks he could have saved Ethan's life if Ethan had confided in him. There's no basis for him thinking that, but he still feels it, and like you, he's convinced that this man, Swain, had nothing to do with Ethan's death. He says it was a set-up, a conspiracy. And I'm sure he thinks the same about poor Katya's death as well, which I read about in the newspaper, although I haven't seen him since that happened.'

'Why? Why does he say it was a conspiracy?' asked Trave, trying to keep the excitement out of his voice.

'Because Ethan wrote the letter from West Germany and not from England, and so Jacob says that Ethan must have discovered something there that led to his death. Jacob may well be right. After the trial in London a stranger came here to this building and told me to warn Jacob to stay away from the past. Jacob wasn't here, fortunately, or there might have been violence, and after the man's visit we moved.'

'What did the man look like?'

'Not tall; thin; small, cold, watchful eyes. He kept on his hat and had the collar of his raincoat turned up around his ears so I couldn't see much of his face. He came in the evening, and it was getting dark outside my apartment, so I doubt I'd recognize him again. But I know what kind of person he was. I've seen men like him before when the Germans were here, people who worked for the security police. He spoke in Dutch, almost like a native. But not quite,' she added thoughtfully. 'Languages are my speciality – they're how I made my living once upon a time, and they're also the one thing Jacob seems to have inherited from me. I don't think the man who came here was Belgian by birth – German maybe.'

'Did he give a name?'

'No, of course not. People like that don't have names,' said the old lady, giving a hollow laugh. 'He didn't stay long – just long enough to make his meaning clear. And I was frightened – I don't mind admitting that, and so I told Jacob. I wish I hadn't now. The man's visit just made him more determined to find out who killed Ethan. And by then he'd become convinced that Titus Osman was behind it all, which made *me* angry . . .'

'Why? Why Osman?' interrupted Trave, leaning forward in his chair.

'I don't know. It's difficult to understand when someone's so wrong-headed. I suppose it's because Ethan went to stay with Titus to find out more about his parents and ended up dying in Titus's house, and because he went straight back there after posting the letter to Jacob, but I think most of all it's because Titus arranged for Jacob's parents to escape from Belgium and they ended up getting caught. That's the root of the trouble, you see – Jacob blames Titus for his parents' deaths, and so he blames him for everything else as well. It was awful at Ethan's funeral. Titus came to pay his respects, as was right and proper, and Jacob practically accused him of being a murderer in front of all the guests. Titus was very good about it, very kind and understanding, but it didn't change what Jacob had done. He had shamed me, shamed our family, and after that it was never the same between us. But now, now I wish he would just come back.'

The old lady's voice caught, and she took a small white handkerchief from the sleeve of her black cardigan and dabbed her eyes.

'Why are you so sure Jacob is wrong about Titus?' asked Trave. He felt a little ashamed of persisting with his questions when the old lady was so visibly distressed, but he couldn't bring himself to stop their conversation just when it had become so interesting to him.

'Because I wouldn't be here speaking to you if it wasn't for Titus,' Aliza said quietly, recovering her composure. 'He saved my life and the lives of my grandchildren, and for that he deserves our gratitude, not slander. He arranged everything: the false papers to get us into France and the guides who cut the wire and took us through the woods into Switzerland in the early morning with diamonds hidden in the heels of our shoes. Without the diamonds the Swiss would never have let us stay. At the border you had no chance – they handed you over to the Germans without a second's thought, but in Zurich it was different. We paid money, and they put us in a labour camp. It was hard, but at least we were safe, and my son and his wife could have been there with us if Avi hadn't been so stubborn, so pig-headed about staying in Belgium. It was Avi's fault what happened, not Titus's. He waited nearly a year, until the winter of 1943, and by then it was much harder to get out. Switzerland had become impossible, and so Titus tried to send them through Vichy and across the Pyrenees to Spain, but the borders were tighter and they were stopped, sent back . . .'

'Why did your son wait?' asked Trave. 'He must have known how dangerous it was here.'

'He thought he would be safe because he and Golda were Belgian citizens, and for the first year after the deportations began in 1942 the Germans had a strict policy of only taking foreign Jews. It was easier for them that way. Almost all the Jews in this country were refugees, and exempting Belgian citizens kept the local population guilt-free. And the Germans were clever that way. They did everything gradually so as not to make us panic. They came in in May 1940, but it was two years before they made us wear the yellow stars. Registration was the key. Once we'd registered they knew where to find us when they were ready. They made a camp at Mechelen. Do you know where I mean?'

Trave shook his head.

'It's a pretty town – twenty kilometres from here on the road to Brussels. There are good rail connections into Germany and from Germany to Poland. And Mechelen's where they told the Jews to report for deportation to labour camps in the east, except it wasn't a labour camp they went to. You know where they went, don't you, Inspector?'

'Yes, I know,' said Trave, bowing his head, experiencing

that same sense of empty despair that he always felt when he thought of the Holocaust.

'Many Jews suspected too, I think,' said Aliza. 'They went into hiding, and when only a few thousand answered the work orders, the Germans began the round-ups, the razzias – beating down people's doors, dragging them from their beds in the middle of the night.'

'And yet your son stayed?'

'Yes, for more than a year. Like a fool he believed he was safe even while the Shoah was occurring all around him. And he didn't want to leave his home, his business – everything that he'd worked so hard to achieve.'

'But surely he wasn't able to carry on his business?'

'He used gentiles to run it as a front. And that worked for a while. Until the Germans changed their minds and went after the Belgian Jews too. And then Avi and Golda went into hiding, sewed diamonds into their clothes, and got caught at the border. They were on one of the last convoys that went from Mechelen to Auschwitz, and they didn't come back. Almost no one came back.'

Auschwitz: the dread name that Aliza had hitherto avoided using fell like a stone into their conversation, reducing them both to silence. Outside the sun had set, and the fire's blaze had died down so that Trave could hardly make out the expression on the face of the old lady. She seemed far away, lost in places where he could not follow.

'How do you bear it?' he asked her. 'This terrible suffering – how do you go on?'

'Because I must,' she said simply. 'It is my fate, the fate of my people. I have a choice – to live or to die. I cannot choose to live *and* die.'

Trave shook his head, thinking of his own life – the death of his son, the loss of his wife, all the murdered men and women whose deaths he'd been called on to investigate, but it was all as nothing compared with what had happened in the war. Auschwitz was beyond measure – it stripped the world of meaning.

'It's not easy,' said Aliza, looking at Trave as if she understood what he was thinking. 'My life has been hard, but there's been good as well as bad amid all the wandering. My name, Aliza, means "merry and joyful" in Hebrew. I think my parents called me that because they were so pleased to have me. My mother had had difficulties before – several miscarriages. Many times during my life I have thought of changing my name, but I never have because it is who I am, who my poor parents intended me to be, who I must try to be despite all the suffering.'

'You said you wandered,' said Trave. 'So you are not from here?'

'Antwerp? No. I came here from Poland after the first war, fleeing from pogroms, dreaming of America, but I ended up staying like so many others. I got work at the bourse, the diamond exchange, as an interpreter. I met my late husband there and we had Avi. And Antwerp became my home. I could have gone to Israel after the war, but I had to come back. They say that Antwerp is now the last shtetl in Europe . . .'

'Shtetl?' repeated Trave, not understanding.

'It means "little town" in Yiddish. Like one of your villages in England where everyone knows each other and everything is familiar and yet life is always fresh and new and colourful.'

Trave nodded, remembering the vivid bustle of the Jewish Quarter earlier in the afternoon.

'But perhaps I was wrong,' said Aliza meditatively. 'Perhaps I was selfish. Maybe in Israel the boys would have looked forward rather than back. Every day in Switzerland they waited for their parents to come, and then in Antwerp they thought constantly of what might have been.'

'Were they close, Ethan and Jacob?'

'Yes, they were inseparable, even though they were so different. Ethan was two years older, and he was more like me I suppose – steady, patient, persevering – whereas Jacob is headstrong, ruled by his emotions, in love with extreme positions. After Ethan's death he left our synagogue and became a Hasid, and then two months later he gave that up and said he was a Zionist. I don't know what he is now. Or where he is . . .'

'Has he written to you, telephoned you, made any kind of contact since he left?' asked Trave.

'No, nothing. As I said, our relationship deteriorated after Ethan's funeral.'

'Do you have a photograph of him? I saw Jacob once when he gave evidence in London, but a picture would help with finding him.'

'Yes, I thought of that,' said Aliza. She leaned forward to pick up an old weather-beaten black bag that was lying on the ground by her feet, and the white cat on her lap stretched and jumped softly down, looked quizzically at Trave for a moment, and then stalked away out of sight.

Aliza took a small framed picture out of the bag and handed it to Trave, who got up from his chair to take it from her.

'It was taken two years ago,' said the old lady. 'And Jacob wears glasses now. He was always short-sighted like his father, but it got a lot worse at the beginning of last year. I've written my address and phone number on the back.'

A young, good-looking man with thin cheeks and wide eyes stared back at Trave out of the photograph. He was neither smiling nor scowling, but the line of his mouth was resolute and his chin was firm and set. He looked like a man on a mission, Trave thought – a soldier about to go to war.

'I will look for him,' said Trave slowly, feeling like he

was taking a vow. 'I can't promise anything, but I will try, and if I succeed, I'll tell him your message.'

'Thank you. That's all I ask,' said the old lady, holding out her hand in farewell. 'I feel you are a good man, William Trave. I think you have suffered too like me and so you understand what I have told you. May God go with you and be your guide.'

CHAPTER 17

Vanessa shivered, pushing her hands deep into the pockets of her overcoat. She'd wrapped up warm to come out, but it still wasn't enough to keep out the stabbing cold. There'd been a forecast for snow in the morning paper, but for now there was only the cold and the clinging mist that hung over the river beside which Vanessa was sitting, rendering the line of black, leafless trees on the far bank into tall, ominous shadows that filled her with unease.

Vanessa hated January – the month when winter seemed like it would never end and it was dark by half past four in the afternoon. It was like an annual endurance test – bedraggled Christmas trees awaiting collection at the end of the road, the ground hard and barren, nothing to look forward to but more of the same. It made Vanessa think, as she often did, that she'd been born in the wrong country, that she was a southerner at heart, forever longing in vain for the warm sun of the Mediterranean or the hot countries beyond.

She knew, of course, that she could go there now on a cheap ticket, lie on a beach for a week, burn the cold from her bones. She had some money saved up, and she was sure Titus would go with her if she asked him. He'd jump at the idea. But something held her back. It felt too much like an escape, an abdication of responsibility. Because it wasn't just the winter that was making her feel anxious and hemmed in. Her unease had deeper roots. She felt she was at a crossroads in her life and would soon have to choose a road to go down for better or worse. And yet she distrusted the signposts, feeling unready to make a decision.

Titus had been patient with her for months, but she could sense that soon he would press her for an answer to his marriage proposal. Vanessa believed she loved him – certainly she thought of him constantly when he wasn't there and looked forward with hungry anticipation to their evenings together. But was this a basis for married life? She'd loved her husband with all her heart once, years ago, and yet their union had failed. Vanessa was burdened with her past: however hard she tried, she was unable to free herself of her life experience. She feared commitment and yet could no longer enjoy the independence that she'd worked so hard to achieve in her little flat behind Keble College. She was always restless now, taking long, directionless walks after work, and at night she was oppressed by loneliness, turning on the radio beside her bed to fill the vacant space and then waking up in the small hours to the sound of alien, disembodied voices discussing the parlous state of the world.

But she knew that it wasn't just indecision over her future with Titus that had upset her peace of mind. It was guilt too – a gnawing guilt that was eating away at her inside. The months had passed since David Swain's arrest, and now his trial was fast approaching, and yet she still maintained her silence about what Katya had said to her that September night in the drawing room at Blackwater Hall. Vanessa remembered the terrible effort the girl had made to reach her, to get her words out before she lost consciousness. 'They're trying to kill me,' she'd said. And a few weeks later someone had killed her, and yet Vanessa had stayed quiet. Why? At first because Titus had asked her to, but that was all right because at that early stage she'd only agreed to think about what to do; she'd made no binding commitment. And then when Franz Claes had pressed her on the issue a week later, her immediate instinct had been to rebel against his pressure and tell Titus that she had decided to go to the police. She had always thought of her husband as essentially a fair man, and she'd been unable to credit the idea that Bill would twist Katya's words to try to implicate Titus in the murder because he was conducting a jealous vendetta against his wife's lover. But then within hours of her conversation with Claes she'd been forced to revise her opinion. Vanessa shuddered even now, months later, at the memory of her husband lying sprawled on his back in the courtyard of Blackwater Hall like some pathetic, angry schoolboy who'd just lost a playground fight. It was obvious he couldn't be trusted, and so she'd reluctantly agreed to remain silent when Titus raised the matter with her again later that day. And she'd felt bound to stay quiet even when her husband was taken off the case.

Then, as the weeks passed and Swain's trial got closer, she tried to tell herself that her silence didn't matter because the case against the defendant was so overwhelming, but her conscience kept getting the better of her. She couldn't suppress the memory of Katya's white, agonized face from her mind, and every day she felt more torn between her need to do what was right and her desire to protect Titus.

What troubled Vanessa most was that she wasn't just shielding Titus; she was shielding Claes too. Vanessa had no doubts that Titus was entirely innocent of all wrongdoing, but she was far less sure about Claes. She had always disliked Titus's brother-in-law with an intensity that she didn't understand, and at their most recent meeting the previous Sunday their unspoken mutual antipathy had almost erupted into open hostility.

They'd been in the dining room at Blackwater – Osman at one end of the polished oak table and Claes at the other, with Vanessa and Claes's silent, severe-looking sister sitting on either side between the two men. Outside, it had been raining all day and the atmosphere was heavy and oppressive. Vanessa had to force herself to eat the roast beef and Yorkshire pudding that Titus always liked to have served on Sundays in a strange culinary homage to his adopted country, and she was counting the minutes until Titus and she could be alone. With dessert they began a desultory conversation about politics and the state of the world. It was not a subject in which Vanessa had any great interest, but she had enjoyed watching the Kennedy inauguration on the television a few days earlier and had felt infected by the mood of excitement and hope inspired by the new young president.

'He will have to be ready,' said Claes in his strangely formal English. 'The Russians will attack – maybe this year, maybe next. Khrushchev, Stalin – they are all the same.'

'What do you mean – the same?' asked Vanessa, irritated by Claes's doomsday certainty. 'Khrushchev condemned Stalin and the purges. Didn't you read about that?'

'It does not matter,' said Claes with a dismissive wave of his hand. 'They are Bolsheviks. They want to make everyone else Bolshevik. We had the chance to stop them in the war, and now maybe it is too late.'

'What chance? What are you talking about? Without the Russians Hitler would have won. Is that what you wanted?' asked Vanessa, outraged. She threw down her napkin and pushed her chair back from the table, but Osman reached out, covering her hand with his, preventing her from rising.

'Please don't be upset, my dear,' he said in a soothing voice. 'This is all a misunderstanding. Franz did not want Hitler to win. He fought in the Belgian army when the Germans invaded. It's just that he does not like the Communists. None of us do, including your President Kennedy.'

Vanessa sat stiffly in her chair, keeping her eyes fixed on Claes, refusing to be mollified. 'What do you say?' she asked.

'About what?' asked Claes. Vanessa sensed the contempt in his voice, in the way he looked at her. She felt that underneath his rigid exterior he was spoiling for a fight just as much as she was.

'About Hitler? About fighting the wrong enemy in the war?'

Claes smiled thinly at Vanessa, apparently about to respond, but then he glanced away, unable to ignore Osman's intent stare. 'I did not want Adolf Hitler to win the war,' he said slowly, sounding for a moment like a recalcitrant schoolchild reciting a lesson that he'd been required to learn by heart. On the other side of the table, Claes's sister exhaled deeply and put her hand up to the small silver crucifix that hung from a slender chain around her neck, in what was obviously a habitual nervous gesture in such moments of crisis.

Titus, however, had behaved as if nothing had happened, taking Vanessa by the arm and leading her along the corridor to the drawing room, where they passed the rest of the afternoon side by side on the sofa in front of a roaring fire, talking about faraway places where Vanessa had never been and to which Titus was eager to take her.

But now, sitting on the grey wooden bench by the riverbank in the darkening late January afternoon, Vanessa realized once and for all that there could be no future with Titus as long as she kept Katya's words a secret. She could only give Titus what he wanted if she went against his wishes and told what she knew to the police. Not to her husband but to the policeman who'd taken over the case. He didn't have an axe to grind with Titus; he'd be objective, unlike Bill; he'd tell her what to do.

Vanessa thought of telling Titus first but then decided

against the idea. He'd make her change her mind, and she couldn't cope with the guilt of remaining silent any longer. She needed to do what was right. He'd just have to understand.

Vanessa wasted no time once she'd made her decision. She phoned the police station as soon as she got home and made an appointment to see Inspector Macrae the following day.

It felt strange going into the building where her husband had spent his working life. Vanessa had rarely been there while they were together. Police functions tended to be held at a hotel near the station, and Bill had always wanted to keep his professional and personal lives apart. Vanessa thought with sudden sadness how lost he must feel now that he'd been exiled from this place perhaps forever, but then she hardened her heart, remembering how he'd shut her out after Joe's death, leaving her alone with her grief while he worked in his office through the long evenings, only coming home to go to bed.

Macrae came out into the entrance hall, introduced himself, and led her back down a series of twisting corridors to his office. She appreciated his consideration but nevertheless felt put off by the man. Sitting across the desk from him, she couldn't put her finger on the reason. Perhaps it was the way his eyes seemed so cold and watchful, detached from what he was saying; perhaps it was the way he stroked his long fingers together as he listened. But Vanessa was determined not to let an unfounded aversion obstruct the purpose of her visit, and so she pushed it to the back of her mind, refusing to acknowledge its existence.

She began to describe her encounter with Katya in the drawing room at Blackwater Hall four months earlier. It felt like a relief at first to be breaking her long silence and telling this stranger what had happened, but then, faced with her own disclosure, she felt a new surge of guilt for not having spoken before and stumbled over her words, realizing to her shame that tears had started to spring from her eyes.

'I didn't want to get Titus into trouble,' she said. 'He's a good man, and he was just trying to help Katya, but I knew that Bill, my husband . . .'

'Would take it the wrong way,' said Macrae, finishing Vanessa's sentence. She nodded her head and bent down, taking a handkerchief from her bag to dry her eyes.

'I can understand your concern, Mrs Trave,' Macrae continued. 'Your husband hates Mr Osman, and now, meeting you, I think that I can understand why.'

'What do you mean?'

'I mean that you are a beautiful woman. Your husband cannot bear the fact that you have left him for Titus Osman, and so he wants to paint Mr Osman as a murderer when he is nothing of the kind.'

Vanessa flushed, not knowing what to say. She resented Macrae's personal remarks, and yet she realized that he was only articulating what she had long thought herself.

'It is a tragedy,' Macrae went on. 'Your husband was once a very good policeman but he has lost his way, and now I fear it may be too late.'

Macrae sounded regretful, but the expression in his grey eyes didn't seem to match his words. She sensed a cruel humour in them, as if Macrae was secretly enjoying himself, but then with an effort Vanessa dismissed the impression as an illusion. 'I came here to talk about Katya, not about my husband,' she said firmly.

'But your husband is the reason you didn't come forward with the information before. Isn't that right, Mrs Trave?'

'Yes,' said Vanessa reluctantly. It was true – mistrust of her husband was the reason why she'd stayed quiet, but the spoken acknowledgement felt like a betrayal. She was saying that Bill was not to be trusted, that he had lost his objectivity, that he had become dishonest; and she was saying it here, in this place where he had worked so hard for so many years to do what was right. Vanessa looked up and felt for a moment as if Macrae had read her mind, as if he entirely understood the significance of her admission and was savouring it with relish.

'But I am telling you now,' she said, trying to regain control of the conversation. 'And I need your advice about what to do . . .'

'To do?' repeated Macrae, appearing puzzled. 'There's nothing you need do, Mrs Trave. You see, this case is very simple. David Swain killed Katya Osman. There are no conspiracies, however much your husband would like to uncover them. By all accounts Katya was a very unhappy person. She took drugs and generally abused herself in places where no self-respecting girl should go, and her uncle, to his great credit, tried to help her by looking after her at home. It is not his fault that she had become too unbalanced to appreciate his efforts and made wild allegations to you one evening, and he does not deserve to have those allegations aired in public. No, Mrs Trave, there's been too much muddying of the waters already in this case. We don't need any more.'

'So we do nothing?' asked Vanessa, surprised. It was the outcome she'd hoped for, and yet it left her strangely dissatisfied, unable to reconcile all her soul-searching and guilt with this easy happy ending.

'Just that – nothing at all,' said Macrae with a smile. 'Justice will take its course up in London, and you and Mr Osman will live happily ever after at Blackwater Hall. He's a very lucky man.'

'Nothing is decided yet,' said Vanessa defensively, getting

up to go. There was nothing she could put her finger on, but once again she had the impression that Macrae was taunting her, enjoying her discomfort.

'Of course not,' he said evenly, holding out his hand. Reluctantly she took it, noticing again the policeman's long, tapering fingers and his effeminately shaped nails. She made to let go immediately, but he held his grip, looking her in the eye. 'A word of advice, Mrs Trave,' he said softly. 'You've done well to come to me, but now I would let the matter rest. Idle talk costs lives – remember what they told us in the war.'

Macrae dropped Vanessa's hand and walked over to the door, opening it to let her pass. A burly overweight man in police uniform was standing outside, apparently waiting to come in. He'd cut his chin shaving, and a big sticking plaster disfigured his already ugly face.

'Ah, Jonah,' said Macrae, addressing the big man with easy familiarity. 'Please, could you show Mrs Trave out?'

Wale glanced over at Vanessa with a leer when he heard the name and then turned without a word and began walking away down the corridor. Vanessa followed in his wake, thinking that there was something half-bestial about the man's lumbering gait. And then out in the foyer he looked her up and down and smiled – a thin, cracked smirk of a smile that set her teeth on edge.

'Thank you,' she said more curtly than she intended. But he just grinned and turned away, disappearing back into the interior of the police station.

Vanessa didn't quite know what to feel in the days that followed her visit to Inspector Macrae. She'd at last done what her conscience demanded and the result had been better than she could have hoped. The policeman in charge of the case had expressly told her to let the matter rest.

Now she could get on with her life, unencumbered by any self-reproach. She wouldn't even need to tell Titus that she had gone to the police. And yet she remained troubled. It had all been too easy. She still felt that questions needed to be put to Claes and his sister, and she remembered with distaste the way Macrae had seemed to take such an unnatural pleasure in Bill's downfall. Her silence had started to feel like a kind of complicity – a further betrayal of her husband with another of his enemies. But then the sense of accountability made her angry. Bill was the one to blame, she told herself – for the failure of their marriage, for the implosion of his career. He had always been stubborn and difficult to work with – it was why he'd never got promotion, dooming them to life on a financial shoestring. And now she couldn't allow him to hold her back. Titus offered her a second chance at happiness, and she had to grasp it with both hands before it slipped away.

Over the weekend the long-predicted snow finally began to fall, covering the world in a dazzling white brightness. It was beautiful, especially down by the frozen river in the University Parks, where groups of laughing students were out skating on the ice, their long, coloured scarves trailing behind their shoulders and their breath hanging in the still winter air like smoke. Vanessa watched them from the bench beside Rainbow Bridge, where she'd felt so despondent a few days earlier. Now she felt alive in every pore of her body, and, leaning down, she scooped up a ball of snow into her gloved hand and pressed it to her forehead, enjoying its sudden cold bite. And then she walked back through the avenues of black trees, delighting in the crunch of the thick-textured virgin snow beneath her feet, got into her tiny car that was parked outside the gates, and drove out to Blackwater Hall, following the golden-red glow of the sun as it sank down into the western sky.

She was early, but Titus had already opened the front door and come down the steps by the time she'd turned off the engine. He'd obviously been watching out for her from the drawing room window, and it warmed Vanessa's heart that he should look forward to her arrival with such anticipation.

He was wearing no hat or coat, and she laughed when she got inside the house, seeing how the snowflakes had settled on his thick hair and beard, making him look like a fashionable Santa Claus dressed in an expensive suit and tie.

'Come on,' he said, taking her by the hand and leading her down the corridor to his study. 'I've got something to show you.'

'Something that can't wait?' she asked, laughing at his excited impatience.

'Something that can't wait,' he agreed, opening the door.

It was a colour photograph lying face-up on the desk. The surface was otherwise entirely empty except for a telephone and a green-shaded reading lamp near the corner. The silver-framed photograph of Katya that Vanessa had noticed on a previous visit had now disappeared.

Looking down, Vanessa saw that it was a picture of an enormous square cushion-shaped diamond with innumerable facets, all glittering with different shades of white and dark light. 'It's beautiful,' she said, staggered by the apparent size of the stone.

'Yes, and extraordinary when you see it in person and know its story,' said Titus quietly. 'Because the great diamonds – and this is one of them – each have their own history. What they have in common is that they travel across the world, passing from one lustful hand to another, and that they tend to possess their owners rather than be possessed by them. That is their nature. Perhaps now people understand this and that is why so many of them are locked up in museums.'

'Like this one?'

'Yes. It's in the Louvre. They have it sitting on an electrically controlled black velvet plinth in a case made of bulletproof glass. Below there is a specially made steel vault, and at a flick of a switch it rises into the light in the morning and descends back into the darkness when the museum closes at night. No one has even tried to steal it,' said Titus with a smile.

'Does it have a name?' asked Vanessa.

'Oh, yes. All the great diamonds have names. This one is the Regent. It was found by a slave worker who dug it out of the Partial mine on the Kistna River in India at the beginning of the eighteenth century,' said Titus, taking obvious pleasure in the pronunciation of the foreign place-names. 'The stone's value was obvious – I mean it was the largest diamond ever found in the world up to then, and the slave was determined to try to keep it for himself, so he cut a gash in his leg and hid the jewel in the bandages he wrapped around the wound. And then, I don't know how, he managed to escape from the mine and found his way to the coast, where he made a deal with an English sea captain to take him to Madras in return for half the value of the stone when sold. But the captain was greedy and arranged to have the slave thrown overboard, and so, as so often, the diamond's history began with a murder . . .'

Osman paused, looking out of the window toward the last golden glow of the sunset as it faded from the sky above the tall black pine trees on the other side of the snow-covered lawn.

'Go on,' said Vanessa impatiently. 'What happened next?'

'It was bought by Thomas Pitt, the British governor of Fort St George in Madras, and he sent it back to England and had it cut.'

'Cut?'

'Yes. Cutting is what changes a diamond, Vanessa: it releases the inner fire. Until there was cutting, the fire was invisible. In the Middle Ages no one understood what lay behind the dull, greasy outside of a rough diamond. The Indians valued the stone for its extraordinary hardness, not its beauty. And then someone somewhere began to use diamonds to cut diamonds, and the fire was released. First there was the rose cut – facets on a flat base like an opening rosebud, and then at the end of the seventeenth century a cutter in Venice invented the brilliant cut, and after that, nothing was the same. This stone, the Regent, was the first great diamond to receive the brilliant cut – fifty-eight facets, thirty-three above the girdle, twenty-five below . . .'

'What's the girdle?' asked Vanessa, interrupting.

'The middle of the stone. Above is the crown, below is the pavilion. And the facets bend the light as it enters and leaves the crystal, reflecting and refracting it so that the diamond dazzles and achieves its full glory. It took two years to cut the Regent, and at the end it was almost flawless. It went from four hundred and ten carats to one hundred and forty and a half, and almost all the cleavage pieces were sold to Peter the Great, the emperor of Russia, but several small rose-cut diamonds remained, and this – this is one of them.'

Pausing for effect, Titus took a small blue velvet box out of his pocket and placed it on the palm of Vanessa's hand. With trembling fingers she opened it and looked down at the most beautiful bright white diamond ring she'd ever seen.

'I love you, Vanessa,' said Titus. 'And I want you to be my wife. Say you will, please say you will.'

The diamond was like a sparkling magnet drawing Vanessa's eye down into its liquid depths. It made her giddy, made her want to throw all her anxiety and caution to the wind. It was the promise of a new world, a second chance at life: all she had to do was nod her head and say yes. And so she did.

'Yes,' she said. 'Yes, I will.'

And quickly, before she could change her mind, Titus took the ring from the case and slipped it on her finger. Then, taking Vanessa in his arms, he kissed her long and hard and then held her close to his body, feeling her heart beating against his chest. She leaned her head down against his shoulder, abandoning herself, and Titus stroked her long brown hair and looked over her head toward Cara, his cat, who had been lying curled up in an armchair in the corner of the room throughout the afternoon. The cat gazed up at her master for a moment and then began to purr, seeing the unmistakable expression of triumph dancing in Titus's bright blue eyes . . .

'Why is it called the Regent?' asked Vanessa later in the evening when they were eating supper by candlelight, sitting side by side at the end of the long dining room table on the other side of the corridor from the study. There had been no sign of Claes or his sister all day.

'Because in 1717 Thomas Pitt sold the diamond to the Duke of Orléans, the regent of France, and thereafter it became part of the French crown jewels. King Louis XV first wore it in public in March of 1721 to receive the Turkish ambassador, and it was said at the time that it surpassed in beauty and weight all the diamonds that had ever been seen in the West before that date. And afterwards the next king's wife, Queen Marie Antoinette, had it set in a black velvet hat . . .'

'She was guillotined,' interrupted Vanessa, frowning. 'Is the diamond cursed? Tell me the truth, Titus. I've read about jewels like that.'

265

'Well, I don't think you need to worry, my dear,' said Titus with a smile. 'What you're wearing on your finger is a tiny fragment of the Regent. And besides, I personally think it is a lucky diamond. A hundred years ago the Empress Eugenie wore it set in a diadem to the opera in Paris. On her way, a gang of revolutionaries threw three bombs at the carriage in which she was travelling, and yet she and her husband were unharmed – even though the coachmen and the horses all died.'

'I like it when you tell me about the past,' said Vanessa, looking at Titus with love and admiration in her eyes. 'You make it come alive.'

'The great diamonds are magical,' said Titus. 'All I do is tell their stories. But you need to see them to really understand. I will take you to Paris for our honeymoon, and you can look at the Regent in the Louvre, see it glittering in all its iridescent glory.'

'No, not Paris,' said Vanessa, looking suddenly troubled. Paris was where she and Bill had gone together so often when they were first married, spending long summer afternoons wandering in the Bois de Boulogne or the Jardins du Luxembourg, listening to jazz bands in the outdoor cafés. Paris was in the past, and she needed to keep it that way.

'No?' said Osman, darting Vanessa a quizzical look. 'Well, we can go wherever you like: Istanbul, Baghdad, Tierra del Fuego – you choose, Vanessa. But I don't want to wait any more – tell me when you will speak to your husband.'

'Soon. I promise,' said Vanessa, feeling suddenly under pressure.

'Will he agree – to the divorce?'

'Yes, I'm sure he will – he's a decent man. But I must speak to him in person. He deserves that much.'

Titus nodded, looking pleased, but Vanessa turned away,

266

hiding the look of anxiety that had creased her face. The prospect of seeing her husband again filled her with dismay. She felt for a moment like a swimmer who had dived into a beautiful river and found it far colder and quick-running than she had ever anticipated.

CHAPTER 18

This was a new prison: Pentonville, in North London. But still there were the same high walls, the same barbed wire, the same iron bars as in all the other gaols that David had passed through in the two and a half years since he had first been incarcerated following Ethan Mendel's murder. He had even been given the same prison number. And yet there was a change from before. He wasn't just a number any more; he was also a name: he heard it being spoken in hushed voices as he passed by his fellow prisoners in the exercise yard or sat alone in the canteen eating his food, enduring their surreptitious glances. They were fascinated by him, and yet they avoided him like he had some kind of horrible infectious disease. And David knew why: he was charged with being a two-time murderer, and if the jury convicted him he'd swing. The Angel of Death was already hovering outside the door of his cell.

For the sake of administrative convenience, the prison authorities had assigned David as a cellmate the only other remand prisoner on a capital charge in their custody. Richard Toomes, he was called, and his trial had already begun. It seemed like a formality: one Sunday morning Toomes had gone over to the house where his wife of twenty years had moved in with her boyfriend and had dispatched the pair of them to kingdom come with two blasts from his shotgun. He'd then walked calmly round the corner to the local police station, deposited the gun on the desk, and made a full confession. Now he seemed resigned to his fate. When he came back from court in the evening, he read his library book on a stool in the corner, mouthing the words silently as he picked over them one by one, and then slept peacefully through the night, snoring quietly in the bunk above David's head. Tombstone, as David had secretly nicknamed him, gave no trouble, and David envied him his peace of mind, because David did not sleep so easily. In fact, as his trial approached, he found he could hardly sleep at all. Instead he tossed and turned through the long prison nights, at the mercy of nightmares spun from his unconscious fears.

One repeated itself over and over again, coming back to attack him in the hour before dawn. He dreamt it was evening, after sunset, and he was alone in the twilight, walking along the narrow path through the woods that led from the road down to Blackwater Lake. The air was still and there was no sound, nothing except the noise of his footsteps on the ground. He could see the slender, silver-grey trunks of the pine trees arching up gracefully to make a canopy of branches overhead, but beyond them his eye couldn't penetrate the shadows of the woods on either side.

Up ahead there was a light. It was where he was going, although he didn't know why, and so he quickened his pace, frightened by the gathering silence. And now on his left he came to the lake, opening out black and wide and still under the darkening sky. He could hear the gentle lapping of the water against the stony bank, but he was looking the other way, over towards Osman's boathouse standing on its wooden pilings, set back from the path, like a prehistoric creature marooned in the trees. That was where the light was coming from – bright and white through a shut uncurtained window at the side, and, standing still, he could hear sounds – a moaning or a wailing rising and falling and returning again clearer than before. He imagined it might be the sound of a night bird crying over the lake, but he knew he was deceiving himself: it was coming from inside the boathouse.

Now he wanted to run away back the way he'd come, but the dream wouldn't permit him to turn around. Instead he was forced forward like a moth toward a flame, until, standing on his tiptoes, he looked down through the dusty window into the interior and saw what he'd seen before: Katya and Ethan naked, coupling like beasts on the floor under the unshaded electric light, turning and writhing and thrusting at each other, oblivious to the world around them. But this time it was different – they were changed somehow in a way that at first he didn't understand: their faces and their bodies were pale white and their hair was lank and they moved like automatons, and there was blood, thick dried blood, on Katya's forehead and all down Ethan's lower back.

David cried out, but his cry did not wake him from his dream; rather it alerted the dead lovers inside the boathouse to his presence. He turned to run but tripped on the uneven ground just as he regained the path, and, picking himself up, he could hear the door of the boathouse opening behind him; he could hear them on the steps coming down. He tried to run, but his legs wouldn't obey his command. He could feel them behind his shoulders now, holding him, forcing his neck down with their clammy hands. And as he fell into the cold black water of the lake, felt it close above his head, and started the struggle to breathe that he knew he couldn't win, he sensed their voices inside his head, telling him he was going to die because they were dead and that there was no coming back, no coming back at all.

Each time the dream was worse. He'd wake panting and gasping in the half light, wildly warding away his unseen assailants until, after a few moments, he'd realize where he was, hearing the steady rise and fall of Toomes's breathing above his head and the footsteps of a night guard walking on the metal landing outside their cell. And then, wiping the cold sweat from his brow, he understood why he dreamt like this about dying, why he woke before dawn with his hands encircling his neck. It was because soon now men he didn't know would come for him at just this time; they would pin his arms behind his back, tie a noose around his neck, and kill him, put an end to David Swain once and for all. And however much he struggled, there would be nothing he could do about it – nothing at all.

The days passed and his fear grew, and on the day before the start of his trial David was called from his cell for a visit. He felt nervous as he crossed the exercise yard: apart from his lawyers, it was the first visit he'd received since the policeman, Trave, had come to see him in Brixton Prison more than a year earlier, and he could not imagine who his visitor might be. His face lit up when he saw that it was his mother.

He kissed her clumsily and sat down, taking in the novelty of her appearance. Instead of the pale blue housecoat she always wore at home, she had on a charcoal-grey dress with smart shiny black shoes. David had only seen the outfit once before – at his father's funeral, when he had been too grieved to really take it in. It suited her, he thought, and he realized with a jolt that his mother had been pretty once and had a life of her own beyond caring for an unreliable husband and an unrewarding child.

He saw that she'd pinned a small brooch close to the lapel. It was nondescript – a small flower of some sort, but David found it oddly touching to think of his mother sitting in front of her dressing table at home and digging in a drawer to find this silly brooch so that she would look better for her reprobate son when she went to visit him in his London gaol.

She sat rigid and erect in her hard-backed chair but

kept her eyes down, fastened on the empty square metal table between them. David noticed how she was holding on tight to the small black handbag in her lap, and he understood with a wrench how much it must have cost his mother to come to see him in this God-forsaken place when she had spent so much of her life struggling to stay respectable.

'How was the journey?' he asked, saying the first thing that came into his head in order to break the awkward silence that had begun to build up between them since he sat down.

'It was all right,' she said nervously, putting out the half-finished cigarette that she'd been smoking when he came in. 'I haven't been to London for a long time. It's bigger than I remembered – more people.'

David saw how she darted quick looks at the other couples sitting at the adjacent tables – the men in their drab prison uniforms, the women decked out in their Sunday best. He wondered whether his mother had ever been inside a prison before – he doubted very much that she had.

'Well, thank you for coming,' he said. 'I know it can't have been easy.'

'No, it wasn't,' she said, glancing up at him for a moment before she lowered her eyes again. 'But it's the right thing to do. I should have come before. I'm sorry.'

'So you're only here because it's right, not because you wanted to come?' asked David, suddenly irritated. He had his dignity too: he didn't want to be an object of pity.

'I'm here because I want to be here,' she said quietly, holding his gaze this time. 'I told you I'm sorry.'

'All right, I'm sorry too,' said David, mollified. 'I'm glad you came. Did you tell Ben?'

'Yes; I don't tell lies. You should know that by now.'

David nodded. 'So what did he say?' he asked.

'He was angry. Shouted and swore. But he calmed down when he saw that I'd made up my mind.'

'He hates me. You know that?'

'It doesn't matter what he thinks.'

'That's not what you thought before though, was it?' said David, unable to leave the past alone. 'Why did you change your mind?'

'Because I saw you, because you came home . . .'

'And waved a gun at Ben, stole his car, terrorized Max . . .'

'Max wanted me to come,' she said. 'He wants to know that you're going to be all right, and I don't know what to say.'

There were tears in David's mother's eyes, and they tore at David inside his chest. He held on to the table hard, resisting an impulsive longing to get up and run back to his cell and shut his mother and his family out of his mind forever, because he had no words of comfort to give them, and he didn't want to think about the future or his lack of one.

'Max is a good kid,' he said, trying hard to keep his voice steady. 'He's a credit to you, Mother.'

'And you're not?'

'You know I'm not,' said David, bowing his head. 'But for what it's worth, I didn't do what they say I did. Like I told you before, I only took that gun with me to protect myself. Fat lot of good it did me,' he added bitterly.

'That's what the policeman said,' she said, nodding. 'He said you didn't commit either of those murders.'

'What policeman?'

'Inspector Trave: the one who was in charge of your case and then got taken off it when he didn't think you were guilty.'

'The one who got me caught, you mean. If I hadn't gone

to meet him in that bloody cricket pavilion I wouldn't be here,' said David angrily.

'They'd have found you in the end. You know they would. And it wasn't that inspector's fault. He didn't know they were following him when he went to St Luke's: he told me that. They've suspended him from duty for what he did. He's probably going to lose his job.'

'Well, at least he's not going to lose his life,' said David furiously, and then immediately regretted his words as he saw his mother blanch and grip on to the table for support.

'I'm sorry,' he said, reaching out and touching her clenched hand for a moment. 'It's going to be all right. I'm innocent, remember,' he added with a thin smile, trying to provide his mother with a reassurance that he didn't believe in himself. She nodded wanly in response, struggling to regain her composure.

'When did you talk to Trave?' David asked, changing the subject.

'A few days ago. He came to the house when Ben was out at work. He said he couldn't come and visit you because prosecution witnesses can't talk to a defendant but that he was going to do everything he could to help you. He wanted me to tell you that. He said he believed in you and told me that I should too.'

'Oh, so that's why you changed your mind,' said David with a knowing smile.

'No, it wasn't just that. It was seeing you too. I already said I was sorry about not coming before.'

'I know, I know,' said David, holding up his hand. 'I'm glad about Trave. Perhaps he'll find something out.'

But David wasn't holding his breath. Tomorrow his trial would begin. In two weeks or even less he would know his fate, and he couldn't see any jury acquitting him on the evidence as it stood. In less than two months he could be dead.

'I brought you clothes for your trial – a suit and two clean shirts,' said David's mother. 'They said they'd give them to you in the morning.'

'Thank you,' said David, biting his lip. He remembered his mother ironing his school uniform before the start of term at St Luke's, and now she was buying him clothes for his trial at the Old Bailey. It was too much, too painful. He was grateful to his mother for coming, but now he wanted her gone so he could escape back to the impersonal safety of his cell. He shuddered with relief when the horn sounded for the end of visits and hoped that his mother hadn't read his mind.

'Goodbye,' he said, standing up. 'Thank you for coming. Safe journey home.'

She looked at him hard as he spoke his inadequate words and then silently leant forward and took hold of both sides of his head with her hands and, reaching up, kissed him once on the centre of his forehead.

'I made you,' she said. 'They've got no right to take you away.'

And then, without another word, she turned and walked away down the hall. He watched her until she disappeared from view, but she didn't once look back.

Toomes was still at court when David got back to the cell. He lay down on his bunk and closed his eyes. His mother's visit had unsettled him, and images from the past came floating unbidden into his mind. He tried to drive them out but one remained. It was a winter afternoon nine years earlier, and he was standing by his father's open grave in a far corner of Wolvercote Cemetery. His mother was beside him wearing that same grey dress that she'd been wearing for her visit. It was cold, and a slow, heavy rain had begun to fall out of a grey, overcast sky. David was getting wet but he hardly noticed. Instead his eyes were fixed on the light brown coffin in the hole below his feet, on which the raindrops were falling one after the other – tap, tap, tapping out a steady staccato beat. Each one that fell exploded on impact, adding to the pool of water already spreading on the lid of the casket. David knew that his father was underneath that lid, dressed in a thin black suit, the same colour as David's own, and he wondered if his father was getting wet too, if he was feeling the cold.

There was a small brass plaque screwed into the centre of the coffin bearing the legend JOHN DAVID SWAIN 1900–1952. John David Swain, father of David Swain, lying in a box in a hole in the ground with the rain coming down, while his relatives looked down on him from above. *This is it*, David had thought at that moment. This was the truth – not shops and cinemas and cafés, not fleeting sensations of love or happiness, but this – rain falling on a box. Everything else was nothing more than a pretence, worse than a lie.

He'd stood there beside the grave after the funeral was over and the mourners had drifted away, until in the end there had just been him and his mother standing there side by side in the rain. Finally she'd taken his hand and tried to pull him away, but he'd silently resisted, staying where he was, until eventually she'd given up and walked round the mound of earth at the bottom of the grave and away down the path toward the car. And he'd stayed there alone with his dead father in the gathering gloom until he could hardly see the coffin any more and one of the sallow-faced undertakers had had to lead him away.

CHAPTER 19

Trave sat bent over the kitchen table with his head in his hands and ignored the telephone, which was ringing again for the third time in ten minutes. He felt like throwing it at the wall – he needed some outlet for the anger and frustration that had been boiling up inside him ever since he'd left the disciplinary hearing the day before.

There had been three of them facing him across a long table in a room with a grandstand view of Christ Church Cathedral, of all places – the chief constable in full dress uniform flanked by Creswell on one side and a Home Office lawyer on the other – a little man with bushy eyebrows brought down from London for the day to take Trave apart. And he had done exactly that. Trave had simply not been prepared for the thrusting hostility of the questions, and his answers had sounded flat and unconvincing even to himself. He'd tried several times to explain his doubts about Swain's guilt, but the lawyer had twisted his words around so that it looked like his concerns were just excuses that he'd dreamt up along the way to enable him to pursue his vendetta against Titus Osman.

The trouble was that the evidence all pointed one way. Trave couldn't deny that there had been a conflict of interest, which he had wilfully ignored in his determination to stay on the case. And he could hardly claim that that conflict had not affected the conduct of his investigation when he had chosen to make an unprovoked assault on a vital prosecution witness outside the man's house. And then, worst of all, he had disobeyed an order to stay off the case by setting up a secret meeting with the main suspect. Trave insisted that he had had no intention of assisting Swain's flight from justice, but he could see disbelief etched all over the chief constable's face. Disgust was there too, and on the chief constable's left, Creswell looked like a man in pain. The superintendent stayed silent throughout the hearing and wouldn't look Trave in the eye. It didn't bode well for the final decision, which the chief constable had reserved giving for seven days at the end of the hearing.

Trave had no idea what he would do if he lost his job. The prospect was close now, but he still refused to think about it. His mind was fixated on the Osman case. David Swain's trial had already opened up in London, and he had uncovered no new evidence on his trip to Antwerp. Jacob was nowhere to be found and probably knew nothing anyway, and Bircher, the only tenuous link between Blackwater Hall and the prison escape, was dead – written off as a jumping suicide. And yet Trave refused to give up: he read and reread the transcript of Swain's first trial until the typed words swam in front of his eyes; and in recent days he had even taken to driving aimlessly around the centre of Oxford, searching the crowd in vain for a glimpse of Aliza Mendel's grandson.

Trave went and sat down on the sofa in front of the television, making an unsuccessful attempt to distract himself from his troubles with the afternoon news. The television was a fairly new addition. Vanessa had bought it a few months after their son, Joe, died. It had helped to fill the silence, providing a buffer between their separate griefs, and Trave remembered how it had been on almost all the time in the weeks before Vanessa finally got up the courage to go. But then she didn't take the television with her when she left: it was as if she didn't need it any more now that she was making a new start. Trave wondered whether Vanessa had a television in her new home. It pained him that she had so entirely disappeared from his life that he couldn't even picture her surroundings – except that soon he would be able to again if she divorced him and moved in with Titus Osman at Blackwater Hall. Trave pressed his hands up against the sides of his head, trying in vain to suppress the images that rushed unbidden into his mind. Each one was worse than the last: Vanessa gone, Vanessa at Blackwater Hall, Vanessa reaching out for Osman's hand as she looked down at him, sprawled on the ground at Osman's feet the last time they met.

He wanted to feel sorry for himself, but he knew that his pain was self-inflicted. He had lost his wife because he hadn't been able to bring himself to comfort her in her hour of need. Instead he had spent every minute he could away from her, investigating other families' deaths as if he could solve his own problems at second hand. He might as well have taken up with another woman: he'd abandoned his wife just as thoroughly by working day and night at his stupid job. It seemed poetic justice that he was now about to lose the job after all these years and would end up alone and unemployed in this big empty house that he'd tried so hard to get away from before.

The doorbell rang. It was an unusual sound, particularly on a Sunday, and it made Trave jump. Since Joe's death and Vanessa's departure, there were hardly any callers at 17 Hill Road apart from an occasional Jehovah's Witness and the man who read the gas meter once a month, and he always came in the mornings. Trave thought of ignoring the bell in the same way as he had the telephone, but almost immediately it rang again, insistently this time. Whoever it was knew he was at home – the sound of the television must have betrayed his presence. Unwillingly, Trave got up and opened the door. Clayton was standing on the step, shivering even though he was wearing an overcoat.

'What do you want?' asked Trave. There was no hint of welcome in his voice: entertaining a visitor was the last thing he felt like at that moment.

'To get out of this bloody cold,' said Clayton, stamping his feet and rubbing his hands together to indicate his distress.

'All right, you better come in,' said Trave, reluctantly standing aside to let Clayton pass. 'I warn you – I'm in no mood for company.'

'I know that: I rang you three times and you didn't pick up. Did the hearing go badly?'

'Worse than badly,' said Trave bitterly. 'Bloody chief constable's getting ready to give me the boot.'

'I'm sorry about that,' said Clayton, looking worried. 'I wouldn't have come over here if it wasn't urgent.'

'What's urgent?' asked Trave, starting for the first time to show some interest in the reason for Clayton's visit.

'I found Jacob. I know where he's living.' Clayton made his announcement like a conjuror producing a rabbit from a hat, and it had the desired effect. Trave was open-mouthed for a moment, unable to believe his ears. He'd given Clayton Aliza's photograph of her grandson soon after his return from Antwerp. Jacob's face was already imprinted on his memory, and Trave calculated that an active policeman would have a better chance of tracking Jacob down than one who was suspended from duty, but it was a long shot, and he hadn't really expected anything to come of it. Trave knew that Clayton was answerable to Macrae, who had no interest in any further investigation of the Katya Osman case now that he had Swain's trial under way, and Trave also had no evidence that Jacob was actually in Oxford: it was only a hunch based on Aliza's account of her grandson's fixation on Katya's uncle.

'How did you find him?' asked Trave once he'd recovered his self-possession. 'Where is he?'

'He's in a one-bed flat off the Iffley Road. He's living there under the name Edward Newman, which is kind of an appropriate alias, given he's got himself a completely new look since that photograph you gave me was taken. He's grown a beard and wears jeans and a leather jacket these days. Oh, and he's got glasses too now, like you said he might, but don't worry – I'm sure it's our man. I found him because of what you said about him being obsessed with Titus Osman. I thought: What do obsessed people do? Answer: They watch the people they're obsessed with. So I went out to Blackwater a couple of times last week and walked along the path by the boathouse and drew a complete blank. And I was just about to give up on the idea when I got lucky: today was going to be my last visit in fact . . .'

'Got lucky how?' asked Trave, unable to contain his impatience.

'There was a scooter hidden in the undergrowth on the other side of the fence from the road, and there he was at the end of the path that goes through the woods, just where it opens out onto the big lawn across from the side of Osman's house. He was standing behind a tree, looking up at the house through a pair of binoculars.'

'Did he see you?'

'No. I'm good at moving quietly – I always won at hide-and-seek when I was a kid,' said Clayton with a smile. 'I just went back to my car, moved it away out of sight, and waited; and then, when he came back to the road, I followed him home, which was the difficult part, given he was on a Vespa and I was driving. They don't teach that at training school.'

'No, they don't,' agreed Trave. He looked his former assistant up and down and nodded once as if pleased with what he saw. 'You've done damn well, Adam. I'm proud of you,' he said, looking Clayton in the eye.

Clayton flushed with pleasure. It was the biggest compliment he'd ever received from Trave, and he filed it away carefully in his mind, intending to savour it when he was next alone. Recent events had done nothing to dent his admiration for his former boss, and sometimes he worried that his affection for Trave and his visceral dislike of Macrae were affecting his own judgement. The trouble was that Clayton couldn't make up his mind about the case. He balanced the heavy weight of the evidence incriminating David Swain against his gnawing concerns about what had happened on the night after Swain's arrest, remembering the passive, deflated way Swain had confessed to Katya's murder, like he was some kind of automaton. And, try as he might, Clayton couldn't form a mental picture of Swain going out into Oxford when he was on the run to buy blank ammunition for his gun, just so he'd look innocent when he was caught. Surely Swain would have been too desperate, too frightened to come up with such a plan, let alone carry it out. But that didn't change the fact that Swain was the one with the motive and the opportunity to kill Katya. He'd been right there at the murder scene, just like he had been when Ethan was stabbed down by the lake. Every day, every night, Clayton went back and forth in his mind. The only thing he was sure of was that he wanted to know more. And maybe Jacob would be able to tell them something . . .

'Have you told Macrae about this?' asked Trave.

'No, of course not,' said Clayton, sounding surprised.

'Are you going to?'

'No, why would I do that?'

'Because you're working for him now, and so it's your duty to tell him.'

'Well, if I tell Macrae, he'll find some excuse to get hold of Jacob and put him somewhere neither of us will ever find him, or at least not until Swain's trial is over and it's too late. The Blackwater case is Macrae's pride and joy, you know. He guards it like it's his private property. And he doesn't trust me with it any more for some reason. My role's limited to giving evidence next week. That's why I've been able to go on all these joyrides out to Osman's boathouse.'

'I wonder what Jacob was doing out there,' said Trave musingly.

'I don't know. Let's go and ask him,' said Clayton. 'That's why I'm here, isn't it?'

Trave nodded, smiling for what seemed like the first time in weeks. 'You'd better drive,' he said. 'You're the one who knows where we're going.'

They arrived outside 78 Divinity Road ten minutes later. Clayton was driving his own car since it was a Sunday, and they parked right across the street from Jacob's house. It was a residential neighbourhood that had clearly seen better days. The tall, narrow nineteenth-century houses that had once been home to affluent families had been split up into small one-bedroom flats after the war, and 78 was in no better or worse condition than its neighbours. Some of the paint was peeling from the stucco, particularly around the portico under which Trave and Clayton were now standing, and above their heads several electric wires hung loose where there had once been an outside light. A few pieces of washing were hanging from a makeshift clothesline rigged up inside the wrought-iron balcony that ran the length of the first floor, and the white garments flapped to and fro occasionally in the intermittent wind like a row of disconsolate ghosts, but there was otherwise no sign that anyone was at home. The sun had set and the last of its light was beginning to fade from the sky, but there were no lights on in any of the windows.

To Trave's right, there were five doorbells with a handwritten name beside each one, and Edward Newman proclaimed himself in neat capital letters as the occupant of Number 5.

'How do you know he's Newman?' asked Trave.

'Because 5's obviously the top flat, and I saw him in the window at the top of the house a couple of minutes after he got back. And I don't think he's Fiona Jane Taylor, who lives in Number 4.'

Trave nodded. 'All right, let's go and talk to him,' he said, and rang the bell. They waited for nearly a minute, but there was no response, and so Trave tried again, pushing the bell longer and harder this time. Still nothing happened. The building remained dead to the world, and behind them an empty brown paper bag blowing this way and that across the deserted street was the only sign of life.

'Makes my road look like the West End of London,' said Trave, blowing on his hands to keep them from going numb.

Clayton laughed. 'I doubt he's gone far,' he said. 'We can come back.'

'You can,' said Trave. 'I'm going in.'

'You're what?' said Clayton, unable to believe his ears. 'You haven't got a search warrant.'

'And I'm not exactly likely to get one, am I? A suspended policeman about to get his marching orders – I carry about as much weight as a wet rag, and you can't do anything official without Macrae's say-so. No, I'm not really too worried about doing things by the book any more, Adam, to be honest with you. You'd better get used to it if you want to stick around me. People are dead and a boy's likely to swing for something he never did; so I'm going to do whatever I have to do to get at the truth. And right now that means breaking into this flat. I'd like to see what Mr Newman-Mendel's got up there before he comes back. Are you coming or not?'

Clayton knitted his brows, looking undecided, but then

suddenly laughed out loud, infected by Trave's mood of recklessness.

'What the hell,' he said. 'I'm in.'

'Good,' said Trave. 'Have you got something plastic or a piece of wire?'

Clayton had neither, but the penknife attached to his key chain proved sufficient to get them through both the front door and the door to flat Number 5, which they reached at the top of three steep flights of uncarpeted stairs. Jacob had obviously just pulled the latch shut when he left – the mortice lock further down the door had been left open. Now the two policemen stood in a narrow hallway running the length of the flat with two doors opening on either side. On the right there was a small kitchen with an old stove, a half-empty fridge, and a low shelf on which various packets with labels from a kosher grocery in the centre of town were displayed in a line. And beyond the kitchen on the same side a sparsely furnished bedroom contained only a narrow iron bed made up with sheet, blanket, and pillow tucked tight together with military precision; a small night table; and a heavy mahogany wardrobe in which Jacob's clothes hung pressed and ready for use on a line of wire hangers. Everything was neat and orderly. It was like a monk's cell, thought Trave: all that was missing was a cross over the bed, but that of course was hardly likely, given that the occupant was a Zionist Jew.

The windows on this side of the flat looked across to the back of a row of similar houses in the next street which were illuminated by a few lights here and there, and down below, in the gathering gloom, the policemen could make out the outlines of a few straggly bushes in the house's disused garden surrounding the shape of what looked like an old Anderson air-raid shelter from World War II that stuck up out of the ground with a humped earthen back like some kind of stranded primeval creature. There was no one in sight and no sound from the floors below.

Leaving the bedroom, they crossed over to the other side of the corridor, to a tiny bathroom and toilet and, next to it, the living room, by far the largest room in the flat. It was twilight now and the soaring spires of the city churches were visible as silhouetted shadows on the skyline outside the window, but inside the room it was almost dark. Here they were at the front of the house, and they knew they could not risk turning on the light since it would have been visible to Jacob on his return if he chanced to look up from the road down below, but Trave had thought to bring a torch, and now he turned it on, circling the beam of light as they took in their surroundings. There was a rectangular pine table in the centre of the room covered with papers. A single chair was tucked into its side, and over by the window a button-back blue armchair faced a small television. The only other pieces of furniture were a large free-standing bookcase in the far corner stuffed to overflowing with books, files, and magazines and, beside it, a tall metal filing cabinet. But up above, all four walls were entirely covered with photographs, newspaper articles, maps, and diagrams so that the place felt like a miniature war room. It was a sinister place, Clayton thought – full and yet empty all at the same time. He had the sense that the man who lived in this room was driven, dedicated – someone who would stop at nothing to do what he had set out to do.

Now Trave focused his torch on the faces looking down at them from the photographs on the walls: David Swain peering out from one of the wanted posters that had gone up around the city after Katya's murder; Eddie Earle in profile – a snapshot inset in an article describing the escape from Oxford Prison; Titus Osman, dressed in a dinner jacket speaking at a charity function the previous month; and, in the centre of the opposite wall, above two photographs of Blackwater Hall, a triptych of blown-up pictures of a man who was unmistakably a younger version of Franz Claes, albeit with no disfiguring scar below his left ear. In the first he was wearing a military uniform, standing on a raised platform in front of a microphone, addressing a crowd. There was a banner above his head emblazoned with big black gothic lettering. It looked like Dutch, and neither Trave nor Clayton could understand a word of it, but at the bottom of the picture 'Flemish National Union 1938' was written in neat letters. Trave wondered for a moment at Jacob's use of English to annotate the picture, but then realized it made sense. Aliza had said that her grandson had inherited her facility with languages, and if Jacob Mendel was going to become Edward Newman, then he would need to immerse himself in his new identity even when he was alone.

In the next picture, the one in the centre, Claes was on the far left of a row of official-looking men in suits seated behind a long table facing two other men in skullcaps who were wearing the Star of David on their jackets. Again there was a handwritten inscription underneath – 'Meeting of Security Police with AJB – Antwerp, July 1942.' But it was the third picture that was the most striking. Here Claes stood between two other men outside some kind of government building. Claes was still in a suit, but his companions were in German uniform, and underneath Jacob had written in thick capital letters: 'Asche, Claes, Ehlers – Sipo SD, Brussels – August 1943 – Last Picture?'

Trave caught Clayton's eye and whistled softly under his breath, but he didn't speak, remaining intent on his inspection of the room. Now his torch was shining on a large map of Europe with a series of coloured lines stretching out west and south from tiny Belgium like an octopus's tentacles.

They were obviously escape routes, thought Trave – ones along which people had got away and ones where they had been caught and sent to the transit camp at Mechelen, and then east. Like Jacob's parents. There was a picture of them with their two sons on the mantelpiece above the gas fire – a framed studio portrait taken when Ethan and Jacob were children. The boys were wearing tweed suits with knee breeches and stood posed on either side of their mother, who was seated, wearing a long ankle-length black dress with her husband standing behind her with his hand on her shoulder. Their expressions were rigid, formal, but the parents' touch was natural – enough for Trave to know that Avi Mendel and his wife had loved each other once years ago, before they were murdered. Trave closed his eyes thinking of the millions of other victims. It was incomprehensible. Photographs were the only way to begin to understand the horror, he thought, with sudden insight – to make some small sense of the meaningless numbers.

Clayton had been standing by the window, dividing his attention between following Trave's torch beam as it travelled across the walls and keeping watch on the pavement down below, which was lit by a nearby street light; but now, as Trave remained immobile, lost in thought, Clayton became impatient and took the torch from Trave's hand and began to look through the pile of papers on the table in the centre of the room. One by one he turned them over: correspondence; cut-out newspaper reports on Swain's trial, including several describing its opening at the Old Bailey the previous Wednesday; a handwritten document listing possible prosecution witnesses marked with crossings out and question marks – Clayton noticed that his name and Trave's had been left unamended; a letter from two months earlier confirming Edward Newman's membership of a local rifle-shooting club; a tenancy agreement for the flat dating from the previous May, this time in the name of Jacob Mendel . . .

'Something must have happened. Jacob changed his name after he got here,' said Clayton, showing Trave the document.

'Yes, can't you guess?' Trave paused, but Clayton shook his head. 'He's our burglar, Adam. The one who broke into Osman's study last summer and had a boxing match with our Nazi friend over there,' said Trave, pointing to the pictures of Claes on the opposite wall. 'There's a pair of glasses in the bedroom, and I'd bet my house they'll turn out to be a match for the ones he left behind at Blackwater. I don't suppose you'll have much choice but to take him in now, Macrae or no Macrae.'

Clayton was about to respond, but the words died in his throat. There was the unmistakable sound of a key being fitted in the front door of the flat, and Clayton cursed himself for having abandoned his watch on the pavement down below. Instinctively the two policemen flattened themselves against the wall on either side of the open door to the living room and waited, holding their breath.

CHAPTER 20

The light went on in the hall, footsteps approached, and Jacob cried out as Trave seized him from behind, shouting 'police' as he did so. But the young man's reactions were quicker than Trave had anticipated. He twisted his body violently to the left, throwing Trave off balance, and then slammed his right arm back, catching Trave a glancing blow on the side of the face, sufficient to make Trave let go of his jacket. And then he took off, running back down the corridor, pulling open the front door of the flat, and taking the stairs three at a time. Clayton set off in pursuit, but Jacob had a head start and would certainly have got away if he'd taken the time to turn on the upper landing light before he began his mad descent of the stairs. Instead he lost his footing in the dark, two flights down, and fell head over heels down the remaining steps, ending up in a heap on the floor of the entrance hall.

By the time he regained consciousness, the lights were on and Clayton and Trave were standing over him, barring his way to the door. Slowly he got to his feet, rubbing his head, and gingerly took a few steps towards a suspicious-looking old lady who had emerged from the ground-floor flat at the other end of the hall.

'It's all right, Mrs Harris,' he said, speaking in fluent English. 'Nothing to worry about – just a silly accident, that's all.'

The old lady looked unimpressed by the explanation. She peered distrustfully at the strangers by the door, and then retreated back inside her flat, closing the door. A moment later there was the sound of a key turning in the lock.

'What the hell do you want?' asked Jacob furiously, turning back to face the two policemen.

'To talk to you. About Blackwater Hall and your brother, Ethan Mendel,' said Trave calmly.

'I don't know what you're talking about. I'm Edward Newman. My name's on the doorbell out there, if you can be bothered to look.'

'Please don't waste our time,' said Trave evenly. 'You're Jacob Mendel. I recognize you from when you gave evidence at the Old Bailey two and a half years ago. And you probably know who I am too, judging from the interest you've been taking in Mr Swain's new trial.'

There was the glint of recognition in Jacob's eyes, but Jacob said nothing, continuing to glower at Trave and Clayton as if trying to work out a strategy for a second escape attempt.

'We can talk down here,' said Trave, 'or upstairs. Personally I'd prefer upstairs. But it's up to you.'

Jacob appeared to hesitate, and then, to Clayton's surprise, he turned and began slowly climbing the stairs, keeping hold of the banister for support. The policemen followed at a cautious distance behind, and then, once they were back in the living room, Jacob pulled out the chair and sat down heavily at the table with his hands folded in front of him, watching silently as Trave turned on the light and then went over to the armchair by the window. Clayton took up position in the doorway on Jacob's other side, barring his route of escape.

'I went to Antwerp to see your grandmother,' said Trave, opening the conversation. 'She's worried about you, wants to know where you are.'

'Well, you can tell her you found me and that I'm all

291

right,' said Jacob with finality, as if there was nothing more to say.

'Why don't you tell her yourself? She's an old lady and she loves you – she told me you're her last living relative.'

'She's old and she's blind,' Jacob burst out angrily. 'Wilfully blind – she believes in Titus Osman and all his lies. Just like Ethan did, and I don't want to hear any more of that.'

'Well, you won't from me,' said Trave quietly. 'I've lost my job over Osman, but I think you already know that, don't you?' he added, pointing up at a newsapaper cutting sellotaped to the wall, describing David Swain's arrest and Trave's suspension from duty. 'We're on the same side, you and I. Why do you say Ethan believed in Osman?'

'Because he had to have done. He wrote me that letter from Munich about finding out something vital and then flew back to England and went straight to see Osman. He wouldn't have done that if he didn't believe in Osman, would he? He'd found out something that affected Osman – that's why he wanted to talk to him, but it wasn't something that shook his faith in the bastard. If it had, he'd be alive today,' said Jacob bitterly. He spoke in a rush, as if relieved to finally have an outlet for the thoughts that had obsessed him for so long.

'And you think that that something he found out was about Franz Claes?' asked Trave, looking over at Claes's photographs on the wall.

'Yes. Who else? Claes was Osman's contact in the secret police. That's how Osman got Jews out, or got them caught.'

'All right, so what you're saying is that Ethan found out something incriminating about Claes and told Osman, who killed Ethan because of it and then set up David Swain to take the blame? Is that right?' asked Trave, speaking slowly as he put the pieces together.

'Yes, exactly right. It's the truth,' said Jacob passionately.

292

'I know it is. I just can't prove it – that's all. Claes is the key. I can show he was involved in Belgian fascist politics before the war; that he was invalided out of the Belgian army after the German invasion and went to work for the interior ministry; that he had dealings with the AJB, the Jewish Council; and that he was involved with the secret police . . .'

'Sipo SD?' asked Trave, pointing over at the photograph of Claes with the two men in German uniforms.

'Yes. Ernst Ehlers, the man on the right, was in charge of the Gestapo in Belgium, and the other one, Kurt Asche, was head of its anti-Jewish department, but Claes was always behind them in the shadows. I don't know what he did. And what I've got on him isn't enough. I'm not sure that it's even a crime; it's certainly not enough of a secret to kill people for. No, the information Ethan discovered was in West Germany, not Belgium, and in Germany I've found nothing. But it's there. I know it is,' said Jacob, making no effort to conceal his frustration.

'Why?' asked Trave. 'Why are you so certain?'

'Because Claes disappeared in late 1943 – just after my parents got arrested at the French border, in fact, although I don't know if there's a connection. And then there's no trace of him until he turns up here a couple of years after the war, living the good life with Titus Osman. But that's not all. He's a man without a beginning as well. There's no record of him or his sister in Belgium before 1931, when he joined the army – no birth certificate, nothing. He came from somewhere else – where I don't know. Maybe he went back to wherever it was in 1943.'

'To Germany?'

'Yes, maybe. But there's no trace of him there or anywhere else in Europe that I can find. And in Belgium I've been to every office and read every document that I can lay my

293

hands on, but I need authority to go further, and it doesn't make it any easier that there's no appetite for investigating the occupation in my country. They want to look forward, not back. I think it's because a lot of them collaborated with the Nazis. Belgian police helped with the round-ups, you know. Just like in France.'

Jacob's bitterness was obvious, and Clayton, watching from over by the door, thought that Jacob was the first real fanatic that he'd ever met. Silent at first, Jacob now couldn't stop talking – it was like a dam had burst, releasing the rage and frustration that had built up inside him through the long, lonely months he'd spent in this room cutting up newspapers and feeding his obsession with Titus Osman, who was almost certainly an entirely innocent man. If Claes had committed the murders in order to conceal his criminal past, then there was no reason he hadn't acted alone or with his peculiar sister. Jacob was even more obsessed with Osman than Trave, thought Clayton. He remembered the shooting-club document he'd seen on the table earlier and wondered uneasily if Jacob had a gun.

'What were you doing out at Blackwater today?' Clayton asked, speaking for the first time. 'I saw you in the woods watching the house.'

Jacob swung round to look at Clayton, and the hostility was back in his eyes.

'I was looking,' he said. 'That's all.'

'But you broke in there last summer, didn't you, and had a fight with Claes? Is that why you changed your name? In case he came looking for you? Or the police did?'

Jacob glowered at Clayton and then turned back to Trave. 'Who's he?' he demanded angrily. 'Does he work for that man who's taken over from you – Macrae?'

'He's with me,' said Trave. 'And there's no point pretending it wasn't you. Your glasses in the bedroom match the ones

Claes knocked off your nose. You broke into Blackwater Hall because you wanted to find evidence against Osman, didn't you? I'd probably have done the same in your shoes.'

Jacob looked defiant, saying nothing.

'So what did you do when breaking in didn't work?' Trave pressed. 'What did you do next?'

'I talked to Katya,' said Jacob flatly.

'Yes,' said Trave quietly. 'I thought you might have done.' He put his hand up to his face and turned away, looking out through the window into the darkness. The image of Katya dead pushed up at him from where it always lay, frozen just beneath the surface of his consciousness with all the other horrors that he tried to keep shut out of his conscious mind. Again he saw her long blonde hair trailing across the pillow, her sunken cheeks, her beautiful, empty eyes. She'd died because she'd found something out, because Jacob Mendel had asked her to look, because he hadn't had the courage to go in there again himself. A wave of hatred for Jacob shook Trave for a moment, but then with an effort of will he pushed it away, clearing his mind of emotion.

'I wish I hadn't,' said Jacob, sensing the accusation in Trave's silence. 'God knows I feel responsible for what happened to her. And to Swain – I've sent his lawyers copies of everything I've got on Claes, but I don't know if it'll make any difference . . .'

'Tell me what happened with Katya,' said Trave, ignoring Jacob's attempt to change the subject. 'Maybe you'll feel better if you get it off your chest.'

'I'd met her at Ethan's funeral, and so she knew who I was,' said Jacob, speaking slowly as if the words were hard to get out. 'We sat in a café down the road from here, and I showed her the photographs of Claes. I told her everything, and she went white, whiter than I've ever seen anyone – white and silent. And then she believed. Just like she believed it was David Swain before. Because that's what she was like – she was passionate, overflowing with emotion. And beautiful too – I understood why Ethan had loved her. And I didn't even have to ask her to look, you know. She said she would – in Osman's bedroom, in Claes's bedroom – places I could never hope to get at. She called me a week later at the time we'd agreed on. She said she hadn't found anything, but not to give up because she hadn't finished searching. And then, after that, I heard nothing until . . . until she died.'

'How long? How long did you hear nothing?' asked Trave.

'Three or four weeks. I don't know. She told me that I'd have to be patient, and there was no way I could contact her without attracting Osman's suspicion. Don't you think I regret it now?' said Jacob angrily.

'Yes, I'm sure you do,' said Trave. 'But breaking into Blackwater Hall won't help.'

'How do you know? Katya found something. That's why they killed her.'

'And if she found something, they've already got rid of it a long time ago,' said Trave. 'You're clutching at straws.'

'Maybe. But that's better than doing nothing – like you,' said Jacob angrily. 'This is the end game, don't you see?' he went on passionately. 'If Swain is convicted of Katya's murder, if he's executed for it, then they've won. They'll have got away with everything.'

'Then you need to give evidence at his trial. Sending Swain's lawyers copies of old pictures of Claes isn't enough. You know that,' said Trave, pointing up at the documents covering the walls. 'You need to tell the jury that you asked Katya to search. Without that they've got no connection between Claes and Katya.'

'But the connection's not enough,' said Jacob. 'Like I told you before, hiding what I've dug up isn't worth killing for.

I need more. That's why I asked Katya to look, for God's sake.'

'The jurors will still need to hear from you. Without you they won't understand why she was vulnerable in that house,' said Trave urgently.

'Assuming they believe me,' said Jacob. It was obvious from his tone that he didn't believe they would.

'Try them. Maybe they will.'

But Jacob didn't rise to the challenge. 'I know what you're saying,' he said with a sigh – 'don't think I haven't thought about going to court, still think about it all the time, but if I give evidence, Osman and Claes will know who I am, and I won't last long after that.'

'They probably do already, and anyway it's a chance you'll have to take,' said Trave. 'You owe Katya that much.'

'I owe her everything. And that's why I can't let them find me. I can't let them succeed. I have to stop them.'

'They – you keep saying they,' said Clayton, unable to contain his irritation. He didn't like Jacob, he realized – didn't like the man's melodrama, his certainty that he knew best. 'You've got no evidence whatsoever against Osman that I can see. Just guilt by association. Why couldn't Claes have been acting alone – if he acted at all?'

'Because he wasn't – my brother died because he spoke to Osman . . .'

'You don't know that. Maybe he talked to Claes that afternoon after he saw Osman,' said Clayton, interrupting. 'Didn't you just say five minutes ago that whatever your brother dug up in West Germany had nothing to do with Osman because, if it had, Ethan wouldn't have rushed back to have lunch with him? You can't have it both ways.'

'I'm not trying to,' said Jacob angrily. 'You're just twisting my words. Claes couldn't have kept Katya a prisoner without Osman . . .'

'Yes, but that doesn't mean Osman killed her. He told us he was keeping Katya at Blackwater for her own good when we talked to him, and we've got independent evidence that that much is true,' said Clayton, glancing over at Trave, who refused to meet his eye.

'You don't see because you don't want to see,' said Jacob, looking over at Clayton with obvious hostility. 'The two of them – they're in it together: they have been from the start. Osman targeted my family; he planned the whole thing. He knew my father was wealthy – he'd dealt with him lots of times at the Antwerp diamond exchange before the war, and he knew that my father had hidden most of his diamonds when the Nazis came, just like the other Jewish traders did. He got me and my brother out of Belgium because he knew he had to get my parents to trust him with their escape. And the plan worked – my parents must have had at least half their fortune sewn into their clothes when Claes met them at the border. And sent them to Mechelen. Do you know about Mechelen, Inspector?' Jacob asked, turning to Trave.

'Yes, your grandmother told me,' said Trave quietly.

'But you didn't go there, did you? You didn't see it?' Trave shook his head. 'I thought not. It doesn't look like anything nowadays – just an old barracks near the railway line with a big enclosed courtyard in the middle. The Belgian army use it as an officer training school. A school – can you believe it? And there's nothing there except a tiny plaque to say what it was, when there should be a monument, the biggest bloody monument in Belgium to stop them forgetting. They shouldn't be allowed to forget . . .'

Jacob broke off, drawing deep breaths to control his anger. And when he resumed speaking, it was in a new, flat, expressionless tone, as if he knew that this was the only way that he could safely talk about the past.

'The commandant there was called Schmitt – Philip Schmitt. He was a sadist – strip-searched the women himself when they arrived and used his big alsation on the prisoners. One of them died from bites. But he was the only one who did. People didn't die in Mechelen. They needed them alive to make up the numbers for the trains. It was easy at first – the Jews reported to the camp themselves, called up for forced labour in the east, and the SS was sending out two trains a week. But then rumours got out about what was really waiting at the other end of the line, and the Jews went into hiding. The Nazis started doing round-ups, night arrests, but still there were fewer Jews coming into Mechelen than before, and so they had to wait until there were enough of them for a convoy. My parents had to wait two months, Inspector. I don't know if they knew where they were going – I pray in my heart that they didn't, but in my head I know they did. And yet they must have hoped, hoped right up to the end that they weren't going where they feared they were going, that they would survive.'

Jacob broke off, looking out into the darkness outside the window, as if he was trying to search back into the past.

'The SS used third-class passenger carriages at first when they began the deportations in 1942,' he went on again after a moment, 'but then people started jumping out of the windows, and so they switched to goods wagons – seventy Jews locked in each truck for two or three days with no food, no water, almost no ventilation, and at the end – the end of the world. Screaming and shouting and barbed wire and arc lights and dogs and . . . and . . .'

'You don't need to tell us this. You don't have to,' said Trave. 'We understand . . .'

'No, you don't. You don't understand,' Jacob interrupted passionately. 'The selections were done straight away at the end of the platform. You probably know that – right to the camp, left to the gas. And my parents – they were split up. My father was selected to live; my mother to die. And so that was their last moment – being dragged apart in that terrible place. I see it through his eyes; I see it through her eyes. On and on and on forever.'

'How do you know this?' asked Trave. 'Your grandmother didn't say . . .'

'I didn't tell her. She's suffered enough – why should she have to live with that knowledge? I found it out from the SS records – the Germans kept lists of everything. That was their way. Both my parents were on the convoy when it left Mechelen, but only my father's name was recorded as entering the camp. And he lasted six months and two weeks – about average for someone of his age – before he went to the gas as well. People didn't survive. It's a myth to say they did. Twenty-five thousand Jews went from Mechelen to Auschwitz in two years, from 1942 to 1944, and a thousand came back; and then no one wanted to hear what they had to say. No one except people like me – orphaned children who'd been hidden or escaped. And it's up to us to make devils like Claes and Osman pay for what they did to our people – even if you gentiles won't.'

'What do you mean by that?' asked Clayton, stirring. He was still standing by the door, continuing to bar Jacob's only possible route of escape.

'I mean you, Detective Whatever Your Name Is,' said Jacob, half-spitting out his words as he fixed Clayton with a hostile glare. 'You seem a lot more interested in me breaking into Blackwater Hall last summer than what those bastards have been doing in there. That's what I mean.'

'Burglary's a crime,' said Clayton, riled. 'And you've got no proof against Osman, or Claes either for that matter. We don't punish people without proof – not in this country.'

'Proof!' said Jacob with an angry laugh. 'Like the proof

300

that you police are using against that poor bastard, Swain, up in London just so that you can hang him for something he never did? I won't let them get away with it, I tell you. I won't let them win – proof or no proof.'

'No one's above the law,' said Trave softly. 'If you've got something else on Claes or Osman, show it to us. I promise you that I want to find evidence against them as much as you do.'

Jacob gave Trave a long, searching look and then glanced back at Clayton. He looked like he was weighing something up in his mind. 'Okay,' he said, as if coming to a final decision. 'I'll show you what else I have.' He got up from his chair and crossed over to the filing cabinet in the corner, using a key on his ring to unlock it. He opened the middle drawer all the way and bent down over it as if searching for something. Suddenly, too late, Clayton sensed what was happening. He rushed toward Jacob but then stopped dead in his tracks as the young man turned round to face him with a revolver gripped in his hand.

'I know where you want to take me,' Jacob said slowly, speaking to Clayton now, not Trave. 'You want to lock me up for that burglary so I don't try it again and take a gun with me this time. Maybe you're right: I've reached the end of my tether and I'll stop at nothing now – nothing.

'Now get over there with the inspector. I'll use this thing if I have to.'

Clayton didn't know whether he believed Jacob, but he wasn't going to put his doubts to the test. Keeping his eyes fixed on the revolver, he edged across the room to join Trave by the window.

Powerless, the two policemen watched as Jacob pulled out a rucksack from behind the filing cabinet. It was already packed, and they realized that Jacob must have been prepared for this day for a long time.

'You're making a mistake,' said Trave. 'Can't you see I want to help you?'

'Yes, maybe you do, although I don't trust him,' said Jacob, indicating Clayton with a wave of his gun. 'But it doesn't matter what you want any more. You've had your chance and you achieved nothing – just got David Swain arrested for something he never did. Osman played you just like he played my father, and now he's got your pretty wife on his arm and my family's diamonds in the bank.'

'What are you going to do?' asked Trave.

'Do? I'm going to do whatever it takes to bring them to justice – I promise you that, Inspector,' said Jacob. He sounded as if he was taking an oath. 'Now I'm going to lock you both in,' he said, backing away toward the door. 'Don't come after me or I'll shoot. I don't want to, but I will.'

He turned out the light and closed the door, and moments later the two policemen heard the front door of the flat closing and a key turning in the lock.

They crossed over to the window and the pale moonlight illuminated their tired, impotent faces as they watched Jacob getting on his scooter down below. He turned on the engine and rode away into the darkness without once looking back.

CHAPTER 21

Jacob had double-locked the door as he left, and it took Trave and Clayton a lot longer to get out of the flat than it had taken to get in. There was no telephone, and hammering on the locked door brought no response from any of the neighbours, and so they had to resort to taking it in turns to shout for help down into the empty street. Lights went on in the neighbouring houses, but it was still a maddeningly long time before people appeared below the window, and then there was a further delay while they had to satisfy a would-be rescuer that they were law enforcers and not lawbreakers. Eventually, however, a ladder appeared out of the darkness and the two policemen were able to climb down to the ground.

Clayton already had his car running by the time Trave had pressed a pound note into the hand of the ladder's owner and had joined him, taking the passenger seat, and Clayton wasted no time in heading off.

'To Blackwater?' he asked, glancing at his companion.

'Yes, you heard Jacob,' said Trave with a sigh. 'That's where he's going. Maybe not tonight, but sooner rather than later. He's convinced himself that there's vital evidence somewhere in the house, and he won't rest until he's found it, although personally I think it's a wild-goose chase. If there was anything, Osman would have got rid of it at the same time he got rid of Katya. No, the evidence exists; it's just somewhere else. That's all.'

'How can you be so sure?' asked Clayton. He'd heard nothing in the flat to convince him that Osman had had anything to do with his niece's murder. Claes was a different matter.

Trave started to respond, but his voice was drowned out by the wail of a police-car siren coming toward them down the other side of the road. For a moment its blue flashing lights illuminated the darkness, and then it was gone.

'I know where they're going,' said Trave with a smile. 'Someone obviously thought we were up to no good back there. Probably that old woman in the ground-floor flat. She's certainly had a day to remember.'

'What do you think Jacob's intending to do with that gun?' asked Clayton nervously, wishing that the police car was following them out to Blackwater Hall instead of heading uselessly over to Jacob's empty flat. Right now they needed all the help they could get.

'Well, I don't think he's going to kill anyone with it, if that's what you're worried about,' said Trave with quiet confidence. 'Not unless Claes fires at him first, and I honestly don't think Jacob's looking for that kind of confrontation. He could have shot Osman and Claes a long time ago if he'd wanted to, but instead he's spent every minute of every day going round Europe searching for evidence against them, because it's justice he's after, not some clandestine murder in the dark.'

'Well, I hope you're right. But whatever he's got in mind, we need to warn the people at the Hall. They've got a right to know,' said Clayton, glancing anxiously at his watch. It was six o'clock already, and Jacob would easily have got to Blackwater by now if that was where he'd gone. Once again Clayton cursed his stupidity for having allowed their prisoner to get away and pressed his foot down hard on the accelerator, trying in vain to extract a little more speed from his old second-hand car.

Trave said nothing, and they passed the rest of the journey in an uneasy silence.

Jacob stood motionless in the darkness with his back to a tall pine tree on the edge of the woods that bordered the wide lawns surrounding Osman's house. The wind had died down since the afternoon but still blew softly through the trees, and overhead the crescent moon peeped out intermittently from behind a veil of clouds, shedding a pale light down onto the well-tended grass. About two hundred yards away the Hall was a great shadowed shape lit here and there by pricks of electric light. The minutes passed and nothing happened, but Jacob showed no sign of impatience. His face was impassive, giving no clue to the feverish workings of his brain.

The Swain trial had already been running for three days, and Jacob had confidently expected Claes and his sister and Osman to go to London to give evidence on the Friday, two days earlier. They hadn't, but the newspaper yesterday had reported that preliminary legal arguments were over and that the live evidence would begin on Monday. And until his unexpected encounter with the police, Jacob had calculated on the three of them being gone for the day, giving him the opportunity to quietly break into the house and search it at his leisure. Osman was a collector, a keeper of trophies – there would be evidence somewhere of his crimes. Jacob was sure of it.

But now the situation was out of his control. Trave might not want to stand in his way, but the other policeman certainly would, and a locked door would not keep them imprisoned in his flat for very long. On his arrival fifteen minutes earlier Jacob had climbed up into the trees and cut the telephone line running from the road up to the Hall, and now all he could do was wait and see what happened next.

Jacob cursed himself yet again for having come out here

earlier in the day. There was no need for it. Monday was going to be his opportunity, and if he'd stayed home that young detective would never have found him. But there was no point regretting his mistake. What was done was done. The house drew him like a magnet – that was the problem. Tonight he would sleep in the boathouse. It was the place where he felt closest to his brother – it was where Ethan had been happy and where he had died, murdered in cold blood by those two bastards who'd already sent Ethan's and his parents to the gas chambers. A spasm of hatred gripped Jacob's thin frame, but it was gone in a moment as he reasserted control over himself. He hadn't come this far to let emotion get in the way of what he had set out to do.

At ten past six the outside light suddenly went on above the front door, and a moment later Claes and his sister appeared on the steps with Osman behind them, wearing a dinner jacket. Jacob watched them through his field glasses as they got into Osman's Bentley. He knew where Jana Claes was going, dressed all in black with a lace mantilla on her head and the old worn prayer book in her hand. He'd followed her before on a Sunday evening to 6.30 Benediction at St Aloysius and sat two pews behind her in the big, echoing church while the tiny congregation abased themselves before the Blessed Sacrament and incense filled the air. Mass in the morning; Benediction in the evening – Claes had his work cut out on a Sunday, Jacob thought with bitter amusement, ferrying his sister back and forth to church so she could confess her family's sins, seek forgiveness for the unforgivable. And then Claes had to drive Osman about as well. Tonight the master of the house looked like he was on the way to some gala dinner or other in the city, where he would no doubt be treated like visiting royalty. Jacob had done his research – he'd traced the way Osman had spent the last fifteen years building himself a position in local society with carefully targeted charitable gifts, trading his ill-gotten gains for his neighbours' respect, until now no Oxford ball or banquet could be judged a real success if Titus Osman wasn't present as the guest of honour.

The headlights of the car raked the trees for a moment as Claes turned the wheel, and then they were gone, disappearing into the darkness up the drive. Jacob hesitated. He knew the house was almost certainly empty – there was no live-in staff at Blackwater Hall. It was the opportunity he had been waiting for, and yet still he hung back, unwilling to take the risk that Claes might come back unexpectedly and find him. Jacob hated Claes, but he feared him as well. He remembered the man's wiry strength when they had wrestled together in Osman's study the previous summer. He'd only just managed to get away.

And yet Jacob knew he had to try his luck. The chance was too good to miss. He stepped out onto the lawn, feeling the crunch of the frosty grass beneath his shoes, and had just reached the side of the house when he came to an abrupt halt, flattening himself against the wall as a car drew up in the courtyard. Looking cautiously around the corner, Jacob saw two men going up the steps and then heard them knocking hard on the front door. It was what he'd feared: the moonlight was just sufficient to enable Jacob to recognize Trave and the other young detective – they'd escaped their captivity quicker even than he'd anticipated.

Trave stopped his knocking for a moment and then started it up again, this time even louder than before. A minute later the younger policeman took over. Jacob thought they would never give up, but finally they turned around and went back to their car. The doors closed and Jacob waited expectantly for the sound of the engine gunning into life, but nothing happened. He cursed his luck: it was obvious what was happening – they were going to sit there and wait for Osman and Claes to come home so they could warn them about him. And there was nothing Jacob could do about it except stand shivering in the cold and watch.

The minutes passed agonizingly slowly. It was too dark for Jacob to be able to see his watch, and he dared not risk his torch. An owl hooted several times somewhere high up in the trees, but there was otherwise no sound to break the silence until the bell in the tower of Blackwater Church on the other side of the hill began to toll out the hour of seven. It was like a signal: almost immediately a light went on in the car, and then, several minutes later, the younger policeman got out and went up the steps again. He didn't knock on the door this time; he was doing something else, which Jacob couldn't see in the darkness, and, once he'd finished, he went back to his car and drove away.

Jacob held his breath. Benediction was a short service, and Claes and Jana could easily be back by now; they could still meet the policemen's car further up the drive, and all would be lost. But Jacob heard nothing. Once again he was entirely alone. Stealthily, he crossed the courtyard and went up the steps. There was a folded piece of paper tucked into the letter box. Jacob let out a sigh of relief – the young detective had obviously thought his note was more likely to attract Osman's attention hanging on the outside of the door rather than posted into the interior. Carefully lifting the brass flap, Jacob picked up the note, put it in his pocket, and went back to the trees, where he read it by the light of his pocket torch.

It was addressed on the outside: 'To Titus Osman/Franz Claes' and marked 'Urgent.' Inside there were four sentences signed by 'DC Adam Clayton':

*I waited for you but you were out. I came to warn
you that Ethan Mendel's brother, Jacob, is the man
who tried to break into your house last summer and
he is likely to try again very soon. He is armed
and dangerous. Please call the police station as soon
as you get this letter.*

Jacob put the note in his pocket and smiled for the first
time that day. If he'd been this lucky now, he'd be lucky
tomorrow. He felt certain of it: he'd find what he was looking
for because he was meant to find it. From down the drive
came the sound of a car's approach, and Jacob watched as
Claes and his sister got out and went into the house. Then
he turned away with a satisfied smile and headed back down
the path toward Osman's boathouse.

Clayton would've preferred to wait longer. He didn't share
Trave's confidence that there was nothing immediate to fear
from Jacob, but he did agree that he needed to alert the
station to what was happening – keeping the information
about Jacob to themselves was clearly no longer an option,
given that the man was armed, had broken into the Hall once
already, and intended by his own admission to do so again.

Clayton drove back into town via North Oxford, dropping Trave at his house on the way to the police station.
Trave had been warned to attend court on the Monday
afternoon to give evidence at the Swain trial, and they agreed
to talk again the following evening.

The station was almost deserted – hardly surprising on
a Sunday evening. Clayton tried without success to get hold
of Macrae and Creswell on the phone, and the operator
reported that there was a fault on Osman's line that couldn't
be investigated until morning. Clayton drank some black
coffee and spent an hour typing up a statement of the day's

events, but halfway through, his fatigue finally caught up with him, and he fell asleep with his arms on his desk, only waking up in the small hours when two night-duty policemen brought in a pair of angry drunks who'd decided to finish off the weekend in style with a bare-knuckled fight on Broad Street. It was too late now to drive back out to Blackwater and wake up Osman, and Clayton assumed that the station would have heard something if there'd been any trouble. He told the night-duty sergeant to be sure to wake him if there were any developments and then drove slowly home, letting the cold air blow through the open car windows to keep himself awake. Once inside, he made a sandwich, set his alarm clock, and fell into bed, where he tossed and turned all night, at the mercy of a series of nightmares in which he was always a minute too late to prevent terrible things from happening to people he was responsible for but couldn't help.

Jacob woke with the first rays of the bright winter sun in his eyes as it shone across the still, blue-grey waters of Blackwater Lake and in through the curtainless windows of Titus Osman's disused boathouse. His limbs ached from the hardwood floor and the cold, but he was oblivious to the pain. Adrenaline coursed through his veins at the thought of what lay ahead. Today was going to be the day – he was sure of it. And he was not mistaken. At just after seven o'clock Osman and Claes emerged from the house wearing overcoats and suits and got into Osman's Bentley. There was no sign of Claes's sister: she'd obviously not been warned to attend court that day, or perhaps the prosecution wasn't calling her as a witness in any event. Jacob had no way of knowing, and it didn't matter. Thinking about it, her presence in the house was actually an advantage. She wouldn't be armed like her brother, and there would be no burglar

310

alarm to fret about. Jacob had already cut the telephone wire, and so there was no risk of an alert being sent to the police station, but he had been concerned about the possibility that he wouldn't be able to stop the alarm bell ringing on the side of the house. Now he needn't worry – all he had to do was wait for Osman and Claes to drive away and then walk up the steps, knock on the door, and wait to be let inside.

Jana answered almost immediately. She was dressed as usual in a long black woollen dress with not a hair on her head out of place – she'd obviously been up for some time. 'Remember me?' asked Jacob brutally, as he pushed past her into the hall and then turned and shut the door with a hard shove of his hand.

Jana didn't respond. Terrified, she recoiled from Jacob into the corner, looking about wildly as if searching for some non-existent means of escape. Jacob laughed, enjoying her fear. He had no idea how much she was involved in all that had happened, but she was Claes's sister, and that was crime enough.

'Perhaps it's the beard that's throwing you off. Facial hair changes a man, doesn't it?' he said, fingering the thick black hair on his cheek and chin. 'No? All right, well then let me remind you,' Jacob continued, looking down at Jana's shaking hands with unconcealed amusement. 'I was here last summer in Titus's study having a wrestling match with your Nazi brother – remember now?'

'What do you want?' asked Jana, stuttering over her words. She spoke hoarsely, as if fear had taken away her voice.

'Want? I want everything,' said Jacob with a humourless smile. 'I want to know where you were when Katya died, whether you were involved in my brother's death, what you did in the war – all your sins and secrets. But you aren't going to tell me about them, are you? Not unless I make you, and luckily for you I haven't got time for that. So let's just settle for you telling me where Titus keeps his papers. Not his phone bills; his important papers. You know what I mean.'

Jacob stared into Jana's frightened eyes, demanding a response, but she said nothing, just slowly shook her head from side to side.

'You won't say? Well, you'll show me then.' Abruptly Jacob leaned forward and took hold of Jana's wrist, squeezing it, pulling her towards the back of the hall. 'Come on, let's start with his study. I know where that is.'

Inside the study he let go of her and went over to the desk. To his surprise, all the drawers except the one in the centre at the top were unlocked. He pulled them open one by one, rifling through their contents while Jana stood watching, looking appalled, like she was watching an act of desecration in a church. But there was nothing. Pens and stationery, headed letter-writing paper with an absurd golden crest at the top as if Osman was some kind of lord, a bundle of bank statements – everything that he wasn't looking for.

Only the top drawer remained. Jacob didn't bother asking Jana for the key. Instead he took the revolver out of his pocket, stood back from the desk, and carefully fired a bullet into the keyhole, smashing the lock and the wood. Jana screamed in terror, but he ignored her. Instead he swept aside the dust and looked inside, but there were only cheque books and Osman's passport – and of all things a photogaph of Katya in a silver frame. He didn't touch it – the impact of the bullet had smashed the glass.

'Where are they – the documents, the diamonds?' asked Jacob angrily, fastening his eyes on Jana again. Her face was white now, and he noticed how she kept fingering a silver crucifix hanging from a chain around her neck. It was obviously an unconscious gesture – something she did in moments of stress – but the reminder of her hypocritical religion made Jacob hate her even more. He went over to her. She tried to turn away, but he took hold of her face in his hand, forcing her to look at him. It was as if he was trying to read her mind.

'There's a safe, isn't there?' he said softly after a moment, letting go of her chin. 'That's where he keeps his past. Where is it? Tell me where it is.'

Jana turned away without answering, but not before Jacob had had time to see and understand her first reaction to his words. He knew what her rapid anxious glance up toward the ceiling had meant.

'It's not in here, is it?' he said, speaking as if to himself. 'It's upstairs – upstairs where he sleeps. Show me where he sleeps.'

Jana stood rooted to the spot, ignoring Jacob's order. But whether it was resistance or fear that had immobilized her, Jacob neither knew nor cared. He put the revolver up to the side of her head, pressing its muzzle against her temple. 'Move,' he commanded, and this time Jana moved – up the stairs to the first floor and down the corridor to the left until they came to the door at the end. She hesitated outside, but Jacob reached in front of her, turned the handle, and pushed her inside.

It was a grand room with an elaborately carved cornice surrounding its high ceiling. The furniture was ornate French Second Empire – an armchair and a four-poster bed that had not yet been made from the previous night and, on the nearest wall, two matching wardrobes decorated with pastoral scenes that stood on either side of a small oil painting of Blackwater Hall as it had appeared a hundred years earlier. However, the real glory of the room lay in the views from the tall rectangular sash windows hung with exquisite pale white silk curtains. At the front was the tree-lined drive leading up to the gates, and beyond that, across the invisible road, the green hill climbing up to Blackwater village. And through the window to the right there was the same view as from the drawing room below, except this time from higher up, so that on a clear day such as this the eye could take in the full expanse of Blackwater Lake and the pine woods beyond, disappearing down into the distant valley. This was what Osman woke to every morning, thought Jacob with disgust, while those he had wronged lay buried in the dirt, seeing nothing.

'All right, where is it?' he demanded, raising the gun threateningly toward Jana's head. Petrified, she pointed over to the picture between the wardrobes with a trembling hand.

Jacob's eyes flicked over to the wall and back to Jana. He gestured with the gun, and, following its instruction, she backed away to the front window. Then, keeping the revolver trained on her with one hand, he lifted the picture from off its hook, revealing a steel wall safe surmounted by a small black-and-white number dial. His eyes lit up and he audibly exhaled, sensing how close he was now to the summit he had been struggling towards for so long.

'I don't know the code,' said Jana in a whisper, pre-empting his question. He went up close to her again, but this time she held his gaze and he knew she was telling the truth. He returned to the safe and began twisting the dial this way and that, trying every combination of significant numbers he could think of – Osman's birthday, the date the war ended and when it began, the registration number of Osman's Bentley. Nothing worked. Finally, maddened with frustration, Jacob took aim and fired his revolver at the safe, but the bullet just ricocheted off the silvery surface and embedded itself in the opposite wall.

He would have shot again, but from down below there

was the sound of someone knocking on the front door. Jacob and Jana both froze. Jacob was the first to recover. 'Get away from the window,' he ordered, but she did the opposite, flattening herself back against the glass, refusing to obey. Jacob advanced on her, seizing her arm, trying to drag her away, but she took hold of the curtain and stood her ground. She was surprisingly strong, and Jacob pocketed his gun, realizing he would need two hands. Straight away, Jana took advantage of the momentary loosening of his grip to twist around and bang on the window with one of her hands, trying to attract the attention of the man in the courtyard down below.

When he heard the noise Adam Clayton was just walking back to his police car. He'd requisitioned it from the station earlier that morning when he had gone in to try and track down Macrae, who was still nowhere to be found. Now, turning around, he looked up and saw Jacob Mendel locked in a struggle with Jana Claes. For a moment they were framed, silent and contorted in the first-floor window on the far left of the house. And then they disappeared, as if they had never been there at all.

Clayton looked about wildly for something with which to break a window, and then thought of the wheel jack in the back of the car. He'd got it out and was about to use it when Jana reappeared in the window above his head, pulling it up open wide. 'He's gone,' she shouted, leaning out. And at that moment, to his left, out of sight and round the side of the house, Clayton heard the sound of another sash window opening; seconds later, he caught sight of a figure running fast across the wide lawn towards the trees. Clayton reacted instantly. He ran to his car, reversed it into a three-point turn with a screech of tyres, and set off up the drive, arriving at the fence where the path from the boathouse met the road long before Jacob

315

could have got there on foot. Mindful of Jacob's gun, Clayton moved his car further down the road out of sight and radioed in for reinforcements. Then he got out and stood behind a tree, watching. He knew his job wasn't to arrest Jacob but to keep track of him until armed police arrived.

A minute passed and then another, but nothing happened. Everything was still and silent. Clayton was sure he was in the right place – from where he was standing he could see the bushes where Jacob had hidden his scooter the previous day. Cautiously, he crossed the road and climbed over the fence. He searched all the nearby undergrowth carefully at first and then with a rising panic, but there was no sign of the scooter. He looked anxiously down the path leading to the boathouse. It was narrow and uneven, unsuitable for riding, but perhaps Jacob had wheeled his scooter down there this time. Nervously Clayton started walking, stopping at each corner to check the way ahead. But there was nothing, until he came in sight of the boathouse and looked out across the lake to where a rowing boat was fast approaching the weeping willow trees lining the bank on the other side. There was one solitary figure pulling on the oars, and Clayton didn't need the man to turn his head to know who it was.

Clayton walked slowly back up the footpath. He knew there was no point in hurrying now. Jacob would have disappeared into the Monday-morning traffic long before the pursuing police could catch up with him on the other side of the valley.

Osman and Claes returned to Blackwater Hall in the late afternoon, followed shortly after by Macrae. Clayton had spoken to his boss on the phone at the Old Bailey soon after he had got back to the house, but Macrae had decided to remain at the Swain trial, where he was required on a daily basis as the officer in the case, once he had established that Jana Claes was shocked but otherwise unharmed and that nothing had been taken.

'Well, Mr Osman's very grateful to you, Constable,' said Macrae once they were alone, standing out in the courtyard in the gathering twilight. 'You're quite the hero, aren't you, stopping an armed burglary and saving the damsel in distress? Almost worth a medal if you can just answer me one question.'

'Sir?' asked Clayton, feeling he had a pretty good idea of what was coming next.

'Just this,' said Macrae mildly. 'How did you know to come here? What gave you the idea that this Jacob Mendel character was going to be breaking into Blackwater Hall at seven o'clock in the morning? Was it your sixth sense or something a bit more specific?'

Clayton swallowed apprehensively. He knew that he had no option but to put Macrae fully in the picture, given the seriousness of what Jacob had done and was likely to do again, but he also realized that a full report was not going to do anything to help his career prospects.

'I saw him here yesterday watching the house,' he began nervously. 'And I followed him back to his flat – it's off the Iffley Road. There were a lot of documents on the walls – photographs and newspaper articles about Claes, about him working with the Germans during the war . . .'

'Ah, so that's where all that came from,' said Macrae, looking interested.

'What came from?' asked Clayton, not understanding.

'Allegations that Swain's barrister put to Mr Claes today in cross-examination. Just a sideshow – they didn't amount to anything,' said Macrae with a dismissive wave of his hand. 'Carry on – I'm sorry for interrupting.'

'Well, it was like Mendel was obsessed with Osman and

Claes, and his glasses matched those that the burglar left behind last summer when he broke into Osman's study. I was going to arrest him, but he pulled a gun and got away. And so I came out here and left a note to warn Osman, but Mendel must have removed it, and the phone line was down . . . I tried to call you as well, sir, but you weren't home,' Clayton spoke in a rush, trying unsuccessfully not to sound defensive.

Macrae looked at Clayton quizzically as if assessing whether he was telling the truth and then nodded as if temporarily satisfied. 'All right, I understand why you came back here this morning,' he said in the same easy-going tone as before. 'But what I don't quite grasp is what you were doing here yesterday when you saw Mendel watching the house. Can you enlighten me on that, Constable?'

'I was looking for him,' said Clayton.

'Why?'

'Because I thought he might be the one who broke in here last summer.'

'So you've been devoting your valuable time to investigating a six-month-old failed burglary?' asked Macrae with a sneer. 'I'm afraid you'll have to do a bit better than that. I'll repeat the question: Why were you looking for Jacob Mendel out here yesterday afternoon?'

'I thought he might have something to do with what happened,' said Clayton reluctantly. He felt like he was being slowly backed into a corner.

'Happened to whom?' asked Macrae. There was a dangerous edge to his voice.

'To Katya Osman.'

'But we know what happened to her,' said Macrae, making no effort now to conceal his anger. 'She was brutally murdered by Mr David Swain, who's being prosecuted for the offence up in London, while you're busy trying to undermine the prosecution case against him down here. Just like your ex-boss tried to do, and now he's about to become an ex-policeman. I'd say you're in way over your head here, Constable.'

Macrae stared at Clayton, who looked away, determined not to rise to Macrae's challenge. But Macrae hadn't finished. 'Look at me when I'm talking to you,' he ordered, raising his voice. 'Were you alone when you went to Mendel's flat yesterday? Tell me the truth.'

'No,' said Clayton quietly.

'Who were you with?'

'Inspector Trave. I was with Inspector Trave, sir,' said Clayton, suddenly defiant. Macrae could do what he liked. In his conscience Clayton didn't feel he'd done anything he should be ashamed of. He was keeping an open mind, trying to find out the truth. That's what a detective was supposed to do, after all.

'I thought so,' said Macrae, who clearly didn't see it that way. 'Trave never gives up, does he? Well, you've hitched your horse to the wrong wagon this time, Constable. I'm not a good enemy to make. Trave'll tell you that. And just to think that you told me I could count on your loyalty. I thought you had a bright future, but it looks like I was wrong.'

Macrae paused for a moment, sizing Clayton up as if deciding what to do. 'I'm sure I'll regret this,' he said quietly, 'but I'm going to give you a chance to make up for your misconduct. Find Mendel. You've done it before and you can do it again, and this time you'll have Jonah to help you. Find him fast, and when you've got him, bring him to me. Don't ask him any questions, just bring him to me. And stay away from Trave if you want to stay a detective. I'll be watching you,' Macrae added with a thin, spiteful smile before he turned away and went back into the house, leaving Clayton alone in the gloomy courtyard.

CHAPTER 22

On the same Monday morning that Jacob Mendel broke into Blackwater Hall, Vanessa Trave finally forced herself to make the phone call to her husband that she had been putting off from day to day ever since she had promised to marry Titus Osman two weeks earlier. She did not fully understand her own reluctance. She had no wish to go back to her husband, and yet she found it extraordinarily hard to make the formal break with her past that was now required. It felt like she was closing the book not only on her husband but also on her dead son: divorce was not just an acknowledgement of failure but also somehow an act of cruelty, a betrayal of the past. She hadn't been able to explain any of this to Titus when he'd gently but insistently pressed her about her continuing inaction during dinner in Oxford two days earlier, but she realized that the delay was only making it harder to do what she had to do, and so she went straight to the telephone almost as soon as she'd got out of bed, determined to seize the bull by the horns.

Trave answered on the second ring, and she was momentarily at a loss for words. She hadn't spoken to her husband in months, and the sudden sound of his voice disconcerted her. When she said her name it hurt that he sounded so pleased to hear from her.

'Could I see you?' she asked. She knew that she couldn't tell him what she had to say on the phone. As she'd told Titus, he deserved better than that.

'Now?' he asked. 'I've got to be in London this afternoon.'

'Yes, all right,' she said, taken aback. And yet it was better this way, she thought – an amputation should be done quickly or not at all. And she didn't need to be at work until ten.

She named a coffee house on St Michael's Street – neutral ground where they had never met before – and noticed that her hand was trembling when she put down the receiver.

She dressed carefully. Her instinct was to wear black but eventually she compromised, settling for a simple grey dress that she'd recently bought in a second-hand store in the market, with her old black overcoat on top. Frowning, she looked down at the two rings on her hands: the simple gold wedding band on the right and the perfect diamond on the left: Bill's ring and Titus's. Worlds apart, and yet set in permanent conflict. Slowly and carefully she took both rings off and put them away in a small jewellery box by her bed. Today she'd be herself only, she decided. It was better that way.

Trave was already sitting in the café when Vanessa arrived, and he insisted on queueing up at the counter to order her a coffee while she sat opposite his half-drunk mug at the table by the window, feeling more awkward by the minute. She wished there were set rules for this kind of meeting: she'd come here to tell her husband that she wanted a divorce, not to drink coffee. And yet here she was sitting amid a throng of women and their shopping as if she was just meeting an old friend. It was all wrong. She wished she'd chosen some sombre venue – the back of a church or some out-of-the-way corner of the public library. But it was too late now – she'd have to get on with it.

When Trave finally sat down, Vanessa was struck by how run-down he looked. There were dark circles under his eyes, and his suit was crumpled as if it hadn't been hung up in weeks. And something told her the dishevelment was not just superficial. He'd aged since she'd last seen him, turned some corner in his life that she hadn't been there to see.

'I'm sorry about your job,' she said. She really was sorry, but her words sounded awkward, artificial.

'It doesn't matter,' he said, even though it was obvious that it did. 'You can't keep making compromises forever. I'll find something else to do.'

'What?' Vanessa asked, genuinely curious. The concept of Bill as anything other than a policeman was inconceivable to her.

'Something,' he said with a sad smile. 'You look wonderful, Vanessa. Better than you've done in years.'

She flushed, touched and yet upset by the genuine pleasure in his voice. And she couldn't cope with the way he looked at her so intently, as if memorizing every detail of her face. The meeting was painful, more painful than she could have imagined. She needed to tell him why she was here, to get the words out while she still could.

'I need a divorce,' she said. She spoke softly and didn't know at first whether he had heard her. He looked away out the window, averting his face, gazing sightlessly at the people hurrying by in their winter overcoats. And when he turned back, there was an awful desolation in his pale blue eyes, which made her feel suddenly sick, as if she was an executioner disgusted by her own handiwork.

'You want to marry Osman,' he said. It was a statement, not a question.

'Yes,' she said. 'He's not like who you think he is, he's . . .' Vanessa stopped in mid-sentence, seeing the weary disbelief in her husband's eyes. 'It's a second chance,' she said. 'Everyone deserves a second chance.'

'Yes,' said Trave quietly. 'You do deserve that. You deserve the sun and the moon and the stars, Vanessa. And what I regret most in my life is that I failed to give you any of them.'

Vanessa wanted to cry. Her husband had never said anything as simple and loving to her before in all the years they had been married. He'd saved it up for now, when it was all too late. She couldn't bear it. She steeled herself against him. She knew she had to if she was going to survive.

'So you'll help me,' she said. 'It'll have to be your petition with Titus as co-respondent. There's no other way.'

Trave nodded, and then he reached out and took hold of her right hand, the hand that was now missing its wedding ring. 'Be happy,' he said. 'Try to be happy, Vanessa.'

She nodded, squeezed his hand once as if sealing an agreement, and got up to go. But then, at the doorway, she turned back, unable to leave him when she felt so in the wrong. He looked up, surprised, when she got back to the table, taken aback by her sudden return.

'Titus didn't kill Katya,' she said, blurting out the words. 'You believe it because he's with me. Admit it, Bill. That's why you've done all this.'

'Done all what?'

'Ruined your career, been so pig-headed.' She spoke accusingly, harshly, but he also sensed the desperation in her voice, as if she was pleading for exoneration, and that was something he could not provide.

'No,' he said, shaking his head. 'I hate Osman because of you. That's true. But that's not why I think he killed Katya.'

'Why then?' she asked, challenging him.

'Because I don't believe David Swain killed her or Ethan either for that matter,' said Trave, choosing his words carefully. 'Swain's a fool, an angry fool, but he's no murderer. But Claes is. I know he is. In fact I think he's been responsible for many people's deaths, even though I can't prove any of them,' he added bitterly. 'And if Claes killed Katya, then he couldn't have done it without Osman.'

'No, that's where you're wrong,' said Vanessa vehemently. It was years since Trave had seen her so passionate. 'Maybe you're right about Claes. I don't like him either. He's got some hold over Titus which I don't understand, but that doesn't mean Titus knows what he's doing. Titus isn't like Claes. I know him and you don't. That's the difference. He was taking care of Katya after she'd gone off the rails. It wasn't his fault she blamed him for keeping her at home. He did it to help her, for her own good.'

'How do you know she blamed him?' asked Trave, leaning forward.

'Because she told me,' said Vanessa quietly, lowering her eyes.

'Told you what?'

'She said: "They're trying to kill me." It was ten days before her death. I was there for dinner and she came into the drawing room. I was on my own, and that was all she said. She was in a bad way and she fainted afterwards. Titus said his sister-in-law had tried to give her a sedative, and he explained about the state she was in, about why he was so worried about her, about why he had to keep her at home for her own good.'

'I'm sure he did,' said Trave sarcastically. 'He's an expert at playing the do-gooder. The man's a professional philanthropist.'

'I knew you wouldn't understand,' said Vanessa angrily. 'That's why I didn't tell you. I knew you'd have used it against Titus when he hasn't done anything wrong. I know he hasn't,' she added fervently.

'It doesn't matter what you think. You should still have told me.'

'I told that inspector who took over from you.'

'Macrae?'

'Yes.'

'When?'

'A couple of weeks ago.'

'And I suppose he told you to say nothing?'

'Yes.' Vanessa sounded defensive now.

'And you felt okay with that?'

Vanessa stirred uneasily in her seat, not answering. She resented the cross-examination, and yet she also felt its justification. Her interview with Inspector Macrae had not set her conscience about Katya at rest, however much she had hoped it would.

'You're going to have to tell that court up in London,' said Trave quietly. He spoke as if what he had to say was obvious, not a subject for argument or discussion.

'I can't. I won't,' said Vanessa, refusing to see it that way. Her eyes blazed with defiance, but Trave stood his ground.

'It's your duty. You know it is,' he told her. 'A man's on trial for his life. If Osman loves you then he'll understand.'

'And you hope he doesn't, don't you?'

'I hope you'll do what's right. That's all.'

Vanessa looked at her husband and suddenly the fire went out of her, extinguished in a moment. Her sharp retort died on her lips and she bowed her head, realizing that he was right: she had no choice. She wished with all her heart that Katya hadn't crossed her path that night at Blackwater Hall, but she had, and in those few moments the girl had placed her under an obligation that she could only ever discharge by standing up and telling the whole world what Katya had said. Until she had done that she would have no peace. Bill had only told her what she knew already.

Vanessa felt exhausted suddenly. It was like she'd finally put down a burden that had been weighing her down for months and only now realized how heavy it had been. She needed to be alone, to gather her strength for what lay ahead. She stood up and leaned across the table, bending down to kiss her husband on the cheek.

'Thank you,' she said. And as she turned and walked away it occurred to her that she didn't know whether they were parting on her terms or his.

That day and most of the next went by in a blur. Vanessa went to work and did her job, typing letters and filing correspondence on automatic pilot, while underneath her mind raced from one thought to another as she tried to work out what she could say to Titus to make him understand her decision. She knew that this time she could not delay. The Swain trial was already into its second week, and Swain's lawyers would need to take a statement from her before she gave evidence. But she couldn't go to see them without telling Titus first. She owed him that much. Several times she picked up the telephone, intending to dial Blackwater Hall, but then replaced the receiver like it was hot to the touch, reproaching herself for her cowardice. It wasn't that she was frightened of Titus; it was that she was frightened of losing him. She wished she could abandon her conscience, discard it into the waste-paper basket on the floor beside her desk, but she knew she couldn't. She was who she was, and perhaps Titus would understand that. But she knew she would have to see him to explain. A telephone call was not enough. And so after work on Tuesday she got into her car and drove out to Blackwater with a heavy heart.

Jana answered the door. Dressed as always in funereal black, Claes's sister showed no warmth of recognition when she saw Vanessa on the step, shivering in the cold. There was something frozen about the woman's face, Vanessa thought – as if it was a door that had been shut and locked against the world. It unnerved Vanessa, and she felt forced to explain herself, to justify her visit.

'I wanted to see Titus,' she said, stumbling over her words. 'Something important has come up that I need to tell him about. Is he here?' she finished lamely.

Jana opened the door wide without saying anything and moved aside to let Vanessa pass. It was warm inside and Vanessa rubbed her hands together to restart her circulation, and then, looking up, she was surprised to see a uniformed policeman come through the doorway at the end of the hall and go up the stairs to the first floor. There were several voices talking somewhere out of sight, but Vanessa couldn't tell if one of them was Titus's.

'Has something happened?' she asked, turning to Jana. 'Is Titus all right?'

'A man broke in here yesterday, trying to take things. But the police came and he ran away,' said Jana in her slow, heavily accented English.

'Who was here?' asked Vanessa, horrified.

'I was. Please wait in here,' said Jana, opening the door of the drawing room. 'I will tell Titus you are come.'

Vanessa had innumerable questions to ask, but something in Jana's tone prohibited further conversation, and Vanessa did as she was told, taking a seat on the same sofa where Katya had lain unconscious five months before, having placed Vanessa under an obligation that, try as she might, she seemed unable to escape.

The grey, overcast afternoon was now dissolving into an early evening gloom, and the drawing room felt cheerless and forlorn. There was no fire, and Vanessa did not turn on the lights. She felt like she was in some kind of medical waiting room and that there would be no good news when she finally got to see the doctor.

She idly picked up the newspaper that was lying in front

of her on the coffee table. It had obviously been read already since it was folded in on itself with an inside page now at the front, and the headline explained why it had attracted the previous reader's attention: 'Blackwater Murder – Witness's Nazi Connections'. Osman came in when Vanessa was halfway through the article.

'Is this true?' she asked, leaning away as he bent down over the back of the sofa to kiss her.

Osman glanced at the newspaper over her shoulder and sighed with obvious irritation. 'That Franz was a Nazi?' he asked, straightening up and heading over to the drinks tray in the corner.

'Yes. Was he?'

'I don't know, to be honest with you. He certainly worked with them. He had no choice if he was going to keep his job in the interior ministry, but I've never asked him if he was actually required to join the party. I didn't think it was any of my business.'

'That he was, is, a Nazi,' said Vanessa, looking appalled. 'What could be more important?'

'Nothing, if he really was one,' said Osman evenly. 'But the truth is he only worked with them so as to do good things. For Belgium and for Belgian Jews. Yes, that's right, Vanessa,' Osman went on, seeing the look of disbelief on his fiancée's face. 'Without Franz I would never have been able to help all those poor people to escape. I needed someone on the inside with power . . .'

'A Nazi,' said Vanessa interrupting. 'You needed a Nazi.'

Osman turned away without answering, concentrating on mixing himself a drink. Vanessa shook her head when he offered her one too. It was only quarter past five according to the clock on the mantelpiece.

'I'm sorry, my dear,' he said, coming over to sit beside her on the sofa. 'I'm not at my best right now. This has not been an easy couple of days. Franz and I had to give evidence at the trial up in London, which was stressful, particularly for Franz' – Osman gestured toward the newspaper – 'and then when we came back we found the house had been broken into and Jana had been terrorized by a man with a gun. He fired a bullet into my desk and another one upstairs. Thank God the police came, or I don't know what would have happened.'

'Who was it?'

'Ethan's brother, Jacob Mendel. It's not the first time he's been here. He blames me for Ethan's death. I don't know why. The police need to catch him before he does something really stupid.' Vanessa caught the note of anxiety in Titus's voice. It was strange when he was usually so confident, so much the master of the situation.

'I'm sorry,' she said. 'I wouldn't have come if I'd known it was a bad time. I wanted to talk to you because I saw Bill, like you asked me to. I had coffee with him in town yesterday morning and . . .' Vanessa hesitated, searching for the right words.

'Did he agree – to the divorce?' Osman asked, suddenly eager.

'Yes.'

'I told you he would,' said Osman, smacking the side of the sofa with his open hand. 'He's . . .'

'A decent man,' said Vanessa, remembering the word she'd used to describe her husband to Titus on the day that she'd agreed to marry him. Now she felt ashamed of its inadequacy, it felt obscurely like a betrayal. It was Titus's triumphalism that was making her uneasy, she realized. It made her feel cheap, as if she was a prize won in a game of chance, as if Bill's agreement to the divorce was Titus's victory, not hers.

'There's something else,' she said. 'I agreed to give evidence myself.'

'Give evidence. What evidence?' asked Osman, not under-standing her meaning.

'About what Katya said. About people trying to kill her.'

'You can't,' said Osman, horrified. 'You can't do that to me, Vanessa. You said you wouldn't.'

'I know I did, and I shouldn't have done. I have to do this, Titus,' she said sadly. 'I can't be with you otherwise.'

Osman got up and walked away to the window. He stood with his back to her for a moment, looking out, and Vanessa could sense him battling to keep control of his emotions.

'Your husband put you up to this, didn't he?' he said finally, turning round. There was a cold, hard edge to his voice that Vanessa had never heard before. It frightened her, but the fear only made her more determined to go through with her decision. She knew she would have no peace otherwise.

'He made me see what I should have seen for myself. That's all,' she said.

'Very clever,' said Osman. Again Vanessa had that fleeting sense that Titus was playing a game, reacting to a surprise move of his opponent. 'Wasn't going to Macrae enough?' he asked angrily.

'Macrae! How do you know about Macrae?' asked Vanessa. Now it was her turn to be astonished.

'Because he told me. Macrae wants to do what's right, unlike your husband, who'll do anything to hurt me. Can't you see that?'

Vanessa shook her head and got up from the sofa, heading toward the door. She wanted the scene to be over. She wanted to be on her own. But Titus blocked her path, taking hold of her arm.

'I love you,' he said desperately. 'Doesn't that mean anything to you at all? Why do you have to ruin everything? Swain killed Katya. Everyone knows that.'

Vanessa heard the appeal in her lover's voice, and perhaps she would have answered it if at that moment the door hadn't opened. It was Claes. No doubt he'd heard the raised voices coming from inside. Vanessa looked at him and remembered what she'd read in the newspaper minutes earlier, and she thought of what he had said about the war that day at lunch the previous month. He was a Nazi. She knew he was. It didn't matter what Titus said. She wanted to be gone, far away from Claes and his limp and his scar and his thin-lipped, silent sister. Pulling away from Titus, she ran to the door and then out through the hall and down the steps to her car and drove away without a backward look.

CHAPTER 23

Trave drove up to the Old Bailey immediately after seeing Vanessa on the Monday morning and then spent the entire afternoon pacing the police room, waiting to give evidence, but the summons to attend court never came, and he had to wait until the next morning to take the stand.

Almost all his testimony was going to be uncontroversial, but the jury still needed to hear about what he'd found at Blackwater Hall on the night of the murder and the various investigations that he'd carried out and ordered until Creswell took him off the case. The previous week he'd insisted on making a further statement about John Bircher's connections with Claes and Eddie Earle, realizing that the defence would then be able to elicit this information from him in cross-examination, but he didn't seriously anticipate that this would make any major difference to the outcome of the case, given the strength of the evidence against the defendant. The jury would dismiss Bircher's involvement as a minor coincidence, just as the allegations of collaboration with the Nazis that the defence had thrown at Claes the day before – using the material sent by Jacob – would do no more than muddy the waters.

Trave had heard from Clayton when he got back from court the day before about Jacob's botched break-in at Blackwater Hall, but he thought it unlikely that the young man had found anything worthwhile in the house, given that Osman's safe had apparently survived intact. It might conceivably make a difference to the outcome of the trial if Jacob came to court himself and told the jury that he'd sought out Katya a month before her death and asked her to search Osman's house for incriminating evidence, but Trave wasn't holding his breath about the likelihood of Jacob's showing up. According to Clayton, Jacob had disappeared into thin air after the break-in, and there was no way of knowing where he was now holed up.

Vanessa, on the other hand, would give evidence – Trave knew his wife well enough to be sure that her conscience would not allow her to do otherwise. But Trave doubted that her testimony would be enough to save Swain. The prosecution would recall Osman to explain away Katya's words, and Vanessa's continuing determination to marry Osman would provide him with a gold-plated character reference. And that would be that. One fine morning David Swain would have his neck broken for him in Pentonville Prison, and Trave's wife would marry the man whom Trave believed should be hanging there instead. Trave felt the frustration pressing hard down onto his chest like a physical weight, but there was no relief to be had from the pain. And he knew he was running out of time.

It was the same Old Bailey courtroom in which David Swain had been tried for the murder of Ethan Mendel two and a half years earlier, and Trave found the sense of déjà vu almost overpowering. There was a different judge and defence counsel this time around, but hawk-like Laurence Arne had again been instructed for the prosecution. Unwinding himself from behind the files of evidence that covered his table, he was just as imposing and dominant as before, and he seemed even more determined to secure a conviction now that the defendant faced the ultimate penalty for his crime. Hanging was the prescribed punishment for a murder by shooting, and Swain could expect no mercy given that this was the second time he'd killed with premeditation.

Trave looked over at the defendant, sitting between two prison officers in the dock. It was the first time he'd seen Swain since their desperate meeting in the cricket pavilion the previous October. Surprisingly, Swain looked better than he had then, notwithstanding his terrible predicament. The wild, haggard look had disappeared from his face, replaced by an air of quiet resolution. Dressed in a sombre dark suit, he gazed at Trave intently, leaning forward on the railing of the dock as Trave answered the prosecutor's questions. Trave found it hard to concentrate. He felt a terrible guilt about his inability to help an innocent man, about his unwitting role in Swain's capture.

During a pause in the questioning, he glanced over and caught the eye of Macrae, who was sitting at the same side table where Trave had sat when he had been the officer in the case at the first trial. The look of unconcealed triumphant glee on his successor's face was intolerable. It made Trave want to be sick. He felt suddenly claustrophobic in the windowless courtroom, with its wood-panelled walls and bright white lights, and longed to be outside in the bracing winter air.

And yet he lingered for some reason in the empty courtroom after his evidence was over and everyone had left for lunch. He sat in Macrae's chair at the police table and stared over at the witness box, trying to reconstruct a memory of Katya that had been on the edge of his consciousness ever since his conversation with Vanessa the previous day. He remembered the girl lying on her narrow bed in that sparse, cleaned-up room at the top of Blackwater Hall – so thin she had been and fragile and gone forever. It was a vision that never left him, waiting always on the surface of his subconscious, ready to spring out at him like a permanent reproach. But this was another kind of memory – a detail, elusive and minute. He thought perhaps it was something

334

Katya had said when she'd given evidence from this same witness box, staring over so angrily at her former boyfriend in the dock, convinced of his guilt. And yet he couldn't be sure – maybe it was just his imagination, feeding on the intensity of his desire to find a key to unlock the case when perhaps there was no key to be found. The uncertainty made him nervous, and, picking up his hat, he headed for the door.

Back at the house a letter was waiting for Trave on the doormat. The envelope was typed, official-looking, and he knew what it contained even before he'd ripped it open.

> *Dear Mr Trave,*
>
> *The Chief Constable regrets to inform you that it has been decided to terminate your employment with the Oxfordshire Police forthwith in the light of a finding of gross dereliction of duty following the hearing last Saturday. You have fourteen days to appeal . . .*

Trave didn't bother reading any further. He screwed up the letter and threw it across the room and then proceeded to get as drunk on neat whisky as he'd ever been before in his entire life.

He woke up on the sofa the next day with the morning sun burning in his eyes. He had a blinding headache, and the telephone was ringing insistently in his ear, filling his head with yet more pain. It was Creswell.

'Did you get the letter?' asked the superintendent.

'Yeah,' said Trave, remembering with a feeling of renewed sickness the reason why he'd drunk himself into a stupor the night before.

'I'm sorry, Bill,' said Creswell, sounding genuinely upset. 'I did my best, but they wouldn't listen to me.'

'I know. I didn't think they would.'

'Look, you have to appeal. I'll try again. Dismissing you isn't fair. It's too harsh.'

'I don't know,' said Trave. 'I don't think it'll do any good. It's cracking this case that would change things . . .'

'Don't be a fool,' said Creswell, sounding angry now. 'It's your pig-headed obsession with Titus Osman that led to all this. If you'd been a bit more contrite . . .'

'But I've never been much good at that, have I?' said Trave. 'Look, sir, I appreciate you calling, and I know you're trying to help, but I'm not feeling at my best right now.'

'Okay, I understand. But you'll think about what I've said, won't you? About not giving up?'

'Yes,' said Trave. 'Of course I will.'

But Trave stopped thinking about the appeal as soon as he'd got off the phone. He was touched by the superintendent's concern, but now he had other things to worry about. Something had been on the edge of his mind when he woke up, and he needed to concentrate before it slipped away. He went upstairs and showered in ice-cold water until his head was clear of alcohol and self-pity, got dressed in a pair of old gardening trousers and a patched jersey, and made a pot of the strongest coffee he could tolerate. He drank down a cup, and then, with a second in his hand, he finally sat back down with the transcript of David Swain's first trial across his knees. It was dog-eared now, the pages crumpled from overuse. Trave turned to Katya's evidence and began to read:

Evidence of Katya Osman

Witness is sworn

PROSECUTION COUNSEL, MR ARNE: *Please tell the court who you are and where you live.*

WITNESS: *I am Katya Osman and I live with my uncle at Blackwater Hall. It's near Oxford.*

COUNSEL: *Do you know the defendant sitting over there? (Counsel points toward the dock.)*

WITNESS: *Yes, we used to be friends.*

COUNSEL: *Friends?*

WITNESS: *He was my boyfriend for a year, but then I broke up with him after I met Ethan.*

COUNSEL: *Ethan Mendel?*

WITNESS: *Yes; he came to stay with my uncle last year. We fell in love. And David hated us for it. He sent me letters – horrible, threatening letters. I've got them here – six of them. I got the last one a few days before he killed Ethan. I brought them with me— (Witness produces bundle of handwritten letters.)*

COUNSEL: *My lord, these will be exhibits 17 through 22. Copies have been made for the jury, and with your lordship's leave the witness will now read them into the evidence.*

JUDGE: *Very well, Mr Arne.*

Trave impatiently turned the pages of the transcript, looking for the resumption of Katya's evidence. It was what Katya had to say that he was interested in, not David Swain's childish, impassioned rants.

COUNSEL: *The defendant refers in his letters to meeting you at 'the boathouse'. Please tell us where that is, Miss Osman.*

WITNESS: *It's by the lake. You get to it across the lawn and along a path through the woods. No one goes there.*

COUNSEL: *But you did with Mr Swain. Why?*

WITNESS: *Because no one goes there. My uncle didn't approve of David, and so I couldn't see him in the house.*

COUNSEL: *Never?*

WITNESS: *I took him there once when my uncle was away. Otherwise we met at the boathouse or in his room in Oxford.*

COUNSEL: *How often did you meet Mr Swain at the boathouse?*

WITNESS: *Lots of times.*

COUNSEL: *And how did Mr Swain get there if he wanted to avoid your uncle seeing him?*

WITNESS: *There's a place on the road before you get to the main gate. You can get over the fence and walk down the path to the lake. That's how.*

COUNSEL: *Did you use the boathouse after you ended your relationship with Mr Swain?*

WITNESS: *With Ethan you mean?*

COUNSEL: *Yes.*

WITNESS: *Yes, we did. I liked that it was our place, our secret. It was romantic with the lake and everything.*

COUNSEL: *I understand. Did you ever see the defendant at or near the boathouse after you ended your relationship with him?*

WITNESS: *Yes, once. It was in the evening. Ethan was writing something, and I went outside to look at the sunset. David was in the trees further up the path, watching. It was horrible, creepy. I never saw him again after that – until now.*

COUNSEL: *When was this?*

WITNESS: *The third of April – three days before Easter.*

COUNSEL: *How can you be so sure?*

WITNESS: *It upset me, and so I wrote about it in my diary. It helps to get things out of my system.*

COUNSEL: *What did the defendant do when you saw him?*

WITNESS: *He ran away back towards the road. I could hear him in the undergrowth.*

COUNSEL: *Did you tell Mr Mendel?*

WITNESS: *Yes. He was angry at first, worried. He wanted to go and see David about it, but I didn't want him to. I thought it would make things worse. And so he didn't. We stayed away from the boathouse for a while after that, but then we went back because it was beautiful and it was our place and David had no right to try and take it away from us. (Witness breaks down, distressed.)*

COUNSEL: *I'd like to move forward now to the period immediately leading up to Mr Mendel's murder. What was the state of your relationship with Mr Mendel at that time?*

WITNESS: *We were in love; we were happy, although Ethan was preoccupied with something. He wouldn't tell me what it was. He went away to Europe for a week. He didn't tell me where he was going, but I assumed he was going to see his family in Antwerp. And then on the day he came back, I was out shopping in Oxford with Jana and so I never saw him. (Witness breaks down again, distressed.) I don't know why he sent that note to David. Perhaps it was because of David's letters. Ethan knew they upset me; he knew I was scared. I wanted them to stop.*

COUNSEL: *I want to show you the knife, the murder weapon – it's exhibit three, my lord. Have you seen it before, Miss Osman?*

WITNESS: *I may have done. David had several knives similar to this in his room in Oxford. I can't say if it's the same one.*

COUNSEL: *Thank you, Miss Osman. If you wait there, my learned friend will have some questions.*

Trave got up from the table and made himself some more coffee. He glanced around the room, grimacing at the dust and disorder: unwashed dishes stacked up by the sink, piles of unanswered correspondence balanced precariously on his desk in the corner. He didn't need to be told that the mess was a symptom of the way his life was spinning out of control, as recorded in jottings on the Oxfordshire Police Force calendar hanging on the opposite wall – *disciplinary hearing; Vanessa; give evidence* – he might as well add *lost job* under today's date.

Calendars, records – Katya had kept a record, a diary – it was how she'd been able to remember the date when David Swain had come stalking her and Ethan at the boathouse. And it wasn't just an engagement diary; it was a fully fledged journal that she used 'to get things out of my system'. That was what she'd said. The reference to the diary was what Trave had been trying to remember in the courtroom the day before – he was certain of it. But where was the diary now? Trave wondered. Had Osman found it? Probably – Trave remembered the cleaned-up feel of Katya's room on the night of her murder. But then again, not necessarily – perhaps Osman didn't know about the diary. He'd hardly have looked for it if he didn't know it existed, and Katya was a girl who loved secrets – her meetings with David Swain behind her uncle's back and her attachment to the boathouse itself were part of the same pattern. 'I liked that it was our place, our secret.' That was what she'd said.

And yet she'd also been prepared to tell the world about the diary when she gave evidence, unless of course she'd answered Arne's question about the date without thinking, regretting the immediacy of her response later as she rode home in the back of her uncle's car, hoping no one had noticed what she'd accidentally revealed. Trave paced backwards and forwards across his living room as his mind turned the scraps of evidence this way and that. He knew perfectly well that it was all speculation and that he was clutching at straws, just like he'd accused Jacob of doing two days earlier. But if straws were all he had, then he also knew he had no choice but to clutch at them, however pointless the exercise. Doing nothing was the alternative, and that was intolerable.

But if Katya had kept a secret diary that survived her death, then who was to say where it was now? Trave knew he couldn't follow in Jacob's footsteps and break into Blackwater Hall in the hope of finding something. Apart from the fact that Claes and Osman were now on high alert for intruders, he wouldn't have the first idea of where to look. Katya's bedroom had been cleaned up before her death, and the forensics team had gone through it with a fine-tooth comb on his orders afterwards and found nothing. If the diary was in there, it was concealed in some ingenious fashion that had eluded both her uncle and the police. To find it Trave needed to talk to someone who knew about the hiding place, someone in whom Katya had confided. Because Trave knew from his years of criminal investigation that that was the way of secrets: they existed to be revealed, to be disclosed in hushed whispers to those we love or think we love. And who had Katya loved? Ethan – but he was dead – and before Ethan, David. Trave remembered the transcript:

'My uncle didn't approve of David, and so I couldn't see him in the house.'

'Never?'

'I took him there once when my uncle was away.'

What had happened when Katya had taken her first lover up to the house that one time? Trave wondered. It was an act of defiance on Katya's part, a way of telling David that she valued their relationship more than her uncle's wishes. And once inside, once they were upstairs in her bedroom, would she have wanted to do more – to show David things, to share her secrets with him so that he would know she cared? Perhaps. It was a long shot, but worth asking David about, if he could just find a way to talk to him. Except that that wasn't going to be easy. Prosecution witnesses were not supposed to talk to the defendant during the trial, and even if he could find a way past the court gaolers, David might not be prepared to see him. They hadn't parted on good terms in the cricket pavilion the previous October, and Trave didn't know whether David still blamed him for his arrest. He remembered how David had stared at him so intently while he was giving his evidence the day before – now he couldn't make up his mind whether the stare was benevolent or hostile. But whichever it was, Trave knew he had to try.

He looked at his watch. It was already twelve o'clock, but he didn't trust himself to drive after all the alcohol he'd drunk the night before. He rang up the police station, hoping to find Clayton, but was told that Clayton was out with PC Wale. And so without further delay Trave called a taxi to take him to the railway station. If Clayton couldn't drive him to London, he'd have to take the train.

It was mid-afternoon when he got to the Old Bailey, and some of the spectators had already gone home, making it possible for Trave to find a seat at the back of the public gallery above Court Number 1. Down below, Eddie Earle was in the witness box. The prosecution's star witness was still a serving prisoner, but someone, Macrae perhaps, had equipped him with a suit and tie, making him look almost respectable.

To Trave's surprise, Eddie seemed to enjoy giving evidence – he clearly had no shame about selling his old cellmate down the river. He was Easy Eddie again, wallowing in the attention of the courtroom, reliving the glory of his escape from Oxford Prison, and the prosecutor had to cut him off several times – or he would have been on the stand for the rest of the week describing his exploits.

Trave watched as David's barrister did everything he could to shake Eddie's credibility when his turn came to cross-examine: he made the obvious point that Eddie was lying to obtain leniency for his escape offence; he read Eddie's long list of previous convictions to the jury; and he questioned Eddie about his connection to Claes's friend, John Bircher. But Eddie was somehow able to deflect the attacks with ease. And looking down, Trave could see that what really held the jury's interest was Eddie's tale of his late-night conversations with David in their prison cell. Try as he might, David's barrister couldn't change the ring of truth with which Eddie described David's gathering rage against Katya, whom he blamed for all his misfortunes. There was no denying it: Eddie's evidence showed beyond doubt that the defendant was highly motivated to commit the crime with which he was charged.

Trave gazed down at Eddie and wished he could turn back the clock to the interview room in Oxford Police Station, to that moment when he'd been so convinced that Eddie had been on the verge of telling him the truth. About Bircher and Claes; about driving David out to Blackwater

Hall and giving him the gun loaded with blanks. Before Creswell came in and took him off the case. Trave remembered Macrae smiling at him from behind Creswell's shoulder in the corridor, just like he was smiling now, watching the noose tightening around David Swain's neck. Trave knew what was happening in the trial – the evidence that mattered was all one way. It was like the defendant was falling down a deep stone well and the points that his barrister made were no more than the scratches of his flailing hands on the walls as he fell.

At half past four Eddie finished his evidence and the judge adjourned the case for the day. Trave knew that it was now or never. He watched as the gaolers led David Swain down the stairs from the dock, and then he slipped out the back of the public gallery, ran down five flights of stairs until he got to the basement of the courthouse, and rang the bell beside the big iron door marked *Cells*. It was a busy time of day with the prisoners being got ready for the vans that would return them to their different prisons for the night, and Trave had to wait nearly five minutes for the door to open, but he knew better than to keep ringing to be let in. He needed the gaolers to be accommodating if he was to have any chance of an interview before David was taken back to Pentonville.

He was lucky. The young gaoler who answered the door seemed entirely satisfied when Trave waved his warrant card and said that he was a police officer come to see Swain – the prisoner on trial in Court Number 1. Trave signed his name in the book and took a seat in a small glass-fronted interview room. Opposite, across the corridor, a man with a scar across his face was gesticulating wildly at a barrister still dressed in his horsehair wig and gown, and through the open door Trave could hear a cacophony of shouts and footsteps and jangling keys.

Finally, just as he had been about to give up, David Swain appeared in the doorway.

'You again,' he said, sitting down heavily in the chair across the table from Trave without shaking his hand. 'I thought you weren't allowed to see me, you being a prosecution witness and all. That's what my mother told me.'

'She's right. I lied to get in here.'

'What did you say?'

'That I was a police officer.'

'Well, you are that.'

'Not any more. I got fired this morning.'

'I'm sorry. Katya hasn't done either of us much good, has she?' said David, looking Trave in the eye for the first time. Trave was relieved to see that there wasn't hostility in the young man's expression, just a fathomless suffering in his eyes that had aged him by years in the months since they had last met. 'God, I've had enough of this. Every day it just seems to get worse,' David went on in a weary voice without waiting for an answer to his question. 'Eddie's a professional liar, and yet the jurors were hanging on every word he said. I could see it in their eyes. The trial's a charade. That's what it is. Claes and Macrae have got it sewn up between them.'

'What about Osman?' asked Trave.

'What about him? I don't know if he's involved or not. Claes has probably got him duped as well. I wouldn't put it past him. Claes is the one behind it all, you know. It was him who was there waiting for me each time, not Osman. At the boathouse when Ethan died, outside Katya's room when I came out. He's a clever bastard – I'll say that for him. Too clever for the likes of us, I'm afraid. You should face it, Inspector – we're all played out. They should have done with the fancy wordplay and hang me tomorrow.'

'No,' said Trave fiercely. 'I won't let them.'

David looked at Trave for a moment as if he was some

345

kind of lunatic, but then his expression softened. 'You mean well,' he said. 'And you want to help me. I know that. But the trouble is you can't. You're out of your league this time, Inspector. Accept it.'

'No, I tell you,' said Trave, shouting now as he seized hold of David's hands across the table. 'There is something – a chance.'

'What chance?' asked David, pulling his hands away, taken aback by Trave's sudden outburst, his unnatural excitement.

'Katya wrote a diary. Maybe it still exists; maybe Osman never found it. Did she tell you about it? Did she?' asked Trave insistently, but David looked blank.

'What about the afternoon she took you up to the house, up to her room – when Osman was away? Did she show you something then?' demanded Trave, refusing to give up. His eyes bored into David's, searching for a response, and slowly, as if in answer to a prayer, a light of understanding began to dawn in David's face.

'Yes, she kissed me,' he said, speaking rapidly as if in the grip of a memory that he'd entirely forgotten up until that moment, 'and she took out a big book from the shelf and opened it – and it was hollow. And there was another book inside with lots of tiny writing, her writing, and she went to a page in the middle and showed me a picture she'd drawn. It was a picture of us, and it was like we were in our own house and we didn't need to hide all the time, like we had a future . . .' David broke off in mid-sentence, putting his head in his hands to hide his pain, and behind his back the door of the interview room opened. It was another gaoler – an older, more senior one this time. 'Time's up,' he said in a voice that brooked no argument. 'The prison van's here.'

'What book was it?' asked Trave as David got up to go. 'What big book?'

'I don't remember. It was a long time ago. Like it was in

another lifetime, like it happened to someone else,' said David sadly as he held out his wrists for the gaoler to put on the handcuffs.

Trave sensed the return of David's despair and wanted desperately to say something encouraging, but the words died in his mouth. It was just so damned hard to maintain hope when the cards were all stacked the other way, and he felt his heart sink as he watched David shuffle away down the corridor like a beaten man.

Just as he reached the top of the stairs leading up from the cells, Trave came face-to-face with Macrae.

'What were you doing down there? Have you been up to something you shouldn't?' asked Macrae with a smirk on his face.

Trave thought of punching his enemy but knew that he'd be playing into Macrae's hands if he did, and so contented himself with simply barging Macrae out of the way with his shoulder as he headed across the foyer toward the exit.

'Sorry to hear about your job,' Macrae shouted after Trave as soon as he'd recovered his balance, but Trave showed no sign he'd heard the taunt as he headed out the door into the cold darkness of the late afternoon.

CHAPTER 24

Macrae arrived first. He left Wale in the car, checked his coat, and followed the maître d' to a table in the corner set for two. He liked this place – the reflections in the big mirrors on the high white walls, the shine of the silver, the deference of the waiters in their tailcoats. The restaurant made him feel that he mattered, that he had weight in the world.

Methodical as always, he read the menu in its entirety, his thin lips moving silently as he enunciated the foreign words, savouring each one as he went about making his choice. And so he didn't notice Osman until his host was in the act of sitting down opposite him at the table.

'Well? What did Arne say?' asked Osman expectantly once the waiter had poured them each a glass of wine from an expensive-looking bottle that had followed Osman to the table.

Macrae sipped it with interest before he answered with a question of his own: 'Couldn't you get her to change her mind?'

'No, I already told you that,' said Osman impatiently. 'There's no point in even trying. It'll just make it worse. Bloody Trave – he's got right under her skin with his mind games.'

'Well, it won't matter,' said Macrae, patting his mouth delicately with his napkin. 'Sir Laurence understands that you have a perfectly good explanation for your niece's hysterical outburst. The fact is she was irrationally angry with you because you were preventing her from going back to the life of self-abuse from which you'd rescued her before.

You can give evidence of that after Mrs Trave has said her piece; and then, as you know, we've got documentary proof of Miss Osman's drug use and low-life associations, which we can also put in front of the jury. Sir Laurence says all this is a hiccup – nothing more than that.'

'A what?'

'I know. Not the word I'd have used either,' said Macrae, raising his eyebrows in amusement. 'But the point is you've got nothing to worry about. Swain'll swing just like he deserves to, you'll get the girl, and Trave'll drink himself to death thinking about it.'

'That's the part that appeals to you, isn't it?' said Osman with a contemptuous look.

'Yes, I'm not ashamed of it,' said Macrae evenly. 'We're trying to see justice done. That's the difference between us and Trave. He's a self-righteous prig, and he deserves exactly what's coming to him.'

'Because he was in your way up the greasy ladder, I suppose?'

'Not as much as he's in yours,' said Macrae with a dry smile. Turning to the hovering waiter, Macrae made his order, but Osman waved the man away. He didn't know what it was about Macrae that irritated him so much or why he should feel so demeaned by their association. It was enough that he did, and he had no intention of prolonging their meeting any longer than he had to.

'What about Jacob?' he asked, pouring himself another drink from the bottle but purposefully leaving Macrae's glass empty.

'He's gone to ground, but we'll find him.'

'You'd better. Before he finds me. He's got a gun, remember.'

'I remember,' said Macrae, sounding unperturbed. 'Do you think it was him or Trave who sent Swain's lawyers the stuff about your brother-in-law?'

'I don't know. Both of them maybe. I'm not a clairvoyant,' said Osman, making no effort to conceal his irritation as he got up from the table. 'Just find Mendel, okay? Before he does any more damage.'

Without waiting for an answer, Osman extracted an envelope from the inside pocket of his jacket, dropped it on the table, and then walked away without a word of farewell. Outside, he almost ran into the burly figure of Jonah Wale, who was standing on the pavement. Wale said hello, but Osman barely nodded in response as he got into his Bentley, letting out a sigh of relief as Franz Claes put the car in gear and drove away.

Macrae watched Osman's departure through the window and then picked up the envelope and glanced with satisfaction at its contents before turning his attention to the pâté de foie gras that he had ordered to precede the coq au vin. It gave him pleasure to know that Jonah was watching him through the window as he ate.

Three and a half miles away ex-Inspector Trave was eating too – a cold dinner cobbled together from the remains of the two previous nights' dinners, washed down with a glass of water from the tap. He ate mechanically, registering neither pleasure nor displeasure as he chewed and swallowed the food. His thoughts were elsewhere, focused obsessively on Katya's missing diary. The last few days had been exhilarating: chasing down the elusive memory in his mind, finding the line about the diary in the transcript of the girl's evidence, and getting the information about the hiding place from Swain of all people, right under Macrae's nose. He'd acted on a hunch and been proved correct, but that didn't mean the diary still existed. Trave knew from personal experience that happy endings were few and far between in real life. If the diary contained anything of note, Osman had almost certainly found it when he and his lackeys spring-cleaned Katya's bedroom after her murder, or before when he caught his niece looking through his things. Because that's what must have happened, Trave thought. She must have found something out, or Osman wouldn't have needed to have her killed. It was an article of faith for Trave now that Osman was responsible for his niece's death. He couldn't conceive of any other explanation, and it mattered to him not one jot that the only person who shared his view was Jacob Mendel, who was now in hiding somewhere, a fugitive from justice.

The diary had probably been destroyed. Going in search of it was probably a wild-goose chase. But a probability was not a certainty. There was a chance it was still there, sitting inside a hollowed-out book in Katya's book-case, waiting to be discovered. There had been big books as well as small books on the shelves in Katya's bedroom – hardbacks as well as paperbacks. Trave was sure he remembered them under the framed picture of her parents at the seaside that the doctor had asked him about. But was the right book there? Waiting?

There was only one way to find out and that was to look, but Trave knew it was hopeless for him to even consider going out to the house himself. He had no power to search openly, and Osman and Claes would be doubly on the watch for burglars after Jacob's antics three days earlier. No, the only person with a chance of getting in and out of Katya's room undetected was Vanessa.

Trave felt sick every time he thought of asking his wife to look for the diary, and yet he couldn't leave the idea alone. He remembered the cold hatred he'd felt for Jacob when the young man admitted to persuading Katya to search for evidence, and now here he was contemplating asking his wife to do the same. Except that Vanessa didn't need to be caught. A few minutes would be all it would take. Surely to God she could find an excuse to go upstairs for just a couple of minutes. The risk was minimal if she kept her wits about her.

He had to know one way or the other, Trave realized. And so he had to ask her. It was that simple. He'd already made his decision. For better or worse.

Vanessa didn't answer her phone when he called her in the morning, and so he went over to her flat to find her. It was in a little street behind Keble College that he'd never been to before. She'd given him the address when she first moved there so that he could forward her mail, but this was the first time that he'd ever visited it. There was no one home, and so he wandered the streets aimlessly, wondering what he would find to do to fill his days now that he was officially an ex-policeman. He made a pint of beer and a cheese sandwich in the Gardeners' Arms last half the afternoon and found Vanessa just returned from London when he knocked on her door again at half past three.

'Hullo, it's me again,' he said, stating the obvious as he stood awkwardly on her doorstep, twisting his hat in his hands. He felt horribly nervous suddenly, with his heart beating hard and a hot red flush spreading across his face. It didn't help that Vanessa didn't seem pleased to see him. She seemed like someone he didn't know any more, dressed in a black business suit and high heels, with her hair tied up above her head.

'This isn't a good time,' she said. 'I just got back from court, from giving evidence.'

'How was it?'

'Bad. I had to go. I know that. But I wish I hadn't – had to, I mean.' It was unlike Vanessa to muddle her words, and Trave saw how she looked upset, like she might be going to cry, and wished that he had chosen another time for his visit.

'I'm sorry,' he said. 'I phoned earlier but you weren't home. I wouldn't have come if it wasn't urgent.'

'All right, I suppose you'd better come in,' she said reluctantly, standing aside to let him pass before following him down the narrow hall into a small living room at the end of the corridor. Vanessa's pictures covered the walls – places he knew and didn't know rendered in vivid lines and bright colours. The paintings shocked Trave. He thought of the dark, unremarkable interior of the house two miles away up the road that they had shared together for more than twenty years. It bore no relation to this place. He'd never guessed at the energy, the creativity locked inside his wife; he realized with a jolt that he'd never helped her try and release it.

'They're beautiful,' he said, pointing at the walls. 'You should never have given it up.'

'Well, it's not too late to start again,' she said and then stopped, not intending her words to sound so harsh. She was overwrought. That was the problem. And her husband's visit felt like an invasion. Her flat, her carefully created new surroundings, were an attempt to start again, but they were also a barrier against the past, against memories that she couldn't cope with in the present. Just his presence posed a mortal threat to her peace of mind.

'I'm sorry,' she said. 'Like I said before, this isn't a good day. What is it you want, Bill? Why are you here?'

'I found out something – about Katya Osman. She kept a diary.' Trave spoke hesitantly, sitting perched on the edge of a low armchair and looking up at Vanessa where she stood, taut and unforgiving, with her back to the window. It was partly her lack of warmth that made him nervous, but he also wondered once again whether he had any right to ask her to place herself in danger on what might well be a fool's errand.

'She mentioned it in her evidence at the first trial,' he went

353

on when Vanessa did not respond. 'And it might still exist. In her bedroom out at Blackwater. It might show what really happened,' he ended lamely, unable to bring himself to ask Vanessa outright to go out there and look for the diary.

'What really happened!' Vanessa repeated her husband's words with an angry, exasperated edge to her voice. 'What really happened is that David Swain went and put a bullet in his ex-girlfriend because she didn't love him any more, and now he hasn't got the guts to own up to it.'

'I don't believe that,' said Trave quietly.

'No, of course you don't. You believe in some crazy conspiracy theory about Titus because you can't stand the idea of me being happy. Don't I deserve a life even if you're determined not to have one? Don't I?' Vanessa shouted, stamping her foot.

'Yes, of course you do,' said Trave, taken aback by his wife's sudden fury. 'I told you I want you to be happy.'

'You know I waited outside that courtroom for two hours today while Swain finished giving his evidence, and then I was in there for five minutes,' she went on, refusing to be placated as she gave full vent to her frustration. 'That's all it took – five minutes to burn my boats and go right back to where I started. Titus'll never marry me now,' she burst out, unable to control her bitterness.

'Well, if so, he's a fool,' said Trave. 'If he loves you, he'll understand you went to court because you had to. Because Swain's jury needs to hear all the evidence. There can't be any justice otherwise. It's the same reason why I want them to see Katya's diary. Except I can't get it. Only you can do that.'

'No, I can't,' Vanessa snapped back. 'Can't you get it through your head, Bill, that Titus and I have quarrelled? I'm not welcome at Blackwater Hall any more, and so I can't go snooping round there even if I wanted to, which I don't.'

'He'll make up with you. You know he will,' said Trave stolidly. 'And I'm not asking you to snoop around. I just want you to find an excuse to go up to Katya's bedroom for a couple of minutes – it's halfway down the corridor on the top floor, looking out to the front. All you've got to do is look in one bookcase and see if there are any large books with hollowed out insides. And if you don't find anything I won't ever bother you again. I promise.'

'Why? Why should I?'

'Because then you can be happy. Look, maybe I'm wrong. Maybe Osman's innocent; maybe Swain did kill Ethan and Katya; or maybe Claes did it and acted alone or with his sister. If you find the diary you'll know what happened one way or the other. You wouldn't have gone to London today if you didn't have doubts.'

Vanessa looked hard at her husband and then shook her head. 'No, Bill,' she said, getting up from her chair. 'I've done enough. If Titus comes back I shall marry him, and you know why? Because I don't need any diary to tell me who he is. He's a good man, an innocent man, and if you've any decency, you'll stop hounding him and leave him alone.'

Trave felt sick. He wished he hadn't come. He hadn't been prepared for the reality of Vanessa's new separate existence. There was something obscene about its negation of their shared past. He had no place here among these pictures, which screamed reproaches at him from every wall, and if he was to survive, he knew that he needed never to come here again.

But at the door, as he was leaving, he summoned his strength for one final effort. 'It's not for me that I'm asking you,' he said. 'It's for the dead who can't defend themselves: for Ethan and Katya – and yes, for the soon to be dead, for David Swain too. Think of them before you make up your mind.'

'I have,' she said. 'And I've thought of the living too.'

There was nothing more to say, and so she closed the door, shutting her husband out as he stood looking back at her, committing the lines of her face to his memory one last time.

Vanessa was already upset after her ordeal in London, and Trave's visit had made the strain almost intolerable. She'd had to appear convinced of Swain's guilt in order to get her husband out of the flat, but beneath the surface she felt deeply confused, at sea amid a storm of conflicting emotions. She took a walk; she had a drink; she turned on the radio – but nothing helped. Try as she might, she couldn't escape her recollection of that windowless Old Bailey courtroom with all those silent strangers hanging on her every word. Yes, it had only taken five minutes, but they had been five of the longest minutes of her life. She hadn't been prepared for the sombre formality of the place – the wigs and the gowns and the antique language – and she hadn't anticipated what it would be like to come face-to-face with David Swain for the first time. Until today he had been only a name. But now he was real – a living, breathing human being sitting only a few yards from where she stood giving evidence, a young man who probably only had a few weeks left to live, even though he was perfectly healthy. Sooner rather than later he was going to be turned off a gallows with a black hood over his head and his hands tied behind his back and left to swing until he was finally cut down. That was why the spectators' gallery in the courtroom was filled to the rafters – it was the same reason why great crowds of people had always turned out to watch hangings when they were still carried out in public: a fascination with death that was as old as humanity itself.

Until today Vanessa hadn't had to contemplate any of this, but now, by coming to court, she knew she'd become part of the process. She was involved, complicit, whether she liked it or not. And it was as if Swain instinctively knew this too. His eyes had never left her face all the time she was in the witness box, and she'd found she couldn't resist his stare. She kept looking back at him as she answered the barristers' questions; she could see the whiteness of his knuckles on the brass rail in front of the dock as he leaned over it toward her; and, as she walked past him down the aisle at the end of her evidence, she read his lips as he mouthed the word 'thank you' toward her, not once but twice.

Now she couldn't get his face out of her mind, however hard she tried. He might well be guilty; in fact he probably was, but yet she couldn't be sure. Bill had been right – she'd gone to London partly to assuage her conscience and partly, as he'd said, because she had doubts about Swain's guilt, and denying her uncertainty to her husband had only served to make her doubts more insistent than before. They weren't doubts about Titus – just like she'd told Trave, she was quite certain that he had had nothing to do with his niece's murder, but what about Franz Claes? She remembered the cold, disgusted way she'd caught him looking at her sometimes in unguarded moments – in the rear-view mirror of the Bentley or when she entered a room. And she knew it wasn't just her he hated; it was all women, except his sister perhaps, and she was as sexless as a woman could be. What must Claes have made of Titus's passionate niece, Vanessa wondered, when Katya started asking awkward questions, poking her nose into Claes's private affairs? Because Claes had secrets. That much was obvious. After quarrelling with Titus that evening at Blackwater, Vanessa had bought all the newspapers she could lay her hands on. She'd read every word about what had been put to Claes in cross-examination the day before; she'd looked at the blown-up photographs of his Nazi associates who'd ruled Belgium with an iron fist during the German occupation, pronouncing their harsh-sounding names to herself – Ehlers, Asche, Reeder. What had Claes been doing all those years, she asked herself – helping Jews or sending them to their deaths? And if the latter, what would Claes not do now to keep his secret?

Had Katya found out something about him? Vanessa wondered. Had he killed her because of that and set up Swain to take the blame? And had Katya known what he intended? Was that the meaning behind her desperate words – 'They're trying to kill me'?

Vanessa was quite sure that Claes, acting with or without his sister, was more than capable of murdering Katya, but was he actually guilty? Maybe Bill was right. Perhaps Katya's diary would tell her the truth. Perhaps she should look for it – climb the stairs to the room that had once been Katya's bedroom and look in her bookcase for a hollowed-out book. But for that she needed Titus to come back to her. Without him she could never return to Blackwater Hall, without him her future seemed suddenly black. Vanessa was filled with a sudden visceral longing for her lover. She wanted to feel his arms about her; she wanted to wear his ring again; and as if in answer to her prayer the telephone rang beside her hand and it was Titus asking to come over.

He came with flowers, a multitude of them that temporarily hid his face and body until she had taken them out of his hands and filled all the vases in the flat with purple and pink and yellow and blue – a riot of colour to match the pictures on the walls that her husband had complimented her on earlier in the day.

'I'm sorry,' said Osman, watching her arranging the stems from the doorway of the kitchen. 'I was rude to you in my own house, when you were my guest. I am ashamed of myself. Can you forgive me, Vanessa?'

He stood up straight and spoke formally, as if he was making some kind of public confession. She could tell he was nervous about what she would say. It was endearing how much he cared.

'I already forgave you. About five minutes after I drove away from your house,' she said with a smile, reaching out to caress his cheek as she went past him through the door with a bunch of flowers in her hand.

'I was taken by surprise,' he said, following her into the living room. 'That was the problem. When I thought about it, of course I understood that you had to do what you thought was right. But by then you were gone, and I felt nervous about coming after you.'

'It was Franz,' she said. 'If he hadn't come in I wouldn't have left. I can't stand him, Titus,' she burst out, unable to control her feelings any longer. 'I can't stand the way he looks at me; I can't stand who he was. You worked with him so you could help people escape. I understand why you did what you did. But I can't make compromises like that. It's not who I am.'

'I know: it's the same reason you gave evidence,' said Osman gently, taking hold of her hands. 'You are true to yourself through and through, you're like a perfect diamond. It's what I love about you; it's why I want you to be my wife.'

'And that's what I want too,' said Vanessa agitatedly. 'But not with Franz there. He can't live with us, Titus, when we're together. I don't want to see him, or his sister.'

'You won't have to. I promise,' said Osman, placing his hand over his heart like he was taking an oath. 'Now, do you feel better?'

'Yes. Like a new woman,' she said, laughing as she returned his kiss. And it was true. She felt wonderful suddenly, like everything was finally going to turn out all right. Titus had given her what she wanted without even hesitating. What greater proof could she have of how much he loved her?

But the feeling of euphoria didn't last. Perhaps it was Titus's nervousness at dinner that unsettled her. He insisted on sitting at the back of the restaurant that he had chosen in an out-of-the-way backstreet and kept glancing over towards the door whenever any new customers came in.

'I'm sorry, my dear. It's this man, Jacob Mendel, that I told you about, who's got me on edge,' he explained. 'The police still haven't found him. He's gone into hiding, but that doesn't mean he won't try something again. Like I told you before, he's got a gun and has no qualms about using it. God knows where he got it from. They're not easy things to get hold of in this country. You need a licence.' Osman's anxiety was obvious, and it unnerved Vanessa. She wanted Titus to be a rock, strong and invincible like he was before, not the bundle of nerves that he had turned into tonight.

'You said he blamed you for what happened to his brother. Why? Why would he do that?' she asked, thinking how pleased her husband would be to know that someone else shared his obsessive suspicion of Titus.

'I don't know. It makes no sense,' said Osman. 'Maybe because Ethan was my guest and I didn't protect him, but how could I? I had no idea that Swain was coming. Just like I didn't know with Katya. God, if only I had,' he said, pressing his hand over his eyes as if trying to shut out an unwanted memory.

'It's not your fault,' said Vanessa, taking Titus's hand across the table. 'But what about Franz? Are you sure *he* didn't know . . .' She stopped in mid-sentence, but her meaning was obvious.

'Yes, of course I'm sure,' said Osman, recoiling. 'I know you don't like Franz, but he had nothing to do with what happened to Ethan or Katya. He couldn't have done.'

'But he didn't like Ethan, did he?' said Vanessa, persisting with her questions despite Osman's discouragement. 'Ethan was Jewish.'

'That had nothing to do with it,' said Osman quickly.

'And what about Katya? What did he think of her?' asked Vanessa.

'They didn't get on very well. But that doesn't mean anything. He's not good with women. I already told you that. Swain committed both those murders, Vanessa. You've got to understand that,' said Osman in a voice that brooked no opposition. He was holding his wine glass so tight that Vanessa thought it would break.

She nodded in apparent acquiescence, dropping her eyes, keeping her doubts to herself. Secretly she hoped that Swain would be acquitted of Katya's murder, but she wasn't going to tell Titus that. He obviously had a complete blind spot where his brother-in-law was concerned, and she had no wish to risk another quarrel. And yet, try as she might, she couldn't contain her sense of unease. Over coffee she returned to the subject of Titus's niece. The girl had a hold over her mind, and Vanessa didn't seem able to stop thinking about her.

'What was Katya like?' she asked. 'You never talk about her.'

'It's painful,' said Osman. 'We didn't get on a lot of the time, and now that she's gone I wish I'd handled our relationship differently. But it's too late, and so I try not to think about it, even though I know that's wrong.'

'It's understandable,' said Vanessa sympathetically. 'Why didn't you get on?'

'Because it was my duty to step into her parents' shoes after they died, and she wouldn't go along with that. She got into trouble at school and with boys, and I tried to stop her; and then, each time I crossed her, she resented me more. It got much worse at the end after Ethan died, but I already

361

told you that. "You're not my father" was her favourite phrase,' said Osman sadly. 'And we often didn't seem to be able to get much beyond our angry words. But what's done is done. You can't bring back the dead.'

'Did she leave anything behind? Anything that you could remember her by?' asked Vanessa.

'No, hardly anything. But she was like that – quick and darting and slender, like some wild bird. I had her photograph on my desk, but then I put it away. It was too painful.'

'Painful': it was the second time that Osman had used the word in connection with Katya in less than a minute, and Vanessa felt oddly dissatisfied by the inadequacy of his description of his niece. Vanessa had only met Katya twice, the second time for only a few moments before the girl fainted away, and yet she had left an indelible impression on Vanessa's mind, and Vanessa knew instinctively as she got up to go that she would never have any peace of mind until she knew for certain who it was that had murdered the poor girl in her bed the previous September.

'Why did Inspector Macrae tell you I went to see him?' Vanessa asked as Osman went to kiss her goodbye at the end of the evening. 'I thought it was confidential.'

'I suppose he wanted to help me,' said Osman slowly, thrown momentarily off-balance by the suddenness of the question. 'He wanted me to know that he was doing all he could to make poor Katya's murderer pay for what he'd done.'

'By concealing evidence?'

'Yes; he was wrong. And so was I,' said Osman. 'And you forgave me for that, remember?'

'Yes, I remember,' said Vanessa, and, putting both her arms around Titus's neck, she kissed him long and hard. It felt that good to have him back.

CHAPTER 25

The trial was moving inexorably towards its end, towards the day when David Swain would finally know his fate. The evidence had all been heard, recorded word for word by the shorthand writer sitting crouched over at her table under the judge's dais. All that remained now was for the judge to give his summing up and put the defendant in the charge of the jurors so that they could 'render a true verdict according to the evidence', and choose whether he would live or die.

The evidence included David's testimony as well. He'd stood in the witness box for a day and a half at the end of the previous week, wearing the black suit and tie that his mother had brought him from Oxford, and told the silent jurors 'the truth, the whole truth and nothing but the truth'. But his words had sounded flat and hollow and unconvincing even in his own ears, and he'd seen how they had kept their eyes averted as he spoke, looking everywhere except at him, refusing to connect, just like their predecessors had done when he was tried for Ethan's murder in this same court two and a half years earlier. Just like before, the thin-faced prosecutor had been able to cleverly twist his words, and David realized now that the web that unseen hands had been spinning around him for so long was far too cunningly constructed for him to be able to escape its knots by mere assertions of his own innocence.

He knew instead that the only way out of the maze was to examine each link in the chain of events that had brought him to where he was now. There had to be a weakness

363

somewhere – something he'd overlooked that would exonerate him and identify his tormentors. And so backwards in time he went, night after night, scouring his memory for clues, and each time he came face-to-face with the figure of one man – Franz Claes. At the critical moment, at the scene of each murder, Claes had been there waiting for him – limping round the corner of the boathouse, armed with his gun, just as David had taken hold of Ethan's waterlogged body and felt the sticky blood seeping out onto his hands, or emerging from the shadows at the end of Blackwater Hall's top-floor corridor, shooting at David's back as David stumbled out of Katya's bedroom, unable to comprehend the sight of her dead body. Claes; always Claes. And now it turned out that he was a Nazi, or as good as one: he'd spent the war working for the Belgian government, collaborating with Nazis, who were busy sending trainloads of Belgian Jews to the concentration camps. David felt sure that Claes was guilty of Ethan's murder and Katya's too. He just couldn't prove it. That was the trouble.

And what about Titus Osman? Was he in league with Claes, or had Claes acted independently of his rich brother-in-law throughout? David didn't know. At David's first trial Osman testified that he'd seen Ethan for lunch before Ethan left for Oxford. Had Claes intercepted Ethan after he left the Hall or had Osman lied about Ethan's departure? David remembered how Osman had banned him from Blackwater Hall because he wasn't good enough for Katya, and he recalled the smooth, unemotional way Osman had given his evidence, but that didn't amount to a case. Everything pointed to Claes as the man behind the curtain: his career in the Belgian government showed that he was clearly a resourceful man, more than capable of having orchestrated all the events that had brought David to his present sorry pass.

David understood now that all that had happened since

Ethan's death – the highs and the lows, the good luck and the bad – had been no more than his jerking about like a puppet on the end of a string, waiting until the hidden hand that controlled his fate returned to use him once again. That hand had been at work in Oxford Prison, tempting him toward escape: Eddie Earle had to have been involved in the conspiracy. He was connected back to Claes through this John Bircher character, who'd jumped off the top of a multi-storey car park – or been pushed . . .

David realized now how easy he had made it for Eddie. All that had been needed to fuel his anger to boiling point were the few inflammatory words and phrases that Eddie had dropped cleverly into their late-night conversations. Because anger had been the driving force of David's life for as long as he could remember – he had been angry with his father for dying and his mother for remarrying, with Katya for rejecting him, and with Ethan for taking her away. Poor Ethan: David had stayed angry with his rival even after he was dead.

Anger had been David's undoing. It gave him a motive, and it was the reason he'd been chosen to play the part of murderer not once but twice. He remembered every detail of the night of Katya's murder like it was a film that he'd watched a thousand times and couldn't get out of his head. He remembered the exhilaration of the prison escape – the terrible fear of being caught replaced by the explosion of ecstatic triumph as he reached the top of the perimeter wall and came down the other side, and then the unforgettable sensation of the cold night air beating against his face as Eddie drove them down the road to Blackwater, past the sleeping houses. He'd felt utterly alive at those moments because he was free, free when he had never expected to be free again.

What a fool he'd been! He'd taken such comfort in the gun he'd insisted on Eddie providing when he little knew that it was useless – loaded with blank ammunition. Claes had known he was coming. Bircher, the man with the beard, must have called Blackwater Hall straight after he'd left the railway station – those two unanswered calls to the Hall from a public phone box at 12.20 and a minute later had been a prearranged signal. David imagined Claes sitting on his bed in the darkness, nursing his gun in his hands, nodding with a knowing satisfaction as he caught the distant sound of the glass breaking in the study window down below and waited for David's footsteps to pass by his door.

David was sure that Claes had meant to kill him: the bastard would have known that he would be immune from prosecution for shooting down an armed intruder who had just murdered the householder's niece in her bed. But David thought that Claes must also have realized that missing the target wasn't the end of the world either. Let the state do the work instead. David would be just as dead swinging from a gallows as with a bullet in the back of his head. And then it would all be over – wrapped up and disposed of once and for all: Ethan dead and Katya dead and David Swain too, who had killed them both for the sake of an insane jealousy.

David understood the plan. He knew he had been used, set up not once but twice. But he still had no idea why. Ethan and Katya had died for a reason. They had to have found out something – probably a secret or secrets about Claes and his Nazi past. The secret was the key to saving himself. David was sure of it. And yet what could he do to uncover it, locked up in the bowels of Pentonville Prison without a friend in the world?

People had tried to help him. He remembered how Inspector Trave had been so desperate to know about Katya's diary when he came to see him in the cells beneath the court the previous week, but David had heard nothing since. Because what good could Trave do? He wasn't even a policeman any more. And his wife had gone off with Osman.

David was grateful to her. It must have cost her a lot to come to court and give evidence about what Katya had told her. 'They're trying to kill me' – powerful words, but in the end they hadn't made any difference. Osman had just gone back into the witness box afterwards and explained them away in a few short sentences, describing how Katya had gone so far off the rails after Ethan's death that Osman ended up having to keep her at the Hall for her own safety, even though she hated him for it. And the jury had believed him. They'd had to – there was independent evidence to back him up.

David was as good as dead. He knew that. It amazed him that he could be so certain of conviction when he was so entirely innocent. But the prosecution had everything: presence, motive, weapon, even a confession. David did not regret admitting to Katya's murder. He knew he had had no choice. Macrae and Wale had broken him after his arrest that night in the cell with the thick iron door at the back of Oxford police station, broken him entirely, and he knew that he would never be the same person again. He had been naked, and they had been clothed, and Wale had done things to him that he had never imagined one human being could do to another, turning the pain on and off like a faucet at Macrae's direction, but never leaving a mark, until David had finally given up and confessed to everything just to have it over with.

In the witness box he'd told the jurors about the torture, but from the outset he'd sensed their disbelief. He hadn't the power of description to make them understand what it had been like, standing there shivering under the white electric bulb, waiting for Wale to come at him again while Macrae sat on a chair in the corner, watching.

And the memory of Wale's face and Macrae's voice had stayed with him ever since, driving out his anger and emptying him inside as he lay awake at night in his cell, thinking back on all that had happened, trying in vain to find a way out of the web in which he was so tightly enmeshed.

Towards the end the trial became a blur, with the days dissolving into one another, divided only by bumpy rides in the prison van through dark London streets and awful, sleepless nights tossing and turning on his hard, narrow bed. He was alone now: Toomes had been convicted and sentenced to death and moved God knows where to await his fate. And now it was David's turn. After hours spent like a caged animal, walking backwards and forwards across the nine square feet of his iron-barred cell in the basement of the Old Bailey, he was taken upstairs in the late afternoon to hear the jury's verdict, handcuffed between two silent gaolers who had seen it all before. They passed down a neon-lit corridor beneath an arched, whitewashed roof, and David imagined for a moment that this is what his last walk would be like – stumbling along under bright white lights towards a half-open door at the end. But the door this time opened onto an old creaking elevator, not the wooden gallows and the knotted rope that haunted all his dreams.

From the lift, David climbed the short flight of steep stairs into the dock, and suddenly the packed courtroom rushed towards him from all sides as he emerged out into its midst. Everyone was already in their appointed places, and there was nowhere to hide from the stretched, hungry faces craning towards him to get a final look at the man who might be going to die. And above them all the black-robed judge sat quite still in his high-backed chair, brooding with hooded eyes like an old vulture.

The babbling murmur that had greeted David's arrival in the courtroom subsided, and the judge's clerk got slowly to his feet, cleared his throat, and asked the foreman of the jury the centuries-old question: 'Have you reached a verdict on which you are all agreed?'

'Yes, Your Honour,' said the foreman immediately in a high, squeaky, nervous voice. He was a little man with red cheeks and a bald head, wearing a pair of horn-rimmed glasses that were too big for his cherubic round face. He looked like a middle-aged schoolboy, entirely out of place in the role he had been elected to perform.

A pause then – a second or two perhaps while the clerk gathered his robe about him – and David felt the pressure growing on his chest and inside his head like he was going to burst open or shatter into a thousand pieces. It was as if he was drowning, seeing and hearing everything around him through a wall of swirling blue water. He looked up at the picture of the lion and unicorn, the symbol of British justice, hanging on the wall above the judge's head, and prayed for acquittal.

And then the clerk's voice came again, even and measured, reaching him as if from far, far away:

'On the single count of murder, how do you find the defendant? Guilty or not guilty?'

'Please, please, please,' David screamed inside his head. But nobody heard him; all they heard was the foreman's falsetto voice pronouncing that one word, 'guilty', that meant the end of David Swain.

It was what everyone in the court had been waiting for. They exhaled as one in a collective gasp, and then went quiet again as a skeletal man in a frock coat appeared behind the judge's chair and silently placed a square of black silk on top of the old man's wigged head.

And the judge began slowly speaking the words of the sentence, enunciating each syllable as if it was some ancient curse:

'David John Swain, you are sentenced to be taken hence

369

to the prison in which you were last confined and from there to a place of execution, where you will suffer death by hanging, and thereafter your body . . .'

But he got no further. The silence of the courtroom was shattered by a lone voice crying high up in the rafters of the public gallery, and, looking up, David saw his mother standing there, shaking her fist. She was dressed in that same charcoal-grey dress that she had worn for her visit to him in the prison.

'No,' she shouted. 'No, you won't. He's mine, my flesh and blood. I won't let you,' and suddenly she reached down and took off one of her shiny black shoes and threw it through the air down at the judge. It didn't hit him; instead it landed just short of his dais, bounced in the well of the court, and ending up under the feet of Inspector Macrae, who had up to that moment been sitting at the exhibits table with a look of smug satisfaction on his waxy face.

And immediately there was chaos: people getting up and knocking into one another and shouting as the judge and the ancient man in the frock coat disappeared through the door behind the dais, and David was bundled down the stairs from the dock, still uninformed about what would happen to his body after he had been hung by the neck until he was dead.

Back in his cell he knelt down on the hard cement floor and took hold of the toilet bowl in the corner with both his hands, gripping on to it like a drowning man. He felt nauseous, his stomach churned, and he could taste the vomit in his mouth as he retched, but nothing happened. He leant his head down against the cold porcelain and closed his eyes and contemplated his own extinction. He saw the rain again falling on his poor father's coffin at the bottom of that pit in Wolvercote Cemetery, and he thought of being alive one moment, standing on the wooden trapdoor of the gallows, and then being dead and gone the next, blotted out forever. It was like turning off a light switch at the wall except that the light of his life could never be turned back on once they'd broken his neck. Life suddenly seemed so precious: air and sun and water, chestnuts in the pockets of his school uniform, his face in Katya's long blonde hair one summer afternoon, his mother's hand in his, crossing the road to the playground when he was a child. He'd never really understood that she loved him until now, when she'd thrown her shoe in front of all those strangers. He loved her for her defiance, but he knew it wouldn't make any difference. The sand in the hourglass was fast running out.

He hadn't made much of his life. He knew that. He wished he'd used his time better. But he was young. He could change, except that now he wouldn't have that chance. He was going to die not because he had cancer or some incurable sickness but because others had decided that he must. It didn't have to happen, but it would happen. That was what made it unbearable. He'd die and be put in a pit like his father, and the world would go on as before, except that he wouldn't be a part of it any more. Soon he'd be old news, forgotten by everyone except his mother and Max, who'd met his brother one morning and now didn't have one any more.

Tears ran down David's face into the toilet bowl and his back shook and his stomach heaved, but the Old Bailey gaolers didn't pay much attention. Prisoner R137861 was being sick in his cell, and there was nothing very remarkable about that. He'd just heard that he was going to swing, and that took some getting used to. They understood these things because, after all, they'd seen them all before.

CHAPTER 26

All through the weekend Vanessa grew more agitated. She tried everything to calm herself down, but nothing worked: she took up her paints and then threw them away in disgust; she spent half an hour reading her book and then realized that she hadn't taken in a single word; and eventually, in despair, she put on her overcoat in defiance of the wintry weather, intending to take a brisk walk down by the river, but ended up envying the regal calm of a pair of swans watching her disinterestedly from the other bank. The only respite from her anxiety came when she went out to the newsagent on Sunday morning and bought editions of all the newspapers, stumbling home with a pyramid of news-print balanced precariously in her hands, and then drank three cups of coffee one after the other while she sat at the kitchen table reading with avid concentration all the accounts of everything that had happened at the Swain trial the previous week, grimacing with worry when each article ended up referring to the strength of the case against the accused.

Vanessa continued to go back and forth in her mind, gnawing at the evidence in a state of ever-growing anxiety. As Bill had said, only Katya's diary could tell her the truth – if it existed, of course, which was a big if. She wished she could read it without having to look for it. Because looking might mean tangling with Claes, and Vanessa was not ashamed to admit that that prospect unnerved her. She knew how much Claes disliked her already, and she was sure that his dislike would soon build into hatred when he found out that Titus was prepared to sacrifice him on the altar of his love for Vanessa Trave. And if Claes was guilty of these murders and found her digging for evidence against him, he wouldn't hesitate about killing her. She knew how cold-blooded he was. He'd wait to get her alone on some deserted street corner or down by the river, and then he'd take her from behind with a hand over her mouth to stifle her screams and twist a sharpened knife in her gut, just like he must have done with Ethan. If he killed Ethan . . .

Vanessa couldn't make up her mind about who was responsible. She remained steadfastly unsure of the truth, plagued by doubt and uncertainty, hoping for David Swain to be acquitted so that she could carry on as before and do nothing, even though deep down she knew that Katya's ghost would not permit her to remain inert forever. Sooner or later she'd have to go and look for the diary, but in the meantime she ignored the summons of the telephone that kept ringing in the living room. She knew it was either her husband or Titus. Both of them wanted her to go out to Blackwater Hall, albeit for different reasons, and that was the one place she didn't want to go near, at least until the trial was over.

The weekend finally came to an end, and work on Monday morning did help provide some temporary distraction from her inner turmoil. For the next two days she stayed long hours in the office, filing and refiling her employer's correspondence, answering letters that didn't need answering, but under her professional exterior she was finding the uncertainty of the trial's outcome harder and harder to cope with. And on Wednesday, after reading two newspaper summaries of the judge's summing up of the mountain of evidence against the defendant, she decided she couldn't stand it any more and stayed home from work. All day she paced the rooms of her flat like they were a prison cell, listening to the hourly news broadcasts on the radio, until the verdict was finally announced at five o'clock, complete with a description of the pandemonium that had broken out in the courtroom when a member of the public had thrown her shoe at the judge, just when he was halfway through pronouncing the defendant's death sentence.

Now Vanessa didn't hesitate. She knew what she had to do. She turned off the radio and rang up Titus. He sounded ecstatic to hear from her.

'I've been worrying about you,' he said. 'You didn't answer my calls. Have you been all right?'

'I had some kind of virus,' she lied, 'so I went to bed and took lots of medicines and unplugged the telephone, but I'm better now. Can I see you?'

'Of course you can. When?'

'Tomorrow for lunch? I can get the day off.'

'Wonderful,' he said. She'd never heard him sounding so happy.

'Good, I'll see you then.'

She rang off, realizing that she'd said nothing about the verdict, and that she hadn't even asked about the man with the gun whom Titus was so worried about. Still, she knew there'd be plenty of time to discuss these topics and others at lunch the next day – before she found an excuse to slip away and look for Katya's diary at the top of the house.

She awoke the next morning to a dense white fog that had enveloped the city in a damp, sightless embrace. The red brick neo-Gothic towers of Keble College that usually dominated the view from her living room window were now no more than vague shapes in the mist. All morning she hoped that the fog would clear, but if anything it was thicker than before when she finally screwed up her courage and got in her car to go to Blackwater.

The journey took much longer than usual since she had

to drive very slowly, feeling her way tentatively along the roads, and Osman was waiting anxiously for her when she finally pulled up in the courtyard and turned off her headlights. He came hurrying down the steps, opened her door, and, taking her arm, steered her through the haze into the warmth of the hall. She felt a surge of relief as she took off her coat and preceded her lover through the door of the drawing room, but then stopped dead in her tracks as she caught sight of Claes standing in front of the fire. She was rooted to the spot, unable to go forward to take Claes's outstretched hand, but Claes didn't seem in the least put out by her rudeness. Instead he smiled broadly, and the tightening of his facial muscles stretched the white scar running down beside his left ear and the mutilated red skin below his jaw, giving him an almost obscene appearance that Vanessa felt sure was a calculated effect, since there was no warmth in his grey eyes to back up the smile on his lips. She felt as if some invisible portion of the fog had followed her inside, wrapping its tendrils around her body.

Osman didn't seem pleased with Claes's presence either, but Claes remained apparently impervious to his companions' obvious wish to be alone. Lunch in the dining room was a miserable affair. Vanessa kept looking towards the door, getting ready to excuse herself so she could go upstairs and search for the diary, but then each time she was about to open her mouth, she caught Claes looking at her out of the corner of his eye. She felt irrationally certain that he could read her mind. And so she dropped her eyes to the table and watched his bony hands holding his knife and fork as he methodically cut up the meat on his plate, and imagined him cutting into her flesh too, sawing her, watching her bleed.

She couldn't eat. She felt weak, helpless in the face of her fear of Claes. What if there was no diary? she asked herself.

What if Swain was guilty – just like the jury had said? But then she remembered the way Swain had mouthed 'thank you' at her as she left the court, and she thought of how young he was – not much older than her own son who had died. She imagined him on the gallows, waiting for the trap to give way beneath his feet, and she went back to toying with her food.

'Have you heard about the verdict, Mrs Trave?' Claes asked, breaking the silence.

'Yes,' she said, refusing to meet his eye.

'And what do you make of it?' he asked. 'You must be disappointed in the outcome after your efforts for Mr Swain's defence.'

'No,' she said quietly. 'It's for the jury to decide, not me.'

'Quite right, my dear,' said Osman, coming to her rescue. 'These trials are very unpleasant. We have to do our duty and give evidence, whether it's for the prosecution or the defence, but that doesn't mean we enjoy the experience or what comes after. Personally I do not like the death penalty, but I understand why some people think it's necessary.'

Claes snorted, as if unable to believe his ears. 'What are you talking about?' he asked. 'You can't have law and order without it. They should use it more, not less. And for scum like Swain the rope's too quick, if you ask me. They should throttle him to death for what he did.'

Vanessa looked up, appalled by Claes's sadism, and was in time to see a look of fury on Titus's face before it vanished, replaced by a thin smile.

'Well, I suppose there are exceptions,' he said in a measured voice, keeping his eyes on Claes. 'Colonel Eichmann for instance. Have you been following that story, Vanessa?'

'Yes, a little.' Vanessa wasn't going to admit it, but she'd read a great deal about Adolf Eichmann since his capture by the Israeli secret service in Buenos Aires the previous May. There had been an international outcry about the kidnap, but Vanessa had been overjoyed. Now his trial was fast approaching in Jerusalem and there'd be a chance for some tiny measure of justice for the millions of men, women, and children that the monster had had transported across Europe to their deaths in the Nazi concentration camps.

'Perhaps there are some criminals whose crimes are so, how do you say, heinous – yes, that's the word – that they should suffer the ultimate punishment,' Osman went on, speaking in the same precise way, as if he was taking part in an organized debate. 'What do you think, Franz?'

Vanessa glanced over at Claes and saw that livid red spots had appeared in the centre of each of his pale cheeks and that his hands were clenched into tight fists. He looked Osman in the eye, but he didn't reply.

'Well, perhaps we should change the subject and discuss something more pleasant,' said Osman, shrugging his shoulders. 'Have you been doing any painting, Vanessa?'

But Vanessa had no chance to respond. The doorbell rang, and a minute later Detective Clayton and Constable Wale were shown into the dining room by a housemaid.

'I'm sorry to bother you, sir,' said Clayton awkwardly, 'but we wanted you to know we were here, taking a look around.' He spoke to Osman but glanced over at Vanessa, as if surprised by her presence.

'Thank you. I appreciate your consideration, Detective,' said Osman. 'Have you any particular reason for thinking Mr Mendel's going to be showing up here today?' he asked in an apparently casual tone, although Vanessa could tell that he was more interested than he was letting on.

'Just that when I talked to him before in his flat he seemed to attach a great deal of significance to the outcome of the trial up in London,' said Clayton, picking his words carefully.

'Significance – what significance?' demanded Claes.

'Well, he said that if Mr Swain was convicted, then "they'll have won; they'll have got away with everything". Those were his words,' said Clayton reluctantly. 'He implied that he would have nothing left to lose.'

'And we are they, of course,' said Osman with a faint smile. 'Well, that certainly sounds rather ominous, Detective. I hope that you and Constable Wale manage to find Mr Mendel before he does anything else stupid.'

Vanessa looked past Clayton to where Wale was standing in the doorway. She remembered him now from when she'd gone to visit Inspector Macrae at the police station and he'd shown her out. He'd had that same ugly, smirking smile on his face then as he had now. It felt like he was mentally undressing her, and she turned away with a shudder.

'Are you all right, Mrs Trave?' asked Clayton, noticing Vanessa's grimace without understanding its cause. He'd seen how nervous she looked when he first came in.

'I'm fine,' she said, refusing to meet his eye. She was all too aware of Claes staring at her across the table.

'Bloody foreigners! They get all the luck,' said Wale with a harsh laugh once they were back outside. 'I bet Trave finds it difficult getting much shut-eye at night thinking about his missis tucked up with old Casanova in there. She's quite a looker for her age, I'll give you that.'

'Shut up, Jonah. And keep your foul thoughts to yourself,' said Clayton angrily.

'All right, keep your hair on,' said Wale, getting into the police car beside Clayton. 'You're a grumpy sod, aren't you?'

Clayton stayed quiet, sensing the car's suspension settling down under Wale's weight. He knew better than to allow himself to be needled, knowing that he'd only be providing Wale with free entertainment, but even after a week in Wale's company he still found it hard to get used to the mean, crude way in which the man's mind worked.

Their complete lack of success in tracking down Jacob Mendel hadn't helped Clayton's mood either. But he had an instinctive feeling that today would be the day that Jacob would show himself if he was ever going to, and he was determined to make as thorough a search of the grounds as the fog would allow. Ignoring Wale's complaints therefore that it was 'a bloody waste of time', Clayton drove down to the road and parked under the trees by the path that led up to the boathouse. And then, leaving Wale in the car, he climbed the fence and set off into the mist.

Back in the dining room of Blackwater Hall, Vanessa had had enough. The policemen's visit had unnerved Osman, and now he and Claes were talking anxiously about Jacob's possible whereabouts. Vanessa knew it was now or never. Maybe there was no diary, but soon she would run out of courage and would never know one way or the other.

She got up from the table, announcing casually that she was going to the bathroom. Osman raised his hand in brief acknowledgement, and Claes went on talking, apparently unaware of her departure. Outside, she turned quickly down the corridor leading to the hall, and then ran up the staircase to the first floor. At the top of the stairs a corridor opened out in both directions. She knew she wasn't yet on the top floor, but she couldn't see the way up. Blindly she ran to her right, and at the end, round the corner, she found what she was looking for – another flight of stairs going up. She took them two at a time and started down another corridor, narrower than the one down below. Now she went slower, counting the doors on her left until she was halfway along. Tentatively, she pushed open the half-closed door and saw a bed but no bookcase. Perhaps this had been Katya's room;

perhaps the bookcase had been moved; perhaps the girl's books had been sold or thrown out now that their owner had no further use for them. With an effort Vanessa pushed her doubts to the back of her mind – she'd come too far to stop now. The next door down could still count as halfway. This one was shut. Slowly she turned the handle, and there it was, right in front of her – an old brown bookcase filled to overflowing with books of different sizes, and on the top a silver-framed photograph of a middle-aged couple standing by the sea.

Vanessa closed the door and began to search. Bill had said the book was big, and so there was no point looking in the top two shelves, which were lower in height and mostly filled with dog-eared paperbacks. It had to be in one of the bottom two shelves if it was anywhere. One by one Vanessa took the larger books out and rifled their pages, looking for a hollowed-out interior. Soon she had a pile of them beside her on the ruby-red carpet, and she was running out of time. Claes would come up the stairs and find her, and she'd have no explanation for what she was doing. Her hands shook as she began work on the bottom shelf. Still nothing: Tolstoy's *War and Peace*; volume 4 of a children's encyclopedia; a thick atlas of the world that had her briefly excited since it seemed just the right size to conceal a diary; a book of Van Gogh's paintings; and then, just as she'd given up hope, she saw at the back of the shelf, standing on its side, a big hardback copy of Lewis Carroll's *Alice in Wonderland*. She recognized the book – she'd had the same illustrated edition herself since she was a child, and instinctively she knew it had to be the one. It had been deliberately hidden behind the other books – she'd only found it after taking out all the books in front of it, practically emptying the bottom shelf onto the carpet.

She sat back on her haunches and turned the first few pages, past a picture of Alice falling down the well, and came to the cut in the paper. And there it was – a small square red book no bigger than the size of her hand, sitting neatly inside the mutilated *Alice in Wonderland*. With the edge of her fingernail Vanessa lifted the front cover and read the handwritten inscription with a beating heart:

Katya Osman
My Diary
Keep Out

The diary was real. Bill had been right. Now all she had to do was get it out of the house, except that that wasn't going to be so easy. She knew she was running out of time, and so she quickly shoved the books back into the shelves, calculating that no one would notice they had been moved as long as they were in the bookcase. And then, getting to her feet, she opened the door and came face-to-face with Jana Claes.

All the time she'd been in the house Vanessa hadn't once thought of Claes's silent sister. She'd seen her so rarely on her visits to Blackwater Hall, and today her thoughts had all been concentrated on Claes himself. Vanessa cursed her stupidity. She should never have made so much noise going through the books: that's what must have attracted the woman's attention. And now it was too late: Jana was blocking her only route of escape.

'What are you doing?' Jana asked. She spoke with a thick foreign accent, but her hostility was obvious.

'I was looking. That's all. Just looking,' said Vanessa weakly, unable to think of an excuse.

'Looking for what?'

Vanessa didn't answer, and the older woman's glance fell to the big book that Vanessa was clutching to her chest.

'What is that? Where did it come from?' asked Jana. 'You took it,' she said, answering her own question a moment later. 'Give it to me.'

Without warning Jana took hold of the book, wresting it away from Vanessa, who was taken by surprise, unprepared for the suddenness of the assault and Jana's wiry strength. Perhaps Jana hadn't expected to get hold of the book so easily either – she took several steps back, trying to regain her balance. And in that moment Vanessa lost her temper. She hadn't come this far and risked everything just to be thwarted at the last by this dried-up woman who was probably just as guilty as her brother. Reaching out with both her hands she took hold of Jana by the shoulders and shoved her as hard as she could back against the wall behind her. Jana hit it with a thud and fell to the ground. She looked like she'd lost consciousness, but Vanessa didn't care. Her mind was focused on one thing and one thing only – to escape the house with the diary. Stooping, she picked up *Alice in Wonderland* from where it had fallen on the ground and ran back down the corridor to the stairs. At the bottom she paused for breath. Still there was no sound from up above. Treading softly now, she made her way back to the top of the grand staircase leading down to the hall. She looked down, and there was nobody in sight except Osman's black cat, sitting contentedly on the fifth stair up, licking her paws. Vanessa had seen the cat there before and knew why Cara liked the position: it had the widest viewpoint of anywhere in the house.

Vanessa's legs were weak and her hands were shaking, so she held on to the curving mahogany banister for support as she went down, clutching the book in her other hand. She paused just above the cat and raised her forefinger to her lips in a mute appeal for silence, and Cara remained obediently still, her unblinking, luminous green eyes watching

Vanessa intently as she went slowly past. Now Vanessa could hear raised voices to her right – it sounded like Claes and Osman were arguing in the dining room. She started across the hall to the front door, and suddenly there was the noise of shouting coming from up above.

For a moment the adrenaline coursing through her body rooted Vanessa to the spot, but then it released her and she was at the door, wrenching it open. The fog rushed up to meet her, and she almost fell on the steps, but somehow she made it to the bottom and into her car. She could hear running feet behind her as she pulled the door shut and gunned the engine, setting off down the drive with a screech of tyres.

Claes watched her go. He hesitated a moment in the court-yard, looking back through the mist at his sister and Osman, who were standing in the doorway.

'She's got something. From Katya's room. A book,' said Jana, speaking in Dutch. Her voice was breathless, and she was holding on to her side like she was in pain.

Claes nodded, making up his mind. He ran past them into the house to get his keys. In his room he unlocked the top drawer of his desk and took out his revolver. He spun the magazine to check the bullets, put the gun in his pocket with a grunt of satisfaction, and then ran back down the stairs.

'Franz, listen to me. Don't . . .' Osman began, but Claes ignored him.

'I won't be long,' he shouted as he got into the Bentley and set off down the drive in pursuit of Vanessa.

Osman swayed on the step, looking shell-shocked. He leaned against the jamb for a moment before Jana took hold of his arm and led him back into the house. The door closed behind them, and out in the fog-shrouded courtyard the eerie mid-afternoon silence returned until, a few minutes later, a tall figure emerged from the trees at the top of the drive. He hesitated a moment and then went up the front steps and rang the bell.

The fog had been less dense down by the road, but it grew thick again as Clayton pressed forward down the path leading toward the boathouse. Soon he could only see a few yards in any direction. To his left he could hear the water lapping against the shore of the lake, while up ahead the boathouse loomed up out of the mist, silhouetted by the surrounding trees. He didn't know why, but the place drew him like a magnet. Perhaps it was because of all that had happened there – love and death, and now this pressing silence, interrupted only by the mournful cries of a gull hovering above the invisible lake. Clayton went up the wooden steps and glanced inside, but instinctively he already knew that the place would be deserted. There was something else that was calling his attention, but he didn't realize what it was until he'd got back outside. Then he noticed it – the rowing boat was back, pushed in underneath the floor of the boathouse. Clayton got down on his hands and knees to pull it out and a moment later looked down at a brand-new bicycle lying on its side in the bottom of the boat.

Keeping away from the trees on either side, Clayton walked as quickly as the fog would let him down the centre of the path, returning the way he'd come. It was easier going towards the end as the fog thinned out nearer to the road. Wale hadn't moved from the car while Clayton had been away, and Clayton got in beside him and turned on the engine, intending to go straight back to the Hall. He felt sure that Jacob wasn't far away. But then, just as he was about to turn out into the road, he had to slam on his brakes as a small blue car rushed past them at high speed. Clayton recognized Vanessa in the driving seat – she looked crazy, like someone or something had sent her clean out of her mind. And then, less than a minute later, another car came hurtling by. It was Claes, driving Osman's Bentley. Clayton knew Vanessa couldn't match the speed of the Bentley, however hard she pushed her little car. Claes would've easily caught up with her by the time she got to Blackwater village. Clayton hesitated a moment and then reluctantly turned the steering wheel of the police car back in the opposite direction and set off in pursuit.

CHAPTER 27

Claes rounded the corner and eased the Bentley back into fourth gear, increasing his speed as the road bent back around the hill toward Blackwater village. The trees that loomed like black ghostly shadows out of the fog now gave way to open fields covered in low-hanging mist, and Claes knew that Vanessa couldn't be too far ahead.

His anger beat with a quickening pulse inside his brain as he peered forward, searching for the tail lights of her car in the haze. He gripped the steering wheel tight with both hands and imagined gripping her neck the same way, feeling for her windpipe with his thumbs so that he could slowly choke the life out of her as he watched the terror emptying from her eyes. That was the least she deserved for seducing Titus, stealing him away with her woman's tricks – low-cut dresses and flickering eyelids. Titus deserved to suffer too. Claes wasn't a fool: he'd already guessed that Titus intended to throw him over once he'd got the Trave woman ensconced as his wife at Blackwater Hall. But Titus could wait. First Claes was going to deal with the woman. He knew that he should have gone after her before now, once he'd realized that she had got Titus bewitched. But instead he'd sat on his hands like a fool and done nothing while she went off to court and told the world about what that bitch, Katya, had said. And now she had something from Katya's room. What it was he didn't know, but he'd have to make sure he got it back before the police arrived.

Perhaps he'd make her talk, tease her with the gun and let her babble a bit with stupid pleas for mercy before he killed her. A faraway look came into Claes's eyes for a moment as he remembered old times in other countries where he'd had the law on his side. But here it was different, he remembered with a jolt. He couldn't torture her or strangle her or bludgeon her to death. He couldn't even shoot her. Not with no one to pin the murder on. He'd have to content himself with running her off the road, making it look like she'd got in an accident in the fog. The weather was on his side at least. It'd be easy once he'd caught up with her – child's play.

Now he was rushing through Blackwater village and could see tail lights up ahead. It had to be her – he could make out the domed roof of her Citroen 2CV, and he sensed she was going as fast as her little car would go. But not fast enough: the Bentley had twice as much horsepower. He only had to apply the slightest pressure to the accelerator and he was practically on her bumper. He imagined her terror as she kept glancing in her rear-view mirror, hoping it wasn't him, knowing it was. They were approaching the crossroads at the end of the village – the same place where David Swain had hijacked a car five months earlier. Beyond, the road turned sharply westward and the woods began again – just the place to stage a fatal accident far from watching eyes.

Claes had expected Vanessa to slow down at the junction, but he had done the job of terrifying her too well. She shot across the crossroads, and automatically he followed. Too late he realized his mistake. A heavily laden lorry coming up out of the fog from the right just missed Vanessa's car, but Claes wasn't so lucky. The collision was immediate and overwhelming as the lorry drove through and over the Bentley. Even if he had been wearing a seat belt, Claes would have stood almost no chance. Without one he died instantly with his last, highly uncharacteristic sensation of astonishment etched across what was left of his pale, twisted face.

*   *   *

387

Clayton got to the crash site moments later, but he didn't stay long with the wreckage. Leaving Wale to radio in a report to the police station, he delivered the shocked, white-faced lorry driver into the care of the old married couple who ran the grocery store at the crossroads and then squatted down beside Claes's corpse, staring for a moment into the dead man's wide-open eyes. And then, almost as an after-thought, he leant down and felt inside Claes's pockets. There was nothing on the right side, but in the left jacket pocket he found a snub-nosed, silver-plated revolver. It was a Colt Detective Special – a different gun to the one Claes had had before. Clayton didn't need to check to know it was loaded.

'What do you want with that?' asked Wale, looking down at the gun over Clayton's shoulder. 'It's evidence.'

'None of your business,' said Clayton, straightening up and returning to their car. 'Did you get through to the station?'

'Yeah,' said Wale. 'But don't think I won't tell Macrae about that gun,' he added. 'Because I will.'

'Good,' said Clayton viciously, swinging the car into a violent three-point turn before heading back toward the Hall at breakneck speed.

Up ahead, around the turn in the road, Vanessa was entirely unaware of what had happened back at the crossroads. All she knew was that there had been lights blazing into her car from behind and then from the right, and suddenly they were all gone. Now she was alone in the mist, careering along a deserted road with the car's accelerator pedal pinned to the floor beneath her foot. If it had been Claes behind her, she didn't know what had happened to him, but she wasn't going to go back and find out. Instead she leant forward in her seat, yearning for her first glimpse of the spires of Oxford.

She was sure she didn't want to go back to her flat. That was where Claes would come looking for her. Instead she realized that her unconscious mind had already made a decision about her destination: she was heading back to her old home in North Oxford, the one she'd left behind for a new life two years earlier. It was Bill who had sent her into the jaws of death to look for this diary, so let him be the first one to see whether the risk had been worth taking.

She parked the car with a screech of the brakes and then, clutching the diary in one hand, she rang the doorbell over and over again until her husband answered. And, once inside the house, she fell rather than sat on the old sofa in the living room. She was shaking uncontrollably, and she spoke in a rush with her words tumbling over one another as she told her husband all that had happened.

Trave felt dreadful, sick with remorse. He wrapped a blanket around Vanessa and poured her a glass of brandy and wondered how on earth he could have put the person he loved most in all the world into such terrible danger. It was worse than what Jacob had done to Katya – much worse because Trave had the benefit of hindsight. He tried to apologize, but Vanessa waved his inadequate words away. She felt at sea in a storm of emotions – remembered fear; something that bore a strange resemblance to happiness about being back in her old home, or perhaps it was just relief; and above all, a consuming curiosity about what was contained in the little red book that she had taken such a terrible risk to obtain.

With a trembling hand she extracted Katya's diary from inside *Alice in Wonderland* and handed it to her husband. 'You read it,' she told him. 'Start at the beginning and tell me what she wrote.' And she laid her head back against the sofa cushions and closed her eyes, preparing to listen.

Trave soon found that the first half of the diary had been

written years before. Alongside the entries there were pencil sketches of the boathouse and the Hall and of David and later Ethan, and a particularly good one of Osman sitting at his desk with a benevolent smile on his face and a half-smoked cigar burning between his fingers. Then, after Ethan's death, there were several pages of rapid writing in which Katya had recorded her intense distress, and after that the diary was silent for more than two years until it began again the previous August.

Trave found it hard at first to decipher Katya's tiny, spidery writing, but gradually he got used to it, and his voice quickened as he read:

August 17th, 1960:

I think it's time to start writing in this diary again; time to start keeping a record. I've neglected it far too long, just like I've neglected myself. It's time for turning a new leaf, beginning a new page . . .

I saw Ethan's brother, Jacob, yesterday. We sat in a café in St Clement's and he told me things about Franz that made me want to be sick. He showed me pictures of Franz with those Nazi pigs and it was like I was in two places at once – in Belgium with those poor people being rounded up and sent off in cattle trucks and here in Oxford drinking sweet coffee in the sunshine. And I thought of how I lived with Franz all those years when I was a girl and I felt unclean, like I could never wash the shame of it away. Not ever.

And suddenly I knew it wasn't David who had killed Ethan; it was Franz. I don't know why I knew. I just did. It was like I was Saint Paul on the road to Damascus. The scales were lifted from my eyes and I could see. I was in the same place, the

same café, and the earth was going round the sun,
but the earth was different and the sun was too.
Everything was changed.

But then Jacob made it worse. He said my uncle
was involved with Franz, that they had killed his
parents and other Jews for their diamonds, and that
they'd killed Ethan too when he found out about
Franz. He told me that they'd set up David to take
the blame. And I didn't believe him; I couldn't
believe him; I didn't want to. Titus is my uncle. He
brought me up; gave me a home. Without him I
would have nothing. But then Jacob told me about a
letter that Ethan had sent him from Munich just
before his death saying he'd discovered something
vitally important, and I remembered how Titus had
got me to leave with Jana to go shopping before
Ethan came back. Was he trying to get me out of
the way? Is he part of a conspiracy? Could he be? I
don't know now. All I know is I have to find out.

'I'll skip the next bit,' said Trave, looking up. 'It's just a
list of names – German officials that Claes was involved
with in Belgium. Jacob must have told Katya about them.'

'There's no proof in any of this, you know,' said Vanessa,
catching Trave's eye. 'Not against Titus.'

Trave didn't respond, just nodded, and then went back
to the diary.

Jacob said he had already tried to break into the
house to find evidence but he'd got nowhere – Franz
had been on to him as soon as he came through the
window of Titus's study. He told me it had to be
someone on the inside looking. He said it was worth
the risk because the proof was there. He was sure of

it. Proof of what they'd done – to his and Ethan's parents, to Ethan, to David. And I didn't have to think before I agreed. It was easy. My life has a purpose again. And I'll use this diary to record what I find. I'll hide it when I'm not writing in it. In the old place. For the first time in as long as I can remember I am almost happy.

Trave turned the page, going on to the next entry:

August 20th:
  I was sick with stopping the drugs for two days but now I'm better. I closed the door and said goodbye but then I realized there was nothing to say goodbye to. These people I know in Oxford – they're not my friends. And I don't need friends because now I have my mission. I can't bring Ethan back – I know that – but I can do something for him – I can bring him justice. And justice for David too, except I don't want to think about that, about the way he looked at me when I gave evidence against him at the trial. I didn't know, David. I didn't know . . .

'Go forward,' interrupted Vanessa impatiently, sitting up. 'Read what happened at Blackwater. I need to know.'
Trave nodded, skimming across several pages and then started reading again:

August 24th:
  I have begun the search and so far I have found nothing. I took Titus's keyring and searched his desk but found only boring business letters and stationery. And today I phoned Jacob like we agreed and told

*him he must be patient. I will not call again until I
have found something – it is too much of a risk.
Still, I am sure my uncle has no idea of what I am
about. He seems pleased to have me home; it's as if
he wants to believe I'm a reformed character. But
he's obviously got his doubts – says he'll have to put
some weight on my bones and colour in my cheeks
before he takes me out into society which is fine
with me. I've got better things to do than make
small talk with bigwigs. I don't know about Franz –
he watches me, but then again he watches everyone.
Who wouldn't with secrets like he has! God, I hate
him. And his sister too, muttering in Dutch over her
stupid crucifix. I wonder what she knows . . .*

August 25th:
   *Franz and Titus were arguing in the dining room.
Titus has a girlfriend in Oxford, the wife of that
policeman who put David away.*

Trave looked up and caught Vanessa's eye and dropped
his gaze immediately. His wife had seemed so familiar sitting
across from him on the sofa like she used to do that he'd
forgotten for a moment the great divide that now separated
them from each other. He bit his lip and went back to the
diary:

   *Franz doesn't like it; says a policeman's wife is a
bad choice. I wonder why! Of course Franz would
hate any woman Titus brought home: everyone
knows what he is but no one's going to admit it.
More lies. This house is built on them.*

August 28th:

I hate Franz. I hate the way he watches me all the time, the way he sneers at me like he knows what I'm looking for and knows I won't find anything. I can't eat and I can't sleep and I want to go back to Oxford and get fixed and forget, but I can't do that either. I promised myself and I promised Jacob.

I look at my uncle and I can't believe he could be involved. He's always been kind to me; he often treats me like I'm his daughter. But if Franz is guilty then perhaps he is too. I have to know one way or the other. There's a safe in Titus's bedroom behind a picture. Yesterday I saw it open. I was out in the corridor and Titus had his back to me. He didn't see me. I know he didn't. And I went in there afterwards while he and Franz and Jana were downstairs eating lunch. I said I wasn't hungry. That much was true. I tried all the different number combinations – every birthday, every important date I could think of, forwards and backwards, but nothing worked. I need to see him open it. That's my only chance.

August 30th:
Twice now I've risked everything and come away with nothing, and I can't do this any more. I know I can't. Yesterday I lay under Titus's bed for hours and he didn't go near the safe – not once – but today I was lying there in the dust half asleep, daydreaming of Ethan, and suddenly Titus came in and went straight to the picture. I pushed up the counterpane and looked, but he was between me and the safe and I couldn't see the numbers when he opened it. My heart was beating so hard and I was so frightened, and he looked round once and I thought he'd seen me, but then he left. And afterwards my legs

*were shaking so bad I could hardly make it out of
the room. It's so hard and I am so alone. I wish
Ethan was here to tell me what to do because I
don't know about my uncle any more. Maybe he had
nothing to do with killing Ethan; maybe Jacob's got
it wrong. Maybe it's all Franz, but I can't get into
<u>his</u> bedroom. He keeps it locked. Day and night.*

'I told you,' said Vanessa, nodding. 'It's not Titus; it's
Claes and his weird sister who are the guilty ones. But Katya
must have found something. Otherwise they wouldn't have
killed her. Can't you find what it was? It must be in there
somewhere.'

Trave turned several pages and suddenly looked excited.
'Here it is,' he said, and began reading again:

September 2nd:
   *This has been the longest day of my life. I found
what I was looking for and then I lost it because I
was a fool, and now I am a prisoner here in my
own room. And I will die here. I know I will. And
be forgotten. Like Ethan. Unless maybe someone
finds this record after I am dead. I must write down
everything that's happened while I remember, while I
can still write. Thank God they don't know about
my diary. I don't think they even suspect that it
exists.*
   *I was sitting here this morning in despair, and I
took out a letter-writing pad from the top drawer of
my desk to write a letter to Jacob to say it was over,
because I'd gone as far as I could and found
nothing. And the sun was shining down on me so
brightly – it was like it was mocking me, except it
wasn't. I looked down out of the glare and it was*

showing me the outline of someone's writing on the first page of the pad. And straight away I knew it was Ethan's – even though the writing was only a faint indentation. I recognized his big, bold letters, and it was like he was speaking to me, like he's been listening when I talk to him at night.

'Dearest Katya, I've just got back. I need to see you. Meet me at the boathouse at five. Ethan.' That was what he'd written. I looked at it and then I realized what it was. It was the note he must have written to me when he arrived back from West Germany on the day he died, or rather a copy of it that he had made unintentionally when his words indented through the thin paper as he wrote. I know what happened now. He must have come up to my room looking for me as soon as he got back, and then, when he didn't find me, he took the pad out of the drawer to write the note, and when he was done, he put it back where he'd found it. And it's been there ever since, waiting for me – Ethan's message to me from beyond the grave.

And I knew straight away what happened afterwards too. Franz found the note taped to my door and he realized his opportunity. He tore off the top of the note and then used the bottom half to lure David out to the boathouse. So simple and yet so ingenious. And the plan worked beautifully. Ethan's dead and David's in prison serving a life sentence for something he never did.

And I realized something else, something terrible. Franz must have kept Ethan prisoner in the boathouse all through the afternoon waiting for David to come. He couldn't have killed Ethan before or the time of death wouldn't match. My darling was alive

*all day while I was out shopping. Shopping! I
couldn't bear it. I rushed out of the house. I needed
to think. I ran through the woods to the boathouse.
That was where Franz had to have kept him.
Perhaps Ethan had found a way to leave me some
note, some sign before he died. I searched in every
corner, every cranny, every crevice, but there was
nothing, and then I walked back down the path
through the trees, back the way I'd come. Not once
but twice. I went down on my hands and knees in
the undergrowth but still there was nothing. Nothing
at all. And so I went and sat in the boathouse,
laying my head on the table where I'd sat with
Ethan so many times before. I remembered the past
and I forgot about time, and it was like Ethan was
alive again, just beyond the reach of my arms. But
then I heard voices outside on the steps and there
was nowhere to hide when they opened the door.*

Trave paused, glancing up at Vanessa as he turned the
page. She was wild-eyed, sitting forward on the edge of
the sofa only inches away from him with her hands clasped
tight together in front of her chest. There was nothing he
could say to comfort her, and so with a heavy heart he turned
back to the diary and resumed his reading.

CHAPTER 28

For ten days Jacob had holed up in the cheap hotel behind
Paddington Station where he'd stayed once before, back
in the days when he was travelling round the records offices
of Europe digging into Claes's murky past. They took cash
in advance at reception and asked no questions, so he
didn't need to tell them any lies. Every day he read the
newspaper reports on the Swain trial and listened to
the radio and took long walks through the London parks,
enjoying the biting cold air that kept him alert as he waited
for the jury to reach their verdict on David Swain. And
when it came, announced as the first item on the six o'clock
news on Wednesday evening, he wasn't surprised. Instead
he was ready. He got up the next morning, hoisted his
pack onto his back after breakfast, and took the train to
Banbury. He didn't think the police would be watching the
station in Oxford, but there was no need to take the risk.
And from Banbury he rode the bicycle that he'd bought
in London slowly through the gathering fog, taking the
back roads until he came to the far side of Blackwater
Lake and found the rowing boat exactly where he'd left
it, hidden in a grove of evergreen trees growing a little
way back from the bank. His plan had been to avoid the
village and the road that passed by the boathouse and the
Hall, but the thick fog meant that he did not need to worry
about observation. Instead he found it a hard task to
navigate his way across the lake and ended up reaching
the other side a hundred yards up from his target. Still,
eventually he had the boat and the bicycle stowed away

under the boathouse and set off through the woods with his torch.

An hour later, standing hidden in the trees at the top of the drive, listening to the Bentley disappearing into the distance, Jacob allowed himself a small smile of satisfaction. Claes's departure was a piece of luck that he hadn't been anticipating. Now Osman would be on his own, apart from the servants and Claes's sister, and he had nothing to fear from them. He waited a few minutes and then, with his hand cradled round the butt of the gun in his pocket, stepped out into the fog.

This time it wasn't Jana but a maid in uniform who answered the door and asked him his business. Immediately Jacob forced his way past her, demanding to see the master of the house. The noise brought Osman into the hall. He quickly retreated back towards his study as soon as he recognized his visitor, but Jacob ran after him down the corridor and was through the door before Osman had the chance to lock himself in.

With nowhere left to go, Osman sat down behind his desk, as if hoping that a little display of dignity might bring Jacob to this senses, although it didn't help that the top drawer was missing, gone to the furniture maker for repair after Jacob had blasted a hole through it on his last visit.

'How dare you come in here like this?' Osman demanded, trying and failing to give the impression that he was in control of the situation.

Jacob didn't respond, just looked down with contempt at Osman like he was some kind of loathsome insect that he hadn't yet decided how best to dispose of.

'What do you want?' asked Osman. He was unmistakably nervous now – beads of sweat had begun to form in his hairline, and a twitch at the corner of his bottom lip indicated his growing anxiety.

'I want justice – the kind they're not handing out up in London,' said Jacob, pointing to the headline of the *Daily Telegraph*, which was lying folded on the desk between them: 'David Swain to hang for Blackwater murder.'

'I want justice for my father and mother and for my brother and Katya and for all the other men, women, and children that you and Claes have murdered in the last twenty years. That's what I want,' Jacob went on, banging his fist down on the desk to emphasize the name of each of the dead victims.

'I've done nothing wrong,' said Osman in a shaky voice, shrinking into the back of his chair in the face of this verbal onslaught. 'I swear it. David Swain killed your brother and Katya, and I tried to save your parents but I couldn't. I saved you. Don't you understand that? You wouldn't be here now if it wasn't for me.'

'Yes, you're right. But why? Why did you save me, Titus?' asked Jacob, leaning forward so that his face was only a few inches from Osman's. 'Come on, tell me. Spit it out: you know the answer. So that my parents would trust you when their turn came to try and escape across the border. That's why. So they'd bring you all their precious diamonds and make you the diamond king. That's all they were to you: the chance for more loot.'

Jacob could no longer contain his anger. He lunged at Osman, taking hold of his enemy by the lapels of his Savile Row suit, and the fine cloth tore in Jacob's hands as he dragged Osman out from behind the desk and over towards the door. Osman was too shocked at first to struggle; and then, when he began to resist, Jacob threw him down on the carpet, took the gun out of his pocket, and pointed it at Osman's head.

'Get up,' he ordered, speaking through gritted teeth. 'I'll kill you. I swear I will, if you don't give me what I want.'

'What do you want?' asked Osman. It was the second time he'd asked Jacob the question, but now there was desperation in his voice: he'd lost control of his breathing and was panting as he spoke. And he seemed to have hurt himself as he fell: he held both his hands behind his back at the base of his spine as he got to his feet and stood swaying backwards and forwards in the doorway.

'Proof,' said Jacob. 'That's what I want. Proof of what you've done, so all the world can see you for what you are: a thief and a cold-blooded killer, not some big-hearted philanthropist.'

'But there is no proof,' said Osman, reaching out to touch Jacob's arm in a gesture of supplication. 'You've got to believe me: I'm an innocent man.'

'Stop lying. I can't stand to hear it,' shouted Jacob, brandishing his gun. With his free hand he pushed Osman away, back through the half-open door, and then immediately came up behind him in the corridor outside, forcing the gun into the small of Osman's back. It was the place where Osman had hurt himself when he fell, and he cried out in sudden pain.

'You're the least innocent man in the whole wide world,' said Jacob, hissing the information into Osman's ear. 'Now get upstairs. Or I'll do that again; only it'll be worse this time.'

Osman was shaking from head to toe, but he obeyed the order, shuffling forward into the hall and up the stairs. At the top, Jacob directed him to the left, and they carried on their strange procession down the corridor to Osman's bedroom. There was no sign of either Jana or the parlour maid or any of the other servants, and Osman wondered whether they had all fled the house, leaving him to deal with Jacob on his own. He'd been listening hard for the sound of the returning Bentley outside, but he'd heard nothing. 'I won't be long,' Franz had said. So where was he now? And where were the police when he needed them?

Concentrating his mind, Trave resumed his reading of Katya's diary:

Franz looked me in the eye and straight away I knew he knew. It was my fault. I realized what I'd done: like a fool I'd left the writing pad open on my desk when I ran out of the house, and he must have been watching me; he or his foul sister. She was there too, standing behind him on the steps with a smirk on her ugly white face like she was enjoying what was happening, like she wanted to see me suffer. I didn't struggle. What was the point? I know Franz; I know what he'd like to do to me with his hands if he got the chance. I know what he did to Ethan with that knife. I wasn't going to give him an excuse.

I told him that I wanted to see my uncle; that I wanted to tell Titus what I'd found. I was playing my last card but it was like Franz knew what I'd been going to say. He said: 'Certainly.' Just that, and gave a little bow of his head and a wave of his hand like he was being polite, treating me like I was some kind of lady who needed to go first out the door. I wanted to run but I could hardly walk, and Jana was in front of me anyway so there was no way I could have escaped. Franz was behind my back. He wasn't touching me, but I could feel his cold breath on the back of my neck while we walked through the woods and across the lawn back to the house. Back to my uncle waiting in his study.

*   *   *

At the end of the corridor Jacob reached round Osman and pushed open the half-closed door with his free hand, and then shoved Osman forwards into the bedroom. But Osman was ready and didn't fall this time; instead he caught hold of one of the carved mahogany posts of his four-poster bed and then turned to face his adversary, who was standing in the doorway, holding the gun trained on his forehead. Behind Osman, his cat, Cara, who had been sleeping on the bed, opened her green eyes wide in surprise. She'd never seen her master pushed across a room before.

'Open it,' commanded Jacob, pointing with a quick side-ways motion of the gun towards the oil painting hanging on the wall between the two matching wardrobes.

'Open what?' asked Osman, playing for time even though he knew perfectly well what Jacob was telling him to do. Jana had given him a detailed description of her gunpoint encounter with Jacob and his inability to get in the safe ten days earlier. God, what an idiot he'd been, Osman thought, cursing himself for his stupidity. He should have known Jacob would come back, just as he should have known neither Franz nor Macrae could be relied on for protection – instead of finding Jacob they had left him here defenceless to face this maniac on his own. Too late, Osman realized he should have hired guards or left Blackwater altogether until Jacob was caught. Now he was caught himself with no means of escape.

'Open the fucking safe!' Jacob repeated his demand with a snarl in his voice; and then, when Osman did not imme-diately comply, he turned the gun a fraction of an inch and fired through the window overlooking the courtyard, shat-tering the glass with the bullet. A wave of cold air blew into the room, and Osman's legs gave way beneath him as, unseen, the cat disappeared under the bed.

Slowly, Osman got back to his feet and took the picture

down off the wall with shaking hands. He glanced across at Jacob and then twisted the knob, entering the coded numbers one by one until the steel door clicked and he pulled it open. Behind Osman, Jacob leaned forwards, looking in at the lines of small blue silk bags, each with a different tiny white number embroidered on its side, and, behind them on a shelf, taking up most of the space at the back of the safe, three thick, dark green, leather-bound books.

'Get those out,' ordered Jacob, pointing at the books. 'Show them to me.'

'They're my accounts. That's all – who I've sold to, who I've bought from, my expenses – nothing else,' said Osman as he took out the ledgers. He put the first two down on the ground and then held out the third one, turning the pages for Jacob's inspection, as if he really thought they might convince Jacob that he was indeed an innocent man.

'How far do they go back?' asked Jacob, looking up from the names and dates and the columns of figures recorded in red and black ink.

'This one four years,' said Osman. 'But it's not finished. The other two are five each.'

'Fourteen years. And before that?'

'I don't have records before I came to England. It was the war, you know,' said Osman. He made it sound like the war explained everything.

'No, I don't know. You're lying,' said Jacob, losing his temper as his frustration boiled over. He'd pinned all his hopes on the stupid safe, and it had yielded him nothing. Trave had been right about Blackwater Hall. There was nothing here – no evidence, no proof, nothing. Or at least nothing that he was going to find without Osman's help. And that help would only be forthcoming if Osman really believed that Jacob would kill him if he didn't talk. The bastard didn't believe that at present – that much was obvious. Jacob had to convince him. That's what he needed to do.

'Get down on your knees,' he ordered, stepping back and retraining the gun on Osman's head.

Osman saw the homicidal look in Jacob's eyes and was filled with a mortal terror that he'd never felt before. He couldn't be going to die. Not now when he'd finally got everything he'd ever wanted. He grabbed a handful of the silk bags from inside the safe and pulled open their drawstrings, spilling radiant diamonds of all sizes and colours and cuts into his hand, holding them out to Jacob.

'Here, take them,' he said. 'There are more, lots more. I can sell them for you if you want. They're worth millions, more than you can imagine.'

Jacob looked down at the array of jewels glittering in Osman's outstretched hand and felt like he was going to be sick. He thought of his family members, dying terrible deaths in unspeakable places just so Osman could get hold of these meaningless baubles of crystal carbon and call them his own. They enraged him, and he leant forward with his free hand and dashed the diamonds out of Osman's hand onto the floor. They fell, scattering in all directions across the pale blue Axminster carpet, and such was Osman's obsession with the jewels that he looked down at them for a moment in disbelief, unable to believe that a person could treat such beauty with such contempt. But then he looked back up into Jacob's cold, angry eyes and remembered his situation.

'Get down on your knees,' Jacob commanded again.

But Osman stood his ground: he knew what would happen when he knelt, and he wasn't going to assist in his own death. He closed his eyes and prayed to a God he didn't believe in for rescue, and, as if in direct response, the roar of a police siren rent the silence, followed by the sound of a car coming fast up the drive. And suddenly the fog outside was lit up by flashing blue lights. Doors were opening – car doors and the front door of the house, and several moments later a familiar voice shouted up at them from down below: 'Come out, Jacob Mendel. We know you're in there. Come out now.'

Keeping his gun trained on Osman, Jacob crossed the room and looked quickly down into the courtyard through the shattered window. The fog had cleared a little, and in the lights he could just about make out the faces of the figures down below: the young detective who'd held him in his flat with Trave was the one who had shouted, and a few yards away on the other side of the fountain was a big burly man in police uniform whom Jacob didn't recognize. Beyond them, two figures, who could only be Jana Claes and the maid who'd answered the door, were running away up the drive.

'Fuck!' Backing away from the window, Jacob vented his anger with a series of expletives, and then he noticed how Osman had risen up to his full height again, puffing out his chest like he had nothing left to fear, like he was back to being Titus Osman, the king of diamonds again. He laughed mirthlessly at Osman's lack of understanding, realizing suddenly that the police were an opportunity for him, not Osman. They could be witnesses to Osman's confession. Jacob was grateful for their arrival.

'Get over by the window,' he ordered, pressing the cold, hard muzzle of the gun against the back of Osman's head to force him forward. Down below the two policemen were looking up at them through the mist.

'Now tell them,' ordered Jacob in a steely voice. 'Tell them what you did. Tell them about my parents, about how you betrayed them to the Nazis, about how you sent them to Auschwitz on the cattle train. Tell them about my brother, about how you and Claes put a knife in his back. Tell them about Katya. Tell them, Titus. I'll kill you if you don't. I swear I will.'

406

But Osman wasn't listening. He thought of jumping, but it was too far and he was too frightened. 'Help me,' he shouted, not at Clayton but at the burly man standing behind him. 'That's what I pay you for.'

Below, Wale backed away towards the police car without responding, leaving it to Clayton to do the talking. 'Let him go,' Clayton shouted up at Jacob. 'Claes is dead. Isn't that enough?'

But Jacob wasn't listening. All his attention was focused on the trembling man in front of him. 'Confess,' he demanded, thrusting the gun into the small of Osman's back. 'Confess and I'll let you go.'

'No,' said Osman. 'I'm an innocent man.' He shouted out the words so that everyone could hear them: Jana and the servants on the other side of the courtyard; the policemen down below; and even Osman's cat, who'd emerged from under the bed and now stood watching the man who was hurting her master over by the window, forcing him to cry out in pain. Suddenly Cara arched her back and launched herself through the air, hanging on to Jacob's shoulder with her claws as she sank her teeth into his neck, and, shocked to the core by this utterly unexpected attack from behind, Jacob dropped the gun.

Osman was onto the opportunity in an instant. Displaying an entirely unexpected athleticism for a man of his age, he dived to the ground, seized the gun in his hand, and rolled away towards the door.

Jacob staggered back into the room, struggling to get a firm grip on the cat as she continued her assault, scratching at his face and neck. Finally he succeeded in getting both his hands around her squirming body and threw her against the far wall, from where she fell to the floor with a shriek and then disappeared back under her master's bed.

Jacob couldn't see for a moment. Blood was spurting out

from a line of cuts on his forehead, and he put up his hand to wipe it away. When he opened his eyes he found himself looking straight down the barrel of his own gun.

'Don't move. Don't speak,' said Osman. They were over by the bed, out of view of the people in the courtyard down below.

'So you want to hear my confession, do you?' he asked. His voice was a whisper. His head was inches from Jacob's; it was almost as if he was kissing Jacob with his words, feeling for his fear with the gun. 'You want to be my priest? You want to give me absolution for my sins?'

Jacob looked at his adversary, saying nothing, waiting to hear the truth. Behind him the soft winter breeze blew into the white silk curtains through the remains of the broken window, and down below Adam Clayton took Franz Claes's gun out of his pocket, looked at it a moment, steeling his courage to the sticking place, and then went up the steps and entered the house through the wide-open front door.

'There's a line I can hardly read here,' said Trave. His forehead was furrowed with concentration as he held Katya's little diary up to the light. 'It's smudged like she spilt something on the page, or maybe she was crying.'

'It doesn't matter,' said Vanessa, nearly beside herself with impatience. 'Get on with it, Bill. Put me out of my misery, for Christ's sake.'

And Trave began to read again, slowly deciphering Katya's scribbled words:

> My uncle was sitting at his desk with Ethan's note in front of him. And he looked up at me and smiled and I knew the truth then once and for all. He didn't need to admit it. I knew what he had done.

To Ethan and to David and to Ethan's parents and to all those Jews he didn't save.

'So you found something, little Katya,' he said. He'd never called me that before. 'A whisper from the past. But that's all it is, you know. A whisper; a murmur on the breeze that nobody will ever hear.' And he picked up the writing pad and threw it on the fire and I watched it burn. Burn my proof to ashes; my hope to dust.

I looked at him and I spat in his face and he took out a silk handkerchief and wiped the spit away. He was still smiling, told me he was sorry it had come to this and even looked half-regretful when Franz took hold of me from behind and dragged me upstairs. I can still feel Franz's cold hands on my body even now two hours later: killer's hands they are, with no pity in them at all; no mercy. They're going to kill me. I know they are. Just like they killed Ethan. So why don't they get it over with? What are they waiting for?

'They were waiting to get David Swain out of gaol; that's what they were waiting for,' said Trave, looking up. 'So that they could set him up with the murder.'

But Vanessa wasn't listening. Her face had crumpled up, and her body shook with terrible sobs. Titus was a murderer and she was his accomplice. That was the truth. If she had gone to the police with what Katya had told her the girl would still be alive. She'd been Katya's last chance, and yet she had done nothing, just left Katya to her fate.

Titus had lied to her about everything – even perhaps about the existence of his dead wife and child, and she had believed him because she had wanted to; because she was flattered by his attention and wanted to be the new Mrs

Osman, living the good life out at Blackwater Hall. Vanessa looked down at her hand and pulled Osman's beautiful diamond ring from her finger and threw it away into a corner of the room. But it didn't help; it didn't change anything. The ring was still there, glittering by the skirting board, an indestructible symbol of her complicity, and she knew that she'd never stop feeling ashamed of herself until she was dead and buried and couldn't feel anything any more.

'You want to know why I betrayed your parents?' asked Osman, staring into Jacob's eyes.

'Because they were Jews?'

'No; they could have been Hindus for all I cared. Guess again.'

'For their diamonds?'

'Yes,' said Osman. 'You know the answer. Of course you do, but you don't understand it. Look, look, where you threw them on the floor.' Osman gestured with the gun down at the gemstones glittering like tiny stars all over the pale blue carpet at their feet.

'They're bits of rock. That's all. They're not alive,' said Jacob. 'Not like your victims were.'

'Yes,' said Osman. 'You're right. They're not like flesh and blood; they don't decay; they don't rot. Diamonds are forever.'

Osman smiled, and Jacob knew suddenly what was going to happen next. He thought of shouting but knew instinctively that he wouldn't get the words out of his mouth before the bullet entered his head. Osman would be able to say it was in self-defence – everyone down below in the courtyard had already seen Jacob at the window threatening the owner of the house with a gun.

'Do people mean nothing to you?' Jacob asked, playing for time. 'Katya was *your* flesh and blood. She was almost like your daughter . . .'

410

'She was a fool. That's what she was. Just like you. She couldn't help herself: she had to peep through the keyhole; she had to go where she was forbidden – and for that there's a price to pay; there's always a price to pay. And you know what that price is, don't you, Jacob?' asked Osman. His voice was gentle, almost sad, but the gun was steady in his hand.

Jacob knew what was coming. He closed his eyes, shutting out Osman's hateful face, waiting to hear the gun's explosion in his ears – the last sound that he would ever hear, but instead he heard a familiar voice shouting 'Stop' somewhere to his left. He opened his eyes and saw Adam Clayton standing in the doorway, holding Claes's gun shaking in his hands.

And then everything happened in a whirl of motion that neither Clayton nor Jacob could really unravel afterward. Jacob threw his body against Osman as Osman turned and fired at Clayton, missing the policeman by a hair's breadth. And in response, without thinking, Clayton squeezed the trigger of Claes's gun and killed Titus Osman with a bullet that passed through his heart and flew out through the already-broken window of the bedroom, embedding itself in a high branch of one of the tall pine trees at the top of Osman's drive. It was the first time that Clayton had ever fired a gun, and afterwards he hoped it would be the last.

'Give me the diary, Bill,' said Vanessa, holding out her hand. 'I need to see what happened in the end.'

At first Trave resisted. He was frightened for Vanessa, frightened of what the last entries in the dead girl's diary might do to her peace of mind now that she knew who Osman really was and what he had done. In his moment of vindication Trave felt no sense of triumph at all. He just wished that none of it had ever happened, but, as he'd realized long ago, that was his lot in life. Like all murder detectives he always arrived too late.

Reluctantly he handed the diary over. Vanessa had more right to it than he did after what she had gone through to get it. He sensed that she wanted to be alone, and so he went upstairs to phone Creswell. Osman and Claes and Claes's sister needed to be arrested before anyone else got hurt.

He put his hand on his wife's shoulder briefly as he passed behind the sofa, feeling that he had never loved her as much as he did at that moment and yet had never been more powerless to make her happy.

Once the door closed, Vanessa turned the pages quickly, looking for the entry for September 15th, the day of her encounter with Katya in the drawing room. She soon found it:

September 15th:
  I cannot bear the pain any more. I feel like I'm going mad. I think it would be better to die than to carry on like this. But how? That's the question. Perhaps I can steal the matches from Jana when she comes in to feed me and then we'll die together, she and I. Burn until there's nothing left. There would be justice in that. But I know that at the last moment I won't be able to go through with it; I'll draw back – I know I will. Why? Why, in God's name, why? It's not fear of death that stops me. I know that. It's hope; hope for life. Hope is my curse. It always has been. I see that now. God, how much better I would be without it. How much . . .

Vanessa realized that Katya must have written this entry earlier in the day, before she fought with Jana in her room and escaped downstairs, but none of those events was recorded in the diary. It was like that night had been a watershed. The entries on the pages that followed grew shorter, no longer a record of the days but rather sporadic thoughts and expressions of desperate emotion. Vanessa wondered whether Katya had worried about having the diary open too long at any one time, but it was more likely, she thought, that the girl had just run out of energy and perhaps at the end even hope. There was only one reference to Vanessa by name. It came two days later and consisted of only a few words, but they stabbed Vanessa to the heart with a pain that she felt would never go away:

Will Vanessa help me? Did she listen to me? Or was all I did in vain?

And the last entry in the book was undated – a one-line scrawl:

What's the bloody point?

Vanessa closed the book and looked up at her husband standing wide-eyed in the doorway.

'What is it?' she asked, getting to her feet. 'What's happened?'

'Claes is dead,' he said. 'He was hit by a lorry in Blackwater village. It must have been when he was chasing you. Died instantly apparently. Are you all right, Vanessa?' he asked, noticing how his wife's face had gone white with shock. She shuddered uncontrollably several times and then exhaled deeply.

'Yes,' she said, swallowing. 'It's a surprise. That's all. He'd have killed me if he'd caught me. I know he would. And I never thought I'd hear myself say this about another human being, but I'm glad he's dead. He was evil, Bill, wicked through and through. It wasn't just Katya and Ethan whom he murdered, you know. There were many more in the war

413

– Jews he helped send to the gas chambers without a second thought.'

'How do you know?'

'He worked with Adolf Eichmann. I'm not sure in what way, but I know he did. Titus got angry with him at lunch today and said something about what the Israelis should do to Eichmann. It was deliberate, and Franz looked crazy suddenly, like he was going to kill Titus or something. I think that's why they murdered Ethan, you know – because of what he found out in West Germany about Franz. That's what Jacob told Katya and I think he was right.'

Vanessa looked at her husband, noticing how he was shifting his weight from foot to foot, looking away from her to hide his discomfort.

'There's something else,' she said. 'Something you're not telling me. It's Titus, isn't it?' she asked, her voice rising hysterically as she instinctively guessed at the truth. 'He's dead too, isn't he?'

Trave nodded. And walked slowly over to his wife, putting his arms out to comfort her as she collapsed in tears on the sofa that they had bought together years before.

'I'm sorry, Vanessa,' he said. 'You deserved so much better than this.'

And he held her gently as her body was rocked with wild sobs and she gave way to a terrible grief.

Cara waited under her master's bed for several minutes after Clayton and Jacob had left the room. She sat wide-eyed in the darkness with her heart beating fast, waiting for the silence to return. And then, as the winter sun outside the window sank gently down toward the western horizon, she stepped out, picking her way carefully among the glittering diamonds scattered across the floor until she came to her master's corpse. There she stopped, staring unblinking

414

down into his dead eyes for a few moments before she laid herself slowly down, stretching her warm body over the blood-red stain that was still spreading out across the left side of his starched white shirt.

CHAPTER 29

Superintendent Creswell waited a moment to make sure he had his temper firmly under control and then turned round a large, green, leather-bound book and pushed it across his desk so that it was right in front of Inspector Macrae, who sat perched on the edge of his chair with a pained expression on his stretched, pale face.

'This is Titus Osman's accounts book for the last four years,' said Creswell in a matter-of-fact tone of voice. 'And here on the right is a page entirely devoted to you.' Creswell tapped his forefinger where the name MACRAE was written in capital letters. 'As you can see, there are three entries – fifteen hundred pounds on 4 October of last year, the day after Mr Swain was charged; five hundred pounds on 2 February, just after his trial began; and then another five hundred pounds just over a week ago. What was that last payment for, Inspector – seems a bit early for a third instalment?' asked Creswell, looking up.

'None of this has anything to do with me, and you know it doesn't,' said Macrae defiantly. 'I've never taken any money off anyone.'

'And nor has Constable Wale, I suppose. Adam Clayton tells me that Mr Osman shouted down at him – "Help me. That's what I pay you for" – just before he died. Why would Mr Osman have said that, I wonder?'

'How the hell should I know? I wasn't there. Maybe he was talking about his taxes.'

'Oh, please, Inspector. You can do better than that.'

'No, I can't,' said Macrae angrily. 'And I don't have to. You've got nothing on me. Nothing!'

'So you won't mind us taking a look in your bank account then? You're quite sure we won't find any large deposits round these dates?' asked Creswell, pointing at the ledger.

'You can do what you bloody well like,' shouted Macrae, getting up, but Creswell sensed a burgeoning anxiety beneath his subordinate's outward bravado.

'All right, Inspector. We'll do just that, and in the meantime you're suspended on full pay. I suggest you enjoy the money while you can,' said Creswell, nodding a curt dismissal.

Macrae stood his ground for a moment, but in the end thought better of giving vent to his rage. He opened the door to leave, but then, just as he was about to go out, Creswell called him back.

'I don't know if you've heard about the new evidence that Bill Trave has dug up, but it appears that David Swain may well be an innocent man. And I warn you: if I find out that you or Wale laid a finger on that boy to extort his confession it won't just be your job I'll be after. You may have got away with using the thumbscrews in your last job, but you won't get away with it down here. You understand that, don't you, Mr Macrae?' asked Creswell, emphasizing every word.

Macrae shot a venomous look at the superintendent and then turned away, almost colliding with Clayton in the doorway. Macrae stared at his erstwhile junior with undisguised hatred for a moment and then suddenly put out his hand and shoved Clayton out of his way. And after that, without a backward look, he hurried away down the corridor and disappeared around the corner.

'Are you all right?' asked Creswell, coming out from behind his desk and helping Clayton to his feet.

417

'I'm fine,' said Clayton, brushing himself down. 'I was just taken by surprise, sir. That's all.'

'Well, Macrae won't be working here again if I've got anything to do with it,' said Creswell angrily. 'He can go and join Wale down at Land's End Police Station if he ever gets his job back.'

'Will he?' asked Clayton. 'Get his job back, I mean?'

'I don't know. Depends what's in his bank statements – the entries in Osman's accounts book aren't enough on their own, but I expect you've already worked that out for yourself. We can't prove there's not someone else called Macrae who did business with Osman, even though I'm sure it's him. And of course we'll never know if he was in on Osman's plot to frame Swain for killing his niece. What do you think?' asked Creswell. 'You were there for Swain's interview.'

'I don't know,' said Clayton, frowning. 'Macrae and Wale definitely did stuff to Swain, just like Swain said at his trial – not that we can prove it, but that doesn't mean Macrae knew Swain was innocent. If I had to guess, I'd say Macrae thought he was guilty and Osman paid him for doing a good job making Swain confess. But I could be wrong. It's difficult to get a clear handle on a lot of what's gone on, sir, to be honest with you.'

Creswell nodded and then sighed heavily, sitting back in his chair. 'It was damn brave what you did yesterday, Adam. I'm going to make sure you get a commendation from the commissioner for it. That Mendel boy owes you his life.'

'I think he knows that. He told me how grateful he is when I went to see him in his cell last night. It's funny – it's like what happened with Osman yesterday has knocked the wind out of him, at least for a bit. He couldn't stop talking when Inspector Trave and I saw him in his flat. He was really obnoxious actually. But now he seems to be finding it hard to string two sentences together.'

'Well, seeing death changes people – even the deaths of people we hate,' said Creswell with a sigh. 'And Osman's death is going to catch up with you too, you know, sooner or later. You did what you had to do, but that doesn't change the fact that you're the one who fired the bullet. That's what I wanted to see you about actually. Don't you think you should take some time off? Maybe talk through what happened with someone qualified to help. There are good people I can recommend you to if you're willing. You can have as long as you need.'

'Thanks, but I'd prefer not to, sir, if you don't mind, at least for now,' said Clayton, biting his lip. 'It's work that's keeping me going at the minute.'

Creswell drummed his fingers on his desk, trying to make a decision. 'Well, maybe you know best,' he said eventually. 'God knows, I'm going to need all the help I can get if we're going to save Mr Swain from his appointment with the hereafter. Thinking he's innocent is one thing; convincing those old judges up in London is quite another. If there's one thing they don't like doing, it's interfering with a jury verdict.'

'But surely there's the new evidence for them to look at,' said Clayton, looking surprised. 'We've got Katya's diary now, and then Osman pretty well admitted her murder to Jacob in the bedroom before I got there. Haven't you seen Jacob's statement?'

'Yes. And it's not enough. Like it or not, Jacob's not a credible witness. You can't get away from the fact that he had an oversized grudge against Osman – he broke into the man's house three times; he threatened Osman and Claes's sister with a gun; and he's also got no corroboration. In fact, as far as I can make out, the only thing you and the rest of the people in the courtyard heard was Osman shouting at the top of his voice that he was an innocent man when

Jacob had a gun to his head. And as for Katya's diary, well maybe it exonerates Swain of the first murder, assuming you accept what a dead girl with a drug history has said about a note that no longer exists. And it certainly shows Claes and Osman had a motive to get rid of Katya, but it doesn't do anything to change the fact that Swain had a strong motive too and that he was there in the girl's room with a gun at right around the time she died.

'It's a pity that ballistics can't do any better with Claes's gun. "It might be the one that killed Katya; it might not be" – it's exactly what they said about the gun Swain had. I just wish Osman's safe had contained something to incriminate its owner with the murders. We need more than a dead man's whisper, Detective. That's the truth. Is Claes's sister still saying nothing?'

'Yes; it's like she's had her tongue cut out,' said Clayton, sounding exasperated. 'I've tried everything – shouting at her, appealing to her conscience – but all she does is finger her bloody crucifix and look at the floor.'

'Do you think Macrae could have interfered with her? I told him to stay out of it yesterday.'

'No, I don't think so. She's doing it herself; she doesn't need any help,' said Clayton, shaking his head.

'Well, we can't hold her indefinitely. Try and think of something to get her to talk. Like I said, we need something more.'

Clayton nodded, trying to look hopeful when he felt nothing of the kind. The superintendent's incisive analysis of the state of play had left him feeling dismally deflated.

'Have you heard from Trave?' asked Creswell as Clayton turned to go.

'No – nothing since yesterday.'

'Well, ask him if he's got any ideas when you get the chance. He's more likely than anyone to think of something.

Swain getting a pardon is the only way he's going to get his job back.'

'I don't really think that that's what's motivating him,' said Clayton, but Creswell had already gone back to his correspondence and was no longer listening.

Despite numerous phone calls and two abortive visits to the house on Hill Road, Clayton heard nothing from Trave for the next two days except for a cryptic telephone message left at the front desk of the police station on the Saturday morning telling Clayton to hold on to Jana Claes at all costs. Clayton complied, even though Jana continued to resist all his attempts to make her talk, instead remaining entirely mute, with the same faraway expression in her eyes that she had worn ever since she'd been told about her brother's death.

Finally, late on Sunday afternoon, Trave called.

'How have you been holding up, Adam?' he asked. 'Are you all right?'

'I'm okay,' said Clayton. He was touched by his old boss's concern, but he saw no point in burdening him with a tale of the sleepless nights that he had been suffering since Osman's death. 'Where have you been?' he asked.

'Israel. I just got back. It was Vanessa's idea, and now I'm dog-tired and flat broke.' Trave laughed – he sounded happier than he'd done in months. 'Did you get my message?' he asked. 'Have you still got Claes's sister?'

'Yes, until tomorrow.'

'Good. Has she said anything?'

'No.'

'All right, meet me at the station in fifteen minutes. I need to talk to you.' And Trave rang off before Clayton could ask him any more questions.

* * *

Trave was already waiting in what had once been his office when Clayton arrived. It was still the weekend, and there were few people around. Trave started talking before Clayton had even had a chance to sit down.

'I want you to let me interview her,' he said. 'Right now.'

'Don't be silly. You know I can't do that,' said Clayton, taken aback by the request. 'You're not a policeman any more. You've got no right to talk to her in here. And besides, if she says anything it'll be completely inadmissible.'

'It doesn't matter,' said Trave urgently. 'It's not evidence against her I'm after; it's evidence against her brother. And once she hears about who he is, she may tell us what he did to Katya.'

'What do you mean "who he is"? Who is he?'

'Let me talk to her,' said Trave, ignoring the question. 'We're going to need more than Katya's diary and a bit of hearsay from Osman to get Swain off. You know that.'

'Show me what you've got, and I'll get her to talk,' suggested Clayton.

But Trave rejected the compromise: 'It's got to be me. I know how to play her,' he said. 'We've gone too far to stop now, Adam. Surely you can see that. You've got to let me see it through.'

Reluctantly, Clayton nodded. It was entirely against his better judgement, but he knew he had no choice but to go with Trave. He'd broken far too many rules already to baulk at breaking one more now.

They interviewed Jana in the same little room at the back of the police station where David Swain had made his confession four months before.

Escorted by Clayton, she shuffled down the corridor from her cell and sat down heavily in the chair opposite Trave. She looked very different to when Trave had last seen her.

Her greying hair was no longer tied up in a bun at the back of her head but instead hung loose and unkempt around her shoulders, and her black dress was wrinkled and stained. There were dark circles under her eyes, which had lit up in brief recognition when she first saw Trave but now filmed over again as she retreated back into herself and dropped her gaze to the floor.

'You remember me,' said Trave, speaking in a reasonable, friendly voice as if they were meeting casually in a coffee-shop somewhere and not in the back of a police station. 'You remember how we talked after Katya died. You remember how you told me that you never took communion, never went to confession in your church, but you wouldn't tell me why. Well, I think you should tell me why now, Miss Claes. I think it'll make you feel better. I think deep down you want to say what happened to that poor girl but you're just too frightened. Isn't that what you feel?'

Jana did not respond, but Clayton saw with surprise that Trave had got her attention. She was looking in his direction and had taken tight hold of the silver crucifix that was hanging from her neck.

'I don't think you knew what Titus Osman and your brother were going to do,' Trave went on in the same quiet, mesmeric tone. 'Not until after it happened, when Franz came and told you. So you see: it wasn't your fault. You didn't know; just like you didn't know who your brother really was. And that's what I'm here to tell you, Jana. It'll help you if you know. I really think it will.'

'Know what? What do you know about him?' Jana burst out. She sounded scared, and her voice was hoarse, raw from not having been used in days.

'Did you go with Franz when he left Belgium in 1943?' Trave asked, answering Jana's question with a question of his own.

She shook her head.

'But you know he went to Germany, don't you?'

Jana nodded.

'Do you know what he was doing there?'

Jana gave another shake of her head, almost imperceptible this time, but her eyes were wide open now, fixed on Trave across the table.

'I thought not. All right, let me tell you. He had a job, an important government job. It was in a place called Referat IV B4 of the Reich Main Security Office at 116 Kurfürstenstrasse in Berlin. That was the department dealing with what the Nazis called Jewish affairs, and your brother was working there for a man called Eichmann, Lieutenant Colonel Adolf Eichmann. Have you heard of him, Miss Claes? I'm sure you have – he's been in the news a lot recently because he's about to go on trial in Jerusalem. He's charged with being the chief organizer of the Holocaust, the extermination of the Jewish people . . .'

'No.' It was a cry more than a word, torn from deep inside Jana's chest.

But Trave ignored the interruption. 'Yes, Miss Claes. When he got to Berlin, your brother was given the rank of Sturmbannführer, a major in the SS. You couldn't hold that rank if you were a foreigner, but then that wasn't a problem because he wasn't really Belgian, was he, Miss Claes? He was German just like you. And so in late 1943 he went back to being Franz Kleissen, which was the name he gave up when he went with you to Belgium in 1931. I don't know why you both emigrated from Germany in the first place or changed your surname from Kleissen to a Belgian name. Perhaps it was to get work during the Depression. Anyway, it doesn't matter now. Franz Claes became Sturmbannführer Kleissen and went to work killing Jews,

424

packing them up in cattle trains and sending them to Auschwitz from all over Europe, not just Belgium.'

'You're lying. It's not true,' screamed Jana, getting up from the table. Her fists were clenched, and Clayton thought for a moment that she was going to attack Trave. But Trave remained unperturbed.

'I'm afraid it is true,' he said. 'And I have documents and photographs to prove it. Look, here's your brother in full uniform standing beside Eichmann. The man on the right is Heinrich Müller, head of the Gestapo. They're outside SS headquarters in Berlin. And in this photograph he's in Auschwitz itself with the commandant, Rudolf Höss. They're standing on the platform at the end of the railroad track, and those are Jews in the background from a *sonderkommando*, collecting the belongings of the men, women, and children who have just been led off to their deaths. It was in Auschwitz apparently that your brother suffered the injury to the left side of his face. One of the prisoners attacked him during an inspection and was hanged for it afterwards, so it's not a war wound at all. And in this photograph your brother's at the camp entrance: you see the sign over the gate, do you, Miss Claes? ARBEIT MACHT FREI – 'Work makes you free'? It's him, Jana. There's no doubt about it. Here, take your time. Look.'

Trave paused, fanning out the photographs across the table.

'Where did you get these?' asked Jana, subsiding back into her seat.

'In Jerusalem. I flew there two days ago to see the investigators preparing the Eichmann trial and they gave them to me. They matched them with your brother straight away when I gave them his photograph and told them what I knew about his background. The Israelis would have loved to put him on trial too if they could have found him, but I told them he's dead now, beyond their vengeance. No one can bring him back, and no one can change what he did. But there is something you can do, one small thing to make amends – now, before it's too late.'

'What? What can I do?' asked Jana. Her voice was barely more than a whisper.

'You can tell the truth. There's a man up in London who's going to hang for a crime you know your brother committed. But if you tell the truth about what happened to Katya, he can go back to his family and have his life back. And you won't have to live with the guilt of his death for the rest of your life.'

'What will happen to me if I tell you?' asked Jana nervously. 'I kept her locked in. I did not tell the truth.'

'I'll do my best for you,' said Trave. 'But I think it's your immortal soul you should be concerned about right now, not the British courts. You don't need me to tell you that you're going to need absolution if you're to have any chance of eternal salvation, and for that you must repent; you must tell the truth. Once we're done here, I promise I'll bring you a priest, and you can make your peace with God. But first you must save the living. It's time, Miss Claes. It's time.'

Trave was silent, waiting to see what effect his words would have on Jana. He wondered if she'd understood him – he'd deliberately used the ornate language of her religion to appeal to her conscience. She closed her eyes tight shut and opened them again and looked down at the crucifix in her hand. And then she took a deep breath, and her body trembled as she exhaled and began to speak:

'Katya was sleeping. Franz came to me; he said: "Stay in your room." And I did what Franz told me to do because he is my brother. Then I heard a bang – a shot from a gun. Franz came again and said he had to do it, because Katya was bad; she wanted to hurt us if she could. And I was crying. But Franz said I must say nothing. He made me promise. He said that a man is coming and I must stay inside, lock my door. And then later the man came and there was more shooting, and running – running all over the house. And then Titus told me the same thing – I must say nothing. And I did what they said because I was frightened, and because I promised, and because it was too late, too late.' Jana began to cry as she repeated the words. Great shuddering sobs shook her body as the floodgates of emotion broke inside her and she wept for what she'd done.

'I did not know,' she said through her tears. 'You must believe me. I kept her in, but I did not know what they were going to do.'

'I believe you,' said Trave, passing Jana a box of tissues across the table. 'Did you know about what they did to Ethan?'

'Yes. Franz told me. At the end after Katya died. He needed me to understand that we had to stay together, protect one another. But now he's dead, and I . . . I am all alone.' Jana's voice, previously not much more than a hoarse whisper, suddenly broke, and she put her hands up over her face.

Trave watched her for moment, realizing that he felt no pity for Jana at all, not one scrap of sympathy, and then abruptly got up from the table.

'Thank you, Miss Claes,' he said in a businesslike voice. 'You'll sign a statement confirming all this, won't you? And you'll tell it to a court if you have to?'

Jana nodded.

'Well, then you can rely on us doing our best for you. Detective Clayton here will show you where to sign. And I'll arrange for that priest to come and see you.'

* * *

Two hours later Trave and Clayton found themselves sitting opposite Sir Laurence Arne, QC, in his chambers at Number 2 Doctor Johnson's Buildings in the Temple. It was Sunday evening, and Trave had rung up Arne's clerk from the police station, hoping at most to get an appointment for the following day, but when he explained his business, the clerk had told him to wait and then returned a minute later to say that Sir Laurence was working late and would see Mr Trave that evening if Mr Trave so wished. And Trave had so wished, repeatedly breaking the speed limit as the pushed his old Ford to the limit on the road up to London so that there would be no delay in showing the prosecuting barrister Jana Claes's statement and Katya's little diary.

Arne finished reading and took off his half-moon glasses. 'You guarantee to me that this is authentic?' he asked, holding up the diary.

'Yes,' said Trave. 'My wife risked her life to get it.'

'And the Claes woman is telling the truth. You're sure of it?' Clayton and Trave nodded.

'Why though? Why would she tell you all this now?' asked Arne.

'Because I told her that her brother worked for Adolf Eichmann in Berlin between 1943 and 1945. I went to Israel on Friday to talk to the investigators there, and they gave me documents that prove it. They didn't know about him until now because he's been living here under an assumed name,' said Trave, reaching into his briefcase and taking out the same file of photographs that he'd shown to Jana Claes earlier in the evening. Arne looked at them one by one and then put them down on his desk with a heavy sigh. He looked shaken and his eyes were troubled.

'Do you think that this is what Ethan Mendel found out in West Germany – that Claes worked for Eichmann? Is this why Claes and Osman killed him?' he asked.

'Yes, I think so,' said Trave. 'Osman had to help Claes because Claes held the secret of his past too. They were tied together by what each of them knew about the other. They must have hated each other by the end.'

'A pact made in hell,' said Arne, nodding. 'But why do you think Jacob couldn't find what his brother found? He obviously didn't leave any stone unturned looking.'

'I think that Claes must have gone to West Germany and destroyed the records after Ethan's death,' said Trave thoughtfully. 'Ethan's mistake was to believe Osman wasn't involved. He sealed his own death warrant when he came back to Blackwater and told Osman what he found.'

'But yet you've found out the truth,' countered Arne.

'Yes, in Israel, not Germany. And the information about Claes and Eichmann only came to light there after the Israelis started interrogating Eichmann last year and preparing the case file for his trial. It wouldn't have been available to Jacob even if he'd had the same kind of official access that I had, which he wouldn't have done of course.'

Arne was silent for a moment and then got up and went over to the window, where he stood looking out into the darkness. 'This is the devil's work,' he said gravely. 'In all my years at the bar I have never seen the like of it. I prosecuted that boy twice for murder, and each time I was sure he was guilty. I thought he deserved to hang the first time. And yet he was innocent, as innocent as you and I. This news makes me doubt myself, makes me doubt our whole system of justice.'

'So will you help us?' asked Trave. 'I didn't know who else to come to.'

'Yes,' said Arne firmly. 'There are people I need to talk to, but I can tell you my recommendation will be not to fight the appeal. You can rely on me for that. And I hope, Mr Trave, that you will soon be reinstated. It is the least that you deserve.'

As Trave shook Arne's hand on the way out, he remembered how he'd once imagined him as a bird of prey hovering over his victim. He looked nothing like that now, thought Trave. In fact, he'd never seen a prosecuting barrister look more human.

Two days later, early on Tuesday morning, David Swain was told to get dressed for court. He was confused. His lawyers had told him that his appeal wouldn't be heard for another week, and yet here he was being bundled into a prison van with no warning. He wondered if it perhaps had something to do with what he'd heard on the radio about Osman's death out at Blackwater Hall. But there'd been nothing in the report about new evidence. David remembered the worried look on his lawyers' faces when he'd asked them about his chances at the end of their last visit. It didn't bode well for the appeal if that was where he was headed.

But there was no point speculating. Instead David glued his face to the window of the van, drinking in sights that he knew he might never see again – a newspaper seller setting up his stand outside Euston Station, the spray of silver water cascading from the fountains in Trafalgar Square, a cyclist weaving in and out of the traffic on Charing Cross Road while an anxious-looking woman gripped the hand of a little boy as they stood waiting to cross at the traffic lights. It could be his mother and Max, thought David with a wrench – how they might look a month from now when he was no longer in the world.

At last, with a lurch, the prison van turned in at the gates of the Royal Courts of Justice. David caught a brief glimpse of silver-grey stone spires and monumental archways before he was taken out and locked up in yet another cell. Iron doors and cement floors and concrete walls and dripping taps and the endless toxic smell of urine and faeces – this was the world where he belonged, far away from sunshine and grass and children playing in parks – other sights he'd seen flashing by the van window that morning on his way to court.

He didn't have long to wait. A jangling of keys and an unlocking of endless doors and he emerged out into the Court of Criminal Appeal. To David it seemed more like a vast, cavernous library than a courtroom. Shelves of antique leather-bound books rose up on all sides from the floor to the distant wood-panelled ceiling, while far away to David's right three old men in black gowns and horsehair wigs were sitting on tall high-backed chairs at a long polished wooden table on an elevated dais. Their bony hands were strangely illuminated by the green subaqueous light from their reading lamps, but otherwise the courtroom was a dark, shadowy place, inspiring in David not hope but despair.

After a moment the familiar hawk-like figure of the prosecutor, Sir Laurence Arne, rose from a bench below the judges and began to speak: 'My lords, I have asked for this case to be called on today in advance of its appeal date as it appears that there has been a serious miscarriage of justice, not just in the lower court but also in relation to the defendant's conviction on another murder charge in 1958. Inspector Trave of the Oxfordshire police has produced to me certain documents, which leave me in no doubt that Mr Swain has been the victim of a wide-ranging conspiracy to make him take the blame for not just one murder but two . . .'

David swayed in the dock, unable to believe what he was hearing. It was a fantasy, a dream from which he would wake in a moment, a final trick of the cruel and malevolent fate that had pursued him for the last three years. The prosecutor's words washed over him until finally a light dawned inside his head and he understood. It was over. He was free. The nightmare was at an end.

His mother was waiting for him outside the court. He didn't recognize her at first because her face was lit up like he had never seen it before. It was as if all the years of worry and toil had been magically lifted from her in one transcendent, cleansing moment. And beside her, gazing up at his half-brother through those same extraordinarily thick glasses, was Max.

'I'm very happy you're free,' said Max seriously. 'Because I have a lot of things to show you at home. Not just robots; other things too. I've made some of them. You are coming home with us, aren't you, David?'

'Yes, Max,' said David, taking a firm grip of his half-brother's hand and smiling over Max's head at their mother. 'I'm coming home.'

CHAPTER 30

Vanessa drove Trave to the ferry in her Citroen 2CV. She had become very attached to the car since her escape from Claes in it a month earlier, and swore that she intended to keep it until it died a natural death.

'And then I suppose you'll bury it in the back garden?' said Trave with a smile.

And Vanessa started to laugh too, but then stopped because there was no outside space at her flat, and he could only be referring to the garden of their old home in North Oxford.

But then the awkwardness passed as they came out onto a wide stretch of road with fields of wheat on either side waving in the breeze, and it was impossible not to feel happy about the coming of spring. There was a warmth between them now that sometimes reminded Trave of the days when they were young and had travelled through France and Italy in a car like this one, putting up at tiny auberges or even sometimes sleeping out in the open under the Mediterranean moonlight.

They were older now, scarred with their different experiences and kept awake at night by different kinds of guilt. But what they had both been through also made them more understanding of each other, and for the first time in their lives it seemed like they were really friends.

Trave worried about Vanessa. There was nothing he could do to change the fact that she had been seduced by Osman and had failed Katya in her hour of need, but he knew that he had failed Vanessa too. He had abandoned her when she needed him after their son died. And this time he was not going to make the same mistake. She needed comfort and support, but he also knew she needed space and time to think. She still stayed most nights in her flat, and he understood why that was important to her. Like her job, the flat was an achievement, an expression of her ability to be a person in her own right, outside her husband's shadow. And in fact he enjoyed the evenings when he went to dinner there at her invitation, amazed by her newly developed culinary skills and the pictures on the walls that spoke of a talent and passion that he had hardly guessed at until now.

Trave encouraged his wife quietly and comforted her when she grieved, and he tried hard to live in the moment and hope for the best. Creswell had rushed through his reinstatement, which was accompanied by a fulsome letter of apology from the chief constable himself, and the return to work gave Trave's life a renewed purpose. Sometimes he caught Clayton, newly promoted to the rank of detective sergeant, looking at him out of the corner of his eye, anxious that his boss was about to have another hunch, but so far there had been nothing to disturb their working harmony. Crime in Oxford this March was considerably down from the previous year.

Trave and Vanessa stopped for lunch on the way and got to Harwich with only minutes to spare, so that Trave was almost the last passenger to board the boat. He carried his small suitcase down the gangway and waved to his wife from the deck. 'Next time you'll come too,' he shouted, but his voice was drowned out by the sound of a horn. And almost immediately the ship moved off, groaning as it left its moorings. Trave smelt the sea in his nostrils and was suddenly exhilarated. 'I love you,' he called to Vanessa's receding figure, and this time he was sure she'd heard him. He saw her face light up with a smile as she put up her hand and waved back, and he thought that she had never looked as beautiful as at that moment, with her dark brown hair blown up around her face in the gathering wind.

He got to Antwerp in the early evening and went to bed early. He'd arranged with Aliza to pick her up in the hired car at nine o'clock the next morning, and he wanted to be rested for the day ahead.

Aliza was as he remembered her – old and frail and extraordinarily alive. As before she was dressed in black, but today she had a coloured prayer shawl over her shoulders. She looked straight ahead as he drove, as if preparing herself for what lay ahead.

'It is hard to know I was so wrong about Titus. It hurts my faith in human nature,' she said quietly, breaking the silence when they were halfway to Mechelen. Trave had phoned straight away to tell her about Osman's death and Jacob's arrest, and since then he had written her a long letter describing how the truth about Osman and Claes had emerged afterwards. And it was in response to that letter that she had invited him to Antwerp.

'It's your faith in human nature that has enabled you to survive,' said Trave. 'And I admire you for that.'

'I survive because I survive,' said Aliza sadly. 'There is no secret to it. Some of us do and some of us don't. But I thank God and your deputy, Mr Clayton, for sparing me my grandson. Do you know how much longer he must remain in prison, Inspector?'

'Not too long, I hope. He will have to do some gaol time for the burglaries, but the court should give him credit for pleading guilty and will have to take account of his motivation for committing the crimes. It'll be hard for the court to be too severe on him when he was simply trying to obtain a justice that the legal system played such a role in denying him.'

'I hope you are right. He has written several times to say that he will return to me when he is released, and I am already weary with waiting,' said Aliza with a smile that belied her words. Trave couldn't imagine impatience getting the better of the old lady. He felt he had never in all his life met a person who radiated such inner calm.

'Follow the road by the river,' she directed when they arrived in the outskirts of Mechelen a few minutes later. 'It'll take you there.' And she was right – Trave didn't need any further directions.

He parked in a corner of the square and held Aliza's arm as they crossed the road and stood across from the entrance to the barracks. He was surprised by the building – it was an eighteenth-century classical design, pleasing to the eye and very different to the soaring gabled Renaissance Gothic architecture that dominated the rest of the town. There were three storeys with rectangular windows at symmetrical intervals all around the four enclosing white-painted walls, and inside, through an arched entrance, Trave could see a quadrangle in which men in uniform were walking to and fro. He remembered what Jacob had told him – that the barracks were now used as a training centre for the Belgian army.

'We come here in September,' Aliza said softly. 'And stand in a circle with candles and say the names of our dead. Because this is where the railhead was, where they put them on the trains. This is where they left Belgium never to return.'

'Would you like to go inside?' asked Trave. But Aliza shook her head. Instead she pulled her shawl over her head, slipped her arm out of Trave's, and clasped her hands together in prayer. She bowed her head and then, looking over at the barracks, she began to sing, or rather to chant, in a language that Trave didn't understand but knew must be Hebrew. The chant was beautiful, suffused with an infinite sadness that went straight to Trave's heart.

'What is it?' asked Trave when she had finished. 'It's like you were grieving for the whole world.'

'In a way I was,' said Aliza, looking up. 'It is from the Book of Lamentations. The prophet, Jeremiah, is weeping for the fate of Jerusalem after it was sacked by Nebuchadnezzar of Babylon. He says: 'Alas, she sits in solitude! The city that was great with people has become like a widow. She weeps bitterly in the night and her tear is on my cheek. Those who I cherished and brought up, my enemy has wiped out.' It is the song we sing on Tisha B'av, our day of mourning, when we remember all that has happened to our people. But we are also commanded to hope and to believe, and so when those we love die we extol the name of God and we say that He is good. We say Kaddish for them, and we refuse to give in. Come, Inspector, say it with me. I will pray in English.'

Aliza held out her hand, and Trave took it and went to stand beside her, thinking for a moment how strange they must seem to anyone passing by – an old lady and a middle-aged man standing hand in hand praying outside an army barracks in the morning sunshine. He smiled at the thought and Aliza smiled back; and then, holding her hand in his, he repeated each line of the Kaddish after her, looking up at the plaque by the entrance arch, the best memorial Belgium could offer to the twenty-five thousand men, women, and children who had been sent away from this place to die:

MAY HIS GREAT NAME GROW EXALTED AND SANCTIFIED IN THE WORLD THAT HE CREATED AS HE WILLED.

MAY HE GIVE REIGN TO HIS KINGSHIP IN YOUR LIFETIMES AND IN YOUR DAYS, AND IN THE LIFETIMES OF THE ENTIRE FAMILY OF ISRAEL SWIFTLY AND SOON.

BLESSED, PRAISED, GLORIFIED, EXALTED,
EXTOLLED, MIGHTY, UPRAISED, AND LAUDED BE THE
NAME OF THE HOLY ONE BEYOND ANY BLESSING AND
SONG, PRAISE AND CONSOLATION THAT ARE UTTERED
IN THE WORLD.

MAY THERE BE ABUNDANT PEACE FROM HEAVEN
AND LIFE UPON US AND UPON ALL ISRAEL.

HE WHO MAKES PEACE IN HIS HEIGHTS, MAY HE
MAKE PEACE, UPON US AND UPON ALL ISRAEL.

AMEN

AFTERWORD

Following conviction at his trial in Jerusalem, Adolf Eichmann was hanged at a few minutes before midnight on May 31, 1962, at a prison in Ramla, Israel. His body was cremated and his ashes were scattered in the Mediterranean, outside the territorial waters of Israel so that he would have no memorial and no country would serve as his final resting place.

In Belgium the Eichmann trial briefly ignited interest in the fate of the Jews who had been imprisoned in the Dossin de St Georges Transit Camp in Mechelen and then transported across Europe to their deaths in the Auschwitz-Birkenau Concentration Camp in Poland. But the interest soon subsided, and the Dossin barracks fell into disuse after they were abandoned by the Belgian army in 1975. However, in recent years, a museum has been established in one wing of the barracks, and in 2007 a widely praised exhibition was mounted outside the walls showing the enlarged photographs of 1,200 of the 1,631 men, women, and children who left the transit camp for Auschwitz on 16 April, 1943, on Convoy 20. Among those who also made this terrible journey on twenty-five other trains between 4 August, 1942, and 31 July, 1944, were 23,285 other Jews and 351 Gypsies – and only 1,221 of those transported survived the war.

Fifteen miles from Mechelen the Jewish shtetl in Antwerp continues to thrive today, and Antwerp diamonds remain famous all over the world. It is one of the only such communities that now exists in Europe, and it serves as a reminder of what might have been if Eichmann and those who served him both in Germany and in the countries occupied by the Nazis had not been able to carry out their program of genocide.

Let us not forget.

COMING SOON,
THE INHERITANCE
BY
SIMON TOLKIEN

PART ONE

1959

PART ONE

One

Detective Inspector William Trave of the Oxfordshire CID felt the pain as soon as he'd passed through the revolving entrance doors of the Old Bailey and had shaken the rain out from his coat onto the dirty wet floor of the courthouse. It hurt him in the same place as before – on the left side of his chest, just above his heart. But it was worse this time. It felt important. Like it might never go away.

There was a white plastic chair in the corner, placed there perhaps by some kind janitor to accommodate visitors made faint by their first experience of the Old Bailey. Now Trave fell into it, bending down over his knees to gather the pain into himself. He was fighting for breath while prickly sweat poured down in rivulets over his face, mixing with the rain-drops. And all the time his brain raced from one thought to another, as if it wanted in the space of a minute or two to catch up on all the years he had wasted not talking to his wife, not coming to terms with his son's death, not living. He thought of the lonely North Oxford house he had left behind at seven o'clock that morning, with the room at the back that he never went into, and he thought of his ex-wife, whom he had seen just the other day shopping in the Covered Market. He had run back into the High Street, frightened that his successor might come into view carrying a shared shopping bag, and had ducked into the Mitre in search of whisky.

Trave wanted whisky now, but the Old Bailey wasn't the place to find it. For a moment he considered the possibility of the pub across the road. It was called the Witness Box, or some fatuous name like that, but it wouldn't be open yet. Trave felt his breath beginning to come more easily. The pain was better, and he got out a crumpled handkerchief and wiped away some of the sweat and rain. It was funny that he'd felt for a moment that he was actually going to die, and yet no one seemed to have noticed. The security guards were still patting down the pockets of the public just like they had been doing all morning. One of them was even humming a discordant version of that American song, 'Heartbreak Hotel.' A rain-soaked middle-aged policeman sitting on a chair in the corner, gathering his breath for the day ahead, was hardly a cause for distraction.

A sudden weariness came over Trave. Once again he felt weighed down by the meaninglessness of the world around him. Trave always tried to keep his natural nihilism at bay as best he could. He did his job to the best of his ability, went to church on Sundays, and nurtured the plants that grew in the carefully arranged borders of his garden – and sometimes it all worked. Things seemed important precisely because they didn't last. But underneath, the despair was always there, ready to spring out and take him unawares. Like that morning, halfway down his own street, when a young man in blue overalls working on a dismembered motorcycle had brought back the memory of Joe as if he had gone only yesterday. And fallen apples in the garden at the weekend had resurrected Vanessa stooping to gather them into a straw basket three autumns before. It was funny that he always remembered his wife with her back turned.

Trave gathered himself together and made for the stairs. When he got time, he'd go and see his doctor. Perhaps the GP could give him something. In the meantime he had to carry on. Today was important. *Regina v. Stephen Cade*, said the list on the wall outside the courthouse. Before His Honour Judge Murdoch at twelve o'clock. Charged with murder. Father murder – patricide, it was called. And the father was an important man – a colonel in the army during the war and a university professor in civilian life. If convicted, the boy would certainly hang. The powers that be would see to that. The boy. But Stephen wasn't a boy. He was twenty-two. He just felt like a boy to Trave. The policeman fought to keep back the thought that Stephen was so much like Joe. It wasn't just a physical resemblance. Joe had had the same passion, the same need to rebel that had driven him to ride his brand new 600cc silver motorcycle too fast after dark down a narrow road on the other side of Oxford. A wet January night more than two years ago. If he'd lived, Joe would be twenty-two. Just like Stephen. Trave shook his head. He didn't need the police training manual to know that empathizing with the main suspect in a murder investigation was no way to do his job. Trave had trained himself to be fair and decent and unemotional. That way he brought order to a disordered world, and most of the time he believed there was some value in that. He would do his duty, give his evidence, and move on. The fate of Stephen Cade was not his responsibility.

Up in the police room, Trave poured himself a cup of black coffee, straightened his tie, and waited in a corner for the court usher to come and get him to give his evidence. He was the officer in the case, and, when the opening statements were over, he would be the first witness called by the prosecution.

The courtroom was one of the oldest in the Old Bailey. It was tall, lit by glass chandeliers that the maintenance staff needed long ladders to reach when the bulbs blew out. On the wood-panelled walls, pictures of long-gone nineteenth-century lawyers stared out on their twentieth-century successors. The judge sat robed in black in a leather-backed armchair placed on a high dais. Only the dock containing the defendant and two uniformed prison officers was at the same level. Between them, in the well of the court, were the lawyers' tables; the witness box; and, to right and left, the benches for the press and the jury. The jurors were now in place, and Trave felt them slowly relaxing into their new surroundings. Their moment in the limelight, when they stumbled over their oath to render a true verdict in accordance with the evidence, had come and gone. Now they could sit in safe anonymity while the drama of the murder trial played out in front of them. Everyone – members of the press, the jurors, and the spectators packed together in the public gallery above the defendant's head – was focused on the prosecutor, Gerald Thompson, as he gathered his long black gown around his shoulders and prepared to begin.

'What time did you arrive at Moreton Manor, Inspector?' he asked, 'on the night of the murder?'

'Eleven forty-five.' Trave spoke loudly, forgetting for a moment the acoustic qualities of the Old Bailey.

'Were you the first policeman on the scene?'

'No. Officers Clayton and Watts were already there. They'd got everyone in the drawing room. It's across from the front hall.'

'And the victim, Professor Cade – he was in his study. On the ground floor of the east wing.'

'Yes. That's right,' said Trave.

There was a measured coldness and determination in the way the prosecutor put his questions, which contrasted sharply with his remarkable lack of stature. Gerald Thompson couldn't have been more than five feet tall. Now he took a deep breath and drew himself up to his full short height as if to underline to the jury the importance of his next question.

'Now, tell us, Inspector. What did you find?'

'In the study?'

'Yes. In the study.'

Trave could hear the impatience in the prosecutor's voice, but he still hesitated before beginning his reply. It was the question he'd asked himself a thousand times or more during the four months that had passed since he'd first seen the dead man, sitting bolt upright in his high-backed armchair, gazing out over a game of chess into nothing at all. Shot in the head. Detective Inspector Trave knew what he'd found, all right. He just didn't know what it meant. Not in his bones, not where it mattered. Pieces of the jigsaw fitted too well, and others didn't fit at all. Everything pointed to Stephen Cade as the murderer, but why had he called out for help after killing his father? Why had he waited to open the door to his accusers? Why had he not tried to escape? Trave remembered how Stephen had gripped the table at the end of their last interview in Oxford Police Station, shouting over and over again until he was hoarse: 'I didn't do it, I tell you. I didn't kill him. I hated my father, but that doesn't make me a murderer.'

Trave had got up and left the room, told the sergeant at the desk to charge the boy with murder, and walked out into the night. And he hadn't slept properly ever since.

Thompson, of course, had no such doubts. Trave remembered the first thing the prosecution counsel had told him when the case was being prepared for trial: 'There's something you should know about me, Inspector,' he'd said in that nasal bullying tone with which Trave had now become so familiar. 'I don't suffer fools gladly. I never have and I never will.'

And Trave was a fool. Thompson hadn't taken long to form that opinion. The art of prosecution was about following the straight and narrow, keeping to the path through the woods until you got to the hanging tree on the other side. Defence lawyers spent their time trying to side-track witnesses and throw smoke in the jurors' eyes to keep them from the truth. Trave was the officer in the case. It was his duty not to be sidetracked, to keep his language plain and simple, to help the jury do its job. And here he was: hesitant and uncertain before he'd even begun.

Thompson cleared his throat and glowered at his witness.

'Tell us about the deceased, Inspector Trave,' he demanded. 'Tell us what you found.'

'He'd been shot in the head.'

'How many times?'

'Once.'

'Where in the head?'

'In the forehead.'

'Did you find the gun?'

'Yes, it was on a side table, with a silencer attached. The defendant said he'd put it there after picking it up from the floor near the French windows, when he came back into the study from the courtyard.'

'That was the story he told you?'

'Yes, I interviewed him the next day at the police station.'

'His fingerprints were on the gun. That's right, isn't it?'

'Yes.'

'And on the key that he admitted he turned in order to unlock the door into the corridor. The defendant told you that as well in his interview, didn't he, Inspector?'

'Yes. He said the door was locked and so he opened it to let Mr Ritter into the study.'

'Tell us who Mr Ritter is.'

'He was a friend of Professor Cade's. They fought together in the war. He and his wife had been living at the manor house for about seven years, as I understand it. Mrs Ritter acted as the housekeeper. They had the bedroom above the professor's study, overlooking the main courtyard.'

'Thank you, Inspector. All the fingerprint evidence is agreed, my lord.'

'I'm glad to hear it,' said the judge, in a tone that suggested he'd have had a great deal to say if it hadn't been. His Honour Judge Murdoch looked furious already, Thompson noted with approval. Strands of grey hair stuck out at different angles from under his old horsehair wig, and his wrinkled cheeks shone even redder than usual. They were the legacy of a lifetime of excessive drinking, which had done nothing to improve the judge's temper. Defendants, as he saw it, were guilty and needed to be punished. Especially this one. People like Stephen Cade's father had fought in two world wars to defend their country. And for what? To see their sons rebel, take drugs, behave indecently in public places. Stephen Cade had made a mistake not cutting his hair for the trial. Judge Murdoch stared at him across the well of the court and decided that he'd never seen a criminal more deserving of the ultimate punishment. The little bastard had killed his father for money. There was no worse crime than that. He'd hang. But first he'd have his trial. A fair trial. Judge Murdoch would see to that.

'Let's stay with the interview for a little bit longer,' said Gerald Thompson, taking up a file from the table in front of him. 'You have it in front of you, if you need to refer to it, Inspector. It's an agreed version. The defendant told you, did he not, that he'd been arguing with his father shortly before he found Professor Cade murdered?'

'Yes. He said that he went to the study at ten o'clock and that he and his father played chess and argued.'

'Argued about his father's will? About his father's intention to change that will and disinherit the defendant?'

'Yes. The defendant told me they talked about the will but that their main argument was over the defendant's need for money.'

'Which his father was reluctant to give him.'

'Yes . . .'

Trave seemed to want to answer more fully, but Thompson gave him no opportunity. 'The defendant told you in interview that he became very angry with his father. Isn't that right, Inspector?' asked the prosecutor.

451

'Yes.'

'The defendant admitted to shouting at Professor Cade that he deserved to die.' The pace of Thompson's questioning continued to pick up speed.

'Yes.'

'And then he told you that he left the study and went for a walk. That's what he said, wasn't it, Inspector?'

Thompson asked the question in a rhetorical tone that made it quite clear what he, at least, though of Stephen Cade's alibi.

'He said he walked up to the main gate and came back to the study about five minutes later, when he found his father murdered.'

'Yes. Now, Inspector, did you find any footprints to support Stephen Cade's account?'

'No. But I wouldn't have expected to. The courtyard is stone and the drive is tarmac.'

'All right. Let me ask you this, then. Did you find any witnesses to back up his story?'

'No. No, I didn't.'

'Thank you. Now one last question,' said Thompson, smiling as if he felt he'd saved his best for last. 'Did you find any of the defendant's belongings in the study?'

'We found his hat and coat.'

'Ah, yes. Where were they?'

'On a chair beside Professor Cade's desk.'

'And the professor himself. Where was his body in relation to this chair and in relation to the entrance doors to the room? Can you help us with that, Inspector?'

'Why don't you give the jury a chance to look at all this on the floor plan, Mr. Thompson?' said the judge, interrupting. 'It might make it clearer.'

'Yes, my lord, I should have thought of that. Members of the jury, if you look at the plan, you can see the courtyard is enclosed on three sides by the main part of the house and its two wings. Professor Cade's study is the last room on the ground floor of the east wing. It faces into the courtyard, and you can see the French windows marked. The internal door in the corner of the room opens out into a corridor which runs the length of the east wing. You can take it up from there, Inspector,' said Thompson, turning back to his witness.

'Yes. The deceased was seated in one of the two armchairs positioned in the centre of the study, about midway between the two entrances,' said Trave, holding up the plan. 'The desk and the chair with the defendant's hat and coat were further into the room.'

'So the professor was between the doors and the defendant's hat and coat?'

'Yes. That's right.'

'Thank you, Inspector. That's what I wanted to know. No more questions.'

Thompson sat down with a self-satisfied expression on his face and stole a glance at the jury. He knew what the jurors must be asking themselves: Why would Stephen Cade have gone for a walk at half past ten at night? And if he did, why didn't he take his hat and coat? It was obvious he hadn't been wearing them, because not even he could pretend that he put them back on the other side of his dead father's body on his return.

No, the truth was inescapable. Stephen Cade never went for any walk at all. He was in the study the whole time, arguing with his father about his will, threatening him, and finally killing him with a pistol that he had brought along for that precise purpose.

Then, the next day, he'd told the police a ridiculous story in order to try to save himself. But it wouldn't wash. With a little help from the prosecution, the jury would see right through it. It'd find him guilty, and then Judge Murdoch would make him pay for what he'd done. With his neck.

Simon Tolkien is the grandson of J.R.R. Tolkien. After studying modern history at Oxford he went on to become a barrister specializing in serious crime. He now lives in California with his wife and their two children.

www.simontolkien.com